The author of THE RAGGED SCHOOL has written many novels for adults and children under various pseudonyms. This is the third regional saga set in Essex. THE OYSTERCATCHERS'S CRY and THE SAFFRON FIELDS are also available from Headline.

F. K. Salwood comes from generations of Essex farmers and fishermen, and though a traveller for many years, always returns to the awe-inspiring landscapes and natural beauty of the Essex countryside and coastline.

Also by F. K. Salwood

The Oystercatcher's Cry
The Saffron Fields

The Ragged School

F. K. Salwood

KNIGHT

First published in 1995
by HEADLINE BOOK PUBLISHING

First published in paperback in 1996
by HEADLINE BOOK PUBLISHING

This edition published 1999 by
Knight an imprint of Brockhampton Press

10 9 8 7 6 5 4 3 2 1

ISBN 184186 031X

Typeset by Avon Dataset Ltd, Bidford-on-Avon, Warks

Printed and bound in Great Britain by
Mackays of Chatham PLC, Chatham, Kent

Brockhampton Press
20 Bloomsbury Street
London
WC1B 3QA

This one is for my mother-in-law, Betty Bailey,
and her sister Marjorie Wright,
two fine ladies

Chapter One

The shrill rising note of the air-raid siren pierced the walls of the classroom. Rebecca paused in mid-sentence, knowing her words would soon be lost in the following steady wail from Tilbury docks. Rupert Chawner Brooke's 'Grantchester' would have to wait until after the all clear came. Some of the pupils were already putting their things inside their desks and making ready to file out of the classroom into the corridors where the smell of school dinner cabbage still lingered from the previous day.

'Stand!' Rebecca cried over the siren's insistent call. 'Shirley Williams, lead them out.'

Shirley, a sturdy eleven-year-old, marched to the door, opened it, and the class began to file out. They were abnormally quiet on the occasions when they made for the shelter. Not, Rebecca was certain, because they were frightened. The children took these incidents in their stride: air raids were part of their formative years. Eighteen months had passed since Chamberlain's declaration of war and fear numbs with the passing of time. When a bomb landed very close by, or a classmate died in an attack, there were sometimes white faces and tears, but the fear and sadness never remained for long. Children were far more adaptable and resilient than the adults, Rebecca had decided. They accepted things for what they were.

'David, leave Jenny's hair alone,' called Rebecca, noticing a boy tweaking the plaits of the girl in front.

Out in the main corridor, which ran across the whole length of the wide-fronted building, Rebecca directed her children towards the exit that led to the boys' playground. There were underground shelters at the end of this playground, dug into the bank of the railway siding below. Other teachers were now emerging with their charges, shepherding them alongside Rebecca's crocodile until they were three abreast.

Outside it was chill and damp, and the sky overcast. This was the suicide month. People were prepared to kill themselves in wartime, just as in peace, and February's weather helped them make up their mind. An elderly neighbour living in the same block of flats as Rebecca had swallowed a lethal dose of something recently and escaped any further trips to the shelters in the depressingly dull, cold, bleak weather that was February's only offer.

The drone of enemy bombers was heard in the distance. Anti-aircraft guns began to open up, pounding the cloudy skies, hoping inanely for an early fortuitous hit. The mosquito buzz of friendly fighters flying overhead was raggedly cheered by the kids, who wasted no opportunity for a little noise of their own, even though they didn't look up. It was difficult to see anything in the grey murk however, and the children were playing it by ear, so it was a half-hearted yell that went up to the Royal Air Force, not even accompanied by a wave.

An air-raid precaution warden quickly checked the school,

then hurried on to her other ARP duties.

When the pupils were halfway across the playground a stick of bombs fell some two miles away on the edge of Tilbury, close to the docks, and the ground shuddered. Several children squealed after the blast and one or two started to run towards the shelters.

'Stop running!' called the strident voice of the headmaster. 'Walk on, walk on!'

The pace was stepped up, but running was not allowed. The teachers could not control the children at a run and there was the danger of a crush at the narrow-doored shelters, one on either side of the playground. They filed quickly in and sat on the benches in the narrow confines, the teachers being the last to enter.

Stephen Sinclair, the headmaster, was in the same shelter as Rebecca. His was the responsibility for allocating classes to shelters and he had arranged it that way. There was another teacher with them, there being six in the school altogether; she was Miss Simms, a seventy-year-old who took the youngest infant class. Miss Simms was a tiny individual, hard of hearing, a little vague and not very well sighted. She wore a grey cardigan, with which she fussed the whole time, it never seeming to cover her small frame to her satisfaction. It was Miss Simms's job to enter the shelter first and put a match to the candles, their only source of lighting.

Stephen Sinclair was a tall man of around forty-five with a stoop to his body. It was the heavy, impressive nose that Rebecca had immediately noticed when first looking into his face. It seemed to dominate not just his face but the whole topography of his body, like Mount Everest plonked in the middle of the flat sands of the Sahara. It wasn't exactly an ugly feature – indeed it curved magnificently, with a regular outwards sweep – but it was big and aggressive. Its owner seemed aware of its power and force. He used the organ to intimidate, to overwhelm, to domineer.

Rebecca Daniels herself was evenly featured, with a slender body. She was tallish for a woman, at five foot six, with brown curly hair and very deep brown eyes. Her legs, she had long ago decided, were the least impressive items on the inventory of her physical parts, but she had ceased to care about their inadequacy. Silk stockings did nothing to improve them, which was just as well because Rebecca could not afford such items of luxury.

Rebecca had a keen mind, was interested in most subjects, and knew herself to be as clever as the next man's son, brother, uncle or father. What was more, she had a good deal of 'common intelligence', which her mother had always impressed upon her as being more important than either a good pair of legs or a brilliant brain. Common intelligence was what kept warplane pilots alive, ships' captains with a vessel beneath their feet and soldiers with all their limbs intact. Common intelligence was slow-burning, but sure, when flashes of genius were setting fire to their owners.

Rebecca had a problem with Stephen Sinclair. The headmaster believed himself entitled to fondle the young female teachers on his staff and did so with regularity. He had especially picked out Rebecca, a vulnerable twenty-seven-year-old widow with a six-year-old daughter, for his sexual forays.

Once Rebecca's children were all safely inside the shelter, she herself entered. Her daughter Kim, in Miss Simms's class, was squashed in between two pals. Kim had learned not to expect privileges, or even to engage her mother's attention, while in school. Having waited until last to enter, Rebecca had found the only empty space was next to Sinclair. He gave her a tight smile and patted the bench with his heavy hand. Having no choice she reluctantly, with a sinking feeling in her stomach, sat down.

Miss Simms was busily handing out reading books, passing them along the line of pupils on her side of the shelter, while chattering away to Rebecca and Sinclair.

'I don't know, these daylight raids,' she was saying, 'they're not normal at all . . .'

As if there were a 'normal' time to have an air raid.

'Settle down, children,' boomed the headmaster, ignoring Miss Simms and completely obliterating her voice with his own. 'I know it's difficult, reading by candlelight, but I'm informed by the authorities that we'll have electric light in here soon. Then we'll be able to see properly what we're doing, won't we, Miss Daniels, eh? Get on with it, Jameson, get on with it. Leave Drinchard alone, will you . . .'

'Please, sir, he punched me first.'

'I didn't punch – it was just a little push, sir. Jameson was holdin' up the line.'

'I'll bang *both* your heads together if you don't shut up. Now settle down.'

Rebecca did not correct Sinclair's 'Miss' to 'Mrs', knowing that the next time he would slip back to using the wrong title.

During the next half-hour she felt the touch of his hand more than once, but even in the subdued light with another dim-eyed and somewhat dim-witted teacher present, there wasn't much he could do without the children noticing.

Rebecca couldn't make a fuss in front of Miss Simms and the children, so she bore these infuriating surreptitious touches with dignity. Occasionally a near miss would send the whole group into momentary confusion, which Sinclair made the most of in his sly manner.

The air raid, which was mainly centred on the docks, finally ended and the all clear went. Miss Simms opened the door and the cold air wafted in from the outside, welcome for its freshness but disliked for its dampness. Most of the boys had pullovers under their jackets and the girls cardigans, but there were some who were not adequately clothed who were in danger of chest infections. Rebecca led her children straight back to their classroom, where the fire was still glowing in the grate. She put on one or two more pieces of coal to get what little heat she was able into the chilly schoolroom.

'Now, "Grantchester",' she said.

Outside there were buildings on fire, accompanied by the usual shouts and punctuated occasionally by a gas explosion. There was no chaos on the streets, but there was misery and death. Later, when listening to the wireless, Rebecca learned that a bomb had landed near the Bank of England and ripped Threadneedle Street apart.

Back in her little flat, Rebecca felt safe from the unwelcome attentions of the headmaster. Sinclair was not a married man but she detested his advances. A woman surely still had a choice, wartime or not? There remained inside her a strong flame burning for her husband Alan, a lieutenant, killed on the beach at Dunkirk.

Dunkirk had also robbed Rebecca of a father and her only

uncle. The two older men had been crewing a yacht across the
Channel, ferrying soldiers home. On the third voyage, when
the men must have been exhausted and their vigilance at a low
point, the yacht had hit a mine. The captain of a nearby cockle
boat owned by an Essex shellfish family had confirmed the
explosion, searched the area and reported no survivors
amongst the wreckage.

Although she missed her father a great deal, it was Alan
who was constantly in her thoughts. From the accounts given
by his men, Lieutenant Daniels of the Essex Regiment had
been assisting the wounded from his group, helping them into
the small boats, when a German dive bomber swept low over
the sands and strafed the British and French soldiers. Alan had
caught a round in the chest and died instantly.

Alan had been dead for less than a year, though Rebecca
had not seen him for longer than that. There had been training
on Salisbury Plain to go through, then his regiment had been
one of the first to leave for France. She still had his last letter,
posted in Wiltshire, which never left her handbag. Sinclair
could not possibly replace her Alan.

Sinclair had no place in her personal life now or ever, even
if his advances had been serious suggestions of a formal
courtship, which they were not. Sinclair had no intention of
forming a relationship with Rebecca. He simply wanted to
satisfy his need for power by subjecting her to humiliating and
lewd suggestions followed up by the inevitable feel.

'Mummy, the *blackout*,' said Kim, looking up from her
book. 'The ARP man will have your guts for garters.'

'Kim, where *do* you get these expressions from?'

'Jimmy Reynolds, Mummy.'

Jimmy Reynolds was a six-year-old going on twenty-five: a street-wise urchin in Kim's class at school.

'Please, Kim, do not repeat things James Reynolds has taught you.'

'All right, Mummy.'

Rebecca sighed and let the curtains drop, realising she had wandered over to the window without thinking, and pulled them aside to look out over the dark rooftops.

'Sorry, sweetheart, I wasn't quite in England.'

'Well, where were you then?' demanded her daughter.

Rebecca smiled sadly. 'I was – I was on holiday with your daddy, in France. Did I tell you we used to go to France? Oh, we had such fun there, in the Dordogne . . .'

'Door-doing? That sounds like a doorbell.'

'Yes, it does, doesn't it?'

Kim asked, 'What did you do in the Door-doing place?'

'Oh, we drank wine and laughed a lot – and you played with the French children. You were only two so you won't remember. It was sunny, there were wild flowers growing in the hedgerows, and herbs. The whole place had this wonderful scent of herbs about it. Sometimes we took out bicycles and you were put in a little seat at the back of Daddy's saddle. You used to wear a white bonnet with a large pretty frill. Your daddy used to say you looked like a sunflower in it.'

'Did he?' cried Kim eagerly, in that harmless though selfish way that children have of wanting to hear about themselves. 'What else did he call me?'

'He said you were a poppet and a little cabbage.'

'He called me a *cabbage*,' cried Kim, her face dropping. 'What for?'

'Oh, in French, not in English. *Petit chou* means something quite different in French. It's like calling you a – a *primrose*, or a snowdrop or something. It's the most affectionate term the French have for their loved ones.'

'Well, I'm glad we're not French then,' replied Kim, still not convinced that she hadn't been insulted. 'It was prob'ly when Daddy was drunk on wine that he called me that.'

Rebecca ruffled her daughter's fine hair. 'Daddy was never *drunk* – not in that way. He used to get a little merry sometimes, but never drunk. It wasn't that sort of drinking. We used to stay in a farmhouse with an orchard and have picnics under the apple trees. French people always drink wine with their meals, so we did too, while we were there. Even you had some wine – mixed with water of course.'

'Did I?' squealed Kim. 'Did I get drunk too?'

'No one got drunk,' growled Rebecca, 'not even you. Now, off you go and wash, ready for bed. Change into your nightie. I'll be through in a minute to tuck you in. There's another long day ahead of us tomorrow and if we get a raid tonight we won't get much sleep.'

'Can't we stay indoors if the Germans come again? Can't we go under the kitchen table, like Billy Wilson's family does?'

'They haven't got a shelter nearby and we have. Now, off, quickly, young lady, before I become annoyed.'

Kim grumbled some more but eventually went off to the small kitchen, then to the tiny room which held only a toilet. For baths they had to get out a metal hip bath and scrub in front of the gas fire. Two baths a week each was the most they could manage and sometimes one of those would go by the board. A thorough all-over wash at the kitchen sink was the norm, when the water main hadn't been hit and there was water coming out of the taps. Otherwise it was a lick and a promise from water carried in a bucket from the standpipe along the street.

When Rebecca had finished marking her books, she too went to bed, first saying a small prayer for the dead and a somewhat longer one for the living, then falling into a fatigued deep sleep. Her dreams were jumbled, some happy, some not so, but they were blissfully uninterrupted for the first time in several weeks, as the enemy bombers went south to Portsmouth.

Chapter Two

The sound of a bugle playing reveille in nearby Tilbury Fort, which overlooked the Thames, woke Rebecca with a start. She used a bedside torch to look at her alarm clock. It was still only five thirty and probably as black as soot on the other side of the thick curtains. The Home Guard who now used the fort were anxious to be seen doing their bit for the war effort, even though they were considered too old or too unfit for duty in the regular army.

Rebecca attempted to go to sleep again, but remained firmly awake. She sighed and got up, leaving the warmth of the bed for the chill morning air. The lino was cold on her feet as she padded across the room and put on some clothes. Once dressed she was still shivering, but it was pointless lighting a fire. By the time it got the place warm she and Kim would be on their way to school. It would be a waste of precious fuel.

Instead, she went downstairs and put a kettle of water on the gas, happy to find there was both water and gas to be had. Before long she was sipping a cup of weak tea and sorting through her ration coupons. There was a strip of sweet coupons left which Rebecca knew Kim would have counted. Rebecca worried about Kim's teeth, but there were too few treats in life these days to deny her daughter a visit to the sweetshop.

Rebecca then read a women's magazine, enjoying a 'William' story by Richmal Crompton. Finally it was time to wake Kim and make some breakfast. Rebecca had already decided on porridge. It was warm and thick and would keep them both stoked up until lunchtime.

It was still dark when they left the flat to brave the Essex river mists. They caught the bus to school but there was little they could see through the folds of net curtains put up to prevent flying glass should the bus be caught in a blast. Rebecca sat back and dreamed of better times and Kim was lost in a six-year-old's visions of life during a world at war. There were few mornings when they felt like communicating with one another, though Rebecca often felt guilty about this state of affairs. But mother and daughter were not morning people and were often much too fuzzy-minded at such an hour for any sort of conversation.

Once at school Rebecca had to wake up fast. She entered a noisy classroom to find children throwing things across the room at each other, yelling, and one boy even standing on his desk.

'Silence!' she yelled, as she entered the room. 'By your desks, all of you!'

There was a general scramble as the children stood to attention by their desks. Rebecca feigned terrible anger, the only attitude she found effective in gaining control, even though she didn't feel it. She had long ago decided that a schoolteacher had to be a part-time actress too, in order to stay on top. In the first few months of teaching she had occasionally been reduced to tears, but had managed to get through that period when the class could run rings round her. Now, at a moment's notice, she could appear like Medusa on a bad day.

There were forty-two boys and girls in her class, ranging from nine to eleven. They had destroyed the last music teacher, sending him home with a nervous breakdown after six weeks at the school. There were many attractive individuals amongst them but as a group they were ruthless, and between them had less compassion, showed less mercy and more brutality than the barbarian hordes led by Attila the Hun. Far from showing remorse over the music teacher's illness they had turned 'Mr Smith's Breakdown' into a playground game, which ended with one boy staggering around crying, 'I've gone completely nutty – I'm bonkers, I am,' while the rest of the kids cheered and jeered.

'Right,' she said, picking up her chalk after taking the register, 'we're going to do a few fractions before assembly, just to see if you're all awake . . .'

A general groan rippled through the classroom, but they knew better than to argue.

A little later, assembly consisted of prayers and hymns. They sang 'Eternal Father' for the navy, and chanted prayers for the pilots of the Royal Air Force. The army, too, were given a little prayer space, but not a great deal. Stephen Sinclair had brothers in the first two services and none in the last.

Rebecca had difficulty in holding back the tears whenever she sang this particular hymn. The sea had taken members of her family from her and she had not yet surmounted her grief.

She was still climbing that hill. The fact that she had a full-time job now and a daughter to look after did not give her a great deal of time to reflect on her loss, especially with air raids to interrupt sleep and any leisure moments, but at times like these the force of her mourning almost overwhelmed her. It was as if her grief had stored itself into a flood which during unguarded periods was suddenly released.

Once the singing was over, she regained control of her feelings. She wondered what she used to think of during that particular assembly hymn *before* Alan's death. In those days she had been a voluntary teacher, keeping her hand in but with a main eye to looking after her family. Had it sounded as melancholy in those days, when one heard only occasionally of a ship in distress, or lifeboatmen losing their lives? She was inclined to believe that she had probably, in happier times, mentally revised her shopping list while mouthing the words. Had she been that shallow then? She couldn't remember. On the one hand it seemed so long ago, yet at the same time it felt like yesterday. Time and death played tricks with logic, formed contradictions, brought one into conflict with oneself. Half-asleep at three in the morning her hand might stray towards the other side of the bed, in a desperate hope that the war had been just a bad dream, only to find it empty. Yet there were times when she had to force herself to recall the sound of Alan's voice, or his face, and then their life together seemed almost a part of history.

'Let us pray . . .' she heard.

She lowered her head, at the same time as keeping her eyes open and on her pupils. An offensive odour drifted up from the wooden floor. There was always a peculiarly nasty smell in the hall where assembly took place. The hall was used for school meals, plays, music lessons, dancing, games when it was wet outside, and various other activities. Rebecca guessed the odour was a mixture of sweat, dust and overboiled cabbage. It made her want to gag every time she walked into the room. It was ingrained in the whole structure of the place.

Back in the classroom again, Rebecca was handing out books for her lesson when she heard a tremendous racket coming from across the corridor. She felt it safe to leave her own class for an instant to find that Mr Jones's class was without a teacher and the children were running riot. She ordered them to be quiet and follow her back to her own classroom. Since there weren't enough seats in her room, they had to line the walls. Rebecca sent a pupil with a message to the headmaster, to tell him what had happened and what she had done about it.

A few moments after the child had gone on her errand, a yell went up. Through the frosted glass of her doorway Rebecca saw Mr Jones go flying past. She recognised him by his large round shape. The whole school seemed to be in an uproar. There was angry shouting at the end of the corridor and finally her door was flung open by Jones.

'*There* they are!' he thundered. 'What on earth do you think you're playing at, Mrs Daniels? Why are my children in your room? I only left them for a second to visit the headmaster and when I returned they were gone.'

Rebecca said, 'I'm afraid you were gone for rather longer than a second, Mr Jones. Your class was . . .'

'Are you calling me a liar?' he whined. Then to his class, 'Get back into your room, you lot. I'll deal with you in a

15

minute. Mrs Daniels, I'd like you to accompany me to the headmaster, if you will?'

Rebecca began to bristle. 'I'm afraid that's out of the question, Mr Jones. I'm not able to leave my own class at the moment as I'm sure you can't leave yours again. If one of them were to have an accident in my absence, I would be held responsible. I don't intend to let that happen.'

'What's going on here?' said a quiet, firm voice behind Mr Jones. 'Why are these children running around loose?'

It was the headmaster and he was indicating Jones's pupils who were crossing the corridor on their way back to their own classroom.

'Ask Mrs Daniels that,' snivelled Jones.

Stephen Sinclair looked down his great nose at Rebecca and raised his eyebrows. 'Well?' he said.

'I don't see why it should be me offering the explanation,' said Rebecca, beginning to seethe now, 'but if you want it that way – Mr Jones left his class unattended. They were making a terrible noise so I went across and took charge of them in his absence. When Mr Jones returned he hadn't the good sense to enquire where they were, but went charging off convinced they'd absconded. The children are now being returned to him.'

Sinclair looked at Jones, who was trembling a little, both with anger at Rebecca, it seemed, and with fear of Sinclair. The headmaster could be a ruthless autocrat when he felt it necessary. In wartime schools the headmaster was the unquestioned captain of the ship. His was the ultimate power of authority. Since flogging had been abolished in the last century, Sinclair could hardly resort to such punishment of his staff, but the punitive methods he did use were almost as cruel.

Sinclair said quietly, 'On whose authority did you assume control over Mr Jones's class, Miss Daniels?'

'Mrs Daniels,' corrected Rebecca, feeling it was time for a showdown. 'I took my own initiative, since the children were without a teacher.'

'Mr Jones was, at the time, engaged in a short conversation with me,' replied Sinclair. 'If you had but waited a few more moments your intervention would have been unnecessary. As it is, you have disrupted the whole school with your actions. This is a very serious matter indeed, *Mrs* Daniels.'

During this conversation Rebecca's class stared at the teachers with round eyes, as did Mr Jones's pupils. There was a sophisticated battle going on which the children only partly understood, but it was without doubt a fight. The headmaster's presence was enough to keep them sitting at their desks, quiet and still.

His cane was feared by one and all, though Rebecca herself had never sent any of her children to him to be punished. One or two amongst them had fallen foul of the headmaster during assembly and other general school meetings and had no desire to hear the swish of that bamboo rod again. The accounts of their canings had been passed on to others, accompanied by lurid descriptions. Tearstains down their cheeks and livid marks on their palms or bottoms had been displayed as proof of their torture. The rule of rage and rod was real to them.

'I understood,' said Rebecca levelly, 'that no class should be left without a teacher, no matter whether for a few seconds or a much longer period. In fact I had time to listen for a few minutes to the row that class was creating, cross the corridor, usher forty children into my room, and *still* Mr Jones was nowhere in sight. Please don't tell me it was for a few moments – it was nothing of the kind. He was gone for at least a quarter of an hour.'

'Oh, Good Lord!' cried Jones. 'You see what I have to put up with, Headmaster? These kind of accusations . . .'

'Be quiet,' snapped Sinclair at Jones, who immediately shut his mouth and looked away in embarrassment. 'Mrs Daniels, you will see me in my office at four o'clock. That is all.'

Jones threw Rebecca a final hateful look before entering his own classroom again.

In the old days, when Alan was alive, Rebecca could have unloaded this kind of incident on to him over dinner at home in the evening, or during a weekend drive in the countryside, just the three of them, or over a drink in the saloon bar of a smart pub (Alan had loathed public bars) on the odd occasions when they managed to get a baby-sitter for Kim.

Alan might have sympathised with her, or helped her to laugh it off, or threatened to punch someone on the nose, thus trivialising the affair. It used to help her to get things in perspective. In turn Alan might use her as a sounding board for something that had happened to him during his day at work. It was things like these that she missed about married life: the sharing of troubles, the forming of an alliance against the world and the devil, the solidarity of two like-minded people, the support of a partner. It used to help her to focus on the important values of life, instead of becoming embroiled in petty school politics. Life then had been a smooth journey with assistance, love and well-being almost taken for granted.

Perhaps it had been shallow? How sad to think that happiness was actually only skin-deep, while misery went right through to the core of one's being.

At the appointed hour, just as darkness was setting in, Rebecca dutifully went to the headmaster's office. Kim had been told to wait in the staff room, which was empty now that the other teachers had gone home. Rebecca had been going over her own actions in the affair the whole day long and could find no fault with herself on the main issue. It had been her duty to take care of a class that had been left unattended. With this firmly in mind she knocked on the headmaster's door.

'Come!'

She opened the door to find the headmaster seated behind his desk, fussing over some papers. He waved a hand at the chair in front of the desk without looking at her. 'Sit down, Mrs Daniels,' he said pleasantly, 'I'll be with you in a moment.'

For the next quarter of an hour, while Rebecca sat on the edge of her seat, he continued to shuffle through papers, make notes and read, until she was nearly at screaming point.

'Mr Sinclair,' she said at last in an exasperated tone which she failed completely to disguise, 'I have a six-year-old daughter waiting in the staff room. She's a very patient child, but . . .'

He looked up and frowned, interrupting her. 'In the *staff* room? Is that proper, Mrs Daniels? There are certain things in the staff room which it would be unwise to reveal to pupils – progress charts, etcetera. I hardly think it's an appropriate place to leave one of the school's children, do you?'

'Where else would you suggest that I leave her?'

19

Sinclair placed his pen carefully on his desk. 'My dear Mrs Daniels, it is not up to *me* to suggest anything. You have a child – she's your responsibility.'

Rebecca felt like leaping up, screaming and overturning the horrid man's desk. Instead she said, 'I am not *your dear* anything, Mr Sinclair, and I'll thank you to remember that. You may be the headmaster of this school . . .'

'That I am,' thundered Sinclair back at her, his eyes blazing, 'and I'll thank you to remember that. I find your conduct this morning indefensible, I have to say, and I've arranged to bring the matter up before the board of school governors. I could dismiss you here and now, for gross insolence – people like you should be working in the factories, since you're not fit to be teaching children – however, I choose to show you that I'm not a vindictive man. Let the governors decide what to do with you. I wash my hands.'

Rebecca could not believe her ears. *Not fit to be teaching children*? This man was the most vicious creature she had ever come across. She fought back the tears with characteristic strength, though she had never regarded tears as a sign of weakness, simply a way of relieving her emotions so that she could think more clearly. If he wanted to put the matter in the hands of the governors, then she could do nothing about it. The only time she had met the governors was when she was appointed to the post of teacher. She did not know how they would react to this situation, nor how close Sinclair was to them. He was obviously far more familiar with them than were any of the ordinary teachers in the school. She did know that the board was made up of three local shopkeepers, a magistrate and a doctor. The magistrate was a woman, the rest

20

were men. They probably had no idea about the difficulties of running a classroom, or managing forty-odd children for hours on end.

'You must do what you feel is best,' said Rebecca with dignity. 'Now, I have to get back to my daughter.'

'You haven't been dismissed yet . . .' began Sinclair, but she was already halfway to the door.

Just before she left the room, he said to her quietly, 'Of course, you know, there's a way all this can be forgotten. I'm not a malicious man, you know. I can be quite nice if you let me be.'

Her stomach churned at these words and she felt physically sick. 'I'm afraid you *are* a malicious man, Mr Sinclair, and I'm certain you'll go straight to hell,' she replied.

She left without any further comment, having shocked even herself by her own words.

Chapter Three

Over the next few days Rebecca remained in a state of anxiety about her future as well as Kim's. If she was dismissed from her post at the school she would have no income. She could, as Sinclair had suggested, go to work in a factory: there was no shortage of jobs and the work held no fears for her. However, there was Kim to consider. Most of the women in the factories were single or without children. The hours were long, sometimes involving evening and night-shift work, and Kim would be left alone in the flat. It was not a desirable set of circumstances for any responsible mother to contemplate.

Yet what was Rebecca to do? She could ask around her neighbours, find out if any of them were willing to child-mind for her, but surely no one would want Kim all night?

When Rebecca and Kim arrived back at the flat after school, five days following the incident with Mr Jones, there was a letter waiting on the mat. Rebecca sometimes had mail from Alan's parents, who lived in Cumberland, though they were more concerned about Kim than they were with Rebecca. They kept asking if Kim could come and live with them, at their rural mansion in the Lake District. There was no mention that Rebecca should come too, nor was any help with the train fare included in the offer.

Rebecca had often told herself that their seemingly selfish interest was only natural. They wanted close contact with a piece of Alan, rather than the stranger who was their daughter-in-law. They hardly knew Rebecca, who had only seen the old couple once or twice, just after her wedding. They had been less than forthcoming then, since they had disapproved of the way their son had married, without inviting even close relatives to the ceremony. It had been useless to explain to them that the expense of a full church wedding and reception was well beyond her or Alan's pocket.

Alan's father had been the owner of some lead mines, now closed, and though wealthy was incredibly mean. Alan told her his father would pay nothing towards the wedding, had never given him any financial assistance in anything whatsoever in the past, and would not be likely to do so in the future.

'Traditionally, it's the bride's father who pays for the wedding,' Rebecca had said, 'so you can't blame him.'

At the time of the wedding Rebecca's father was out of work, having lost his job as a chartered accountant: a fact that did nothing to enhance Rebecca in the eyes of her future in-laws. Her father had taken to the bottle after the loss of his wife. Rebecca's mother had passed away at the age of thirty-six after suffering for years from a wasting disease and Joseph Cory was a man who had relied heavily on his wife to get through the process of ordinary living. Elizabeth had been his crutch. Once she had gone he needed another, and chose alcohol.

'It's not that,' argued Alan. 'If he had a daughter he wouldn't pay a jot either. He believes in young people helping themselves. He's a self-made man and they're the worst misers on this earth. Even my mother has to practise dreadful economies, even though she has aristocratic relatives and was used to the good things in life before she married Father. He preaches frugality at her the whole time. She never goes against him.'

Rebecca did feel a little guilty about not letting Kim go, but she reminded herself that Kim was *her* daughter, not theirs, and while she acknowledged that Kim's only surviving grandparents were important to her, Rebecca certainly was not going to relinquish full-time caring for her. Rebecca had promised that when her finances improved she would take Kim up to Cumberland for a holiday, and they could at last be together with her, but only on a temporary basis.

The letter on the mat was not from Alan's parents though: the large handwriting, with its many loops and curls, was from another hand. Rebecca made a cup of tea, then sat at the kitchen table and opened the envelope, which was postmarked Hornchurch, Essex. At first Kim came round the back of her chair and stared at the letter over Rebecca's shoulder, but soon became bored and went off to read a comic.

Dear Mrs Daniels,

Perhaps I should first introduce myself? My name is Amelia Sartour and I am your great-aunt on your mother's side. The only surviving one, I believe. Apart from the two of us everybody else seems to be dead now and I myself am an ageing, crusty old spinster of ninety-three. I understand you are a schoolteacher, which I consider the most worthy of professions, having been one myself for some considerable time. Now I run a private girls' school situated just outside the RAF station, but seldom teach these days. What do I know of anything now? The only subject in which I excel is history and then only the events from 1848, for obvious reasons.

I am writing to you for a particular reason. In my dotage I have become overly sentimental and wish my school to remain within the family. Instead of surprising you with an inheritance, as if you were the heroine in a cheap novel (although Mr Trollope was not a cheap novelist, and he was wont to use the device of *deux ex machina*), I am thinking of offering you a position here during my lifetime with the objective of passing the estate on to you after my death.

It is fortunate that you are a schoolteacher, though hardly astonishing since the profession has been in the family for a very long time. I understand your mother taught before you and her brother, your uncle, was a professor at some university or other. Teaching is in our blood and since I pride myself that I was a *good* teacher, I imagine you are too, and nothing would give me greater pleasure than to have my great-niece take the reins from my hands and trot my little school forward into the second half of the century. Even if you were not a teacher it would make little difference: running a school requires business acumen, a flair for administration, and a little faith in God when the incomings do not quite match the outgoings.

You may wonder why I make no reference to the fact that we are at the moment engaged in a war with that devil Adolf Hitler. It is because I have faith in our leaders, Mr Churchill especially, that they will deliver us from the evil that is the Nazi invader. The Germans cannot possibly win: Mr Churchill, our government and the armed forces won't let 'em, so there. My school will survive it all, even though it is close enough to the aerodrome to cause a few palpitations occasionally. The RAF station at Hornchurch is frequently attacked as you can imagine and sometimes the bombs fall uncomfortably close to Gradge Lodge.

If the contents of my letter interest you in the least, I should be glad if you will visit us at the above address, on Saturday, 1st March.

> I remain,
> your aunt,
> Amelia Sartour

'There is a God,' whispered Rebecca, placing the treasured letter on the kitchen table, unfortunately in a pool of spilt tea.

'Is there, Mummy?' Kim said, wide-eyed. 'I thought there was, because of 'ssembly.'

Rebecca laughed, though she was close to tears as well. That this letter should have come at such a time was a miracle indeed. It also seemed strange to her, once she got to thinking about it, how Amelia Sartour seemed to know so much about her and her present circumstances. How did the old woman know Rebecca was a schoolteacher? Who was great-aunt Amelia's informant? With whom was the old lady in contact?

It was all very mysterious. Exciting, but mysterious nonetheless.

Another job! The possibility of another job in another school!

Rebecca knew of the existence of Aunt Amelia through the family Bible, on the front blank page of which had been drawn a short but neat family tree. She took out the small Bible, kept in a small seaman's trunk under her bed, and stared at the tree, to which Kim had not yet been added.

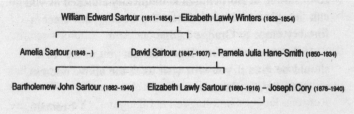

William Edward Sartour (1811–1854) – Elizabeth Lawly Winters (1829–1854)

Amelia Sartour (1848 –)   David Sartour (1847–1907) – Pamela Julia Hane-Smith (1850–1934)

Bartholomew John Sartour (1882–1940)   Elizabeth Lawly Sartour (1880–1916) – Joseph Cory (1878–1940)

Rebecca Cory (1913 –) – Alan James Daniels (1910–1940)

Rebecca knew that William and Elizabeth Sartour, and their two children, had emigrated to Australia in 1854. It was said that the ship had picked up a fever when it docked in Aden and the two adults had died of this while on the voyage across the Indian Ocean. Amelia and David, the two children, had remained in Australia where they had undergone both terrible and remarkable adventures before both returning to England as adults. David Sartour was Rebecca's maternal grandfather; he had died in 1907. The Sartours, Aunt Amelia excepted, were not a particularly long-living family.

Since Rebecca's own mother had died before she herself had reached four years, Rebecca knew very little about the

Sartours, except through family myths, which were sparse. Her father had passed on some vague stories to her, about the Australian orphans being parted and each going into the Australian outback at different times to work on farms, but the recounting had been befuddled by Joseph's permanent alcoholic haze, a state which Rebecca had as a child considered 'normal' in her father since she had spent her formative years under its influence. In any case, the Sartours were from Rebecca's mother's side and no doubt her father had only an indistinct understanding of the biographies even before the drink blurred them further.

She certainly had not known about Aunt Amelia's school. It was all very extraordinary.

'You look happy,' said Kim, taking her mother's face in her little hands. 'Have you had a present?'

Rebecca laughed and hugged her daughter. 'You could say that, sweetie. At least, it might turn out to be a present, who knows? This letter was from my Great-aunt Amelia . . .'

'I read that.'

'Yes, well, she wants us to go to a place called Hornchurch.'

'Where's that?' asked Kim.

'I believe it's near Romford, in Essex – not too far away. A bit more out in the country I think. How do you feel about that? Would you like to live in the country?'

'Will I have to leave Mary and William, my friends?'

Rebecca nodded seriously. 'I'm afraid so. Not for ever, though. We could come and visit them – or they could visit us. We'd have to see. We'd have a nicer life at Hornchurch. Probably a house to live in. What do you say?'

Kim sighed. 'Oh well, if we must.'

'Well, we don't have to, and it still may come to nothing, but we'll see.'

Saturday was only two days away. Rebecca was due to go before the school board on the following Tuesday.

On Saturday the pair, with their ever-present gas masks, took the steam train to Liverpool Street and thence to Romford, where they caught a bus to Hornchurch. The bus conductress, who was a very friendly type, gave Rebecca directions to Gradge Lodge School.

'It's an ever so big house, luv – down Hobblythick Lane.'

It was a delicate, sunny day as Rebecca and Kim walked along the lane close to the airfield. Streaks of white cloud scarred the blue sky – perhaps signs of bad weather to come – but apart from these small blemishes there was a quiet purity about the heavens. The end of the lane, before the sign which said *Gradge Lodge School for Girls*, was lined with chestnut trees which made a leafy tunnel. There were birds having a song-battle in the branches, and a red squirrel performed acrobatic leaps from one tree to another. Both Rebecca and Kim found the scene quite magical. After the oftimes depressing scenery of the docklands, this green place was a different world.

A hundred yards away to the right of the lane, facing the school, ran a high chainlink fence with a roll of barbed wire running along the top. Beyond this fence Rebecca could see fighter planes arranged in a neat row. There was other activity on the RAF station, people moving to and fro, pushing fuel carts, loading things on to platforms, cars and motorcycles whizzing around. There was a control tower in the far corner and a collection of hangars close to the runway.

Some way back from all these was a row of Nissen huts which Rebecca guessed were the living quarters and messes of the personnel who worked on the station and flew the planes. One or two brick-built structures stood overlooking this collection of arched, corrugated monsters, probably the station's HQ buildings.

'Well, here we are,' said Rebecca. 'Your Great-*great*-aunt Amelia's school. What do you think of it?'

They stood outside the ivy-covered estate walls and stared through the handsome, tall, wrought-iron gates. Black poplars shimmered in the grounds, the breezes rustling their leaves like shavings of silver. These towering trees were twice the height of the two-storey building with its hexagonal towers on the two front corners and the Elizabethan spiralling chimneypots endeavouring to corkscrew the sky. Apart from these great giants there were craggy Scots pines, rhododendron shrubs and rosebushes.

The red-brick edifice was not unattractive, though it was bare of any design. A few circular metal discs were set in the wall: the ends of tie beams and evidence that the house had been bothered at some time by subsidence or soil erosion. On either side of the portals were two neat rows of sashcord windows, their glass panes flashing secret messages to someone on the horizon. The roof was of dark blue slate, adding a sombre note to the scene.

'Big,' said Kim, a young lady of few words. 'I like it, Mummy, don't you?'

'Yes, I think I do,' whispered Rebecca, hardly able to believe their luck. 'In fact, I know I do, poppet.'

31

Entering through the school gateway Rebecca noticed a group of girls battling away with hockey sticks on a pitch close to the airfield fence. She groaned. One thing she had never enjoyed was hockey, which she regarded as a brutal, bloody game intended to kill off the weak members of any girls' school: a kind of evolutionary culling system devised by deviant headmistresses.

They went up to the main doors and rang the bell.

A woman wearing a bun in her hair and a grey dress on her narrow frame answered the door. 'Yes?' she asked, then looking down at Kim enquired, 'Is this a new pupil?' It appeared to take much effort for the woman to muster a smile when she spoke these words. Rebecca felt it was a little like sheet ice cracking under pressure.

'No – at least, not yet,' said Rebecca hastily. 'My name is Rebecca Daniels – I'm here at the request of my aunt, Amelia Sartour.'

The arctic smile remained. 'Ah yes, Miss Sartour is expecting you. I'm Helena Patten – won't you come this way?'

Rebecca, with Kim in hand, was led through a dusty hallway, up a magnificent spiral staircase, to a room above. There Helena Patten knocked on an oak door. There was a muffled sound from within which seemed to mean something to their guide, who opened the door and stood aside to allow them to enter.

Rebecca was first struck by the enormous number of indoor plants in the high-ceilinged room, making the place look more like a greenhouse in Kew Gardens than an office, although there was a mahogany desk in the middle of the floor. It was a light, airy room painted cream and green, which also added to the conservatory feel. There were no curtains at the window. The person who used this room disliked a lot of fussy ornaments and materials around her, but obviously loved live greenery. The aroma was one of vegetation.

A wizened little old woman with skin like a large brown monitor lizard was sitting in a basket chair on the far side of the room by a huge Norman-arch window. She was staring out at the girls playing hockey, her face grim. This was obviously Amelia Sartour, their relation.

'Pass, you silly girl, pass . . .' she was muttering. To Rebecca it might just as well have been 'kill, you silly girl, kill'. Then Amelia turned, as if suddenly realising she was not alone any more. Her face broke into a creased smile. It was as if someone had crumpled an old map. It was a smile full of warmth and Rebecca experienced something quite unlike the feeling she had had when exposed to Helena Patten's north wind.

'Your relatives, Amelia,' said Helena Patten in a flat tone.

Amelia frowned at first, as if searching her memory, then her face broke into a smile of understanding. 'Rebecca and Kim?' she said, reaching out a wrinkled hand like a claw, and Rebecca stepped forward to shake it. The skin had a remarkably silky feel to it, quite belied by its appearance. Amelia apparently noticed that both her visitors were staring at her and Kim especially seemed to be holding back, awed by her.

'The Australian sun isn't kind to a woman's skin,' she said, as if some explanation were needed. 'You don't need to touch me, Kim dear. I'm a little repulsive.'

Kim looked stricken, but stepped bravely forward and shook Amelia's hand with a vigorous motion. 'How do you do, Auntie?' she said, then stepped back again, making Amelia beam.

'Oh,' cried Rebecca, 'you must think we're awfully rude – I'm dreadfully sorry.'

Amelia laughed. 'No need to be sorry, dear,' she said, the Australian drawl sounding surprisingly soft and pleasant on Rebecca's ears. 'I know what I look like. Anyway, get yourselves some chairs, sit down. We've got some catching up to do – more than that, because we've not met before, have we?' She glanced towards the window as if reluctant to give up her attempt to control the hockey match by telepathy.

Kim got herself a chair, scraping it on the wooden floor. Amelia winced but said nothing. Rebecca, seeing this reaction, quickly declined Kim's offer to get her one too and found one for herself behind a big rubber plant. They settled down in front of Amelia.

'Do you want to watch your hockey game first?' asked Rebecca. 'We'll sit here quietly if you like. It's so pleasant to be here – you can't imagine.'

'Do you like hockey?' asked Amelia eagerly.

Rebecca decided to be utterly truthful. 'I loathe it. I regarded it as a form of torture at school. I was always the last girl to be picked for any team during games and they usually stuck me in goal, out of the way, hoping my inert, cowardly body would be enough to stop any shots getting in.'

Amelia's face fell a little, but she rallied immediately. 'At least you're honest. Hockey is a passion with me. I think it trains young women to meet men on an equal footing.'

Helena Patten had entered the room with a tray of tea at this point and was clearly interested in Rebecca's reply.

'If you wish to club a man to death,' Rebecca said, 'yes, I imagine it is good training.'

Helena gasped and almost dropped the tray. Amelia, however, laughed. 'A sense of humour. I like that. Now Helena here hasn't got one. There isn't a humorous fibre in her body – not even in her arms. She had both her humerus bones removed at birth, didn't you, dear?'

Helena said grimly, 'If you say so, Amelia. Now, who would like Earl Grey and who would like Lapsang Souchong?'

Rebecca's eyes widened a little; so did Kim's on seeing a plateful of cream cakes.

Amelia said, 'I hoarded the tea before the war – the cream comes from a local farmer. The Earl Grey only comes out on special occasions, so make the most of it. So what's it to be? Name your choice.'

'Could I have Earl Grey, please?' asked Kim, not knowing what she was going to get.

'I'd like Earl Grey too,' Rebecca said. 'Lapsang Souchong always tastes like stale cigarette ash to me.'

Another gasp from Helena and a grim smile from Amelia. 'Lapsang is my favourite,' said Amelia. 'I see you and I are going to get on well together. We appear to be completely incompatible, which always makes life a little more interesting. Milk? Sugar? Helena, are you staying or going? You're quite welcome to some tea too.'

'Going,' said Helena starchily. 'I have things to do.' She left the room at what could only be described as a marching pace, her arms swinging.

'What about you, young lady?' asked Amelia. 'Do you

dislike hockey? Would you like more milk in your tea? A cream cake?'

'Yes, please,' said Kim, 'milk and cream cake.' She sniffed her cup. 'This tea smells like Mummy's scent.'

'It does have a certain perfumed aroma, I'll grant you,' said Amelia. 'Which is why I find it tame when compared with Lapsang Souchong. It seduces you. It has no bite.'

All of this was lost on Kim, who merely sighed.

Amelia proceeded to serve her guests, asking Kim again, 'And what about my question regarding hockey?'

'I've never played it,' said Kim, 'but it looks good fun.'

'Well, I'm glad to hear it – that it looks like fun. It *is* fun. Your mother doesn't know what she's missing.'

'Oh yes I do,' replied Rebecca, taking her cup of tea, 'and I'm glad I'm missing it.'

'Now then,' said Amelia, getting down to business. 'You got my letter otherwise you wouldn't be here. I must say I'm not the sentimental type, but I'm pleased to meet my relatives at last, especially you, Kim. The younger generation . . .' She sighed. 'If you come here, you may play for England one day. Two of our old girls have, you know.'

Hockey, thought Rebecca. The old woman is hockey-mad. She didn't look as if she could even *lift* a hockey stick, let alone wield one. Perhaps that was it? Perhaps she was living out her fantasies through her students?

' . . . so,' Amelia was saying, 'do you think you could handle a school of this size, Rebecca? Would you *want* to? I understand your job at the moment is not wildly exciting?'

Rebecca said, 'You seem to know quite a bit about me, Aunt Amelia.'

Amelia's slight, wizened frame shuddered. 'Not *Aunt*, please. It's not strictly true in any case. There's a *great* in there somewhere, but that's even worse. Amelia will suffice for now, though you might have to be a bit more formal in front of the staff, if I decide I want you to come here.'

'If I decide I want to come here too,' said Rebecca, which Amelia acknowledged with a slight nod of her head. 'But I would like to know how you came to hear of me.'

Amelia explained. 'I was at a London convention for school heads a few weeks ago and I met this ghastly man who is the headmaster of a state school in Tilbury or some such awful place. I imagine all his pupils to be the children of dockside gangsters, scrap-metal merchants and used-car salesmen, going by his general demeanour. I'm sure no one else would trust their offspring with such a man. He told me his name was Sinclair. Since I could think of nothing else to say to the man I asked him if he was married and he told me he was a "gay bachelor" courting a young teacher at his school.'

A cold, prickly feeling came over Rebecca as she listened to her aunt. It was as if some low-order creature were crawling over her flesh. She could almost anticipate Amelia's next words. She wanted to squash Sinclair, there and then, on the spot. The man was the most obnoxious creature nature had inflicted on the world since the cockroach evolved. She wanted to stamp on him, crush him like a beetle. That he should speak to her aunt in this manner made Rebecca writhe with embarrassment, especially since he had used the word 'courting' which, disgusting as it was to her, was not even true. What he really wanted to do, what he was trying to do, was get her into bed, after which she knew he would discard her like some used item that no longer interested him.

'The name he gave me, of the woman, was your own,' continued Amelia, confirming Rebecca's fears and making her squirm. 'He also mentioned that you had a young daughter who was a pupil at his dreadful school. I heard from your father shortly before he died and he told me of your marriage. Daniels is not an unusual name, but coupled with your Christian name I had a very good idea it was you. I made further enquiries, discreetly, amongst the other headmistresses and headmasters. They informed me that this Sinclair creature was a predator and that if I had a niece who worked in his school I might not do better than to offer her the chance of an escape. I telephoned your school secretary saying I was making enquiries on behalf of the Inland Revenue and asked for your address. You would be amazed, my dear Rebecca, how frightened people are of the Inland Revenue. She gave me the address immediately.'

Rebecca said, 'Thank you for being so frank, Amelia. You're right – I would do anything to get away from that man. Almost anything. He's a walking plague. Far from "courting" me, which revolts me enough, he has . . .' Rebecca glanced down at Kim, who was munching a cream cake and taking in every word that was being uttered. 'He has other, less worthy, designs – to put it politely.'

'What designs, Mummy?' asked Kim.

Amelia patted her head. 'You just eat your cake, young lady – this is adult conversation.' She turned to face Rebecca again, her face a picture of simmering fury. 'So,' she said, 'he thinks he can do as he likes with one of my family, does he? I knew he was a rat the minute I laid eyes on the creature. Odious man. I'll see if I can fix his bracket before too long.'

Rebecca said hastily, 'Amelia, you mustn't take up a vendetta. He's done nothing yet . . .'

'He's made your life a misery, hasn't he?' growled the old woman.

'Yes,' admitted Rebecca, 'he has. But if you do give me a job here, then it'll be the biggest slap in the face he's had in a long time. He won't recover from it easily. I can leave his school with dignity and with him knowing that I'm going on to better things. That would cut him to the quick.'

'Then consider it settled,' said Amelia. 'What I propose to do is this. I'm going to make one of my staff, a woman who's been loyal to me for many years now . . .'

'Helena Patten?' questioned Rebecca.

'No, not Helena. She doesn't teach. She's my companion and my housekeeper. No, this is another member of staff, Miss Francine Knole. I plan to make her my headmistress if you come to us. You shall take the place she vacates, teaching English and history.'

'Not hockey?' asked Kim.

Both women looked at Kim and smiled wryly. 'No, not hockey, Kim,' continued Amelia. 'English and history.' She looked seriously into Rebecca's eyes. 'It wouldn't be fair to make you headmistress over those who've been here many years.'

'I should think not,' answered Rebecca.

Amelia said, 'But, when I die, you will become the school's new owner. That's a different thing altogether. That's an inheritance, which no employee should expect. I'll try not to let that happen too soon, but I am over ninety, though I don't feel it. It may sound funny to you young people but I feel the same now as I did when I was your age. You don't grow old inside, only on the outside.'

'It doesn't sound funny – sometimes I still feel as if I were Kim's age.'

'Do you, Mummy?' asked Kim. 'What, when we play dolls' houses together, you mean?'

'Something like that, darling.'

'Well, there it is,' Amelia said. 'I trust that if you and Miss Knole get on all right together, when the time comes for you to step into my shoes you'll allow her to continue as headmistress, while you see to the running of the school in other ways. It would be a little cruel to reward her with the headship only to have it taken away on my death, which *might* come at any day, despite my attempts to ward it off. It'll be up to you then, of course. You may even want to continue teaching, to keep your hand in. I did, until I became a wrinkled old crone.'

Kim asked, 'Are you a wrinkled old crone? What's one of them?'

'A witch,' laughed Amelia, her eyes sparkling. Then to Rebecca she added, 'Well, what do you say?'

Rebecca could hardly contain her emotion. This very generous offer couldn't have come at a better time. Last week she was looking destitution in the face and now she was being offered a plum job and a future inheritance. It seemed as if God had rolled over in bed, woken up, and reminded Himself that He had to take care of a mortal called Rebecca Daniels.

'I don't know what to say – I'm overwhelmed. Of course I

want to come here, but don't you want some references or something? What if you find I'm a useless teacher? I do have my certificate, but that's no proof of my worth.'

'Nonsense, girl. I'm a good judge of character – and of intelligence. You're as bright as they come. You'll do very nicely, thank you.'

'In that case, I would love to come to Gradge Lodge to teach. I also appreciate your decision to make me a beneficiary in your will, but you don't have to, you know. We've never met before now. Haven't you got a good friend you'd rather leave it to? I don't believe in all that "blood is thicker than water" stuff. Friendship is thicker than both of them.'

'My best friend is Helena, whom I expect the school to take care of until she too dies. It's one of the stipulations of the inheritance. Don't tell her I said that to you. She too is old now. I want the school on young shoulders. Do you understand? I want it to survive in the modern world. Once this nasty war is over Britain will begin to thrive again. It'll have need for young women in business. We must provide those women, from schools like Gradge Lodge. The war has changed the status of women dramatically. Today they work in the factories – tomorrow they will be running those factories.'

Rebecca wondered what she wasn't to tell Helena: that Amelia regarded her as her best friend, or that Amelia's will stipulated that she was to be taken care of in perpetuity by the school. Whichever it was, Rebecca would honour it by saying nothing of their present conversation. As for women in top management jobs, she wasn't sure it was going to be that easy.

The men might let them work on the factory floor, now that they needed them, but once the war was over they would want their old jobs back again. Rebecca could not see men on the shop floor doing what female managers told them to do.

Still, it was nice to dream, and certainly she *was* young and energetic. She could make a wonderful career for herself as owner of Gradge Lodge School. It was just that she didn't want to take the job away from a more deserving person.

'Amelia,' she asked, 'how did you come to own the school? I thought you went to Australia when you were Kim's age.'

'I did, but I made my fortune there. Perhaps it's time to tell the story.' Amelia leaned back in her chair, staring out of the window, not at the girls playing hockey, but at the broad expanse of Essex sky. Then her attention seemed to switch to the tall, lean poplars. Rebecca sensed that the old woman was looking back, into the mists of her own past, and was seeing in those poplars something that triggered old memories, brought them into focus. 'Straight as masts,' she murmured. 'Yes, it's probably time. After all, I don't want to die with it locked in my breast. Yes, I'll tell you how it happened, though perhaps not all at once, not all today. Kim dear, take another cream bun, this is going to be boring for you . . .'

Chapter Four

It was the spring of 1854 and I was six years old. I caught the excitement from my parents, though I hardly understood what was going on at the time. We were emigrating to a land called Australia – a land bright with promise, so my father told my older brother David and me – and we were going there by one of the last great sailing ships, *The Wanderer*. Father was a schoolteacher and he had been promised a post at a school in Sydney, where we were to make our new life. I had read about convicts going to Australia, in one of my reading books, and I asked Father if we were being sent there by our government because we had done something wrong.

'Botany Bay?' he laughed. 'No, no, dear. That stopped some few years ago . . .'

'Not so many,' said my mother, quietly. 'They were still sending convicts to Van Diemen's Land two years ago.'

A gentle but firm argument then started between my mother and father over the merits and demerits of a prison colony, my father initially being for them, my mother against. They were always having 'discussions' like this and neither necessarily believed in the views they put forward. They did it simply for the mental exercise and often changed sides in mid-debate, easily and without faltering, executing a 360-degree turn. Listeners would raise their eyebrows and look at one another in puzzlement, not understanding what was going on between my parents.

My father was a small man with a large moustache and my mother was described as *petite*. They were a formidable couple, despite their small statures, since they did not see giants around them, but dwarves – dwarves in intellect. My father was an intellectual snob and intimidated those with lesser minds. He was not a bully, but his confidence was such that he never allowed himself to be considered anything other than a marvellous man with a marvellous wife. They never ceased praising each other, my parents, and I loved them both. David and I had a wonderful childhood up to that point.

When I first saw *The Wanderer* I was struck with awe. She was a five-masted barque, long and sleek, with rigging everywhere. It seemed to me that she had been caught in a giant spider's web and had not been able to divest herself of the network of threads. David was ecstatic. Once we had come up the gangplank, he ran around the deck in a mad frenzy of delight, seriously getting in the way of the sailors who were trying to make the ship ready to sail. Father called David to heel, though I could tell that he too was feeling the excitement. Mother and I were too ladylike to stoop to such outrageous behaviour and we simply held hands and stared about us.

We set sail at seven in the evening. Once we had been towed out of Portsmouth harbour, up went the sails, cracking as they filled with wind, and the ship leaped forward. She was like some purebred racehorse, at last let rein after long restraint. She fairly cut through the water at what seemed to me to be a fantastic speed. Up aloft the sailors were busy in the rigging, like monkeys foraging for nuts in the trees. They looked so sure of themselves as they did their aerobatics as skilfully as trapeze artists at the circus. David and I had cricks in our necks for hours afterwards through staring up at these clever creatures busy amongst the folds of the sails. Mother and Father were more interested in the sunset and the island we had left behind. It seemed to me that now we were actually on our way to the great land of Australia, they were experiencing regret.

Our awed preoccupation with the sailors and my parents' feelings of grief over leaving Britain did not last long, however, for we were all sick in the Bay of Biscay and interested only in reaching some kind of destination where there was dry land. The boat creaked and moved around, beneath and above us like a live creature, and all I could wail was, 'I want to go home, Mother.'

David complained too, but not as much as I. I'm the world's worst when I'm discomfited. However, I was also the first to recover and was running around the upper deck long before Father staggered out of the cabin and gulped down several breaths of salt air as if he had been starved of oxygen since leaving port. It was still quite choppy that day, with spume as fine as Irish mizzle soaking the lower sails and everything on deck.

By the time we reached the coast of Africa, everyone was well again, and to David's disgust Mother insisted we did our lessons. David wanted to be roaming round the ship, talking to the sailors or fishing with a line from the stern. I was quite happy to do some work, because I was becoming bored with life on board a sailing ship. There was not a great deal for a six-year-old girl to do, apart from sewing or playing with my dolls, and neither of those occupations has ever been a favourite with me.

At Cape Town we were allowed off the ship to walk around. I was amazed at the black people there: I had not seen so many foreign faces in my life. And the English the white people spoke was impossible to understand. They had this strange clipped accent as well as distorting the actual words.

'Can we go into the jungle and see some wild animals?' cried David. 'I want to see a tiger!'

Father looked at him severely. 'This is *Africa*, not India. There are no tigers in Africa, unless they be in zoos. We may have the chance to visit the local zoo to see a lion, if they have one here, which I very much doubt.'

'I want to buy some diamonds,' I said to Mother. 'I want to sparkle all over.'

'At least Amelia has the right continent,' Father replied, 'if unfortunately a rather mistaken idea of the size of the family coffers.'

David glared at me for this and made one of his ugly faces behind Father's back. I didn't care. I just stuck out my tongue and wrinkled my nose at him, which made him more furious than ever. I know he would have pulled my hair if he could have got away with it. Instead he feigned indifference and went to the rail to look at the ships and small sailing craft that were scattered over the still waters of the harbour.

Later, when David had forgotten all about being told off by Father, I went up and kissed him on the cheek. He wiped it away quickly with the back of his hand but I could tell he was pleased. He liked affection from me. It made him feel, I think, like the grand older brother.

'I hope you don't grow up to be a bluestocking though,' he said to me, repeating a phrase he had heard. 'It's not good for girls to get too much learning. You have to be a governess if you do, and you wouldn't like that, Amy.' He always called me Amy when he was feeling affectionate. 'Governesses have to look after horrible rich brats for well-off families.'

'Are we a well-off family?' I asked him.

He screwed up his face in concentration and finally said, 'No, we're just ordinary.'

Soon the ship was sailing again and we made our way up the eastern coast of Africa towards an Arabian port called Aden, a place (I learned in my lessons) which had been secured for Queen Victoria by a Captain Haines, who saw it as a perfect refuelling station for ships on their way to India. By this time we were well used to the pitch and roll of the ship and in fact David announced he was going to become a sea captain once he grew up, 'Which is not so very long away,' he added. 'I'm almost eight as it is and it hasn't taken long to get this far.'

That was before the storm off Madagascar, which tossed the vessel around like a cork and scared even the hardy sailors with the terrible waves it unleashed. The wind shrieked over the planks, through the shrouds and stays, tearing the sails, snapping one of the masts. The waves were like liquid mountains around us, as the ship would go down into a deep trough of water, the ocean like a vertical wall just ahead of the bows. Then *The Wanderer* would rise slowly, as if dragging a thousand anchors with it, climbing up that great wall until it reached the top, only to crash down into another trough on the far side.

The whole world was green madness and everything was

soaked through to the very core. A sailor fell from the rigging and was killed when he struck amidships of the rolling craft. His body was then swept overboard by the torrents that crashed over the decks into that terrible raging sea and was never seen again. I imagined his body washing up on some foreign shore, hair and eyes bleached white by the salt sea and sun, to confound Hottentots and Zulus with the paleness of his form.

Wind found its way into every corner of the cabin: a cold, wet wind with salt on its tongue. It did not let us sleep, nor could we eat, for the seasickness had returned with a vengeance. There was darkness and chaos on the deep, which profoundly impressed me, and I knew then that there really was a God, a Devil, and all the might of Heaven and Hell. We were thrown at the sky, rejected, tossed down into the waters again, spun like a twig in a maelstrom, battered on all sides by waves – everything except turned upside down and shaken out.

Between our bouts of sickness we prayed for deliverance, and one day I fell asleep as a stillness came over the ocean. When I woke there was a gentle mist creeping through the bulkhead into the cabin and a wonderful tranquillity in the air. I went up on to the deck to find that the sea was again flowing calmly, a slight swell from the middle of the Indian Ocean the only movement on the broad expanse of water. Porpoise played in the foam around our bows, and flying fish dazzled us with their oily-coloured wing-fins as they skipped in hundreds over the rocking ocean. We realised we were going to live.

Father came up on deck beside me. 'Well, Amelia, the Lord

has seen fit to let us live. He must intend great things for us. You must thank Him in your prayers.'

I did thank him, though I wondered who had sent the storm in the first place if it hadn't been Him.

Aden, our next port of call, came on to the horizon one sweltering day when the wind was barely adequate to nudge the ship onward. A rugged coastline of brown and ochre rock hove into view, beyond which I could see some greenery, but not a great deal. A huge volcano rose out of the sand and rock, just behind the harbour, and I wondered if it were dangerous. It had a wall running round its lip and fortifications at regular intervals in the shape of small towers.

'Is that a *real* volcano?' asked David of my parents.

'An extinct one,' Mother replied. 'It's so old there's a town built inside the cone, called Adan. Adan is the original fishing village which was there when Captain Haines came. This was the first of Queen Victoria's overseas possessions – did you know that . . . ?'

No, we didn't know that, but we learned that when Captain Haines had arrived, much of the land had been forested with mimosa, tamarisk, camel's thorn and myrrh. This had all been stripped away by the ships passing through, for repairs and fuel. Gone too were the hares, rabbits and gazelles, which had lived amongst the trees.

'Now,' said Mother, 'it's a boiling-hot, dusty corner of Arabia with nothing much to offer. The Queen of Sheba's wells are here, though, which helps to make parts of the landscape fertile, and the Sheik of Othman's gardens are said to be some of the prettiest in the East.'

Father wanted to go ashore once we had moored in the

harbour. The captain was strongly against it.

'This is a white man's grave,' he said. 'You're green. You're not wise to the dangers like a sailor. I should not advise you to step out on to this godforsaken rock. However, if you must, then you do so at your own risk and I would suggest you leave your children in the ship. A land of beggars, robbers and flies is not a place for young children. Besides, here on the deck of the ship they will at least feel the benefit of a cool breeze, while on that harbour, and especially inside the crater, the temperatures and humidity are enough to bring a desert pi-dog to its knees.'

Father stared wistfully at the craggy walls of the crater, hating to miss an experience he might regret not taking advantage of in the future. Mother could see he desperately wanted to go out amongst the Arabs and observe their way of life, if only for a day. My father was always consumed with curiosity, a healthy interest in the lives of others. He considered himself a fortunate man and he grieved for those less blessed.

Eventually Mother said to him, 'Oh, come on, let's ignore the captain's warning. He probably has to say that to all the passengers, to protect himself. Of course something *might* happen to us, but something equally serious could happen here on the ship. Why, that storm almost took us all!'

So, after hugging us both, kissing us and asking us to be good in their absence, my parents took a boat to the shore.

David grumbled at first. 'I wanted to go too – I'm as strong as Father.' But then the Arab bum boats came out to us, with Arab boys who would dive for a small coin thrown overboard, even though the water was full of sharks. The bum boats sold all manner of goods, from wicked-looking daggers to wonderful carved boxes inlaid with mother-of-pearl to brass ornaments and sheepskin rugs.

David and I had no money, of course, but we watched others buying goods. There was an Arab magician – a man in a loincloth with a ragged white turban – called the Gulli-Gulli Man, who performed on deck for us, pulling pigeons out of his turban, doing some amazing card tricks, and finding chickens' eggs in our ears. When he had gone, with the setting of the sun, we watched the landscape turn from brown to red in the twilight. The shoreline was an ants' nest of activity, with Arab dhows sailing in and out of the harbour, unloading their cargoes from Africa and India: herbs and spices, ivory, fabrics, medicines, bananas, and a multitude of other goods.

There was a lot of boat-building in progress on the beaches, where they were constructing Arab booms and feluccas. I could smell the freshly cut timber, drifting over on offshore breezes, the burning of their drills as they cut holes in the wood. There were sailmakers and fishing-net makers on the strand too, sitting in the shade of their palm-tree-leaf huts, their eyes intent on the close work.

As the gloaming deepened, birds called kite-hawks – big brown buzzards – wheeled above the ship and dived for scraps when we threw them into the water. We managed to keep ourselves amused until Mother and Father returned, full of high spirits. They told us how they had wandered through the markets, described the colour and excitement of the dusty town which was full of Bedu from the northern deserts, come to buy staple goods and exotic luxuries with their silver Maria Theresa dollars. There were dromedaries, goats and flea-bitten pi-dogs sharing the houses with the local people. There was gold and silver, and precious stones, and beautiful cloth. Mother had purchased a silk scarf, all the way from China, which she wore round her neck. Father had bought a clasp knife with a whalebone handle. There were gifts for us too – a small lapis-lazuli box for me and a fishing rod for David – and we were ecstatic.

Our happiness was short-lived, however, because three days later Mother and Father fell ill.

'It looks like a kind of typhoid,' said the ship's doctor, 'though I can't tell for sure . . .'

Father and Mother admitted to eating shellfish while they were inside the crater, which might have carried the disease. The ship's doctor seemed powerless to help them. Some of the passengers said he was not a very good medical practitioner, or he would not be on board a ship full of emigrants. I was just bewildered by the speed with which my mother and father sank into a terribly weak condition.

'David,' croaked my mother one evening, as she lay on her bunk looking grey and drawn, her eyes dull, 'if – if we should die, look after your sister.'

David, who was only seven, simply burst into tears and tried to hug Mother. I cried too. I was confused and miserable, not knowing what was going to happen to us.

Father went first, in the middle of the night. He had developed pneumonia a week after the doctor had diagnosed typhoid. His slight frame quickly wasted and he passed away looking ravaged. It was as if some evil spirit had entered him and robbed him of all his vitality, leaving just a shell. They came and took his body away the next morning, holding a swift funeral on deck before letting his canvas-covered body slide into the sea. We sobbed our hearts out, David and I, and prayed for our mother.

Two days after Father had died, Mother seemed to rally, but this was a false encouraging sign. Her fever rose immediately afterwards, she kept calling for water in a ragged voice, and she died with her eyes blazing and two bright red blotches on her cheeks. She screamed, 'God help my children!' and raised herself up on to her elbows before sinking back and sucking in her last breath. Her face, the colour of stale bread, seemed to have collapsed in on itself, and she looked like an old woman. They buried her at sea shortly afterwards, the small package slipping down into the waves to disappear below them in the wake of the ship. Within two short weeks we had been made orphans.

The captain was very kind, but he had his duties to attend to and he asked if any of the other passengers would be willing to look after us. A couple with eight children said that two more would make no difference to them and told the captain they would care for us. Mr and Mrs Whitaker came to visit us in our cabin and looked around with eyes like ravens.

'It's nice an' roomy in here, ain't it?' said Mrs Whitaker. 'Ours is so crowded, what with all the kids and everythink. I 'spect it would be a good idea if we moved in here.'

'That's my mother's bunk,' cried David. 'You mustn't sleep in my mother's bunk.'

'Quiet, boy,' snapped Mr Whitaker. 'Yer mother's dead, ain't she? She don't need it now. You've got all this space and we're crowded out. Our kids ain't got a spare inch to put their heads down. We 'ave to sleep in shifts.'

Put like that, it seemed churlish of us to want to keep four bunks to ourselves, so Mr and Mrs Whitaker came and took over our parents' space. Pretty soon afterwards they moved two more of the children in, so that we were topped and tailed in the bunks. While they were there they went through our things, making comments about Father's books and Mother's collection of Spanish hair combs.

'Leather ones look worth somethink,' said Mrs Whitaker, turning over Father's books. 'Might fetch a little bit – you never know. What's it say on the front, child?'

'That's my father's book, not yours,' I said. 'You can't have it.'

Mr Whitaker moved his face close to mine. 'You watch your tongue, missy. If we've adopted you, we need some compensation, see – for our kindness and generosity. This 'ere stuff ain't worth much, so it'll have to do, won't it? We'll sell some of them combs in Hong Kong, to get some food for the little 'uns when we get to Australia. You wouldn't want our babies to starve, would you?'

I said I didn't want anyone to go hungry, but these things were ours to keep, not theirs. Mrs Whitaker laughed and said she would see about that. When David complained to the captain, he said we should be grateful someone was looking after us and that our parents' possessions did not amount to a great deal anyway. 'The Spanish combs are quite valuable,' David told him. The captain laughed at this. 'Well, they may seem so to a young boy like you, but combs? I shouldn't think so.' In fact one of the combs was decorated with a silver inlay and fetched ten guineas from one of the paying passengers. Later the second oldest Whitaker son told us that his mum had been to the captain before David, to prepare that gentleman for any possible objections from us children.

As to looking after us, the Whitakers did nothing except make us into their personal servants, much the same as they had their own children, who were treated only slightly better than David and me. The three eldest enjoyed a sort of officer status, in that they didn't fetch and carry, but acted as overseers, their freedom curbed only through having to supervise the rest of us all the day long, while the parents simply made themselves at home in our cabin, for the most part sleeping, and eating the rest of the time.

At Hong Kong we remained on the ship as before, while the Whitakers went ashore and spent the money they had looted from my parents' possessions. They left their eldest daughter to watch over us. She was a thin, nasty girl of fourteen, who kept pinching me hard on the thighs so that little dark bruises like squashed blackberries appeared, hidden by my dress. When I burst into tears and David objected, she bit him savagely on the hand, drawing blood and making him howl with pain and fright.

'That's prob'ly rabies, that bite,' she sneered at David. 'An' if you tell on me, I'll put a spell on you, so your willy will shrivel up like a rotted fig and drop off.'

We were terrified of her.

When the Whitaker adults came back on board I watched them for signs of illness, hoping they had caught typhoid like my mother and father. Nothing happened. They were just as brash and bullying as ever, encouraging their children to treat us like skivvies. Our clothes were taken and the Whitaker children wore them. One of the boys, just a little older than me, was given my best shift. He tore it the first time he wore it, his boots catching on the hem.

Finally, via Singapore and Bali, we reached Australia, stopping first at Darwin. Then we sailed round the coast until we reached Sydney. The captain asked the Whitakers if they would continue to look after us for a while, thereby discharging duty and responsibility towards us himself, and despite our mumbled protests the Whitakers agreed to keep us until we could be dealt with by the authorities. Once we were off the ship the captain knew he needn't worry about us any more. He had given us to a 'good' family and could wash his mind clean of us.

'We'll take the mites along to the proper Australia office,' said Mrs Whitaker, 'just as soon as we find our accommodations.'

Round about the port however were a number of sheep herders and cattlemen from the outback, looking for sturdy men and women to assist them on their farms. Mr Whitaker took us to several of these men, offering to sell us. An unpaid, farm-raised child – a slave – was invaluable to those who needed helpers. The traffic in such children still goes on today, in 1941, believe it or not. I have continually written to both the British and the Australian governments about it, but of course they are politicians and uninterested.

In those times there was really no one to stop such trafficking in child slaves and, though many of them were well treated, there were obviously cruel people who beat the children, abused them both sexually and physically, and who sometimes worked them to death. These were hard times in Australia, for the colonialists, ex-convicts and the aboriginal natives. The first two were trying to carve a living out of the often inhospitable outback, and the last group were trying to survive being slaughtered to make way for the white man.

So we were peddled like domestic livestock along the quays and wharves of Sydney harbour.

'They're small, admitted,' Mr Whitaker told farmers, gripping us each tightly by the arm, 'but there's good work in 'em. I could let you adopt 'em for a few pounds.'

'Are they your kids?' asked one man.

'In a manner of speakin', yes – adopted, but mine.'

David and I were too terrified to speak out against him. The Whitakers had threatened to beat us and give us to their eldest daughter to do with as she wished if we didn't go along with their scheme. We were two lost and confused children, shocked by the sudden death of our parents and utterly helpless. Eventually, a farmer took David and he was dragged away along the dockside, crying his eyes out, by a burly man in shirtsleeves, flannel trousers and a large-brimmed hat, who said, 'Come on, boy, don't hang back on me now, I got a lot of work to get through today . . . pick your feet up and stop that snivelling.'

Mr Whitaker tried to get someone to take me too, but the farmers eventually took pity on me, crowded round him and told him it was a shame the way he was treating a little girl and if he didn't stop peddling his human cargo they would fetch the law. Whitaker went pale at this and took me down a side alley where he slapped my face for 'being just a useless item of rubbish' and then left me lying there.

I stayed in the alley for the rest of the hot day and wandered out when I became hungry late in the evening.

Then began a period where I became a street urchin, raiding trash outside inns, surviving on crusts and cabbage stalks. During the day I slept in dark corners of the harbour, amongst the rats and cockroaches, coming out at night to scour the back streets and alleys for food. I began to steal things from stalls in the market. This brought me to the notice of the authorities. By the time I was caught I was like a feral creature: ragged, filthy, scrawny. I was so dirty they didn't know whether I was African, Indian or European. I screeched at them like a cat and fought with the hands that tried to hold me until I was too weak to stand.

The police eventually handed me over to an orphanage, who took me in and told me they were going to send me to school.

'My daddy was a schoolteacher,' I told them.

'How nice,' they replied, smiling those smiles that told me they didn't believe a word of it. 'Well, you'll know all about it then, won't you?'

The school they sent me to was down by Sydney harbour, in an area known today as The Rocks. I remember the lintel over the doorway of the small room. An inscription was etched deeply into the granite. It read: *The Ragged School.*

The Ragged School is still there today, if you ever get to Sydney, though it's not in use, of course. I was both pupil and teacher at that school, over the years, but that's another story and for the moment we'll let those years rest. I'm feeling tired now and would like a nap, so if you don't mind, my dears, please indulge an old lady's afternoon habits.

Chapter Five

Travelling back from Gradge Lodge to her flat in Tilbury, Rebecca reflected on the earlier life of her great-aunt. That such terrible events had befallen someone who was still alive, whom Rebecca had seen and spoken with, seemed amazing to her. Amelia was truly a woman from another world, from history, from a time of sailing ships, penal colonies and wars with natives. In some countries the slave trade still flourished. Amelia was still carrying the scars of a time when Australia had only been self-governing for around four years. That she should have survived such a time, with her mind intact, was also amazing.

'Isn't she an *ugly* old lady?' said Kim, taking a child's-eye view of things. 'Her skin's so *wrinkled*.'

'Perhaps she is a little wrinkled, but she's very old, darling – much older than most people – and she has a heart of gold.'

'Does she, Mummy?' Kim said, swinging her gas mask by its strap. '*Real* gold?'

Rebecca laughed. 'I mean she's very kind – she's being very kind to us, at any rate. I think we're going to go and live at Gradge Lodge. Would you like that?'

'Oh yes, I would. I said I would, didn't I? It would be *super*, wouldn't it?'

When they got back to the flat and Rebecca switched on the radio for the late news there was some good amongst it. President Roosevelt had signed a Lend-Lease Bill to help Britain to obtain war supplies, with payment to be deferred. Winston Churchill followed this announcement with a broadcast telling Londoners to hang on. Rebecca went to bed feeling tired but somewhat happier than she had been for a long while. There was a single raid during the night, which kept them awake for an hour or so, but the Heinkel bombers overflew Tilbury.

On the day of the inquest into her so-called unprofessional behaviour, Rebecca was fired with a sense of right. To Sinclair's astonishment she marched uninvited into the room where he was speaking to the school governors. He tried to shoo her out of the room in his usual bullying manner.

'Wait outside, if you please, Mrs Daniels. The board will call for you when they're ready . . .'

'They might call for me,' she said, 'but will I be there? If they have anything to ask me, or say to me, then they can say it now, while I stand in front of them. I'm not waiting outside, unable to defend myself, while you fabricate a lot of nonsense for their ears, so here I am.'

Sinclair raised his eyes and turned to the board with a look that said, 'See what I have to put up with from this insolent woman?'

The governors were a Mrs Delia Jameson, a magistrate; John Procter, an ironmonger; Philip Swan, a butcher; Randolph Parkinson, a saddler; and finally Dr Turner.

'I think, young lady,' crooned the formidable Mrs Jameson, 'you would do well to heed the headmaster's words.'

Rebecca was not to be frightened by a local matron. 'I don't know what the headmaster has told you,' she said, ignoring the magistrate, 'but I have this to say. I was taking my class . . .'

'This is really out of order,' cried Sinclair. 'I'm afraid I can't stand here and listen to lies.'

Mrs Jameson murmured an agreement with this statement, but John Procter, the ironmonger come down from York, held up a rough, calloused hand. 'Just a minute, let's hear what the lass has got to say. I've been sittin' here while Sinclair's been jabbering on for the last half-hour, by heck, and I can certainly sit here another half-hour listening to t'other side of the story.'

'Yes,' said Dr Turner, 'now she's here, let's listen to what she has to say.'

The other two shopkeepers sat back in their chairs, clearly intimidated by everyone else on the board. They said nothing. They were happy to let others speak for them.

'I was taking my class,' continued Rebecca, 'when I heard a disturbance coming from the class across the corridor. It was clear to me that no teacher was in the room. I believe the golden rule has always been: *never leave your pupils alone without a teacher in attendance.* So after a minute or two I went across the corridor and told that class to join my own, until such time as a teacher did appear.'

'Sounds very sensible to me,' muttered Procter.

Sinclair cried, 'You had no *right*, Mrs Daniels, to usurp the authority of the headmaster in this affair.'

'The teacher in question was with you, Mr Sinclair,' answered Rebecca. 'I should have thought you would have made arrangements for his replacement.'

'There was no one available at the time,' answered Sinclair, back-pedalling a little under the onslaught from his teacher, 'and it was only a few moments . . .'

'It doesn't sound like a few moments to me, Headmaster,' said Dr Turner. 'Even *five* minutes can be dangerous, with some of the hooligans we've got in this school. What if one of the children had injured themselves – or somebody else?'

'Nevertheless,' maintained Sinclair firmly, 'and I think Mrs Jameson will back me up on this, permission was not given for Mrs Daniels to leave her own classroom and cause havoc by removing the pupils from the classroom belonging to Mr Jones, who was already on his way back to them . . .'

'I didn't know that, did I?' retorted Rebecca. 'For all I knew they had been left for quite a while and would remain without a teacher.'

Mrs Jameson, clearly anxious to reinstate her favourite's authority, said sharply to Rebecca, 'What steps did you take to inform the headmaster of your actions?'

Rebecca smiled sweetly at the magistrate, who apparently thought she was about to score a victory for her side. 'I sent a child with a message to the headmaster.'

Mrs Jameson glanced angrily at Sinclair, possibly because she had not been informed of this fact.

'It seems to me,' said Mr Procter, gathering up the thoughts of the others on the board and putting them into words, 'that Mrs Daniels acted very properly. I would've damned – excuse me – damned well thanked her, not brought her here on this wild-goose chase, wasting the board's time. What're you thinkin' of, Mr Sinclair? What's it all about?'

Sinclair cleared his throat, about to speak, when Rebecca blurted out, 'Mr Sinclair is a lonely man – he would like the company of those who do not wish to give it. His attentions are unwanted, unfortunately for him, and he saw in this a way to force those attentions on his reluctant victim. The victim wouldn't play and his threat was made good.'

The inference to be drawn from these remarks was fairly plain to everyone but the magistrate, who looked to others to give her some guidance. Since no one seemed prepared to do so, she was left twiddling a pencil between her fat fingers.

Instead of looking ashamed or embarrassed, Sinclair smirked. 'Of course, a poor teacher on no salary to speak of, with a child to keep, wouldn't want the attentions of a headmaster with a house and position to offer her, I suppose?'

Dr Turner was the one who looked embarrassed. 'I don't think we want to go into these matters, which are obviously nothing to do with the board. I suggest we retain the services of Mrs Daniels.'

'Seconded,' snapped Mr Procter.

'All those in favour?' asked the doctor.

Even Mrs Jameson raised her hand, after a moment's hesitation.

Sinclair looked shocked and angry. 'If she stays, I *go*,' he cried.

A stillness in the room followed this remark, during which panic registered on the face of the headmaster. He was saved by the siren sounding, warning of a German raid. Over the rising note of the siren, Rebecca said, 'I'm happy with the board's decision. I hereby give my notice – I'm resigning. I've been offered a post in another school, which I've already accepted. Whether you keep Mr Sinclair is up to you, but I shan't be staying anyway.' A ripple of surprise went through the members of the board. Mr Procter looked amused, while Mrs Jameson appeared slightly affronted.

Once outside the door, Rebecca said to Mr Procter, 'Thanks for sticking up for me – without you I think I should have been dragged over the coals.'

'Oh, I don't like to see injustice done,' he said, smiling. 'And lots of luck in your new job. Is it a good one?'

'Private school,' she answered. 'I'm to be the new owner one day – an inheritance.'

'You have fallen on your feet then.' He held out his hand and she shook it. 'Take care,' he said, glancing over his shoulder at the retreating headmaster, 'there's more than one Sinclair in the world, unfortunately.'

Glad that the ordeal was over, Rebecca hurried to the shelter, deliberately taking the opposite one to the headmaster. So far as she was concerned she never wanted to see the man again. It was her intention to leave that evening, taking Kim with her.

At six o'clock, with their things packed, Rebecca took one last look round the small, poorly furnished flat. She felt a twinge of sadness. Despite its cracked lino and the massive square chipped sink in which when full one could sink a battleship; despite its noisy plumbing, draughty sashcord windows and smoky chimney, its wobbly furniture; despite the shared toilet with its ugly cistern out on the landing, this had been home for a good while. She knew its every nook and cranny, all its spiders and its mice. It is never easy to wave goodbye to familiar surroundings and set out for the unknown, even if those surroundings are not particularly salubrious.

Then she quietly left the place, slipping her key under the

door after locking it. The landlord had his own key to use to get in again. They tried not to make a noise on the back stairs, but the stairs were old and creaked dreadfully: inevitably one or two neighbours opened their doors to say goodbye. Another just peered through a crack and nodded curtly as Rebecca struggled past with her suitcases.

It was quarter to eight when she and Kim arrived at Gradge Lodge with their luggage. Some small bits of furniture would follow on at a later date. Helena Patten showed her to her second-storey rooms: a bedroom for the two of them, and a living room overlooking the playing fields. Kim was to sleep there for the first few nights, with her mother, until she became used to her new environment, then she would join the other girls in a dormitory.

There were thick blue curtains up at the windows, drawn now because of the blackout. The walls were decorated with a light blue wallpaper and white daisies – a little too 'sweet' for Rebecca's taste but ten times better than the faded roses of their last accommodation. Furniture was sparse but adequate. There were one or two thin Indian rugs on the lino, a nice little fireplace with tiled surrounds and a mantelpiece. Among others there was a print of the ancient city of Petra on the wall from a lithograph by the artist and explorer David Roberts. The caption in Arabic and English read: *Petra – The Eastern End of the Valley*. It was one of those places that Rebecca had promised herself she would visit one day, when the war was over and travel was possible again.

'I hope you'll be comfortable here,' said Helena stiffly. 'The kitchen is on the ground floor in the east wing. You may use it during the evening for a snack, but at other times Cook won't welcome you there. Main meals are eaten with the children in the dining hall. Breakfast is at seven thirty, lunch at twelve and dinner at five thirty. Afternoon tea and a bun is taken in the staff room. The staff bathroom is along the hall and clearly marked on the door. Do you require anything else?'

'No,' replied Rebecca, 'I think everything's fine. Helena, I do hope we can be friends.'

'I find that friendship doesn't mix too well with professionalism,' replied the thin lady. 'However, I appreciate the sentiment.'

With that, Helena left Kim and Rebecca to unpack and make the rooms into their own. Rebecca considered Helena's reply and wondered if the woman was upset that Amelia was handing over the school to a stranger, rather than to her. Or perhaps she really meant what she said and was not one for forming close relationships with colleagues? If so, her companionship to Amelia must be an exception.

Rebecca had not seen Amelia since she arrived, but Helena had told her that the old woman was resting and would not appreciate being woken at that time of day. Rebecca had said she quite understood. There would be time enough to become reacquainted with her great-aunt.

The following morning she and Kim went down to breakfast together and Rebecca met more of the staff. There was only one man, a vicar by the name of Simkins who taught Scripture, Greek and Latin, and took services. The rest of the staff were women. Breakfast was toast and porridge for everyone but Amelia, who had kidneys.

'From a local farmer,' she explained. 'Not entirely legal,

but then I'm not going to live long enough to enjoy such things after the war, so I don't have any scruples. You, on the other hand, have a lifetime of kidneys to look forward to.'

Rebecca detested kidneys, especially the odour of urine about them, and wouldn't have had them on her breakfast plate under any circumstances.

While Kim joined her classmates at their table, Rebecca sat next to a bobbed, blonde-haired woman of about twenty-six. The woman was ever so slightly plump, with a round face and an ingenuous smile, and a complexion which Rebecca envied and secretly thought of as 'milkmaid's skin'. She had no doubt that this woman was attractive to men of all types. Apart from her fresh and engaging looks, she had that bouncy, spirited air about her which men often found exciting. Her blue eyes sparkled when she turned them on to Rebecca. Her voice was full of warmth and revealed just a touch of intrinsic gaiety.

'Hello, my name's Fay – Fay Nelson. You must be Rebecca Daniels. Everyone's been talking about you.'

'Have they?' said Rebecca, looking round and panicking just a little. 'Fay – that's a nice name. It suits you.'

Fay laughed. 'You mean sort of light and airy – empty-headed?'

Rebecca was shocked, because Fay had got it exactly right. 'No, no, nothing like that . . .' she tried to fib.

Fay said, 'I don't mind, it's only the impression I give. Actually you'll find I'm quite bright. I teach maths to the seniors and I know my stuff. Listen, are you doing anything this evening? I'm meeting my boyfriend in the Cherry Tree pub, just along the road from the school. He's a fighter pilot. You want to come along, just for a drink?'

Martin Simkins, the vicar, leaned over and said, 'You want to watch her – she'll lead you astray, that one.' He said it jokingly though and winked at Fay afterwards. The Reverend Simkins was about thirty-five, with short black hair and glasses spanning a broad face. Rebecca could tell immediately that he was desperately in love with Fay Nelson.

Rebecca said to Fay, 'Thanks anyway, but I have my six-year-old daughter with me at the moment. Perhaps when she moves into the dormitory? I don't want to leave her alone on her first evening at the school.'

'No, of course you don't. Maybe next week then?'

Rebecca nodded and smiled, knowing she had already made a friend.

Chapter Six

To Rebecca's relief Kim settled down at the school with little fuss. She had obviously left friends behind in Tilbury, but her 'homesickness' lasted only a few days. Rebecca reminded herself that Kim was very young and young children are more adaptable than adolescents, whose formative years are almost past and who cling to peer groups like drowning men to life rafts. Kim was still at an age when her security was invested in the parent and not in her peer group. So long as her mother was there, there was nothing really to worry about.

To Rebecca's surprise, she herself had some difficulty in adjusting to her new school.

For one thing there was the almost continual noise of aircraft to contend with, since the flight path for the runway was over the top of the school when the prevailing wind was more than a breeze. The planes flew too high, however, for the noise to deafen, and the girls themselves had got used to the sound and didn't even lose a step if they were reading from Shakespeare or Robert Burns. Occasionally a Spitfire or Hurricane came in too low and the girls simply paused for a moment to allow the noise to die away, then continued

69

reading. Rebecca took a leaf out of their book and did the same when taking her lessons.

The greatest risk was that a damaged aircraft might crash into the school, but Rebecca had been assured that injured pilots and planes that were badly shot up didn't overfly the building on the normal run-in, but skirted the edge of the playing field. The station CO was well aware of the danger to the school and was careful to avoid any catastrophes.

The girls at Gradge Lodge were less cheeky than the mixed classes she had dealt with at Tilbury, but they were on the whole more intelligent – or at least thought they were which is almost the same thing – and so their disruptions were harder to deal with. They wouldn't destroy a music master with mayhem and disobedience, but they could subtly wear a teacher down with red-herring questions, asked with innocent faces, and divert the course of the lesson. It was a few days before Rebecca realised what was happening to her and managed to put a stop to this undermining behaviour.

With regard to the other teachers, Rebecca was treated with the cool courtesy and suspicion that a newcomer to an exclusive group usually engenders. Without a doubt no one but Helena Patten and Amelia herself knew of Rebecca's relationship to the school's owner. There was no deference accorded her, as would probably have been the case if the staff knew that the newcomer would eventually be their boss. Martin and Fay were the only exceptions to the rule: they were friendly from the start and had no difficulty in accepting her into their ranks. As is normal with such places, cliques had formed, and Martin and Fay seemed to be one unto themselves. Rebecca was welcomed into their small number.

The enemy group, and there is always an enemy group amongst professionals, was led by the games mistress, Priscilla Mohorty, a formidable tweed-and-brogues woman, with the art mistress, Julia Dane, as her lieutenant. There were two others in this group: women of lesser stature and strength. So far Rebecca had not fallen foul of this feared clique, but she had no doubt that one day there would be a clashing of horns.

A fortnight after Rebecca had arrived at the school Hornchurch Airfield was bombed. The teachers and girls had shelters to go to but the attack was sudden and without the usual warning and so they had to file into the underground bunkers while the bombs were actually falling. The coastal watch had not communicated swiftly enough with the airfield and the fighters were caught on the ground. The whole earth shook under the explosions, causing some of the girls to scream in fright.

Amelia was a calming influence. 'Don't worry, girls, our boys will soon be up there and shooting the beggars down, don't you fret.'

A Stuka strafed the perimeter fence as the last of the teachers were going down into the shelters, the cannon shells ripping up turf and wire. Several stray shells hit a water tank nearby, puncturing the steel, the *plunk, plunk, plunk* sounds counter-pointing the noise of the bombs going off. Water poured from the torn holes in the tank, gushing down into the third shelter and threatening to flood it. Rebecca couldn't believe there was so much liquid in the metal tank: enough to drown everyone in the bunker.

'Everybody out!' yelled Martin Simkins. 'Off you go,

quietly now, into the shelter next door.'

The girls began to file out though the bombs were still falling, pale-faced but outwardly calm now, fighting against the flood which flowed down the steps in a series of waterfalls, and then streamed into the underground room. Rebecca stood ankle-deep in water at the top of the steps outside, taking small children that Martin hoisted up to her and setting them down so that they could run to the neighbouring shelter, into which they were cramming themselves.

A bomb fell on the airfield's edge and Rebecca heard the whine of hot metal in the air, then a peppering sound as a spray of shrapnel showered one of the horse chestnut trees not far from the schoolhouse. For a moment she felt like running, her basic survival instincts telling her to panic and get the devil out of there to somewhere safer, but her reason prevailed and overcame this primitive impulse.

'Come on, girls,' she shrieked, causing Martin to look anxiously at her, 'out we come.'

The bombs rained down, many of them falling beyond the village in the fields, several failing to go off but simply hitting the ground with solid thuds. These unexploded bombs would be dealt with later, by the army. Gradually Rebecca got herself under control. She realised she was shaking badly and she hardly felt Martin's hand on her arm.

'Are you all right?' he asked, ushering the last child down the second shelter.

'Yes,' she lied. 'I think so.'

'You look a bit shocked – take care. Shock can be a nasty thing.'

'I've been bombed before.'

'But not out in the open, I suspect. Come on, let's get down there with the others.'

She felt ashamed of herself for almost panicking and the image of her running away while young children were in trouble was subsequently quite terrible to her. She spoke of it in the shelter to Fay, who whispered, 'We all get those moments, Rebecca – no one would blame you if you *did* run. It's a natural thing, to be afraid when there's all that noise and confusion going on around you.'

'But I think I would have died of shame.'

'But you *didn't* run, so don't worry for nights over what *might* have happened. Goodness me, I wince at some of the things I *might* have done, but I don't let them get to me.'

So Rebecca tried to put the incident out of her mind.

The last thing she had seen before going down the second shelter was the RAF Hurricane fighters taking off from the airfield in a ragged scramble, then rising up to meet the German bombers, who were by that time racing back for the coast. She thought how brave it was of those young men to jump into flimsy machines and throw themselves at heavily armoured monsters bristling with weapons. But the fighters were like determined wasps, absolutely bent on stinging the creature that had just attacked their nest, infuriated by the audacity of the giant who had dropped heavy litter all over their nicely lawned airfield.

That evening Rebecca finally accepted Fay's invitation to go to the pub. They set out for the Cherry Tree at six thirty and arrived to find it packed with airmen, nurses and land army girls. Fay said, 'Let's elbow our way in – they'll part soon enough.'

'All right,' replied Rebecca dubiously. 'If you say so.'

It was hot and stuffy inside and though Rebecca was wearing only a summer dress with a short coat over the top, she was soon too hot and removed the coat. Fay was trying to look over the heads of the crowd and finally caught the eye of the person for whom she was searching.

'Bill! Over here!'

'Hi,sweetheart,' cried a tall, dark-haired man in a flying jacket. 'Coming over. What does your friend want?'

'Drink?' asked Fay of Rebecca.

'Oh, anything – half a pint of mild.'

'Not a short?'

Rebecca shook her head. 'No, that'd be far too expensive – just a half of mild.'

'Shandy for me,' cried Fay, 'and half of mild for Rebecca.'

'Let's stand by the door,' said Rebecca. 'The air's fresher and cooler there.'

They moved back to the doorway and Bill joined them soon afterwards, balancing a tray of drinks above the heads of chattering males and females. Bill was a Canadian from Moose Jaw, Saskatchewan, six foot tall, with a strong, broad forehead. Rebecca, having learned the ranks in order to repeat them to her pupils, saw that he was a flying officer. He winked at her and said in a booming timbre, as if shouting down a mine shaft, 'Rebecca, eh? Nice to meet you. Grab your drink, will you, I'm likely to spill it.'

She did as she was asked just as someone else stepped out from behind Bill's broad shoulders. He was a shorter, slimmer man with fair hair that flopped over his forehead. On his battledress, casually slung over one shoulder, were the three stripes of a sergeant. On his face was an extraordinary grin. He looked as if he'd stolen the cat's cream and was damned if he was going to put it back again just because he'd been caught.

Fay said, 'What have you done, Luke?' in the way that she might to one of her pupils.

'Nothing,' he said, holding up his hands in mock innocence. 'I just caught sight of my date for the evening, that's all.'

He smiled at Rebecca and held out his hand, saying in a strong West Country dialect, 'Luke Adams – how do you do?'

Rebecca blinked at him and then turned to Fay. 'Just a minute, I'm not anybody's date,' she said. 'Did you arrange this, Fay? What's going on?'

Fay kicked Luke lightly on the calf. 'No, he's not your date – he's not even supposed to be here. I thought you were on leave, Luke?' She turned back to Rebecca. 'Luke is Bill's best friend. Luke's a mad Cornishman, from St Mawgan . . .'

Luke sipped his pint and said, 'Leave? What's that? Oh, you mean that promise they break at the drop of a hat? Or rather, at the drop of a bomb. Today's raid cancelled all leave. We lost five aircraft on the ground.'

'Oh, you poor thing, never mind. It's nice you can be here to drink with us, isn't it, Rebecca?'

Rebecca felt she ought to be polite, but she was still not sure she hadn't been set up. Fay was just the kind of person to try to get favourite people together. Luke seemed nice enough but Rebecca wasn't yet ready to meet men in that way. She was happy to talk to them, but she didn't want any romance, not now – perhaps not ever. It was too soon after Alan's death to start thinking in that direction. And there was Kim to think of – she had lost a father whom she adored. It would not be kind to Kim to start messing around with other men.

Rebecca said, 'Pleased to meet you – forgive my outburst but I'm not yet ready for dating or anything of that sort.'

Luke's face immediately registered seriousness. 'I'm sorry – lose someone close?'

'My husband,' answered Rebecca, feeling her eyes water. She still couldn't talk about it, especially to strangers, without feeling a surge of emotion go through her. Every time she had to tell someone about Alan's death, she felt she would be able to do it without a change in expression – yet without fail the unseen fist of sorrow struck her right on the heart and made her crumple inside and feel like weeping.

'Ahhh,' said Luke, turning away slightly. 'Sorry about that, m'darlin'.'

'Don't call me that,' said Rebecca, bristling again.

Luke looked surprised, as did Bill. They turned to Fay with raised eyebrows. Fay shook her head.

'It doesn't mean what you think it means, Rebecca. Cornish people call everyone "darlin' " – it's just a local expression, like cockneys say "love".'

'Well, I don't like it, it's too personal,' said Rebecca. 'I don't even like the expression "love". It's condescending and patronising.'

'Men use m'darlin' with each other,' said Luke, 'so it's hardly patronising.'

There was an embarrassed silence among them for a few moments, then Bill glanced through the doorway, looked up and said, 'Bad weather coming in – at least we won't be flying tonight.'

Rebecca felt she had put a damper on the evening so she decided it was up to her to make things right again. She asked Bill, 'I hear you're a fighter pilot?'

'You hear right,' he smiled. 'We're Hurricane people – me and good ole Lukey here. Have to hold our own against the Spitfires, eh, Luke?'

'You mean Luke services your plane?' asked Rebecca. 'How lucky that you should be together.'

Luke laughed. 'I wouldn't service his plane if he was the last flying officer in the RAF, would I, m'darlin'?'

He turned to face Rebecca and his expression had changed again to one of seriousness. He held open his battledress and pointed to a pair of wings above the left breast pocket. 'I'm a sergeant pilot – I fly Hurricanes too.'

Rebecca realised she had made a snobbish assumption and created a rather sorry *faux pas*. 'How – how come,' she faltered, 'Bill is an officer and you – you're . . .'

'A ranker?' finished Luke with a wry grin. 'Why, he's been to uni-ver-sity, that's why. I stayed home and followed the plough, while Bill here went to Cambridge, ploughed into books instead, and earned himself a right proper degree, didn't you, William, m'darlin'? He was punting young ladies down the River Cam, through the curtains of weeping willows of a fine summer's day, while I got dirt under me fingernails, got burned by the wind and wet with the rain, cut through by the leather harness on me back as I walked behind the great shires, the workhorses that plodded their weary way across the fields, leaving the world to darkness and to piskies. Luke the Ploughman, that's me, m'dar' – he hesitated, seeing she was not altogether amused by his acting – 'Rebecca.'

'What young ladies?' demanded Fay, in mock-righteous indignation.

'There weren't any,' Bill said. 'It's all in his imagination.'

'Why, you great liar you,' cried Luke, in a very broad dialect. 'You told me you had dozens of 'em, in the shade of those very willers I just spoke on, jugs of zider at thee elbow, a silk stockin' at thee knee.'

Bill nodded. 'You'll get me into trouble, you will.'

They all laughed, all except Rebecca, who was feeling quite out of it by now.

Later she asked Bill, 'I'm impressed, but why Cambridge? What was wrong with a Canadian university?'

She had phrased it rather badly and Bill replied a little stiffly, 'Nothing wrong with Canadian universities. It was a dream my mother had – to have one of her offspring go to either Oxford or Cambridge. My mother's English and a bit of a snob where education's concerned. I happened to get lucky and fulfil that dream for her. Myself, I'd just as soon have gone to Quebec or Vancouver . . .'

The evening ended on a slightly better note, when Fay suggested they all walk back to the school together and, instead of walking ahead or behind with Bill, hooked her arm into Rebecca's, while Bill went on the other side of her and Luke linked arms with Fay. They marched home singing, 'Pack up your troubles in your old kitbag . . .'

Chapter Seven

Despite the anxiousness she had felt, Rebecca found that in retrospect she had enjoyed the evening. She decided that Luke had laboured the 'm'darlin' thing a bit too much, especially with Bill, but she knew he was trying to overcompensate for having upset her in the beginning. And why was she upset? It was a very trifling thing after all. Yet she knew she had been, probably because Alan had only called her 'darling' two or three times in their relationship and it was a word she loved to hear from the lips of her husband.

It wasn't that Alan hadn't loved her; it was just that he always had difficulty in showing his affection and fondness for her, never using words she had really wanted to hear. Alan had been a very intelligent man, full of wonderful inventions and bright schemes, but he was reserved, possibly afraid of loving and being loved in any overt fashion. He had been undemonstrative, a person who showed his love in ways other than words. He had been good with his hands, making her things: a pine double-bed; a jacket out of an old blanket; a tall stool so that she could sit at the sink, rather than stand.

Some men, she decided, were like that. It was not that they loved any less than those who were free and easy with their

79

declarations – possibly a man like Luke to whom words seemed to come without difficulty – it was rather that they couldn't allow themselves to show it, as if they were afraid of leaving themselves vulnerable, unprotected, if they put their feelings into words. Alan *had* loved her deeply, she was sure. He had also been a fine man from a good family: well bred, genteel.

She admired good breeding in a man, she told herself, because it made them thoughtful, solicitous and impeccably mannered. She wasn't a snob, exactly, but a farmhand-cum-sergeant was not her idea of a gentleman. He seemed barely educated, unlike his friend Bill.

A few days later she met Luke, on his own, in the village while she was shopping with Kim. It was a cold day, slightly overcast, with promising shafts of sunlight occasionally breaking through clouds. Rebecca was not expecting to meet anyone as she strolled along the main street, admiring one or two of the houses with their dormer windows. Just when her defences were down, Luke stepped out of the village shop doorway.

'Well, hello,' he said. 'And how's Becky?'

Rebecca felt a hotness behind her eyes. 'I'm sorry?' she said tartly.

Luke immediately knew that he had made a big mistake in using a shortened name. 'I'm sorry,' he said, 'we're not yet on those sort of terms, are we? Rebecca then.'

'We're never likely to be on the kind of terms that will allow you to call me by a nickname – even my husband didn't do that.'

'Oh,' Luke said, shaking his head a little. 'That's a bit sad. You mean he didn't have a pet name for you, or wouldn't you let him call you anything but Rebecca? Rebecca's a big mouthful for a man wanting to be sweet.'

'Daddy used to call me his little cuddly bear,' confided Kim to this stranger talking to her mother. 'Even though my name is Kim Elizabeth Daniels.'

Luke grinned at her and stooped down to shake her hand. 'How do you do? I'm Luke. I think that's a nice pet name. It suits you.'

'Not now, because I'm much bigger,' Kim corrected him.

'Well, that's true. I expect you're at least eight years old, aren't you?'

Kim looked pleased with this remark. 'I'm only six, really.'

Luke feigned surprise. 'Good Lord, are you? I'd never have guessed it . . .'

'That's enough now, Kim,' said Rebecca. 'Well, if you'll excuse us, Sergeant Adams, we have a lot to do.'

'Whoa, what's the rush, Mrs Daniels? – it's Saturday. Why not come and have a cup of tea with me at the cake shop? I bet Kim would like a cake, wouldn't you?'

'Stop using my daughter to manipulate me.'

Luke's grin faded from his face as this remark obviously hit home. Instantly she regretted it, but it was too late, he had taken offence. He touched his cap. 'Please excuse me, I'm sorry – I made a mistake.'

He strode past her into the shop, leaving her feeling ill mannered and ungracious. Of course Kim would like a cake – Kim was a little girl – and Rebecca could see he had only offered it out of kindness. It wouldn't hurt her in the least to take him up on the offer. What harm was there in taking tea?

When he came out of the shop again, with some tobacco in his hand, she said, 'I'm sorry, that was quite uncalled for on my part – yes, we would like some tea, thank you.'

Instantly his face was covered in a smile. 'Fine, let's go,' he said. 'I don't know what sort of cakes they'll have, so we'll take pot luck, shall we, eh, Kim? What sort do you like? I'm rather fond of the creamy ones myself, Cornish cream of course – that's where I come from – Cornwall. It's a land of giants down west.'

'You're not a giant,' said Kim.

'Ah,' he cried, wagging a finger, 'that's where you're wrong! I *am* a giant. I'm one of the smallest giants in the world. In fact, young lady, I'm probably the smallest giant ever to come out of Cornwall. Now you should see my friend Bill – he's one of the biggest giants.'

'You're silly,' laughed Kim, clearly delighting in Luke's company. 'Isn't he, Mummy?'

'Very silly,' smiled Rebecca. 'You mustn't believe a word he says.'

'Except when I say I couldn't be in nicer company,' said Luke to Kim, without looking at Rebecca.

Rebecca found him the most infuriating man she had ever met. He said nice things, but he made them into personal statements which irritated her. It was as if from the moment she had seen him she knew she had to be wary of him. He appeared to be looking for a relationship and she had the feeling that *any* woman would do, so long as he got a response. Well, Rebecca told herself, I'm not in the market for romance, or anything of the kind, so he can look elsewhere for his liaisons.

When they were sitting down with their Camp coffee, the only beverage available, she asked him how old he was. Kim was sipping an orange juice and eating a bun. Her attention was on another child at the neighbouring table.

'Twenty-five, why?' he asked.

She gave a hollow laugh, thinking she was about to put him out of the game for good. She was certainly much too old for him. She even added a year to her age to make her argument that much more substantial.

'Well – you're just a youngster, aren't you? I'm twenty-eight you know. And women are supposed to be at least three years ahead of men, in maturity, so that makes me six years older than you.'

'Rubbish,' he said, so forcefully that she felt she was being chastised like a child. 'In formative years perhaps the female of the species is ahead on points, but not when you reach our age. What's two years? Nothing. When I'm seventy and you're seventy-two, it'll make no difference, will it?'

'I said I was twenty-eight,' she said. 'That's *three* years, by my reckoning.'

'Yes, but you weren't telling the truth, were you? You're only twenty-seven. You're not twenty-eight until July.'

She blushed to the roots of her hair, mortified that he had caught her lying so easily. She was sure that even Fay didn't know her age or birthday, so how had he found out?

'All right, you've got me, but how did you know?'

'I asked your Aunt Amelia . . .'

'*Great*-auntie,' corrected Kim, her attention coming back to the table for a moment. 'My *great-great* auntie.'

'I stand corrected. Anyway, she's a particularly good friend of mine. I'd actually ask her out for a date if she wasn't so frail. I'm particularly fond of older women, especially those in their nineties, but more especially those in their late twenties. More coffee?'

Infuriating man. Absolutely infuriating.

'You know Amelia?'

'She visits the base occasionally and chats to us fly boys,' answered Luke. 'Nice lady. I went to see her the night before last. I've offered to run a stall in the next jumble sale. I've done the last two jumble sales for the school, so I'm quite an old hand at jumbling. Anyway, what with one thing and another, we got round to talking about you, and I showed her a poem I'd written for you. I asked her if it was wise to give it to you. She told me it would be a disaster. The poem was quite good, but the subject, she said, would have a blue fit. I decided she was right.'

Despite herself, Rebecca was flattered. 'You wrote a poem for me?'

'Yep – roses are red, that sort of thing. I tore it up though. I was angry with myself.'

'Oh.' She felt disappointed. It would have been interesting to see a poem which concerned her personally. What on earth could he find to write about? He had only known her for a few hours. Perhaps it was just as well the poem had been destroyed. It was probably a 'roses are red' thing: a greetings-card ditty with banal rhymes. It was probably in very bad taste and would have soured her thoughts for the next few days.

'I wish you wouldn't do these things,' she said.

'What things?'

'Show my aunt poems. I'm not in the least bit interested, you know, in you or your poems. Now my aunt will think I'm trying to attract you. It's very upsetting. I just want to be left alone.'

'No you don't,' he replied, his blue eyes boring into her.

'You only think you do. Actually, it would be a terrible thing for a woman like you to close herself in and lock out the world . . .'

'Men are not the whole world.'

'True, but they're half of it. I'm not saying I'm the man for you, though I'd like to be, even on so short an acquaintance, I know that much, but give yourself a chance, Rebecca. The nunnery is no place for a woman with your love of life.'

Kim sucked on her straw and said, 'What's a nunnery?'

'Look,' cried Rebecca, 'you're upsetting my daughter now. I have no intention of becoming a nun. When the right man comes along, I'll know. Until then, I would prefer not to be harassed every time I go out of the school gates.'

'Is that what I'm doing, harassing you?'

'Yes.'

Luke shrugged. 'I suppose I am, but it's with good intentions.'

'Oh, I wish you'd go away, Luke. Please go away.'

He stood up and smiled down at her. 'I'm going. Got to fly anyway. Doing a patrol at three. Look, I'm sorry if I've said things to annoy you. And I know it's too soon for you – after your husband's death – but fate brought us together *now*, not at an appropriate time in the future. I like you – a lot – so please think about it for a bit, eh? Don't just dismiss any idea of seeing me again. Oh, and here's a couple of lines of the poem. Couldn't bear to chuck 'em away. They're rather good, I think. Well, not bad.'

He pushed a piece of paper into her hand and then tweaked Kim's hair, saying, 'Bye-bye, tiger.'

He strode out of the shop and into the street.

Rebecca unfolded the screwed-up piece of paper to see that there were in fact quite a few lines. They read:

> Inside her are leopards
> prowling close to her skin –
> they move to her eyes
> and stare out suddenly,
> to stop me gunshot dead,
> before entering her hands
> to mark me with tribal scars
> or stripe my flanks like quarry
> in the fullness of the hunt.
> Their souls are there too,
> red as blood, but cold,
> shadowing our understanding
> with all the antipathy
> of greater cats for men
> in the quick, arcing defence
> of some hidden vulnerability.

Rebecca was astonished. This really was quite good poetry. Had he written those lines himself? Or had he found them in some obscure book of modern verse, knowing that she would be unlikely to find them except by extreme chance?

She stuffed the piece of paper in her handbag, determined to search for the poem amongst the books of poetry in the school library. If he could find it, so could she. In the meantime, she had to put him right out of her mind. He was becoming too familiar with her and she really didn't want that, even if it meant going into a nunnery.

Chapter Eight

Two days after Rebecca had seen Luke, Kim developed a high fever. Her forehead was hot and dry, but her body was drenched in perspiration. She went into a dreamful state of near sleep, crying occasionally but for the most part fretful and twitchy. Rebecca sat up with her all night and in the morning the doctor was called to attend the sick child. He arrived at ten o'clock. Rebecca should have been teaching, but Helena Patten looked after her class for her while she dealt with the doctor.

The doctor was a man in his mid-thirties by the name of Bates. He arrived with a flourish, sweeping into the room and plonking his bag on the bedside table. There was about him an air of indolence which might have been found in a nineteenth-century man of fashion. He certainly dressed well and had the good looks to carry it off.

'Now, where's my little patient?' he said, sitting on the edge of the bed and immediately lifting Kim's eyelids to look at her pupils.

After a brief but thorough examination he quickly reassured Rebecca that Kim wasn't seriously ill. 'You're new aren't you?' he asked. 'Where did you live before you came to Gradge Lodge?'

'Tilbury – some not very nice flats overlooking the docks.'

The doctor nodded. 'Were the conditions a little unsanitary?'

'The drains and toilet backed up occasionally,' admitted Rebecca. 'It used to be a problem.'

Dr Bates smiled at her. He was a tall man with dark, wavy hair and a lop-sided smile. His arms appeared a little too long for his body and his movements were deliberate, almost lazy. Rebecca noticed that his fingers were superb: long and tapering. As he took Kim's temperature she admired his hands. Kim's sweaty head, with its damp, limp hair, flicked back and forth on the pillow. She muttered and moaned, occasionally asking for a drink. The little girl was neither conscious nor asleep, but in a restless place somewhere between the two. Her teeth kept clashing together, so it was no use putting a thermometer in her mouth. She would have bitten it in two. Instead, the sure hands took the instrument, shook it, then placed it carefully under Kim's left arm. Those same hands tucked back the sheet very neatly when it was all over and he was reading the thermometer.

'Hundred and two,' he murmured. 'Well, not good – but not terrible either. I'll give you some medicine to get her to sleep and once she's resting properly I hope the fever will come down of its own accord. I think it's just some nasty germ she's picked up from those drains of yours. We'll soon have her back on her feet, don't worry.'

'But why *now*?' asked Rebecca. 'I mean, we've been at the school some time.'

'Probably a dormant strain of something.'

'Can't you be more specific?'

He sighed, packing his bag. 'If I could be, I would. I can see you're an intelligent woman. I'm not trying to patronise you. Children pick up all sorts of bacteria and succumb to them. Like as not you yourself picked up the same bug, but being an adult your system just shrugs it off. It's all part of children building up an immune system – once she gets over this, she probably won't ever be bothered by the same little germ again. I'll look in tonight.'

She said, 'Thank you, Doctor.'

'Christopher – your aunt calls me Christopher, so there's no reason why you shouldn't.'

'Yes there is,' she smiled. 'I don't know you.'

'Well, it's about time you did, because I come to dinner here quite often. Your aunt and I play chess together occasionally.'

'My aunt seems to have all sorts of – of young men at her beck and call.'

'Your aunt is a fascinating woman,' Christopher said. 'Now I must be off. Got some more calls to make. Take the prescription to the chemist and give her two teaspoonfuls every six hours. 'Bye.'

'Goodbye,' said Rebecca, seeing him to the door of the room.

'Don't worry,' he called as he went out on to the landing, 'I know my way. I'll let myself out.'

Rebecca went back to Kim's bedside and a few moments later Amelia came into the room, assisted by a stick.

'How is the little mite?' asked Amelia. 'Any better?'

'No, but Dr Bates has given me a prescription for some medicine that he says will help her sleep.'

'Young Chris has been, has he? What did you think of him?'

'I – I thought he was a nice man,' said Rebecca guardedly. 'He seemed to know what he was doing.'

'Oh, he's a good doctor all right,' chuckled Amelia. 'Here, give me that prescription. Cook will be going to the village soon to buy vegetables. She can pick up the medicine then. She won't be long with her shopping, so she'll be just as quick as if you'd gone yourself.'

Amelia took the prescription and went out of the room, but she was back again shortly. She sat down on the other side of the bed and patted Kim's hand with her own grizzled, lizardskin palm.

'Poor little mite,' she said again, in her Australian drawl. 'I remember when I was sick on that boat going out to Aussie. I thought I was going to die. Instead it was my parents that died, not me. Anyway,' she turned her attention fully on to Rebecca, 'you seem to have collected a couple of beaux since you came here. They must like your regal bearing or something, because you're not exactly full of life, are you?'

'I don't know what you mean,' replied Rebecca, taken aback, both by the subject and by the insult. 'What beaux – what men?'

'Well, there's Luke running around like a dog who's found the bone,' chuckled Amelia, 'and Dr Christopher Bates MD just left the house whistling "Dixie". If I'm not mistaken you've got the vicar staring at the moon too.'

'Martin Simkins?' cried Rebecca, aghast.

'That's the fella,' Amelia said, leaning with both hands on her stick and then resting her chin on them. 'The one with the dog collar. Quite a collection, eh? A vicar, a doctor and a fighter pilot? More than I ever had. The only bloke who ever fell in love with me was a dried-up old sheep farmer from the outback. Still, he was good enough for me, and I took him.'

'Amelia,' said Rebecca, 'why are you slipping into vernacular speech?'

'Oh, I do it sometimes, to remind me where I've come from. I may be grand now, but I wasn't always.'

'I thought you never married?'

Amelia snorted. 'Never did, never wanted to.'

'But what about this farmer you mentioned?'

'Jim? I never married him – just lived with him – and you can take that shocked look off your face. We're talking about Australia in the middle of the last century now, not prim and prissy Blighty. When I went off with old Jim, there wasn't a preacher within a thousand miles, so who was going to marry us, even if I let them? Once we'd taken to each other we considered ourselves good and married anyway.

'My advice to you is to live with one of those young men, if you feel inclined, but don't get married to any of them. Marriage turns a man into a different kind of animal – thinks he owns you then. If you don't tie the knot then you've always got a lever. They're always wary of you. You hold a trump card in your hand and they have to toe the line or they might lose you. Of course, a wife can run off too, but it's much harder. They say things like "you've got to come home, you're *my* wife", instead of "please come back, I'll be good".'

'I think that's a very cynical view of marriage,' said Rebecca. 'My marrying Alan was the best thing that ever happened to me.'

Amelia, on looking into Rebecca's eyes, immediately softened her tone. 'Yes, Alan was your husband, wasn't he? You're not over him yet, are you? Tell me what happened.'

Rebecca fought back the emotion that was welling up inside her. 'Alan was killed at Dunkirk. I don't think I shall ever be over him. I don't want to be over him. I loved him very much, you see. I still do.'

'I do see – but then,' Amelia went on gently, 'does love have anything to do with marriage? You can love a man to bits, my dear, without marrying him. I'm not against love, I just think the idea of marriage is obnoxious.'

Rebecca made no reply to this, still locked in a struggle with her emotions.

'I suppose I am rather cynical,' sighed Amelia. 'You see I have this theory that men don't *want* to walk all over you, but if you lie down under their feet, then they feel they've got to. They respect a woman with independence, treat her like one of themselves. Marry them and they lock you out of the club of responsible people, start making decisions for you, treat you as if you had the brains of a donkey. Remain single and they say to themselves, "This one's a bit different, knows what she wants. Better be careful here, treat her with respect." '

'Well, it wasn't like that for Alan and me . . . not exactly. I mean, he did like making the decisions, but he always consulted me first.'

'Before he went ahead and did what he wanted to anyway?'

This was too close to the truth for Rebecca, and she said quickly, 'Anyway, let me assure you that I have no intention of – of flirting with any of those men you mentioned. I think you're being a little absurd anyway – Martin? I don't think so.

And if the doctor was whistling "Dixie" it was because he – he was feeling good about something . . .'

'About meeting *you*. I'm not daft.'

Rebecca mopped Kim's brow with a cool damp flannel. 'No,' she replied, 'you're not *daft* as you call it, but you're mistaken, Amelia. The only man who's been pestering me is the fighter pilot, as you call him, Sergeant Luke Adams. I think we've squared that one away for good.'

Amelia's head came up and she frowned. 'Oh, surely not? You've made up your mind already? You've only known him five minutes.'

'That's precisely why I've told him not to bother Kim and me again.'

'I mean,' growled Amelia, 'you shouldn't tell a beau to take a running jump until you're absolutely sure you don't want him.'

Rebecca found all this very disconcerting. And what had her aunt meant by Rebecca not being 'exactly full of life'? She asked Amelia for an explanation.

'Well, it's the way you walk and everything, I suppose,' said Amelia. 'You can tell you've never played hockey. All hockey players have been humbled at some time by the big stick in the hands of an unbeatable foe. You've got a walk like the Queen of Sheba, as if all around you are creatures of lesser rank. I know you don't mean it – you're probably not really a snob – but it makes the fellas go wild. You represent some sort of nut to crack, I suppose. Or rather a glacier to melt. Yes, that's a much better metaphor.'

'I don't particularly like either,' said Rebecca, appalled, 'but if I had to choose I suppose I prefer the second one. I don't think I'm regal – I certainly don't *intend* to act stately or haughty or anything like that.'

'I know, that's the beauty of it,' cackled Amelia. 'You don't do it on purpose. If you did, they'd see through you in a minute. They'd know you were just a vulnerable woman underneath. But it looks so real, all that poise. You do it accidentally. I'm jealous. It's worth a fortune. I could have done with some of your posture in my time, I can tell you. I would've had a few of those curly-headed boys between my sheets if I'd had some of your bearing . . .'

'Amelia!' said a voice with a frosty edge.

Rebecca and Amelia turned to see Helena standing in the doorway, holding a bottle of medicine.

'Oh, Helena,' Amelia murmured, only slightly abashed. 'Good of you. Leave it on the table, will you?'

Rebecca got up and took the bottle from Helena, saying, 'It's all right, I'll give her some immediately. Thank you for bringing it, Helena.'

'I didn't have any choice,' snapped Helena, and walked briskly from the room.

Amelia chuckled as Rebecca pulled the cork of the medicine bottle. 'She doesn't like you, you know. That's one conquest you haven't made.'

'Well, I'm sorry for that,' Rebecca replied. 'Now, if you'll excuse me, Amelia, I have to give Kim some medicine. You keep saying rather disconcerting things and I don't want to spill any of it.'

'Meaning I agitate you, I suppose? Oh well, it won't be the first time. I'm going back to my room. Please let me know when Kim's fever breaks, will you?'

Her aunt had gone back to her normal formal way of

speaking and Rebecca nodded her thanks.

The good doctor called again in the evening. Kim's fever had already subsided a good deal and a little after he left it broke completely. While he was there Rebecca tried not to think about what Amelia had said to her, but found herself staring at the back of his head as he bent over Kim. Christopher Bates was a very good-looking man and it would have flattered Rebecca to know he was interested in her.

After Dr Bates had gone, Rebecca went to Amelia's office and told the old woman that Kim's fever had broken.

'Thank God,' said Amelia, her face clearly registering relief. 'I was worried about her.'

'But Dr Bates said it wasn't serious.'

'I'm afraid Chris is one of those doctors who hate to alarm people. I don't believe doctors honestly *know* in cases like this. Outback fever, bushwater fever, Tilbury drains fever. How are they supposed to know? They can't. They just make a guess on the evidence available and that's pretty flimsy in a lot of cases, especially where fever's concerned.'

'Doctors are highly trained for this sort of thing, surely?' said Rebecca.

'Pah! Body mechanics, that's all. Don't you get the idea that they've got a gift from God into the workings of the human physique. They're just as bewildered as us most of the time, but they've got appearances to keep up, a mystique to maintain. They tell themselves it's to protect us, so that we'll have faith in them, that they keep up this pretence – but in fact it's to protect their livelihood. They all want to be priests as well as body mechanics.'

'You *are* a cynic,' said Rebecca.

'I hope so.'

'Well *I* hope we don't have a raid tonight,' said Rebecca. 'I'm really tired.'

'The fortunes of war are pretty boring, aren't they?' said Amelia, suddenly looking very old. She was sitting in her chair, leaning over her stick. 'If I'd stayed in Australia, like a sensible woman, I'd be sitting out in the sun now, knitting or something. Instead I'm stuck in a boring war, waiting for boring old bombs to blow me to bits, in a place where the weather is the most boring in the world.'

Rebecca stared at her aunt. 'Why did you come back?'

'Oh,' Amelia gave a little chuckle, 'I thought I had something to prove, I suppose. Show the old country how a woman from the new world has lifted herself up by her bootlaces.'

'Don't you think Britain has anything to offer?'

Amelia nodded. 'Spring, summer, autumn, winter. The seasons are beautiful here, when the fog isn't covering them or the rain isn't washing them away. I hate the grey skies, but when the weather is fine, it's absolute heaven. And the hockey is good. No competition down under. Not enough people.'

'Hockey!' Rebecca rolled her eyes.

'God's own game,' said Amelia, and both women laughed.

There was no raid but Rebecca found she had difficulty in sleeping all the same. She was thinking of the doctor and of Luke Adams. She thought how superior Christopher Bates was to the young airman. He had a worldly, sophisticated air about him, while the fighter pilot seemed raw and gauche. Luke was after all just a farm boy.

She thought too about those lines Luke had written down

for her. Even if he had copied them from a book, they were well chosen, and he had at least taken the time to read a book of poems to find them. That was worth something in her eyes. Perhaps Luke had a sensitive vein running through him, which he had not yet developed? She admired men who could *feel* things, as well as act them out.

Unfortunately Alan had not been a man whose feelings were evident, but Rebecca was not prepared to judge her deceased husband. He was as he was and she had loved him anyway. Any future man in her life, however, would have to conform to certain standards she had since drawn up. She had a daughter to think of now and love, such as it was, was a secondary factor. If she was to consider remarriage, then Kim's future must be her priority.

Rebecca was inclined to believe that a professional man was worth more than a pilot, whose occupation after the war would be the cultivation of root crops, not even for himself, but on behalf of another man, an employer.

Perhaps she *was* a snob? she thought to herself as she dropped off to sleep. So what?

Chapter Nine

Once Kim was better and back in class Rebecca returned to teaching. Miss Knole, the headmistress, had already been a little scathing about teachers who put their family concerns over their work. Priscilla Mohorty, the games mistress, took up on this in the staff room.

'Been on your holidays then?' she said to Rebecca at break time on the first day back.

'My daughter was ill,' Rebecca said, wondering why it needed saying.

'If she did a little more outdoor sport and a little less reading, she might be a bit healthier,' snorted Mohorty.

'My daughter enjoys outdoor sport,' replied Rebecca, looking Mohorty directly in the eye. 'It's me that loathes it and anyone to do with it.'

Thunder gathered in Mohorty's face. 'Really? You've got a big mouth for a newcomer, that's for sure.'

Martin Simkins interrupted with, 'I don't think that kind of talk is appropriate for the staff room.'

'No,' said Mohorty, 'it should be reserved for the women's lavs, where priests aren't around to poke their noses in.'

Julia Dane, the art mistress, sniggered.

Rebecca was shocked at the lack of deference towards Martin in the staff room, but gradually she came to realise that most of the teachers at Gradge Lodge were a tough breed, strong-minded, independent women, some of them atheists with no regard for either the vicar's profession or his gender. Several of them considered men to be one of the lowest forms of life – somewhere between a jellyfish and a lizard in the chain of being – and being a priest did not exclude Martin from their contempt.

Rebecca knew she could give as good as she got amongst other women, but she did feel sorry for Martin, who was already hampered by being a man, and doubly so because he was a priest. He didn't know how to fight on these terms or what weapon to use.

Rebecca was one of the last to leave the staff room, and before she went Priscilla Mohorty whispered in her ear, 'I've got your daughter for hockey tomorrow. We'll see how she shapes up.'

There was a threat in there somewhere and Rebecca whirled Mohorty round by the arm. White with anger, she spat her words at the games mistress.

'You'll treat my daughter in exactly the same way as any other pupil in this school, Miss Mohorty, or you'll be in trouble – any kind of trouble I can make for you. Do you understand? I'll destroy you. I won't have my daughter bullied, not by you or any other teacher in this school.'

Mohorty smiled a little and said, 'Oh dear.'

A stinging slap from Rebecca wiped the smile completely from her face to be replaced by a look of rage. 'I'll have you dismissed for that!'

The only other person present in the room, Julia Dane, let out a gasp as the two livid women faced each other.

'Please do go to Miss Knole, and we'll have the whole thing out in front of her,' said Rebecca. 'Perhaps you'll be able to justify threatening my daughter.'

'I did no such thing – you heard what I said, Miss Dane?'

Rebecca cried, 'It wasn't what you said, it was the way you said it, and I'm certain it's not the first time you've been like this with another teacher. I'm counting on the fact that you've got a reputation for stirring up trouble' – there was a hint of having struck home in Mohorty's face and Rebecca sailed in – 'so please do go ahead and see who you like. In fact, why leave it at Miss Knole, let's go all the way to the top, to Miss Sartour.'

'Miss Knole knows me better than some high-and-mighty newcomer who's just spent a week lazing around because her daughter's sick,' offered Mohorty, lamely.

'Miss Knole might not approve of me taking time off, but she certainly won't approve of victimisation,' snapped Rebecca. 'Miss Knole is a fair woman.'

'I think I know her better than you,' Mohorty answered.

Rebecca smiled, menacingly. 'You knew her when she was an ordinary teacher, but she's the headmistress now. She can't afford to have friends. She has a position to maintain and protect. Try it. Let's see how it comes out. I've got nothing to lose.'

Mohorty remained silent, realising she was beaten.

Rebecca brushed past her. 'Don't mess about with people from the docklands, dearie, they may be tougher than you expect,' she said, 'even though they're more of a woman.'

When she reached her classroom, Rebecca was trembling. The battle had taken it out of her and she was more shaken than she would like to have admitted. The girls sensed a weakness in her and went on the attack a little, but Rebecca was too old a campaigner in the classroom to let them get away with it for long and she soon re-established order.

Not that there was any riot or anything of that kind. The girls at Gradge Lodge, Hornchurch, were much more subtle than those at Tilbury: they wore you out by degrees, with small tricks like dropping pens time after time, stuffing blotting paper in their neighbour's ink well, splaying the nibs on their pens, losing their rulers for a while. All these little annoyances could be wearisome when they came in multiples, unless a teacher put her foot down and demanded attention.

'Please, miss, my nib's bent.'

Giggles from the rest of the girls.

Rebecca raises her head slowly, lets the girl see uncompromising eyes that have no sympathy in them.

'Then write with it as it is, Celia, and if your handwriting is poor, then you'll receive a low mark, won't you?'

'But, miss, it's bent.'

'I heard you the first time, Celia. Your nib is bent. This is a great tragedy – greater even than Shakespeare's *Hamlet* – but, as with Hamlet's dilemma, what is to be done?' The giggles this time are for the teacher, who has scored a point over the enemy. 'If you speak again, Celia, I shall give you demerit points. Now get on with your work.'

Rebecca bends her head over her desk and notices that the girl gets up a few moments later, goes to the class monitor and negotiates quietly for another nib. The whole incident is over without too much fuss. Had Rebecca sympathised, told Celia to change her nib there and then, there would have been a victory for the other side as Celia made the most of going to the monitor loudly and with flourish, causing the maximum disruption to the class and receiving giggles from the others as her reward.

After classes Rebecca went to her room and lay down to think about the attack from Mohorty. It was really only another of those staff-room fights which flared up out of nothing but a spark. The strain of nightly raids caused tension amongst the teachers and small incidents tended to get out of proportion. Mohorty did not like Rebecca, though, and it was going to be a long, hard haul while they put up with each other's presence in the school.

The following Saturday Rebecca was on duty, but Fay asked her if she would like a trip out on Sunday.

'We could skip chapel – Martin won't mind for once. Bill's managed to borrow a car. The four of us can drive down to the coast. What do you say?'

'The four of us?' Rebecca repeated.

'Of course – Luke, Bill, you and me. You can bring Kim if you want to. She'll enjoy it too. It would do her good.'

Rebecca considered the proposition. She would have to put up with Luke's light-hearted banter, but it was true that some fresh sea air would do Kim the world of good. The child was over her fever, but she still looked a little peaky to Rebecca. However, though Kim was her daughter, she was also a pupil at the school. Was it fair to take only one girl out for a trip? She said as much to Fay.

Fay replied, 'Look, they've all got *parents* who come and take them out from time to time. Why shouldn't you take your own daughter out for the day? I know what you're thinking – Mohorty – but she'll cause trouble anyway, whatever you do, so there's no point in trying to tiptoe round her.'

'I wasn't thinking of Mohorty,' said Rebecca, slightly annoyed at Fay. 'Mohorty can go to the other place, for all I care.'

'That's the spirit. Well, you're coming then?'

Rebecca smiled. 'You really are kind, Fay, to think of us like this.'

'Nonsense – we're getting to be good friends, aren't we? I haven't had a good friend since I left East Ham – not a girlfriend. Until I was eighteen I had nothing *but* good friends and relations, up and down the street. I suffocated in good friends. The East End is like that. It's tribal. You know everyone within half a mile radius. Then I left and I was completely alone. I can't tell which is worse – being suffocated or being alone. They're both as bad.'

'I didn't know you came from the East End – what, from a poor cockney family?'

Fay grinned. 'Not 'alf, love. No one dahn our street fought I'd ever make a teacher, did they? Me mum used to talk to Lil three doors dahn wivout even leavin' 'er kitchen sink. She just used to yell "*Lil? You there?*" at the top of her voice and they would have a good natter, shriekin' at each. Me dad works on the railways and me bruvvers were all tallymen before they joined the army. Me eldest sister 'ad a bun in the oven before she was seventeen and 'ad to get married . . .'

'Crumbs. How did you get out?'

Fay's brow wrinkled. 'I worked hard at school, then got my teaching certificate. I had to work early mornings and weekends in the market to see me through, but I did it. Then when I left teacher's training, I couldn't get a job because of my accent. You don't have to speak BBC English to be a teacher, but the one dialect which is forbidden is cockney. So I ironed it out. I saw an advertisement in the paper for this job and got it, mostly because Miss Sartour doesn't care *where* you come from, so long as you can teach. She's a jewel, that one.'

'She is indeed,' said Rebecca, marvelling at Fay's strength of character. 'All right, Kim and I will be happy to join you. Thanks for asking.'

Fay smiled. 'Great – see you in the morning at ten.'

But when Rebecca sought out her daughter, she found Kim outside on the sports' field with a hockey stick in her hand practising corners with a friend. On having a word with her Kim's face crumpled. 'Oh no, Mum, I've got my first big junior hockey game tomorrow – Miss Mohorty says she's counting on me.'

Rebecca was faintly shocked at her daughter's defection to the enemy camp. 'Oh really? You want to play?'

'Of *course* I do.'

'Well, of course you must then. Do you – er – do you get on all right with Miss Mohorty?'

Kim looked at her mother as if she was a little batty. 'What do you mean?'

'I mean – oh dear – well, does she treat you like all the other girls?'

Kim's eyes opened wide in puzzlement and she shrugged. 'Yes, I suppose so, Mum.'

'You don't dislike her for any reason?'

Kim's face returned to its serious expression. 'I think she's one of the best teachers in the school – 'cepting you of course, Mum,' Kim added loyally. 'You're quite good too.'

Rebecca was dumbfounded. Finally she managed to blurt out, 'Well, I'm gratified that you think so, Kim – but then you're a little biased, since I'm your mother.'

'That's true,' smiled Kim ingenuously. 'Well, see you later, Mum.'

Rebecca watched for a few minutes as her six-year-old daughter wielded a shortened hockey stick, whacking the ball with a determined expression and great ferocity, then jumping up and down when she managed to get it past her friend in the goal, gloating, 'Take that! Next time it'll be even *harder*.'

'She's not my daughter,' mumbled Rebecca to herself as she walked away unnoticed. 'She's definitely not my daughter. There was some mix-up at the hospital and I took the wrong baby home, that's all.'

It wasn't until she was back in the schoolhouse that Rebecca realised she would still have to go on the outing tomorrow. She had promised Fay. She gritted her teeth and thought of Luke.

I'll simply ignore him, she thought to herself. I'll just answer his questions in a cold but polite manner, hardly even acknowledging his presence.

Then he'll just call me a snob, she reflected, which would be true in a sense.

There was worse to come. When she entered the main hall, Dr Christopher Bates was walking through, presumably having visited a patient. He acknowledged Rebecca with a wave. 'Hi,' he said, smiling. 'How's Kim?'

'Oh, fine, thanks,' replied Rebecca. 'Thanks to you.'

'Hummm. I bet Amelia didn't give me much credit.'

Rebecca laughed. 'No, she didn't. She called you a body mechanic.'

'She would – she doesn't trust professionals, even though she's one herself. Listen,' he said, suddenly becoming serious, 'my sister's coming to see me tomorrow. We're going out to the pub for a few drinks. Would you like to join us?'

Rebecca stared at the tall, handsome man and inwardly kicked herself. 'I'm sorry,' she said at last, having fought a battle of loyalties within her, 'but I promised Fay Nelson I would go out with her. Her boyfriend's managed to borrow a car.'

'Not Flying Officer Bill Ryker?' said Chris, his jaw visibly dropping.

'Yes, that's it – Bill is Fay's boyfriend.'

Chris gave an ironic laugh. 'That's *my* damn car he's borrowing. I thought I wouldn't need it.'

'It is?' cried Rebecca, brightening. 'Well, then, you could invite yourself along. There's only four of us.'

'There's my sister to think of, and it's only a small Morris – it won't take five, let alone six. And to think I invited my sister for the day, just so you would feel you were chaperoned – well, there's bad luck for you . . .'

'Did you really?' She could think of nothing else to say at that moment. 'Oh, well.'

Chris shrugged and said, 'Maybe next time,' then he left by one of the side doors.

'Damn, damn, damn, damn,' growled Rebecca.

* * *

The next day at ten o'clock she duly met with Fay, Bill and a grinning Luke. Their gas masks were thrown into the boot of the car and they set off. They had decided to visit Leigh-on-Sea at the mouth of the Thames, then take a spin round the Essex countryside. It was a clear April day with grey-edged skies, not too cold. As they drove eastwards the sky seemed to grow softer and warmer and Bill reminded them all that Great Wakering, a few miles from Leigh-on-Sea, was the driest area of England.

'Technically a desert,' he said. 'Under six inches of rainfall a year.'

'I don't believe that,' said Luke, 'but so long as it stays dry today I shan't argue with you.'

Luke was in the back seat of the small Morris, with a stiff and uncomfortable Rebecca sitting beside him. He hadn't tried to put his arm round her though, or press his thigh against hers, the way some men might have done, so gradually she began to relax and enjoy the passing scenery. Although the Morris was a little oily, she could smell the scent of early wild flowers and herbs in the air. Migrating birds were returning from warmer climes, bringing with them the promise of summer. Out in the quiet of the deep Essex countryside, with its shallow-dipping landscape and sudden woods, it was difficult to remember there was a war on.

Plans had recently been announced to conscript twenty- and twenty-one-year-old women into industry and the auxiliary forces. They had previously been in both in a voluntary capacity. British forces had also withdrawn from Greece as the Germans advanced. There was very little good news around.

The landscape had changed, and now they were in the flatlands, in estuary country, and the birds became waders and shore birds: dunlin, shanks, knots, seagulls and terns. The birds were untroubled by the war – it didn't matter to them who lost or won – but the rabbits by the wayside disappeared daily into pots as the meat shortages grew worse.

They arrived at Leigh-on-Sea in time for lunch and had a pint and a snack at the Crooked Billet before tasting the wares of the shellfish stalls. Many of the cockle, whelk and other fishing boats had taken part in the Dunkirk rescue; some of them had never returned and certain closed stalls along the parade of shacks testified to the loss.

As an East Ender Fay had often come at weekends to Leigh-on-Sea, to sample the shrimps and prawns and other shellfish. She was a seasoned campaigner when it came to gnawing on rubbery whelks or winkling out reluctant winkles. She said she loved the place, with its rotting hulks sticking out of the smelly mud reaches all the way to Canvey Island, the mountains of cockleshells outside the steaming kitchens of the shacks, the squawking seagulls feeding on flyblown fish heads, and the seagoing ships moving up and down the Thames hooting their foghorns.

'It stinks,' she said, wrinkling her nose, 'but I love it – all East Enders do.'

'I think it's quaint,' said Bill loyally. 'Reminds me of Cape Cod in the US. Everything smells of fish. We don't have anywhere to match it in Canada, though I went to a backwoods maple syrup party, where everything smelled of syrup.'

'A rather tenuous connection – sweet and fishy smells,' said Luke.

'Well, yeah,' admitted Bill, 'but you know, the maple syrup has to be boiled in vats and kind of distilled. There's steam coming out of the shacks, same as here. April's the main month too, though the ice on the St Lawrence is only just breaking up and there's a foot of snow still on the ground – it's not warm like it is here now.'

'What happens at a maple syrup party?' asked Fay, hugging his arm. 'Do you smear it all over each other and then lick it off?'

'Fay!' protested Rebecca. 'Please!'

'Oh, you,' said Fay, 'stop being so prim.'

'Nothing so exciting,' laughed Bill. 'We just go into forest shacks where they put maple syrup on everything – mashed potatoes and sausages, in the coffee, on the puddings . . .'

'Yuk!' cried Fay.

' . . . we have music, accordion music usually, or a fiddle, and there's some backwoods dancing and singing, all in Quebec French of course. Then finally we go outside into the cold and fill troughs with snow, making small round holes in the snow. We pour maple syrup into the holes and put a stick in before it hardens. *Voilà* – maple syrup toffee apples – without the apples and toffee. It's great.'

'Sickening, you mean,' cried Fay. 'Give me whelks and cockles any time.' She breathed deeply of the putrid odours of decomposing fish as if they were life-sustaining. 'This is my spiritual home – the spiritual home of all the East Enders. This is where our bodies should be laid to rest – on platforms out on the mud, on raised tiers like Red Indians.'

'Well, I lived in Tilbury,' replied Rebecca, 'and I never came here – I can smell why now.'

'I don't know how you can eat those things,' said Luke to Fay, who was still busily gobbling down jellied eels, winkles and cockles with gusto. 'Yuk. You know cockles still have their digestive systems intact when you eat them? No one removes the innards, you know. All that river estuary muck.'

'Thank you, Luke,' said Fay, 'I can do without the biology lesson. I'm enjoying myself.'

Rebecca said, 'The longest pleasure pier in the world is right before your eyes, Luke, and all you can do is put Fay off her *disgusting* shellfish.'

'Disgustin' is it?' cried Fay, falling into her cockney. 'It's luverly stuff – the whelks is rubbery and slimy and – oh Gawd,' she groaned, 'I don't wanna eat any more.'

They drove along the seafront to Southend pier, then walked the one and a quarter miles to the end, where Fay pointed out another construction right across the mouth of the Thames, from the Essex side to the Kent shoreline.

'What's that?'

Luke said, 'The new boom defence – stops German submarines from entering the Thames.'

'Does it work?' asked Fay.

'Who knows, m'darlin'?' He leaned over the rail suddenly and stared intently at the water. 'Hey!' he cried, pointing to the middle of the river. 'What's that?'

'What's what?' asked Bill, frowning deeply.

They all stared at the surface of the water. The rippling tide, which had been out almost beyond the pierhead, was now beginning to come in and faint wrinkles had appeared on the flat, calm sea. Dark shadows of overhead clouds began chasing across the wavelets, as if in search of each other.

There was a deep silver channel further out, where the current was coursing more strongly and firmly upriver.

'Over there,' said Luke dramatically. 'Is that a periscope?'

'Gee, you could be right, Luke,' replied Bill. 'Hey, cripes, it's heading this way! A submarine! It's come to torpedo Southend pier!'

Both men ducked down behind the rail and hunched against each other as if expecting a blast.

Rebecca felt a flutter of panic and didn't know what to do, flatten or run, until she looked at Fay and saw that her new friend was shaking her head as if in great disgust.

'Schoolboys,' Fay said. 'We have to date schoolboys.'

The men got up, grinning, dusting down their uniforms. 'Well, Rebecca fell for it,' Luke said.

'I did not,' lied Rebecca hotly. 'I was – I was just going along with the joke.'

'Sure you were,' grinned Bill maddeningly.

In the afternoon they drove to South Fambridge, on the River Crouch. Even as they were driving along the country roads of the flatlands they could see white sails in the distance. There was the illusion that boats were sailing across the fields, but this was because the river was contained by high dykes and the water was not visible. Dutch engineers in the seventeenth century had reclaimed most of the flatlands from the sea and braided rivers, and now earthen walls were needed to keep the waters back.

The four companions sat on a turfed dyke and watched the boats going up and down the waterway. The grasses were already tall and green with the spring growth. On one side was the high water, covering the reeds and bladderwort-covered mud islands, busy with river traffic. On the other were the fields, now showing a green furze as the crops began to poke their shoots through the rich soil. In the distance was a low ridge, the only real bump on the landscape, on top of which were the villages of Canewdon, Ashingdon, Hawkwell and Hockley, separated by dips down into shallow valleys or road cuttings.

'The sky is so *big* here,' sighed Rebecca.

'And peaceful – at the moment,' added Fay.

Luke said, 'It's funny – if you look at landscape paintings by continental painters – say, one of Cézanne's paintings of Provence – they really *are* landscapes. Sort of portraits of rusty sandstone ridges and yellow ochre outcrops of rock, with definite bushes and shrubs, and even trees. But an artist from around here doesn't do a landscape – it's more of a smudgy black wavy line at the bottom of a picture of a turbulent sky. It's a skyscape. There isn't any real landscape to paint – it's the skies that are huge and magnificent ...'

Despite her prejudices about Luke, Rebecca was impressed by this speech. A little while later Fay and Bill got up and wandered away towards a patch of elders. They were locked together in one another's arms. Rebecca felt a little uncomfortable about this, but it would be churlish of her to grumble about two people in love showing their affection for each other. However, it did leave her with the problem of dealing with Luke. As it happened, she needn't have worried. Luke made no move towards her but simply lay on his back staring up at the sky with a thoughtful expression.

'You know about painting?' she asked, picking an early-flowering buttercup and holding it under his chin.

He looked up at her and she quickly removed the buttercup, realising she was being a little too intimate for her own comfort.

'A little – not much. I find it helps with my poetry studying the paintings of good artists.'

'Your poetry?' she said.

'That's right.' He came up on his elbows. 'I told you I write poetry, didn't I?'

'Well,' she said sceptically, 'you gave me those lines you said you wrote for me.'

He lay down again and laughed. 'Oh, yes – *those* lines. Did you think they were accurate?'

'They had a certain insight, yes,' she replied, still not believing that he had actually written them himself.

'Good. I'm glad you think so. I've sent them off to the *Literary Review*. I think they'll print them.'

Now she was quite certain he hadn't written the poem. The *Literary Review* was the most respected literary magazine in circulation, publishing such poets as Siegfried Sassoon, W. H. Auden and, until he had died recently, A. E. Housman. It was unlikely that they would publish a poem by a Cornish nobody, even if the poem was above average. It was some trick he had devised. He was going to show her a back number of the *Literary Review*, with a famous poet's name under the lines, and then say to her, 'Of course, this is my pseudonym, I don't actually write under my real name of Luke Adams.'

'Well, if and when they do,' she told him, 'I'll come out on that date with you – how's that? But it's got to have the name of Luke Adams under the poem – no other.'

He went up on his elbows again, selected a piece of grass

to stick in his mouth like a rustic, and studied her intently.

'Are you bargaining with my *feelings*?' he asked her.

She felt disturbed under his gaze and stared at the pub, The Anchor, which was nearby. 'I don't know what you mean,' she eventually replied.

'You – you're haggling with my emotions. I don't know whether I like that. Still, it looks like it's the only chance I'm ever going to get to take you out alone, without those two along. All right, it's a deal. It's a long shot because I'm not sure whether the *Review* . . .'

She smiled knowingly. 'Sure – they might not take it.'

'Well, that's true,' he said, seriously. 'But then again, they just might, so don't count your chickens.'

'I shan't,' she said.

Shortly after this Fay and Bill came strolling back from wherever they had been, still hugging one another.

In the car on the way back to Hornchurch, Luke said, 'Rebecca's promised me a date if I get a certain poem published in the *Literary Review*.'

The moment he said it, Rebecca wished she had demanded secrecy as part of the deal.

Fay said, disapprovingly, 'It sounds a bit like the Queen of Sheba dispensing favours.'

Rebecca blushed. 'Yes, it does, doesn't it? I thought this was to be a secret between Luke and myself. It's just a fun thing you know – not serious. I don't want to sound imperious or anything.'

'You never said it should be secret,' Luke protested.

'No, you're right, I didn't. That's my fault, not yours.'

'Bit reckless of you, Rebecca, I should say,' said Bill with a grin as he drove along the winding roads with their low hedges. 'Luke here, why he's a damn good poet.'

Rebecca nodded to herself. So Bill was in on the joke too! She might have guessed it was a conspiracy. 'And you think so too, I suppose?' she asked Fay.

Fay shrugged. 'I'm no judge of poetry.'

'Yes, but,' Rebecca persisted, 'you know that Luke has had hundreds of poems accepted by respectable publishers?'

'He's had a few taken, I know,' said Fay, 'but I don't think it's hundreds . . .'

So, there it was, the three of them ganging up on her, trying to matchmake. Well, it wasn't going to work. Rebecca wasn't going to fall in with this game. She was, she admitted, a little unhappy that Fay was lining up with the boys against her, but she supposed her friend had been put up to it by Bill.

When they arrived back at Hornchurch, Bill and Luke went to return the car to Christopher Bates, leaving the girls at the pub.

Fay whispered to Rebecca, 'Bill and I are staying here for the night.' She said it fiercely, as if she expected opposition.

Rebecca shrugged. 'All right, I'll cover for you at the school if it's necessary.'

'You're not shocked?' asked Fay, surprised.

Rebecca smiled. 'Should I be?'

'Well, you're always so . . .'

'Prim?' finished Rebecca. 'I'm an old married woman, Fay – I know what it's like to be in love, you know. Alan and I went to bed together several times before we got married. And this is wartime – Bill – well, you know.'

It was left unsaid. One day, Bill might not return from one

of his flights. Then Fay would have bitterly regretted remaining chaste in anticipation of marriage.

'Thanks, Rebecca,' she said, touching her friend's cheek. 'You're a pal.'

'Think nothing of it, pal,' smiled Rebecca.

Luke and Bill returned and Rebecca allowed Luke to walk her back to the school, where they shook hands and said good night.

'Remember our bargain,' Luke said.

'I shall,' she replied stiffly. 'Good night, Sergeant Adams, and thank you for a nice day.'

He shook his head and grinned. 'You don't melt easily, do you, Miss Iceberg? Sergeant Adams? Using my rank and surname to keep me at bay while we're here alone in the dark, two little intimate souls frightened of each other.'

'Frightened of each other?' she questioned.

'Or something – something inside us,' Luke murmured.

'Nonsense,' she said. 'Good night, Luke.'

'Good night, Rebecca.'

She left him standing at the gates, watching her while she walked uncomfortably along the driveway to the schoolhouse

Mohorty was duty teacher and was waiting in the hallway. 'Where's the other one,' she said.

'Other one? Oh, you mean Fay Nelson. She came back ages ago,' lied Rebecca. 'Didn't you see her come in?'

Mohorty looked annoyed. 'No, I didn't . . .'

'Have you been standing there all evening?' asked Rebecca.

'Well, not the whole time.'

'Shall I fetch her for you? She's probably in her room,

117

though she gets annoyed when she's woken up. I'd have to tell her it was you who wanted to see her.'

Mohorty grimaced. 'Forget it,' she said. 'Go to bed – you're the last. By the way, your daughter's team won today. She would have liked you to see her play.'

Rebecca felt suitably guilty. 'Did she? Oh, well done.'

'Yes,' said Mohorty with some satisfaction, 'she's a little barbarian on the field. I was proud of her. She's not like you at all, is she? Kim's got grit.'

Rebecca said nothing, knowing that any reply she could think of would only open up the argument further. Instead she nodded shortly and went upstairs to her room.

'Bloody Mohorty,' she said savagely to herself as she undressed. 'I hope her bloody corsets rot on her . . .'

Chapter Ten

Fay's decision to spend the night with Bill at the pub was more momentous than Rebecca had realised. Fay had actually not made love with Bill and that night would be the first time she had ever been to bed with a man. She was in fact a virgin, coming as she did from a prudish East End family.

The kind of working-class family Fay came from, although not churchgoers, had strict moral rules. The women in the family were expected to be purer than nuns until the wedding vows had been taken, and men like Fay's father were as unbending as the Pope when it came to daughters and sex. The unwedded female could drink at the Covent Garden pubs until all hours, show her legs to the men in a Mother Brown knees-up, enjoy herself to the hilt, but she was not permitted to let any part of any man's anatomy between those legs, be it hands, knees or Hampton Wick.

The women were the tribe's property and if they were violated, with the consent of the woman or not, the men in the tribe took drastic action. It was possibly not so much a stand on high moral ground as an unbending pride. A man who took one of your women was trespassing, had no respect for you, and had lowered your status in the neighbourhood. The woman was usually beaten and her violator would be lucky to escape being crippled for life. Certainly he would be battered with weapons such as iron bars or hammers, so that all would know when he hobbled down the street after leaving his hospital bed that he had been punished for his encroachment.

All this was very much in Fay's mind as she perched her bottom on the cold lip of the bath and carefully removed the precious stockings given her by Bill.

She spoke to him from the bathroom. 'Bill, you realise this has to be a secret between the two of us.'

Bill's deep, good-humoured voice came back with, 'Sure, honey – I'm not going to brag about it in the locker room. I'm in love with you, for heaven's sake.'

He appeared in the bathroom door in his khaki jockey shorts, big and husky, and stared down at her. 'Do you mind if I watch you get undressed?' he said, softly. 'I mean, if it bothers you, I'll go back into the bedroom.'

Fay did mind, a little, since she had never taken off her clothes in front of a man in her life, not since the age of five. Even male family members were taboo after that age. There were always uncles and cousins from the extended family around the house. Incest wasn't unknown in one or two families in the East End, and it was always felt better to be safe than sorry.

'No, I don't mind,' she said, blushing furiously and staring at the pattern on the lino.

'Thank you,' he said huskily. 'I – I've never seen a woman undress before. It seems to me to be a beautiful thing, like the unveiling of a work of art.'

'You just feel lusty, that's all,' she said, still not looking at him as she peeled off the second stocking.

'No, no – I admit it's making me excited, but it means something more than that – something *profound*. I think you're the loveliest woman on this earth, Fay, and I want to see if you're actually *real* or not. If you appear before me in a flimsy silk negligée . . .'

'A cotton nightie, I'm afraid.'

' . . . whatever – I'll think you've been wafted down from Olympia and I won't be able to do a thing except worship you from the other side of the room.'

She smiled through her embarrassment. 'Well, we can't have that, can we? I'm expecting you to do your bit for Canada.'

She continued undressing while he chatted and watched her. Fay was glad they were both speaking through the performance, otherwise it would have been unbearably mortifying for her. As it was she finally got down to her skin and then she shooed him out of the bathroom while she washed.

When she finally entered the bedroom he had switched off the lights and opened the curtains so that the moonlight shone through the window and lit the room. The rooftops of the village were visible outside, leading up to the green, with the church beyond. All was quiet and still.

'How romantic,' she breathed. 'Oh, Bill – I do love you, darlin'. I do so love you.'

'I love you too, sweetheart – you don't know how much.'

She climbed into bed and nestled in his arms. She ran her fingers from his neck down the coarse hairs of his chest to his abdomen, then stopped short of entering the black tangle of the region below his navel. He gently took her hand and placed it on the stiffness below the point where she had halted. It seemed to her that it was enormous and she was suddenly very frightened that it was going to hurt her badly.

'Oh, Bill,' she whispered. 'I'm scared.'

'Sweetheart, sweetheart, don't be frightened,' he murmured. 'We don't need to do a thing if you don't want to. We'll just lie here in one another's arms all night, telling each other childhood secrets . . .'

Gradually the fear subsided and she said, 'We don't have any childhood secrets left to tell, do we? I don't. I think I've talked them all out with you. Bill, are you *bigger* than other men – down there?'

He laughed. 'Heck, I would like to think so, but when we had showers at the university, I found to my dismay that I was merely average, honey.'

'Even – even in that state?' she said in wonder.

'Well, I can't say that I saw the others in this state as you call it, but I know men mostly come out about the same.'

'It seems so *big*,' she growled, gripping it in her slim hand. 'If other women can take it, so can I.'

'Hey!' he cried. 'Are you insinuating that I've had lots of other girls?'

'You better not have, you big lunk. I meant *generally*.'

She felt his own large, rough hands now, roaming tenderly over her body, and she started to feel the excitement welling up inside her. There was a feeling of being swollen herself, like a ripe fruit, ready to split into revealing her inner self. His fingertips circled her nipples, making them ache with anticipation. She began to breathe harder, her breath coming out hot and musty-smelling. He too was becoming more ardent, as his hand went down between her thighs and began to caress the most sensitive part of her body.

'Oh Christ!' she said, more loudly than she intended, as a feeling of urgency came over her. 'You'd better do it now, Bill.'

'Not so fast,' he murmured. 'Enjoy it.'

His calloused fingers were beginning to make her sore and her own hand went down, pushed his aside, and she began to touch herself the way she had done before, when there was no man. He didn't seem to mind in the least and concentrated on her breasts, kissing them, running his tongue over the nipples, then down to her armpit, and with his teeth nipping the soft flesh just below where she shaved the hair. Then he bit her earlobe, her cheek, the point of her chin, oh so tenderly.

'*God!*' she yelled. 'Bill!'

She opened her legs and he entered her slowly and carefully, but still it hurt. For a moment all the beautiful sensations that had been thrilling through her were gone and all she could feel was a sharp pain.

'No . . .' she said, pushing at his chest, but then she realised he was inside her. He was actually there, moving in and out rhythmically. She could hear him growling in the back of his throat with the ecstasy of the moment and though the pain remained in the background, not bad, but still there, she felt powerful. She had this great hairy beast of a Canadian male in her thrall, and she owned him, if only for now.

'Fay – oh my – Fay? – oh, God . . .'

She knew that at this precise point in time he would have done anything for her, promised her the moon and stars, killed for her, died for her, and the enormity of her power over him awed her. He was like a small vulnerable boy in her arms, completely captivated by her whole being, body and soul, and had she wanted to she could have cast him down into hell with just a few simple words.

He gave an enormous shudder, a grunt, and then he was like a dead weight upon her breast.

'Bill . . .' she murmured, pushing him.

He rolled away, his chest heaving for breath. She no longer owned him wholly, possessed him completely against all reason on his part, but there was love there. She could feel him loving her, loving what she had done for him. It came in waves from him, washing over her, like a warm tide. It made her feel good, feel warm and tender towards him too. She went on top of him, on top of his bulk, and lay there like a leopard on a rock in the sun, hugging his inert form.

'You – didn't – make – it,' he said, sounding disappointed as he fought for breath.

'No,' she replied, 'but don't worry, darling. I enjoyed it just the same. I'll get there, in good time. It's enough to have you inside me at the moment. I feel – oh, I don't know – fulfilled enough as it is.'

'But I'm getting all the fun.'

'It's still fun for me too – I still get thrills – just not the big one.'

'Maybe I'm failing you?'

She giggled. 'You are such a big soft idiot, Bill Ryker. Forget your manhood for once and listen to me. I – don't – care. I enjoyed it. It was my first time with any man and I'm glad it was with you. At the moment I don't ever want it to be with any other man, either. Just you.'

'At the moment?'

'You can't ask for any more than that, you're not entitled.'

He agreed this was the case but repeated the offer that he had made behind the elder bushes that afternoon.

'Please marry me, Fay.'

'After the war's over. I don't want to be a widow – or you to be a widower. A bomb could fall on me and you could certainly be shot down any day. I know we could be run over by a bus in ordinary times, but it's not so likely. It's silly to get married now. When we get wed, Bill Ryker, I want it to be all flowers and love, and no bloody bombs – you hear? I want you to be able to carry me off somewhere for a lovely honeymoon then to Canada where I can meet your mum and dad. I don't want the air to be thick with fear and death.'

'I get your point,' he sighed.

'Well, there you are then, love. Until then, it's dirty weekends and sneaky nights.'

He rolled her off him and went up on one elbow until he was looking down into her eyes in the moonlight.

'When you asked me to keep this a secret, you meant from everyone, didn't you?'

She stared up at him seriously, reaching with her hand to play with the black curls over his forehead.

'Yes I did, love. 'Cept of course Luke and Rebecca – we could hardly hide it from them, could we? Fact is I come from one of those big families in the East End that would kill a neighbour for touching their women. If my dad found out, or one of my brothers, they'd break every bone in your body.'

'I might have something to say about that.'

She shook her head. 'You wouldn't stand a chance. There's too many of them and they don't fight clean. They'd get you in some back street or quiet dockland area when you were least expecting it and kick you senseless.'

'Sounds like some hillbilly community.'

'Yes, that's it. Terrible feuds, people not speaking to each other for a lifetime, that sort of thing. When you live in a close community, you've got a certain protection from the outside world, but you have to obey the rules and put up with the petty fights that go on inside that community. If you don't, they can be merciless. They stamp down their own kith and kin with no conscience when they feel it's necessary.'

'OK, I'll remember to keep my mouth shut.'

'If someone comes down here, we're just courting, all right?'

'Just courting. All honourable and above-board.'

They lay and cuddled for a few hours, making love once more, before the dawn crept into the room like a grey ghost. Bill was flying just after first light, so he left her, got dressed and then kissed her goodbye.

'You be careful up there,' she ordered fiercely, clinging to him longer than usual. 'You can't just take a woman like you did, then get out of it by being killed.'

'Wouldn't dream of it,' he promised. Then he was gone, ducking under the low doorway out of the bedroom. She listened to his boots on the wooden stairs, heard the back door open and close, then she burst into tears.

'I hate him going,' she snuffled. 'Bloody war.' She conveniently forgot that if it hadn't been for the war she would never have met Bill at all. She wanted him now to reject that war, come to her arms, hand in his notice. None of this was rational, she knew. It was all impossible. Yet she would have cheered had he been as foolish as she and suggested it.

Later she got dressed and made her way to the school. There were faint stirrings inside. Had someone met her on the stairs Fay would have told them that she'd been unable to sleep and had gone out for a walk as soon as the dawn came up. As it was, she met no one. She changed into cleaner clothes, then went down to breakfast. As she descended the stairs, planes roared over the school rooftop. Bill was up there, patrolling the skies, a target.

'Good morning, Miss Nelson,' said a voice.

Fay turned to see a smirking Priscilla Mohorty and Julia Dane following behind her. 'Good morning,' she replied.

'Have a nice night?'

A cold feeling went through Fay but she was prepared to bluff it out. 'Not really – I couldn't sleep.'

Mohorty said, 'I'm not surprised – I never can when I've got company.'

Fay went on the attack, the East End bitch instantly coming out in her. 'You mean when Miss Dane sneaks into your bed? You think I don't know about you two? People in glass houses shouldn't throw stones.'

Julia Dane stuttered, 'I – I never . . .'

'Yes you bloody do, and if you start making unfounded allegations against me, you'll get more than you bargained for, understand?'

Mohorty raised her eyebrows but said no more and the three of them went into the dining room together, looking as if they were all good colleagues discussing interesting aspects of the job of helping young ladies to become educated.

'Let us love our neighbour,' said Martin Simkins that morning during prayers, 'and we don't just mean someone who lives in our street, do we? We mean we must love all and any other man and woman, even those who have done us harm . . .'

Chapter Eleven

On 27 May the German battleship *Bismarck* was sunk. Rebecca heard it on the wireless in the common room. Some of the staff let out a cheer, but Rebecca as always had mixed feelings. She wanted Britain to win the war, of course, but she couldn't stop the disturbing images of drowning sailors from entering her head. Her own father had died that way. She was a little happier to learn that the battleship had been scuttled after being hit by torpedoes, which no doubt meant that the bulk of the crew had managed to abandon ship.

Rebecca delivered this news to Amelia, and was invited to stay. Amelia said she wanted to continue the story she had begun, of her earlier life in Australia.

The old woman looked frailer than usual, her hand shaking as she drank her tea. Rebecca admired Amelia greatly, for her grit as much as anything else. Amelia never complained about aches and pains, the way some old women did. Rebecca often noticed that she rubbed her joints, probably subconsciously. When Rebecca mentioned it once, Amelia retorted very sharply that she was perfectly all right and didn't need fussing over.

There was nothing wrong with her voice though. She told

Rebecca, 'I think it's necessary you should know how and why I founded this school, if you are to become its new owner, Rebecca. The history of the school is very much my personal history – the two are inseparable – and I would like this history to remain alive after I'm gone.'

'I shall see to it that it's not forgotten,' promised Rebecca.

There was only one teacher at Sydney's Ragged School in the middle of the nineteenth century and her name was Frau Stumpf. She was the Austrian wife of a store clerk. She was both cruel and kind, having it in her to beat us if she was angry with us, but would reward us with hugs and kisses if we did well and pleased her. I don't think she was unusually brutal, when you look at the times. People were hanged for very little, so a little beating here or there was not considered to be a terrible thing. It was called good discipline in those days and was considered necessary by the authorities. If a child was disobedient or idle, you beat them into obedience and activity.

Of course, as one of the victims, I went in fear of the birch. I can feel it now, if I try hard enough, stinging my bare back. I probably still carry the scars of that bunch of twigs on my flesh, like a badge of dishonour. Not that I've bothered to look for years, my flesh not being the most pleasant thing to look at in the mirror.

'What's your name?' Frau Stumpf demanded as I was dragged into the classroom. 'Name, child?'

I stood there in my tattered little dress and glared at this big, raw woman with meaty, red arms and tight hair.

'Shan't tell,' I shouted.

Her eyes turned to flints. 'Insolent child,' she snapped, and the birch came whistling down on my thin shoulders.

I screamed at the pain. It aroused such a fury in me I shook off my captors. The older orphans who had brought me, laughed and backed away, as I lashed out with a foot at the ankle of this demon with the whip.

I can smile now at the memory of the horrified expression on Frau Stumpf's face. That a pupil of hers had the temerity to fight back while being thrashed was unbelievable. It was almost beyond her experience and understanding. A waif, an urchin from the orphanage, had dared to kick her. I don't think it even hurt her, physically, but it was more than her pride could bear. She grabbed me by the hair and walloped the living daylights out of my backside, while the class jeered and shouted, then she started lashing out at some of them too.

I fell on the floor in a heap of tears and anger. No one had ever hit me like that before. My own parents had showed me nothing but love and this thrashing was so humiliating to me I could hardly raise my head afterwards. I just lay curled on the stone floor, weeping my heart out, until I felt myself being lifted up and carried to a seat. There I was placed and left until eventually my sobbing ceased.

The class of ragamuffins had gone quiet all around me, once Frau Stumpf had restored order.

When school finished for the day, at twelve noon, and the other children left the room, Frau Stumpf came to my desk. I winced and put an arm over my head to protect myself. She peeled away the arm and hugged me, saying in her harsh voice, 'You mustn't be naughty, you hear? If you are naughty I have to thrash you. You must be a good child. I like good children. Tell me you will be good.'

'I will be good,' I sniffled.

'Ahhhhh,' she hugged me again, crushing me to her great bosom, 'you are really a *sweet* child, I can see that. You smell and your skin is dirty, but inside you are sweet.'

She then took me outside and washed me in the horse trough, my dress too, letting me dry naked on the dockside in the sun while my poor shredded frock flapped from the school windowsill. Then she dressed me again, combed my hair, tied it up with a piece of red rag and sent me back to the orphanage.

'You must wash yourself,' she ordered. 'I want no fleas in my classroom.'

I did as I was told from then on. Frau Stumpf actually liked me, because I was bright. My hand flashed up to answer questions and later when I told her my father had been a schoolteacher she believed me. I also asked if I could see my brother but she said that was impossible. No one knew where he had been taken. I was told to forget him.

I was still hit from time to time, but never as badly as when I had kicked my teacher.

Frau Stumpf was actually quite a good teacher, though she tended to make us learn by rote, smacking her desktop with a ruler to mark the time of learning our times tables:

'One seven is seven,
two sevens are fourteen,
three sevens are twenty-one,
four sevens are twenty-eight,
five sevens are thirty-five . . .'

We chanted this in a singsong voice, like monks intoning prayers at matins, until the whole of the times tables, from two to twelve, was instilled in our brains. We did the same sort of thing with English grammar, learning it by rote, without understanding anything about it. Frau Stumpf's spoken English was not perfect but what she didn't know about English grammar could have been written on the back of a postage stamp. She taught us German too, which I can still speak today: a subject not many orphans had the opportunity of learning.

By the time I was thirteen I was the brightest pupil in the school and was assisting Frau Stumpf with her lessons. I found I liked teaching and it made me want to get on in the world.

At the orphanage itself I was beginning to have trouble with one of the male staff. He was a greasy middle-aged man and he tried to get in my bed one night. I screamed the place down and the woman in charge came up. The man was discharged but I got a beating for 'encouraging' his behaviour. That night I ran away from the orphanage and never returned.

They didn't really care whether I was there or not – it was one less child to look after. I took to the road and finished up on a sheep farm in the outback, some six months later, as a cook for the travelling shearers when the shearing season was on.

It was hard work but I felt independent. I knew that at last I'd shrugged off my childhood and become a woman.

I was just fourteen.

The farm was a dusty old set of shacks and the farmer a willowy bachelor of thirty-five, already a dry, grizzled man, sapped to a husk by the heat and grit of the Australian outback. There was an emptiness behind his eyes and a slight curve to his back, as if he'd already borne the worst of what a lonely life in the wilderness had to offer. Underneath the black straggly beard he'd grown I don't think he ever smiled.

He wore a tattered, floppy, broad-brimmed hat, a dirty undershirt and baggy flannels. In those days I never saw him in anything else and I think he took his baths in the creek with those clothes still on his back. Around his ankles he had wrapped some filthy bandages: he was terrified of being bitten by one of the many venomous snakes. He told me he hated wearing big boots in the heat, but they were useful for stepping on funnel-web and redback spiders. That poor man went in fear of snakes and spiders all his life, though mostly such creatures kept out of the way and meant no harm.

One day I was up to my arms in greasy dishwater. It was a stinking hot day and the flies were a damned nuisance. I was thinking of the new dress I was going to buy with the money I was earning when Jim – the farmer – he came to me and said, 'You want to come and play, girl?'

'What do you mean?' I asked, suspiciously.

There were no more shearers on the farm, the season having finished, and we were alone together with a thousand miles of empty landscape surrounding us.

'Come and shoot my gun, eh? It's a cracker. See?'

Jim held up an old but servicable single-shot rifle with which I had seen him shoot kangaroos and other game. I had nothing to do which couldn't wait, so I followed him out to one of the shacks. He put a tin can in the mouth of an old iron potbellied stove stuck out in the yard. Then the pair of us stood on the veranda of the shack, in the shade.

He aimed at the target and the gun gave off a loud bang that had my ears ringing. The bullet punctured the tin can and clanged around inside the potbellied stove.

'Have to use that to save money,' he said, pointing to the

stove. 'I make my own bullets, see. This way we don't lose the lead if we're just practising – we can get it back from out of the stove. Now you have a go.'

He put another bean can in the mouth of the stove, then he loaded the gun for me and told me to rest the barrel on the edge of the veranda rail. I aimed it just as he told me to, keeping the little knob on the foresight resting in the notch of the back sight. Then I squeezed the trigger.

The recoil nearly took off my shoulder. It threw me back against the wall of the shack. My ears were singing with the sound of the explosion. My eyes were sore with the fumes from the cordite. I was as mad as hell.

'That hurt!' I yelled at him.

Jim grinned for the first time since I had come to work for him. He pointed to the stove. 'You got her, girl – you hit the can smack in the middle. Can you play cricket? I got a good bat in the house, from England. Good willow. I've been keeping her oiled. D'you play, girl?'

'I don't know.'

He felt my arm. 'Bit skinny, but I reckon you could bowl a few spinners to make it interesting. What about it?'

'I could probably learn, I suppose.'

'Fair do's,' he said, punching the hot, still air of the afternoon with his fist. 'Will you marry me, then?'

'What?' I said.

'I said, marry me, girl.'

'Where are we going to get a vicar from, right out here?' I asked him.

'Does that mean you're saying *yes*?' he cried, taking my little hands in his own.

I remember that at the time it was not his words that held my attention, but two fingers of his right hand. They were crooked, as if someone had snapped them at the joints and they hadn't reset properly.

I said, 'How'd you hurt your fingers, Jim?'

He looked down at his scrawny hands and shook his head in impatience. 'What the hell does that matter? I broke 'em in a fight outside a boozer – some fella wanted to kiss a girl in the street who didn't want to be kissed.'

'That's romantic, Jim – you were protecting her.'

'You marry me, Melly, and I won't let no bloke touch you, so help me God. I'll protect you from everything.'

'Except spiders and snakes, eh, Jim? I don't need protecting anyway,' I told him, 'I can look after myself. I'm an educated woman. You get some books in the house and I'll never leave you, Jim. Not till one of us is dead, so help me.'

'You don't wanna get married?' he asked me, surprised. 'Well, that's fine by me. I'm not that dead set on the idea meself. Sort o' silly, out here in the back of nowhere, ain't it, wedding licences and stuff like that? Besides, we ain't got no wedding clothes, have we? Not proper ones. You don't need a bit of paper to stay with me, girl.'

'Yes I do,' I told him. 'I need your last will and testament, leaving the farm and all its holdings to me. I don't want to spend my life out here in the heat and dust and then find that some nephew of yours who's been sitting on his backside in Sydney owns the home I've been keeping clean for fifty years.'

'You got it, girl,' he told me. 'The farm's yours when I kick the bucket. It's half yours now.'

So that was that. We became husband and wife in fact, if not in name. Jim was a good old boy. He treated me well. He was as good as his word in getting the books. We sent all the way to Sydney for them. I was just fourteen at the time and we both knew we'd got a bargain. I came with nothing but the faded old dress I was wearing and Jim was getting a young hard worker for a wife. It suited us both. He taught me to play cricket – I didn't know about hockey then – and I could send down leg breaks that would have him swiping air, so help me. I could bat too. Jim said I could have played for Australia, if they ever took girls, which of course they never did.

Some years later I asked old Jim, 'Did you want to marry me just because I shot the bean can?'

'Naw, girl,' he told me, 'I'd been thinking of it for quite some time, but hadn't the guts to say anything. I needed a sort of, well, an intimate moment, so to speak.'

'Some men might have picked a bunch of desert flowers and caught me coming out of the dunny,' I told him. 'I'm always feeling vulnerable after a visit to the dunny box, where there's a chance of being bitten on the bottom by a funnel-web.'

'That's not me, girl,' he said. 'You know your old Jim. Nothing so romantic. I thought if I could get you on my ground, so to speak, I'd have you. Then I got so excited when you shot that bean can. I said to meself, "This is the girl for me – she's a natural dead shot." And that was that.'

That was that. Jim and I lived together for the next twenty years. I was thirty-four when he got bitten by a snake and died in my arms. 'Farm's all yours, girl,' he said as he was fading away.

'I'm thinking of getting rid of it, Jim, and going back to Sydney,' I told him.

'Best way, girl,' he said. 'You and those books – you're part of each other. Go where the books are, girl.'

'I won't have any other man, you know, Jim. You're the only man I ever wanted.'

My Jim, he died with a smile on his face, he did – and I cried for three days after that. Then I buried him and wrote to an agency in Sydney. They sold the farm for me in six months and I returned to my old city in triumph. I went to see Frau Stumpf. She was old, but still alive, and she hadn't forgotten me. The Ragged School had closed because she could no longer run it and no one else wanted to. I reopened it, with myself as headmistress, and I employed one other teacher.

Anyway, that's a story for another day.

Chapter Twelve

At the beginning of June it was announced that clothes were to be rationed. Since most of the teachers at Gradge Lodge School didn't earn enough to go wild in the dress shops, not many of them were much concerned. Fay grumbled a little and Rebecca was not especially happy about it, but teachers like Mohorty wore tweed skirts and trousers that would last until doomsday, so they saw no need to get excited over a rationing of clothes.

During June there were nightly raids, which had everyone walking around looking like zombies. There was never a night without uninterrupted sleep, when they either had to go down to the shelters, or at least were woken up by the noise. The school was in danger once or twice, when the airfield was attacked, but for the most part it was simply just enough to make life miserable.

Luke Adams and Bill Ryker were kept to an intense routine of patrolling the skies over London and making forays out into the North Sea after German shipping. Many of their comrades were shot down, some were killed, some survived. The pair seemed to be lucky, but as Rebecca heard the Spitfires and Hurricanes taking off day by day, listening to them roar overhead, the sound of their engines fading to nothing as they headed off north, south, east and west, she couldn't help but feel a pang of guilt regarding Luke Adams. Luke was up there, offering his life on a daily basis for the safety of his country, and she knew she had treated him badly.

The trouble was, she still couldn't shake off the attitudes instilled in her by her mother. Rankers in the forces were like bus drivers or railway porters, wonderful when you needed them, but you didn't socialise with them and you certainly didn't date them. This snobbish view of a band of men of mixed intelligence and abilities persisted with Rebecca, even though it had its origins in earlier centuries, when privates and non-commissioned officers were indeed drawn from the poor, uneducated classes.

Christopher Bates, on the other hand, would have been most acceptable to Rebecca's mother. He was educated, he spoke well, and no doubt could converse as easily in French as in English. He knew which knife and fork to use at a formal dinner. Christopher Bates was the kind of man her father had imagined pumping by the hand and congratulating on marrying his daughter. He was the kind of man she herself had envisaged as a husband, when she was an adolescent. There was absolutely nothing about him that was unacceptable to Rebecca.

One day, she received a note from Christopher asking her if she would like to see a London show.

She wrote back saying 'yes please' immediately, hoping that Luke would hear she was being pursued by this eminent and very eligible bachelor. With luck it would put him off for good and keep him out of her hair.

Luke called at the school the day before Rebecca was due to go to London with Christopher. He was on his way to see Amelia and Rebecca met him in the corridor. In his hands was a cardboard folder which appeared to be full of papers.

He gave her one of his usual grins. 'Hello,' he said, 'how are you? Haven't seen you at the pub lately.'

'Actually,' she told him quickly, with a rush of blood to her face, 'I'm tied up. I'm busy tonight and Dr Bates and I are going to London to see a show tomorrow.'

Luke raised an eyebrow but there was still humour in his voice when he said, 'I wasn't asking you for a date – I promised myself not to do that until my poem was published in the *Review* – I was simply saying it was sad we hadn't seen much of you.'

Her confusion almost overwhelmed her. She realised she was being very stupid and making the most awful bungle of trying to put Luke off. The trouble was, she was hopeless at this sort of thing. She wished she were a good liar and could tell Luke that Christopher and she were going out together regularly, but she knew that if she did she would give herself away. She was very poor at telling fibs.

'I'm . . . I'm sorry, I thought you meant tonight.'

'No, I'm flying very early tomorrow morning. I need to get a good night's sleep and wake with a clear head. Can't afford to run the risk of making mistakes in the air, even for the date of a lifetime. Too wise a bird for that.'

She found herself staring into Luke's clear blue eyes. Suddenly she caught a glimpse of the serious man behind the jocular manner. The happy-go-lucky persona was one many of the fighter pilots assumed, probably to hide their real feelings.

A man had to protect himself and others from the truth: that most fighter pilots would not survive a season in the air.

Rebecca was startled to find herself attracted to the real Luke Adams, the genuine man beneath the jester, and immediately fought against those feelings. It was not just a spiritual attraction either. It was much worse than that. In the narrow corridor they were very close to each other and it upset her to discover sensations in herself that a cold corner of her brain told her were not platonic.

'Very wise,' she said faintly. 'Now, if you'll excuse me.' His presence was the cause of ambivalence in her breast, wanting him to go away, yet unable to leave herself.

'Sure, I'm just on my way to see Amelia.'

Despite her need to see him go, Rebecca was curious. 'What for? I mean, if you don't want to tell me . . .'

'No, I don't mind. Fact is, Amelia often helps me proofread my poems, before the galleys go back to the publisher. She's very good at spotting typos. I'm afraid I know the poems too well and simply read through mistakes without noticing them.'

'Proofread?' said Rebecca, a little surprised. 'You mean you've actually got a poem – some poems published?'

She suspected he was probably paying for the printing himself, through one of those vanity publishers. The advertisements were in the Sunday papers every week: *Poets, We Are Looking for Your Work. A Well-known Publishing House Would Be Happy to Consider,* etc, etc. Then, when you wrote to them, they explained that they couldn't bear the costs of the printing themselves, and of course required an administration fee, but they would 'publish' the book.

What that 'publishing' actually meant was they would act

as the middle men between the author and an ordinary printing firm, add their own imprint, such as Dalton Press, and send you the box of books when they had been printed and bound. There would be no distribution, which was the most difficult part of selling a book, and the author would end up giving a dozen copies to relatives and friends for Christmas and birthday presents, and trying to persuade the reluctant proprietor at the local paper shop to sell them from behind the counter.

Luke stared at her. 'Rebecca,' he said, 'you know I write poetry. I wrote a poem for you. It's in this collection, actually. Talbot and Talbot are bringing it out next spring.'

She was stunned. Talbot and Talbot were *the* foremost publishers of poetry and literary works in London. They published all the leading poets of the day and their back list was full of great poets. She waited for the grin to appear, to tell her that he was teasing her, but Luke's expression remained serious.

'Is – is this the first volume you've . . . ?'

'Third,' he said, quickly. 'I'll show you the reviews some time, of the first two collections, if you're interested. They compare me to Auden, which I think is a cheek. We're not the same kind of poets at all – I'm more of an imagist. I don't suppose he likes the idea of being my supposed mentor either.' He looked at his watch. 'Damn – sorry, got to dash. Have a good time in London tonight.'

She was again sceptical, thinking that W. H. Auden wouldn't know or care about a Sergeant Pilot Luke Adams, even if he was a minor poet with Talbot and Talbot.

Luke called over his shoulder, 'I hear there's a good musical on in town.'

'That's the one we're going to see I think,' she said.

'Well, enjoy it.' He hesitated and then added, 'I shouldn't be telling you this, but I'm off to India. Don't know how long I'll be gone. They need some fighters to escort cargo planes over Burma. See you when I get back?'

'Oh, yes, of course – good luck,' she said, surprising herself again by feeling quite upset by this news.

He turned at the end of the corridor and gave her a quick smile and then he was gone, hurrying up the stairs.

Rebecca suddenly realised she was in a hurry too and almost ran to her classroom, wondering whether to believe what she had heard. Once she had started her class on some work, she mulled over their conversation. Luke was spreading it on a bit thick, she thought, using Auden's name.

Finally, Rebecca decided that Luke had probably published his collections with Talbot and Talbot as he'd said, but she had little doubt he was one of their very minor poets, probably a wartime experiment. Perhaps they were trying to repeat the precedent of the 1914–18 War poets, encouraging new but raw talent, some of which might prove enduring, but much of which would be ephemeral. It seemed the most likely explanation.

The next day, once lessons were over, Rebecca hurried to her room and spent a good deal of time with her hair, putting on her make-up and choosing what to wear. The choice was not extensive, but she had some favourites which made her feel good. In the end she chose a dark blue satin dress with a lowish neckline and wore the single string of pearls her mother had bequeathed her. She put her hair up in a French pleat. When she looked at herself in the full-length mirror on the back of the wardrobe door, she was reasonably pleased with the outcome.

The woman staring back at her was a mature and reserved English (no-fripperies) lady, but quite cool and attractive – at least she hoped so. She did not believe she would disgrace anyone, since it was possible they might go somewhere posh for dinner. Even the old dark coat didn't completely destroy the image of the middle-class woman out on the town, though it seemed to be trying its level best.

Once she was dressed, she left the schoolhouse and walked along the driveway to the gates, where Christopher had said he would be waiting for her.

He wasn't.

She stood waiting for him, wondering if she should have called on Kim before she went out. It wasn't really fair on the other girls whose parents weren't able to see them to keep visiting Kim in her dormitory, so Rebecca relied mostly on chance meetings to see her daughter and sometimes have a little talk with her. On open days and parent evenings, Rebecca was often busy, so she believed the school shouldn't begrudge her the occasional in-house visit. However, she knew Kim would have asked a lot of questions tonight, seeing her mother dressed up to the nines, and Rebecca had decided against parading through the dormitory in her finery.

After she had been waiting ten minutes, it began to drizzle. She stood under a horse chestnut tree. It was a light, drifting Irish mizzle that came in from all directions and was impossible to avoid, and though it didn't soak her through, it was enough to uncomfortably dampen her hair and coat.

Christopher arrived three-quarters of an hour later, just

when Rebecca was beginning to despair of ever seeing him.

'Quickly,' he said, flinging open the passenger-side door while remaining in the driver's seat and revving the engine, 'jump in – we're late.'

'Whose fault is that?' she asked, aware of the brittle edge to her voice as she climbed into the little car.

'I'm sorry,' he said, pulling away immediately. 'You know what it's like – doctor. I had a call to make which took longer than I expected. Hazards of the job.'

She allowed herself to be persuaded that he wasn't to blame, though she was a bit upset by the fact that she was feeling like a dishrag.

He turned to glance at her as he drove along. 'You look incredibly beautiful,' he said.

'I might have been, when I started out,' she grumbled, 'but since then I've been for a swim with my clothes on.'

'Should have taken them off then,' Christopher said softly. 'I'd like to see you swimming that way.'

For a moment she was a little shocked, though the remark was harmless enough in its way. It was not the words he used, but the tone. Had it obviously been in fun, she would have dismissed it as one of those remarks that men make when they want to appear risqué, but there was an underlying intensity to his voice which made her feel uncomfortable.

She studied him out of the corner of her eye. He was smartly dressed in a blue serge suit with a sober tie. His dark hair was slicked back in a style reminiscent of the late twenties, early thirties, but it suited him. He was clean-cut and handsome. There was an air of credibility to him, which seemed to tell the world he was a confident man whom one

146

could trust with professional matters. However, it was personal matters that affected Rebecca, not the way in which he dealt with sickness and patients.

'Christopher,' she said, after a little while, 'we don't really know each other very well, do we?'

He looked at her quickly before negotiating a corner. 'And you're wondering what I'm actually like, is that it?' he said, once they were on a straight stretch again. 'You're wondering, *is this the man I think he is?*'

'Yes,' she replied, impressed by his insight.

'Well, we have to find out, don't we? I have to discover who you are, and you have to find out who I am. Then when we know each other well enough, we have to decide what we should do about it. That's what these evenings are for – they're voyages of exploration.'

She was pleased with his response. It meant they were thinking along the same lines. Rebecca sat back and began to enjoy the ride. The warm air from the car's engine filtered through into the interior and began to dry her clothes and hair. They threaded their way through the London suburbs, passing bombed-out buildings and piles of unrecognisable rubble on the way.

The Germans had wreaked a lot of damage on the outskirts of London, and what used to be factories and residential housing were now playgrounds for street urchins and a home for rats. Stray cats and dogs were lodged there too. Such waste areas were still communities of sorts, but the occupants had changed.

They reached a central London pub, The Globe, and had a quick drink there before going to the theatre.

Unfortunately, the musical they had wanted to see had closed. That morning a bomb had exploded just two buildings away and had damaged the theatre. A performance of *Henry V* was on nearby and while Rebecca would have quite liked to have seen a Shakespeare play Christopher said he didn't want culture, he wanted entertainment.

'Never fear, we shall be victorious!' he cried.

They climbed back into the car and he drove them to the Windmill Theatre. WE NEVER CLOSE said the sign outside. The revue was already showing, but they managed to get seats in the back stalls and there they settled for the evening.

After the show, which Rebecca thought quite fun but not very stimulating, they went for a meal at a fashionable restaurant. The menu was not extensive, due to the rationing, but there were some attractive items. They both settled on rainbow trout, with the chef's own recipe sauce. Rebecca liked the candlelight, the linen-covered tables and the French ambience of the place. It was easy to forget that a war was on in such surroundings.

Halfway through the meal, Christopher said, 'Look, a pal of mine has a flat in Hammersmith. He's an army doctor stationed in Wiltshire at the moment. Would you like to spend the night at the flat? It's up to you. I've got a key.'

Rebecca had a forkful of fish on its way to her mouth and his question stopped her hand dead. She stared at the man across the table, seriously considering his words. For some reason however, she was not ready for such a commitment, not yet. It was too soon in their acquaintance. And apart from any emotional barriers, there were serious practical considerations. Unfortunately, instead of saying no, she raised one of these considerations, giving him the impression that this was all that stood in her way.

'I'm expected back at the school,' she said. 'They'll worry if I don't return tonight.'

Christopher leaned across the table and placed his hand over hers. 'Don't worry about that – I'll sort that out with Amelia. We could blame a bombing raid – say we got stuck in a shelter or something. Shall I do that?'

'You certainly will not, Christopher. I don't mean I have to ask permission to stay out all night. I mean I have a daughter there who expects me to take her for a walk early tomorrow morning. If you had this in mind when you asked me out, you should have told me before we left.'

He withdrew his hand and wiped his mouth with his table napkin, clearly put out by her tone.

'I'm sorry – it was a last-minute thing, that's all. I thought that if we spent the night together, it would be a good way of getting to know each other. I want to get to know you better, Rebecca. How do you feel about it?'

'People usually get to know each other *before* they go to bed together.'

'Well, yes,' he smiled, 'but you're a widow, not some simpering virgin. You know what it's all about.'

Rebecca was dreadfully shocked by this remark. For a start she *didn't* know what it was all about. Just because she had been to bed with one man, her husband, didn't mean she knew every aspect of human relationships. It had been a stupid remark to make.

'I don't understand what you mean by that,' she said.

He saw at once that he had made a grave mistake and

immediately sought to rectify it. 'Well, what I mean is you don't have to justify your actions to anyone.'

'I can't just do as I like.'

He began to get irritated. 'Who's to stop you? *What's* to stop you?'

'My own feelings of self-preservation for a start. It's not just a matter of romping between the sheets and forgetting about it. I need to feel it's right for me. I need to feel happy about it. I don't want to get into something that I'm fully committed to and you're treating as a bit of fun. I don't want to be *hurt*, thank you very much. Have you thought that when a woman gives herself she's offering more than just her body – she's offering her whole self?'

'That's a bit strong for me.'

Rebecca stared at him directly in the eyes, which disconcerted him and eventually he looked down. She said to him, 'What about falling in love, Christopher? What would happen if I fell in love with you? You do believe in love, I suppose?'

'Of course I believe in love,' he replied, almost angrily. 'Are you saying you're falling in love with me?'

'No, I'm saying that going to bed might accelerate such a thing, if it were happening. I don't want that to occur unless it's coming from both sides. If I were to fall in love with someone and find it wasn't requited, I would be devastated. Anyone would be. We have to guard against that by not rushing into it blindly. I don't want to find I'm chasing a reluctant lover all over the place, and I'm sure you wouldn't want to be relentlessly pursued.'

'You make it sound as if you'll turn into a predator.'

'I will – believe me, I will – if I find I'm drawn into something and then discarded.'

'Forget it,' he said in an exasperated voice. 'You've put me off the whole idea anyway.'

He clicked his fingers at the waiter for the bill. He paid for the meal and they went out to the car. On the way back to the school they maintained a rather strained silence. When the car came to a stop outside the gates, Rebecca turned to Christopher and said, 'I had a lovely evening, really. Don't let's spoil it by sulking with each other. I'm sorry I disappointed your expectations, but I'm not ready yet for a definite commitment. You do understand?'

'I suppose so,' he sighed. 'Has it put you off coming out with me again?'

'Not at all,' she smiled. 'I like you very much. I'm – I'm just a little frightened of my feelings, that's all. I don't want them to run away with me before I'm sure they're reciprocated. You're not in love with me, Christopher – at least, not yet. You may never be.'

'No,' he admitted, 'not yet – but I might be going that way.'

'I want to be sure of both of us – as sure as I can be – before I let myself go completely. I've just lost a husband, Christopher. I still love him. It's just that he's not there to love me back. Any affair I might embark on at this time would feel like a betrayal, however stupid that sounds. Inside I'm still loyal to him. I have to get over that barrier too. You're right, I'm not some simpering virgin . . .'

He winced and gripped the wheel when she repeated the words that he had used earlier.

' . . . but my feelings run deep.'

'You take sex a little too seriously,' he said. 'At least, more seriously than I do. It's just a couple of people enjoying themselves for a short time.'

'No, it's more than that to me – much more. It's a giving of myself to a man I love above all other men.'

He smiled, wryly. 'That's a very medieval concept – the treasure that you give to one man.'

'You make it sound so very simple, but emotions aren't simple, Christopher. They're very complex, delicate things that can be shattered and rendered unusable. I can't divorce the act from my emotions, in the way that you seem to believe I should be able to. The two are bound together in me. I will make love with the man I love, and no other. I don't think I'm particularly medieval in doing that. I can't take love out of the equation. I'm sorry.'

'No, no,' he sighed, '*I'm* sorry. There's nothing more sordid than a man trying to persuade a reluctant woman into his bed. Let's forget it. Can I call on you again?'

'Of course,' she smiled. She leaned over to kiss his cheek and he turned to meet her, pressing his lips against hers, his hand resting lightly on her breast. She allowed the kiss to develop into something more than just a 'good-night' and then pulled away from him.

'I must go,' she said. 'I'm getting confused. I don't want to be confused at the moment. Good night, Christopher.'

'Good night, Rebecca.'

She got out of the car and walked briskly down the gravel driveway to the school doors. She went inside and up to her room. When she opened the door, Fay was sitting on her bed, the tears running down her face.

'Oh, God,' said Rebecca in a still voice. 'What's happened, Fay? Is it Bill? Is he . . .'

'It's not Bill,' cried Fay, getting up to hug her, 'it's Luke – Luke's been shot down.'

A kind of numbing electric-shock feeling went through Rebecca's body in a series of waves as the words sank in. Luke Adams, the sergeant pilot, had been killed. That should have meant very little to her, beyond the fact that he was a human being she had known, and he was therefore to be grieved over as such. But it seemed to mean much more than that. It shocked her through to the core of her being and she wanted him back, in front of her, so that she could say things to him, things that she had felt but not wanted to put into words.

'Luke's really dead?' she said. Her voice sounded distant and muted to her, as if it were someone else asking the question at her bidding. 'What happened?'

'Luke's been shot down,' sniffed Fay, 'over the Indian Ocean. He was being flown out there for some reason – him and another pilot. They got out an SOS, but then the radio went dead. Search and Rescue didn't find any of them.'

Rebecca felt a sudden ache in her chest at the news.

'Oh, no – Fay, are you sure?'

'There were no traces of Luke or the others.'

A rush of emotion came over Rebecca and she knew she had to get away somewhere on her own. 'I'm sorry, Fay, I have to get some sleep,' she said.

Fay stared at her in disbelief, then walked to the door, opening it and saying, 'Don't you care?'

It was all Rebecca could do to stop from crying, but she

replied over her shoulder, 'Of course I care. I care very much – but I have to – I've got to go . . .'

Once Fay had left the room and closed the door Rebecca fell on the bed and began sobbing into the pillow. She couldn't understand why she was crying. Surely Luke was nothing to her? Surely he was just another airman out of the hundreds of airmen that were being shot down and killed? Was it just because she had known him?

She remembered the day they had gone out in Christopher Bates's car into deepest Essex. She recalled the way Luke had been excited by the big skies out on the flatlands; by the networks of rivers that incised the Essex landscape; by the winding snakes of turf which were the river and sea walls.

'Some people find flat countryside like this uninteresting,' he had told her. 'Well I don't. In Cornwall we have the moors, which are similar to this, though these are more salt marshes than peat hag country. I think marshlands have atmosphere and a wildlife all of their own. They're peppered with a thousand different birds. It's true that they're not beautiful, nor even very pretty, but they have a strong mystical attraction. It's as if the Dark Ages have never left – as if the great warlords of the regions after the withdrawal of the Romans were still somehow exerting an influence over the place. There's a brooding magnificence about the creeks, the wide flat stretches of farmland with the great underbelly of the sky pressing down on them.'

He had pointed out hawks, hovering over the dykes, waiting to drop on mammals in the short grasses.

'The great-grandparents of those raptors could have been

trapped and trained by a Norman nobleman,' he'd said, taking a certain amount of poetic licence.

When she pointed out that birds only live a few years, he had protested at her pragmatism with the reply, 'There's a stillness here, a long pause in the passage of time. If we blink our eyes we could be back in the time of the Norman conquest, with the local Saxons waiting in trepidation for the coming of the invincible armies of William the Conqueror. I feel it in the air – a mighty army coming from the south, from Hastings, to consolidate its victory over the local population. Don't you feel it? That tremor in the air? That waft of wind from the wings of Norman falcons? I feel it . . .'

Now the man who had spoken those words was gone; in all probability he was dead. This realisation opened a floodgate inside Rebecca – a gate she had been forcibly keeping closed for what she believed were rational reasons – and let forth a rush of emotion that threatened to drown her. Luke was dead and she had allowed him to die without being true to him and to herself. She *was* very fond of him, had possibly been in love with him, but he had gone down in his aircraft thinking she detested him for his background and his accent. Rebecca sobbed uncontrollably into the pillow, soaking it with her tears.

The door to her room opened softly, almost without her hearing, and a few moments later she felt an arm round her shoulder. Fay's voice said, 'Oh, Rebecca – I thought you didn't care.'

There was no answer to this and Rebecca did not give one. She simply continued crying until she felt she could cry no more, then she looked up at Fay, whose concerned face was staring down at her.

'I'm crying for my husband too,' said Rebecca. 'It's Alan I'm crying for, not really Luke – but I did like him, you know. And he – he thought I didn't. He thought I was a cold bitch who couldn't stand his humble background.'

'No he didn't,' smiled Fay bravely, stroking her hair. 'And if he did, Luke wouldn't have cared less. He knew he could win you over in the end. His ego wouldn't let him be put off by a few rebuffs, you know.'

Rebecca sat up, dried her eyes and blew her nose on her handkerchief. 'I did notice that. It didn't matter what I said to him – he always came back for more.'

Fay's smile left her face and she became very serious now. 'Well, he was in love with you, you know. I've been close to those boys for a long time and I'd never seen Luke so smitten as he was when he first laid eyes on you. I suppose with him it was a case of first sight.'

'Too late for me to be sorry now,' Rebecca said. 'The trouble was – it was too soon. If I'd met him a year from now . . .'

'Now you know that's not true. You certainly jumped at the chance to go out with Chris Bates, so it's not that, is it?'

'I suppose not,' Rebecca confessed, miserable and confused, 'and yet, I didn't have all *that* much fun with Christopher. I thought it would be wonderful, but it wasn't. It was fairly ordinary. He tried to get me into bed.'

'Huh,' muttered Fay, 'they *all* do that, sweetie.' Her eyes went distant and dreamy for a moment, as she added, 'Still, when you let the right one, it's smashing. It's like floating down a gentle stream into a warm, milky sea . . .'

'Fay!' said Rebecca. 'I don't want to know about your

private affairs. That is . . .' She realised she had chosen her words badly, but Fay seemed not to mind.

Fay smiled again. 'Oh, don't be such a prude – you can't afford to be. You're too young. Shall I sleep with you tonight, love? I mean, to keep you company?'

'No, I'll be all right. It – it was just a shock, that's all.'

'It was a shock for us all. Bill's brokenhearted.'

Rebecca considered Bill Ryker for the first time. Of course he would be absolutely shattered. Luke had been his best friend. 'Oh, of course, poor Bill,' she said. 'How dreadful for him.'

'The worst of it is,' said Fay, 'these pilots pretend they're not affected. It's bad form to talk of missing comrades too much – or grieve for them apparently – because it happens so often. So they all carry on in a breezy fashion as if Luke's merely fallen over and grazed his shin or something. Bill looks as if he's all right, but I know he's really bad inside.'

'He won't crack up, will he?' asked Rebecca fearfully.

'I'm worried he might,' confessed Fay. 'The pressure must be enormous. It's got to come out somewhere, hasn't it? I don't believe he can just brush aside the death of his best friend as if it was just one of those things.'

Fay left Rebecca to get undressed and get into bed. However, once her friend had gone, Rebecca once more lapsed into weeping and eventually cried herself to sleep. There was a raid in the middle of the night, during which she stumbled around in total confusion, hardly knowing where she was. Mohorty remarked upon her mental state, but Rebecca hadn't the heart or mind to reply.

Two days later Bill Ryker gave Rebecca a magazine. It was

the *Literary Review*. She had promised to date Luke if the *Review* ever published his poem to her. She had not believed it possible at the time.

The poem was there, on the second page.

Chapter Thirteen

Several weeks after Luke had been shot down Rebecca was summoned to Amelia's study. When she entered the room Amelia was in her usual position, overlooking the playing fields, watching the hockey.

Fighter planes were zooming in and out of the station, overflying the school and making the windows rattle gently. For a while Amelia said nothing, waiting for a gap in the noise overhead, then she turned in her chair and indicated that Rebecca should sit down opposite her.

'Did you pass a man in the corridor?' asked Amelia in a voice that was becoming increasingly more frail-sounding as the weeks passed.

'Yes – a man in his late thirties.'

'Did you recognise him?'

Rebecca frowned. 'No, should I have done?'

'I suppose not,' said Amelia. 'Anyway, it was Cecil Day Lewis, the poet friend of W. H. Auden. Mr Auden is in the United States, you know – has been for some time.'

'I see,' said Rebecca, wondering what all this was about.

Amelia's brown, creased face broke into a sad smile. 'Mr Auden has written to me to say how sad he was to hear that

Luke Adams has been posted missing in action.'

Rebecca's eyes opened wide. 'Then he really did know of Luke? Auden, I mean.'

'They all did – Luke was a very respected poet, you know. They thought quite a lot of him. I wrote to Mr Day Lewis and told him that Luke had been shot down over the sea. He in turn informed Mr Auden and brought the reply today. I just thought you'd like to know.'

'Is that what you called me in here for?' asked Rebecca.

'No, not specifically – Luke left you something too. I haven't given it to you, because I had hoped we might have news of him. I hoped we would hear he was alive and well somewhere, and merely incapacitated for some reason. That's obviously not going to happen now. So, here's what he left me to give to you.'

It was a small package, wrapped in brown paper. Rebecca took it and opened it in front of Amelia. Inside were Luke's first two volumes of poetry. They had been inscribed with a personal message for her. The inscriptions were not flowery or sentimental. The first said, simply, *To Rebecca, my companion for a day in the wilds of Essex.* The second said, *For Kim, who will astonish us all one day.*

'Oh,' said Rebecca, the tears starting to her eyes.

'Well,' Amelia commented matter-of-factly, 'you'll be able to read what a fine poet he was – that young man – and he hadn't really started. Now, if you'll excuse me, my dear, I become tired very easily these days . . .'

'Yes, of course. I suppose there's still hope – that he might be all right?'

'There's always hope, isn't there?' answered Amelia.

Rebecca nodded but both women knew that fighter pilots shot down over the sea who were not picked up within a couple of days were considered to be dead, even though technically posted as 'missing in action'. The sea was not the kindest of the elements. Even in the Indian Ocean the waters were cold and debilitating. There was very little hope that Sergeant Pilot Luke Adams was still alive.

Rebecca left Amelia's room clutching the two precious books and went to her room to put them beside her bed, to read that evening. She felt confused. That Luke had bothered to arrange such a gift, even while she was showing him the cold shoulder, pricked her conscience. Then she reminded herself that he had written of nothing but friendship, and she was glad to be his friend, even in his absence.

Later that day Rebecca was again at loggerheads with Mohorty. Rebecca had decided to send Kim to her grandparents in Cumberland, for the coming summer holidays. Mrs Dibbs who ran the sweetshop in the village was taking the train north two days before the end of term. Rebecca had asked her if she would take Kim under her wing and the elderly woman said she was delighted to have the company. Rebecca had then asked Francine Knole for permission to let Kim go early, and had received it.

Mohorty had got wind of this from Helena Patten who, though she was a good companion to Amelia, was fond of intrigue and had passed on the information to the games mistress, knowing it would upset her.

Mohorty cornered Rebecca as she was stacking chairs in the large hall after taking a music lesson. The pupils had already gone to another class and Rebecca was on free time.

Mohorty entered the otherwise empty hall from the far end. She confronted Rebecca in the middle of the vast room.

'What's this I hear about your daughter leaving early for the summer holidays?' she hissed.

Mohorty had her back to the large Norman-arched windows that looked out over the playing fields, while Rebecca faced them. There were three large, evenly spaced windows in all; the sills were at ground level and the peaks touched the ceiling. They consisted of small panes, hundreds of them, and they were Amelia Sartour's pride and joy. She said the windows gave the school some majesty.

'I don't see what business that is of yours,' retorted Rebecca, wondering what had got into the games mistress now.

'Kim Daniels is in the team to play St Theresa's School on the last day of term.'

Rebecca realised what all the fuss was about. 'Well, surely it's not *that* important?' she laughed. 'Kim's lot is only the third team after all . . .'

'I never use that word "only" when talking of my teams. They're all as important as each other. Kim Daniels is the best player in the third team – they won't stand a chance without her,' cried Mohorty, hotly. 'I do believe you're doing this on purpose. It's a selfish attempt to get back at me, isn't it? You want the school to lose.'

Rebecca was astounded. The woman was serious. She was genuinely upset that a seven-year-old was going to her grandparents and was unable to play hockey for the school. Rebecca found that incredibly silly. If Kim had been captain of the school team, she might have understood what all the fuss was about, but her daughter wasn't much more than an infant.

'It's nothing of the sort,' she explained. 'Mrs Dibbs at the sweetshop is going to relatives in Carlisle on that day and she's promised to deliver Kim to her grandparents near Lake Windermere. You can't make a conspiracy out of that, Mohorty, no matter how much you try. Anyway, if you want my opinion, hockey is a philistine sport. I'd rather my daughter wasn't crippled before she was ten by one of those little barbarians from St Theresa's, if you don't mind.'

Mohorty swelled about three inches all over. 'Philistine? It's just as civilised as any other subject taught in school. It's character-building. Perhaps that's why insipid creatures like you are devoid of character – because you never played any hockey when you were younger.'

Insipid? Devoid of character? *Creature?*

Rebecca flung the sheets of music she was carrying on to the floor of the hall and put her hands on her hips.

'It may interest you to know, Miss Mohorty, that I did play hockey – and hated every minute of it. So if I have no character, it's not because I didn't play hockey, I can assure you. It's probably because I had women like you for my games teachers – and I'm sure you know what I mean.'

Mohorty's eyes opened wide, then narrowed quickly. 'I'm sure I *don't* know what you mean. Perhaps you'd better explain it to me?'

Rebecca was about to reply when she noticed something behind Mohorty's shoulder. It was outside one of the great Norman windows, high in the sky, amongst the puffs of cloud that drifted over the blue: a wavy line, not much bigger than a tern at that moment, but becoming larger by the second, instantly recognisable by the V-shaped wings. It had come out of a loop and was diving towards the school, sweeping over the countryside at a low altitude. Its cannons weren't spitting, but it seemed to be intent on flying directly into the centre window of the hall and crashing through.

'Stuka!' yelled Rebecca, throwing herself to the ground and flattening her body.

Mohorty remained standing, staring at Rebecca in contempt as she crawled along the floor, trying to get behind a stack of chairs. Out of the corner of her eye Rebecca could see the Stuka flatten its flight pattern above the trees at the end of the playing field, then begin an upward swoop. It was obviously not going to machine-gun the school, but she feared something else.

Her fears were confirmed a second later as she saw a small black object detach itself from the underside of the German aircraft. The object came at a forty-five-degree angle towards the schoolhouse.

'Bomb!' shrieked Rebecca.

Mohorty remained where she was, as if nailed to the spot.

Before reaching the school the bomb hit the ground and exploded halfway down the playing fields. Turf, dirt and stones went flying. The blast shattered the windows behind Mohorty, sending a glistening hail-shower of glass, like buckshot from a gun, the complete length of the hall. Rebecca, hunched behind a chair, heard the tinkle of glass falling like rain throughout the room. Bits of earth and turf followed the blast, splattering against the walls.

It was lucky that Mohorty had been standing between two

windows. When Rebecca turned to look out through the now glassless Norman arches, she saw that the back of the woman's thick tweed jacket and skirt was covered in tiny pieces of glass, glittering like sequins, flashing like diamond chips. Mohorty was decorated with bits of green and brown too, some of the playing field tangled in the curls of her wiry grey-brown hair.

'My hockey field!' wailed the games mistress. 'They've ruined my hockey field.'

Rebecca was astonished by Mohorty's reactions. Whether it had been courage, foolishness or ignorance that had kept her on her feet, Rebecca would never know. One thing was certain, the incident hadn't shaken Mohorty in the least. Her thick clothes and hair had protected her from any serious harm. They were like armour covering her whole back. Only a couple of inches of ankle had been showing below the skirt.

It was fortunate that the blast hadn't broken the old windows into larger slivers, or she might have been lacerated badly. But the panes had completely disintegrated, perhaps due to the age and brittleness of the glass.

Unlike Rebecca, Mohorty wasn't visibly trembling, nor was she searching the sky fearfully for a second run-in by the German aircraft. She was simply agonising over the loss of her sports field.

'Never mind,' said Rebecca, staring without any feeling of emotion at the black pit which moments earlier had been the centre of the hockey pitch. 'I'm sure it won't take long for the turf to grow back, once the hole's been filled.'

Mohorty, clearly still overcome, rounded on her. 'I expect you're glad, aren't you? I expect you're *pleased* the hockey field has been bombed? I shouldn't be surprised if this has answered your prayers.'

People were entering the hall now, staring aghast at the two women standing arguing amongst the debris. Julia Dane gasped when she saw her beloved Priscilla covered in flecks of various-coloured glass. Helena Patten came tripping towards them, tugging at the shapeless cardigan of her twinset with nervous fingers, crunching tiny shards of glass like spilt sugar under the leather soles of her brogues.

Martin Simkins was already organising a sweeping team, telling a group of senior girls to go and get brooms and meet him back in the hall.

'Are you two all right?' he called.

'Yes,' replied Mohorty.

'Yes,' replied Rebecca.

Their replies were short and impatient, since they were eager to be at each other's throats again.

'It might interest you to know,' said Rebecca stiffly, 'that I have far more important things to bother God with than praying for the destruction of your stupid hockey pitch.'

'It doesn't interest me in the least,' snapped back Mohorty, whose back was now being brushed down by the hand of Julia Dane. 'Not in the slightest.'

Dane said, 'Oh dear, oh dear, your ankles are bleeding, Priscilla.'

Mohorty looked down at her ankles with the same contemptuous expression she had thrown at Rebecca when Rebecca had been prostrate on the floor of the hall. 'Nothing that a pair of tweezers and some warm water won't cure,' she snapped. 'Don't fuss, Julia.'

'No, Priscilla.'

Helena Patten stared tight-lipped, first at Rebecca and then at Mohorty. 'Well,' she said, 'if you are quite finished quarrelling, perhaps we can get this room cleaned up.'

Mohorty muttered to Rebecca, 'I haven't finished with you yet,' then walked through the hall and left, followed by Julia Dane, who was still brushing her friend's shoulders as they went.

Rebecca heaved a sigh of relief. 'That woman will be the death of me,' she said.

'Or you of her,' murmured Helena.

'What's that supposed to mean?' demanded Rebecca.

'Oh, I don't know. Don't get into an argument with me too, Mrs Daniels – I'm not ready for one.'

Rebecca was about to protest and then thought better of it. She allowed Martin to take her hand and lead her between the row of sweeping brooms, wielded by the senior girls, and out of the hall.

'Go and get a cup of tea,' said Martin. 'You might still be in shock.'

'What about Mohorty? She didn't even duck.'

Martin smiled wryly. 'It'd take something bigger than a Stuka bomb to shake that old bag.'

'You mean she's tougher than me?'

'Like cowhide,' he said. 'Off you go. Get something hot and sweet inside you.'

Rebecca did as she was told, vowing she would not be intimidated by Mohorty, or anyone else for that matter.

Chapter Fourteen

Fay and Bill had been sleeping together at the Bull Inn all through the summer holidays. Fay was still adamant that she didn't wish to get married until all the fighting and flying was finished. Bill was still trying to get a date out of her nearer than the end of the war. He was one of those who believed the war would go on for longer than a year or two.

'Aw, come on, Fay – we can't wait until doomsday,' he said to her one night as they lay on the overstuffed mattress in the four-poster 'honeymoon bed' at the inn.

There were smells of rotting wood in the room, drying bed linen and mothballs. Bill liked the pubs and inns of England more than the bars of his native Canada, but he didn't want to spend the rest of his life in a room with a rickety floor, plumbing that sounded worse than a submarine's engine room, the noise of drunks hanging around outside after closing time, a washbasin where the taps spat the water in freezing force-ten gobbets, a toilet whose water level rose ominously to the lip of the bowl every time it was flushed, and finally, mice and other house fauna that gnawed all night behind the wainscot.

'You know my thoughts on this, Bill,' said Fay. 'It's not that I don't love you, darlin' – but I'm not prepared to be a war widow. Look what happened to Luke. That could've been you . . .'

She began to get tearful and Bill dropped the subject for a while, raising it again later as they watched the dawn creep through the large gaps between and below the thick, dusty, ill-fitting curtains hanging on the crooked window.

'We could pretend to be married,' he said, 'so we could get a decent apartment in the village.'

'Flat – we don't say apartment. It sounds too big and posh.' She snuggled naturally into his arms. 'No we couldn't – people would be shocked. Anyway, I thought you said you liked pubs? You said you couldn't get enough of the old-world charm and quaint atmosphere of a pub – all that ancient wood, you said, polished by a million rustic elbows, those roaring log fires in the grate, hot enough to roast an ox, the beer on tap all the time, spiral wooden staircases that wind into a maze of upper rooms, with all the creaks and groans of centuries locked in their joints – that's what you said.'

'Did I say all that? I must have been in my cups.'

'No, you were perfectly sober and your eyes were shining with schoolboy delight.'

He held her tightly in his arms before he said, 'Oh, gosh, *then*? That was when I was trying to get you in the sack – I was anticipating being laid, *that's* why my eyes were shining.'

'You – you *rotter*,' she cried.

As he had guessed Fay struggled like mad to get an arm free so that she could box his ears, but he kept a tight hold on her.

'There's another thing,' he said, when she had calmed down a little. 'I want to meet your folks.'

She suddenly stiffened in his arms and he could feel the

panic rippling through her small naked body.

'*No!*' she almost shouted.

'Hey, hey, take it easy,' he murmured into her ear, nuzzling into her hair. 'I've got to meet them some time, honey – you know that. Even if we wait until after the war to get married, I've got to meet them then.'

'That's all right – when we're ready to be married – but they must never suspect we've been to bed together. I told you, there's a strict moral code in the East End, Bill. If my parents knew we'd been to bed they'd kill us both.'

'Both?'

'Well, the men would cripple you, that's for sure.'

'But, sugar, there's a strict moral code *everywhere*. I mean if my own folks knew we'd been to bed, they wouldn't be happy either. I've seen more than one shotgun wedding, I can tell you. Us backwoods Canucks are just as uncivilised as the Londoners of the East End.'

'Uncivilised? My family are positively barbaric when it comes to their women, Bill. They think they own us, lock, stock and big toes. You thought slavery had been abolished, didn't you? Go to the East End and you'll find out that it's still alive and well – white slavery. Female.'

Bill was genuinely concerned. 'How did you get out then? It sounds as if they don't like letting their women out of their sight.'

'My father thinks that Gradge Lodge School is the equivalent of a nunnery. He thinks it's a convent.'

'Why would he think that?'

Her blue eyes looked directly into his. 'Because I told him it was.'

Bill drew back in mock horror. 'You lied to your own father? How could you? The man who sacrificed his life for you, worked his fingers to the bone for you . . .'

'Drank a bottle of whisky the night I was born, just to show how pleased he was that he'd been blessed with a girl,' interrupted Fay bitterly.

'How do you know?'

'He tells me – constantly. "Fay," he says, "your name should've bin Albert, only you was born wivout a tail." '

'Nice guy, your dad.'

'Actually,' said Fay, 'he *is* nice in lots of ways, but he's a product of his upbringing. They've got all these customs, the poor people of the East End, which help them to forget their poverty. It's a kind of club, you see, and if you belong you've got to obey the rules. The women have a worse time of it than the men. The employment situation's the worst factor – it brings the men to their knees.'

'Work's hard to find, huh?'

'Bloody near impossible most of the time, unless you've got a steady job like a dustman or a railway worker. The men are always on the lookout for work, hardly ever finding it, falling into a pit of despair but *never* showing it outwardly, because they're men and men mustn't reveal their weaknesses.

'I can remember the time my mother used to take in washing and do it all hours. I used to wake up wanting a drink of water in the middle of the night, go downstairs and find my mother in the scullery surrounded by mountains of filthy clothes and bed linen, with her red-raw arms up to the elbows in soapy water, scrubbing some other family's dirty underwear.

'I'd end up spending the rest of the night helping her, feeding the fire underneath the big copper, stirring the steaming washing with a thick white stick as big as myself . . .'

Bill kissed her lips. 'Tough life, huh? Well, you don't have to be tough any longer – you've got me. I won't make you do anything you don't want to do, you know that. And if our daughter wants to sleep with a lumberjack before she's married, why – why, I'll – I'll kick the guy so hard on the seat of his pants he'll be arrested for low flying . . .'

'You see,' said Fay, getting a fist free and punching him, 'you're all the same, you men. You can't trust us to make the right choice for ourselves. Well, the time's coming, Bill Ryker, when you won't have any say in what we do. If we want to sleep with a man, we'll bloody well sleep with him, whether the men of the family like it or not.'

At the school only Rebecca knew of the situation between Fay and Bill. She had no idea what her Aunt Amelia would think of Fay's escapades but she was inclined to believe, knowing Amelia's own history, that Amelia would ignore them, providing the couple were discreet.

Fay's greatest fear was that Mohorty would obtain some positive proof of her sleeping out, but Rebecca wasn't so sure the games mistress would do anything about it if she did discover what was going on. As Fay had pointed out to the pair, it would be a case of 'let she who is without sin cast the first stone'. Everyone knew that Priscilla Mohorty and Julia Dane were having an affair and, in Rebecca's opinion, sleeping with another woman in an all-girls school was likely to be viewed with less sympathy than sleeping with a man.

In neither case, however, would the teacher concerned survive if their affairs became public knowledge. Fay knew that she would have to be pilloried by Amelia Sartour, to appease irate parents and convince them the school was not a hotbed of vice.

One night at the Bull Inn, just after Fay and Bill had got into bed together, something rattled against the window.

'What's that?' cried Fay, sitting bolt upright.

Bill said, 'Maybe it's just the wind.'

'It sounded to me like someone throwing gravel,' said Fay, pulling the sheet up over her breasts. 'No one knows we're here, do they? None of your mates?'

'What do you take me for?' asked Bill.

Then a voice came floating up from the pub yard outside. 'Hoy!'

Bill got up and went to the window, but Fay cried, 'Don't open it!'

Bill said, 'Jeez, Fay – no one's going to shoot me.'

He opened the window and peered down into the yard. In the swirling mists of the night, by the light of a street lamp, he could see five men standing looking up at him, three soldiers in uniform and two men in civilian clothes. Iron bars dangled from several hands. The squaddies looked young and fresh, the two civvies were older men.

One of the men in civvies said, 'You Ryker?'

'I might be,' said Bill. 'Who wants to know?'

'Me name's Nelson,' growled the man. 'Get down 'ere and take what's comin' to you, or we'll come in an' get you, Yank. It'll go much worse wiv yer, if we 'ave to come in.'

'I'm a Canadian,' said Bill calmly, 'not an American.'

Fay shrieked and rushed to the window. Leaning out she looked down on three of her brothers in army uniforms, her uncle and her father. It was her dad who had spoken. She yelled at him.

'You touch my Bill and – and I'll never come home again, Dad. I'll report you to the police, I will honestly. Leave us alone.'

Her father looked away, shocked. 'You get somethin' coverin' those titties, young lady,' he gasped. 'You ought to be ashamed, you ought. What wiv your bruvvers and uncle lookin' at you. Go and get some clothes on, for decency's sake.'

Fay was distressed. She rushed back to the bed and found her clothes, putting them on hurriedly. Bill too dressed, but slowly and with less agitation than Fay. When he had on his uniform, he went towards the door. Fay whispered, 'Are you crazy? We have to go out the back window, over the lean-to toilet roof – run away over the fields.'

Bill was smart in his blue uniform, his hat at a rakish angle and his flying jacket making him look as if his chest and shoulders were much bigger than they actually were. His lean, square-jawed face was hard as flint. He stared at Fay for a moment before saying, 'I'm not running anywhere, Fay.'

'But they'll kill you, you fool. At the very least they'll break your legs for you.'

'We'll see about that,' said Bill, quietly.

He opened the door and was about to descend the stairs when the landlord came out of his room on to the landing carrying a candle in a holder. The flickering light cast dancing shadows on the walls of the landing and down the stairs. The publican peered at Bill, lifting the candle aloft.

'Who's that? Flying Officer Ryker? What's going on?' he asked.

Bill replied, 'Some of Miss Nelson's relations from London – sorry to disturb you. We'll get rid of them in a few minutes.'

'Disturbing the whole household,' grumbled the publican, going back into his room and leaving Bill in darkness.

Bill felt his way down the stairs. When he reached the bottom he crossed the bar and unbolted the door. Then he stepped outside to be confronted by the Nelson family. They let him get beyond the step, which had a scrubbed worn hollow dip in the middle, before closing around him.

Bill flexed his shoulders and stood tall, glaring down on the smaller cockneys. This stopped the forward movement. One of Fay's brothers said, 'Big bastard, ain't he?' in a voice that betrayed his insecurity.

At that moment, Fay came stumbling out of the pub, misjudged the worn step and fell forward. Bill stepped towards her quickly and caught her, holding her in his arms. Joe Nelson growled, 'Get your 'ands off my daughter, Yank.'

Bill set Fay on her feet and then turned to face the small, tough-looking old man. 'I've told you once and I won't tell you again, I'm not an American – I'm Canadian, see. I come from Canada. You got that?'

Joe Nelson sneered, 'Yeah, I got it – *Yank*.'

Bill stepped forward and the Londoners all took one step back, crouching like wild animals and wielding their iron bars, muttering, 'Watch 'im, watch 'im,' to each other.

'You leave my Bill be,' cried Fay, stepping in front of her fiancé. 'We're going to be married.'

'Oh, right, I remember bein' told about it, don't I?' said Joe sarcastically. 'I remember bein' asked for me daughter's 'and in marriage. Now when was that . . . ?' He went into mock memory recall as if he couldn't quite recover the date from the back of his mind.

'I'm asking you *now*,' said Bill. 'Mr Nelson, I love your daughter and I want to marry her. We would like your blessing.'

'Oh, *right*,' said the old man in a heavy cynical tone, 'now you're up to your neck in shit, now you fink you're goin' to have seven bells knocked out of you, you're askin' my permission to marry 'er, is that it?'

Bill said evenly, 'I'm not asking your permission – she's over twenty-one – we don't need your permission. I'm asking for your *blessing*. Now, are you going to be a reasonable and responsible father to your daughter, or do we have to kick hell out of each other? Personally, I'd rather beat the hell out of the Germans than my future father-in-law, but if you want it that way, let's get to it.'

'*No!*' yelled Fay. 'Now this has gone far enough, Dad. This isn't the streets of the East End. I'm a respected schoolteacher in this village . . .'

'You won't be, with a big belly and no ring on your finger, will you?' shouted Joe back.

'We've been careful,' Fay said. 'I'm telling you, Dad, I'm going to call the police right now. I won't have it, you hear? I'm not going to have my future husband crippled just to satisfy your stupid ego. Alf,' she addressed the eldest brother present, 'you take Dad home right now, or I'll make your life hell, you hear? You think I don't know about you and Daisy

Tranter? What's good for you is good for me, see. Are you going to marry Daisy? And you, Charlie – you knocked up Phyllis in the churchyard and had to get married. What about that?'

The brothers started shuffling their feet and looking uncomfortable. So did Joe Nelson. Fay's dad knew what she had said was all true, but there were different ways of looking at things. Sons were not daughters. A son could have it away with one of the local girls and be hailed a jack-the-lad, so long as he didn't get caught, but a daughter was supposed to remain chaste until the marriage bed. Then there was the question of foreigners taking what they wanted before going back to America without so much as a by-your-leave or a thank-you. Joe especially didn't like Yanks coming over here and having it away with all the daughters and wives of stout-hearted Englishmen who were off in Egypt or Burma fighting for their country.

'What the boys got up to has got nuffink to do wiv what's been goin' on 'ere,' he began lamely.

'Yes it has!' cried Fay. 'You – you don't know anything, Dad.'

'I don't know nuffink?'

'Anything, anything, anything!' shouted Fay. 'Not *nothing*.' Then she burst into tears.

'I don't understand the difference,' Joe said, bewildered, looking back at his sons and his brother for support. 'Anybody know what's she's on about?'

'Schoolteachers,' said Alf, as if this explained everything, from justifying sleeping with a man out of wedlock to getting upset about poor grammar.

Joe Nelson stood for a long while staring at the Canadian in front of him, then he asked, 'What do you do for a livin'?'

'You mean my job?' asked Bill. 'When the war's over I hope to become a lawyer. Right now I'm in the Royal Air Force – you can see that by my uniform.'

'*Canadian* Air Force?' Alf interrupted.

'No,' said Bill, 'I joined up while I was over here as a student – I'm in *your* air force.'

'*Our* air force,' cried Joe, as if that made all the difference. 'Lawyer, eh? You clever, are you? How much do lawyers earn then?'

'A lot of money,' replied Bill. 'Buckets of the stuff.'

Joe nodded. This made a lot of difference. Some Yank who worked a hot-dog stall was as bad as Fay kipping down with a barrow boy, but a nob of a barrister was different. Barristers went about in Rollers and had big houses in Kensington and Knightsbridge. It was like his daughter was sleeping with English gentry. It could lead to a better life for all of them, if the bloke actually meant to marry her.

Joe made up his mind and pointed a finger at his sobbing daughter. 'You two better get married quick – I'll tell your mother it's already been done.'

'No you won't – I want her to be there, at my wedding,' said Fay stubbornly.

Joe shook his head sagely. 'You always was a lot of trouble, you was . . .'

A relieved-looking Alf had already stepped forward and held out his hand to Bill. Smiling, he said, 'Congratulations, mate,' then seeing Bill's eyes on his other hand Alf sheepishly let the iron bar he had been holding drop to the ground.

Bill nodded and shook Alf's hand. 'I guess you must be Fay's oldest brother,' he said, 'I'm pleased to meet you.'

'Nah,' grinned Alf, 'only the third oldest. There's Jack and Phil before me, only they ain't 'ere. They're on some anti-aircraft battery tonight – couldn't come to the party.' He grinned again.

Bill shook hands with the other two brothers, who melted into the background, and then Joe's brother, Dave. Finally, Bill was facing Joe himself. Joe took his hand in a steel grip and the little man from the East End looked up into the Canadian's face. 'You look after her, you 'ear? If anyfink 'appens to my Fay, you'll be sorry you was even born. Treat 'er fair and you'll always have an 'ome wiv us, on Bakewell Street. Can't say fairer than that, can I, mate?'

'Bill,' said Fay. 'His name's Bill, Dad.'

'Yeah, well, Bill, Willy, Will or William, it's all the same to us, innit? Set the date an' let us know. I'll tell your muvver you never slept with 'im, all right? I'll say it was a load of rubbish, that note . . .'

'Oh Dad, for God's sake, mum's not likely to be . . . What note?' she said.

'The nonimous note we got, saying you two was sleeping together. Got it yesterday.'

'Anonymous?'

'Cut out of bits of newspaper.'

Fay asked, 'What exactly did it say, Dad?'

Joe screwed his face up with the effort of recalling the contents of the note, then said, 'I fink it went like this – *Your daughter's gettin' laid by a foreign bloke* – somefink like that.'

'Bloke? It said *bloke*?'

'Well, somefink like that – no, wait a minute – it was *guy* – foreign *guy*. That was it. Well, we'll be gettin' back now – got to catch the last bus. You let me know, you 'ear?'

'Yes, Dad,' Fay replied. 'Give us a couple of weeks.'

'An' you better be careful,' warned Joe. 'I don't want you walkin' down no aisle with your belly like a barrel.'

With that the Londoners left, making their way through the darkness of the village to the bus stop. Fay took hold of Bill's hand and led him back into the pub. The landlord was standing just inside the door with a shotgun in his hands. He was shaking and he looked tired.

'If they'd started on you,' he said, 'I would've come out.'

'That's fine,' replied Bill, 'I appreciate it.'

Once she got him back in the bedroom, Fay said to Bill, 'I wonder who sent that note?' She looked at him in a peculiar fashion.

'Why do you ask that now?' Bill said. 'I mean it could have been anybody.'

Fay shook her head. 'No, no – the words *laid* and *guy* are Canadian . . .'

'Or American,' Bill pointed out quickly.

'There aren't any Americans here,' Fay countered. 'On the other hand, there is one Canadian.'

Bill looked at her in a puzzled fashion and then his face registered shock. 'You don't think *I* sent the note, do you? Why would I do a thing like that? I mean it was my hide they were after. I'd be stupid to want a fight with your family.'

Fay was deeply suspicious. 'Not if you wanted to get married to me before the end of the war.'

Bill assumed a righteous expression. He was in the process of taking off his shirt and he pulled it back on again. 'Fay,' he said quietly, 'if you believe I would stoop so low as to do a thing like that, we'd better call it quits right now.'

Fay shook her head, bewildered by it all. 'Well – who would do it? Are there any other Canadians in your squadron? Someone who doesn't like you?'

'Yeah!' cried Bill, as if it had just come to him. 'Hey, there's a Yank – a guy from Omaha, who was over here on business when the war started. He joined up and he's on a ground crew. I guess he's jealous of me because I'm a commissioned officer – a pilot – while he's just a non-com.'

'And how would he know you were sleeping with me?' asked Fay, raising an eyebrow.

Bill looked at her nonplussed, then said, 'Well, hey – where else would I be going at night, if it wasn't to get laid? I mean, he knows I go *somewhere*.'

This sounded fairly believable to Fay. She knew what men were like when they were on their own in a bunch. A lot of ribald talk passed between them and even if they didn't brag about their conquests, they implied a great deal. It would have disappointed her if Bill had turned out to be one of those who liked to be known as a ladykiller, but these were only boyish games after all, played by insecure males who needed the approbation of their fellows in order to hold their heads high. Since most males were insecure when it came to women, there was no reason for her Bill to be any different.

'You don't boast about "laying" me?' she asked.

'Hell no,' cried Bill. 'Why would I want to do that? I brag about laying all the other girls, but never about you, darling.

Nothing to brag about – you were too easy.' He grinned at her, to let her know he was kidding.

She punched him on the arm. 'You – you better watch it, Bill Ryker – my sense of humour isn't up to remarks like that.'

'I'm sorry,' he said, looking contrite. 'It was too tempting. You left yourself wide open. Listen, honey, you know I love you to distraction. Why the hell would I want to share something as precious as our love-making with a bunch of stupid flyers? It would be like opening up a box of pearls and scattering them amongst swine.'

She stared at him for a moment, the tears starting to her eyes, then she said, 'I don't know which I prefer – you being funny or you being serious. They both hurt me in different ways. You big lunk! Why can't you just be ordinary and boring like all the other men in the world?'

He smiled. 'I am, deep down, but I've got to keep up this façade of being interesting to keep you by my side. Wait until we get married – then you'll see how ordinary and boring I am. Strictly slippers by the fire, dozing off on a Sunday afternoon in the armchair – you just wait and see.'

She put up her face to be kissed. 'Oh, Bill Ryker, I love you so much.'

He obliged her with a slow kiss. 'I'm glad about that, sweetheart, because I feel the same about you,' he whispered.

They went back to bed.

Chapter Fifteen

Rebecca had to admit to herself that she was envious of the physical relationship between Bill and Fay. Since Alan's death she had come to feel that parts of her had atrophied. That wasn't true, of course. She woke sometimes in the night, not often but occasionally, feeling hot and miserable. At those times she would satisfy herself, but not without a pang of guilt. She had been brought up to believe some things were improper and it was difficult to throw off her conditioning.

It worried her, too, that at such times, when she reached her climax, it was Luke's face that swam before her, and not Alan's. She told herself she couldn't control these subconscious aberrations and that her id was simply pandering to some strange desire to destroy her background. What she *really* wanted, she told herself, was a nice, steady, middle-class man with a profession. Someone like Christopher Bates. Someone with a solid future and a respectable position in society. Luke Adams might have been admired by the leading poets of the day, but he would never be well off or accepted by the establishment. It was important for Kim to find someone who was acceptable.

Fay found this side of her new friend exasperating. 'You like *me*, don't you?'

'You know I do,' replied Rebecca.

'Well, you won't find anyone more common than my family, I can tell you. If you can accept that in me, why couldn't you accept it in Luke? Good God, he was ten times more genteel than I am. He comes from the farming people. I come from the gutter, from the grimy streets of London.'

'Yes, but – well, it's different. I don't have to explain you to anyone, do I? Luke would be Kim's stepfather. He would be important to her.'

Fay sighed. 'I think you're a terrible snob, Rebecca. I like you, but I can't ignore that fact.'

And Rebecca knew she was right. It hurt to know that. It was like being called a bigot. She was prejudiced. She judged people by their class, not by their character. She fought with this side of herself, knowing it was unworthy, often losing the battle.

Rebecca also spent long hours each night trying to remember Alan's features. She found it difficult and couldn't help but decide that she was spiritually weak. She argued that she *should* be able to recall the face of the man she had loved so much and that death was there to be defeated in this battle with her memory. It was inconceivable to her that his countenance and form dissolved into a misty image while she fought to find a definite impression of them her mind.

'He ought to be *part* of me,' she groaned. 'He should be there, inside me.'

She saw it as her failure that he was not. Perhaps, she told herself, I never loved him enough? It seemed wrong that she should let him drift away from her like this. She owed it to her daughter to keep her father's memory alive. She wanted Kim to know Alan, to feel he was still a part of the family, but with every passing day her recollection of him became vaguer.

She spoke to Martin, hoping he would be more sympathetic over this matter than Fay was over Luke.

'Rebecca, Rebecca,' he said softly, his strong hands on her shoulders, 'you have to realise how frail we are. We're not machines that can place an indelible image on our minds so that it's always there to recall.'

'It's not just that,' she said. 'I want to remember other things too – outings we went on with Kim – so that I can tell her all about them later. But I keep getting dates mixed up, and little incidents from one particular time slip into another, so that I get them all confused. Like that time we went to Brighton – I can't remember whether it was chicken or ham we had for lunch. I know it sounds silly, but it distresses me that I've forgotten, when I should be able to remember.'

'Good Lord, Rebecca – you're not supposed to be able to summon up every detail of every day you spent with your husband while he was alive. Reminiscences are bound to be misty, vague recollections. I told you, we're not machines. It doesn't really matter to Kim, does it, whether you had salt or pepper on your lunch the day you went to the boat race? Make things up as you go along, if you want to tell her about those times. Turn them into stories, not history lessons. She'll be much more interested in how you *felt*, rather than in all the items in your hamper that day. Think about it.'

Rebecca was distressed by this advice. 'Surely, that wouldn't be right, would it – to tell lies about it?'

Martin sighed. 'Rebecca, you're still grieving. You're not making sense. Believe me, it doesn't matter to Alan now. He's somewhere else, but he's not looking down on you and censuring you for being unable to remember minutiae. I know what you're feeling – you're feeling bad because you're alive and he's dead, and you want to make up for this in some way. You can't make up for it. It's happened. An act of man or God and all this fussing over detailed memories won't change things. Your job is to bring up Kim to the best of your ability, not try to provide her with a ghost father for the rest of her life.'

Rebecca said, 'I wish I could believe that.'

'You will, as time goes on. It takes many, many years to get over the death of a husband or wife. You may even still be in shock – day-to-day shock – and this is throwing up all sorts of feelings inside you. Take it in easy stages. Stop blaming yourself for things you can't control. My mother always told me never to apologise for the weather. "Oh dear, it's raining, I am sorry" – you hear people say that sometimes. They're always worried that they've done something wrong, though they can't think what it is. Don't get into the habit, Rebecca.'

This little chat cheered Rebecca up and she tried to follow Martin's advice of taking things day by day, not pushing herself too hard, not chastising herself if she forgot about Alan for an hour or two. It was hard. There were times when she found herself laughing over something Kim had done or said and realised Alan had slipped completely from her mind. The guilt feelings would flood back in then, as she thought how unfair it was that she was alive and enjoying life, and he was dead and missing it all. Especially the growing up of his daughter. She felt the least she could do was to try to hold him with her. But she could not. Not continuously. It was very hard.

She had promised him her love would never die. She thought that meant never forgetting, but Martin told her what it really meant was remembering occasionally. It was something she was going to have to learn very, very slowly – but surely.

Chapter Sixteen

Kim had well and truly settled down at Gradge Lodge and Rebecca should have been happier now than at any time in her life since the death of Alan. She had a good job, which she enjoyed, and her prospects for the future were excellent. She stood to inherit a school which even in wartime was proving to be an excellent business. She liked the village of Hornchurch, which stood on the borders of Essex, a county she had grown attached to.

Essex wasn't the prettiest county in England, but it had an atmosphere all of its own. It had once been completely wooded, but even shorn of its forests it was still a place with many mysteries. In the east were creeks, misty rivers, reed-covered flatlands, big skies, small Saxon and Viking villages with thatched wooden churches and stone-towered keeps, saltings and maltings. In the north of the county was rolling country-side, with market towns that boasted churches of cathedral dimensions inherited from the rich wool merchants of earlier centuries, windmills and watermills – Constable country. In the west stood Epping Forest, the remnants of the greater forest of Essex. In the south the Thames industrial strip, down to the estuary at Southend-on-Sea and the boom defence.

Rebecca was in a county she felt comfortable with, in a village she liked, in a job she enjoyed, yet she wasn't happy. She didn't know why she felt so melancholy, but she put it down to the war. The air raids, she told herself, were making her nervy and miserable.

In the middle of September a French officer called Charles de Gaulle formed a Free French government-in-exile, in opposition to Pétain's Vichy government in France. Chris Bates, who had dated Rebecca twice since their London jaunt, was inclined to think that this was just a pointless gesture.

'What can de Gaulle do here? Nothing,' he said, as they drank tea together in the village teashop.

'Well, a government-in-exile is always a thorn in the side of any puppet government,' replied Rebecca. 'It doesn't have to do anything – it can just *be*.'

'I disagree, but let's not fight over it,' laughed Chris. 'I'm enjoying this too much to waste it battling with you.'

Rebecca said, 'I think we can disagree over things, Chris. I mean, it's healthy to discuss such issues and we don't always have the same opinion.'

'Well, I'm bored with the subject,' he said, the seriousness showing behind his smile. 'Let's talk about something else. I was wondering the other day what that school of Amelia's is worth? How much do you think it trawls in a year? Ten thousand pounds? Fifteen?'

'I've no idea,' said Rebecca. She wouldn't have discussed the figure with Chris, even if she'd known what it was. 'It's not really a suitable subject for a teashop, Chris.'

He laughed. 'How conventional you are sometimes. Just a

moment ago you were saying how healthy it was to discuss things.'

'That was a general subject, not the private accounts of my employer.'

'Oh, you're so quaintly stuffy sometimes, Rebecca,' he said, laughing again. 'Now, don't give me that sour look. I can't help being curious, can I? My own business isn't going too well at the moment, and I just wondered how Amelia was coping with the war and everything.'

'Business?' Rebecca said. 'You're a doctor.'

He shrugged. 'Doctoring is a business too. We don't do it for nothing, you know. I have bills to pay, the upkeep on a house and surgery. Money is important, I'm afraid.'

She acknowledged that it was important to keep out of debt, but surely that was all one could expect at such times.

'Yes – and no,' replied Chris, a little frown appearing on his handsome face. 'It doesn't matter. I'm sorry I mentioned it now. So,' he said, brightening, 'what have you been doing with yourself these days?'

'Nothing out of the ordinary. Just teaching school and – teaching school,' she laughed.

'How about you and me going out and getting drunk one night? What about next Thurs . . .'

His sentence was cut short by the wail of the siren.

The young waitress rushed back into the kitchen, almost dropping the tray of dirty dishes she had in her hand. Chris followed her, calling, 'Can we use your shelter?'

''Course you can ' came back the reply. 'Out in the back garden, everybody.'

Chris and Rebecca grabbed their gas masks and followed

the teashop staff out to the back garden, where there was a narrow path between the vegetables growing there. Rebecca admired the enormous cabbages even as she ran through them. Mrs Floodgate, the teashop owner, obviously had green fingers. Most people were 'growing for Britain' but most people weren't any good at it. They ploughed up their lawns and planted seeds, then left them to get on with it.

In the shelter Rebecca sat quietly holding Chris's hand while the bombs fell. Occasionally one dropped near the village, which made the ground shudder and the Nissen shelter creak, but for the most part they appeared to be further south. Rebecca said to Mrs Floodgate, 'You have some beautiful vegetables in your garden.'

'VPA,' said Mrs Floodgate, mysteriously.

'VPA? What's that?' asked Chris.

'Village Produce Association. We all get together to discuss vegetable growing, buying seeds in bulk, the best manure, all that sort of thing. You ought to be in it. Everybody should be. We get people to come and speak,' she said proudly.

'That sounds – excellent,' said Chris diplomatically.

'It is,' insisted Mrs Floodgate. 'We have dances too, and whist drives, and beetle drives. You name it.'

'Welly-boot balls?' Chris said.

Mrs Floodgate, who didn't like being made fun of over so serious a subject, said, 'What?'

'Nothing,' replied Chris. 'Just a little joke.'

'It's no joke, Doctor,' said Mrs Floodgate indignantly. 'This island has to feed itself and it can only do so if people are prepared to muck in . . .'

'A very appropriate phrase,' murmured Chris, but only loud enough for Rebecca to hear.

' . . . because if they're not, they're just parasites feeding on the hard work of others.'

'I entirely agree, Mrs Floodgate,' Chris said. 'I unfortunately have no spare ground in which I can plant vegetables, otherwise I would.'

'The school has, though,' muttered Mrs Floodgate, looking darkly at Rebecca.

Rebecca blinked, realising the teashop lady was referring to the school playing fields. This had not occurred to her before now. That Amelia's hockey pitch should be put under the plough instead of being used to teach young girls barbarous ways of crippling each other was a new thought.

'I take it,' said Rebecca, 'you are referring to the school playing fields? Surely,' she went on, taking the side she didn't believe in, 'young children should have *somewhere* to play their sports? The next generation has to be fit and ready for a possible invasion by the Germans.'

'If they don't have no vegetables to eat,' retorted Mrs Floodgate, 'they *won't* be fit and healthy, will they?'

There was some truth in this. But the vision of Amelia Sartour allowing her precious hockey pitch to be ploughed up and handed over to the VPA was not one which came readily to mind. An image which did come easily was one in which a black-suited Amelia Sartour sat behind a machine gun and defended her playing fields to the death. Amelia, Rebecca was sure, would sacrifice her life and others in the defence of her hockey pitch. Mohorty would stand by her to the end. So would many of the girls at the school.

'I don't think you stand much chance of getting those playing fields, Mrs Floodgate – admirable as your intentions are – it would be over the dead body of Miss Sartour.'

A grunt and a dark look came from Mrs Floodgate, indicating it might very well come to that. 'The parish council has been asked to vote on it,' she said, 'and Miss Sartour might have to watch out for herself.'

Chris said, 'But aren't you on the parish council yourself, Mrs Floodgate?'

She gave him a tight smile in response. 'Precisely,' she said.

When Rebecca got back to the school, she ran into Martin Simkins just outside the room he had made into a chapel.

'Hello, Rebecca,' he said. 'Been out?'

'Hello, Martin – yes, I've been at the teashop with Dr Bates.'

'Was it good fun?' he asked her wistfully.

Rebecca raised her eyebrows. 'Scones and Earl Grey at the village teashop is hardly the event of the year, Martin.'

'No, no, I suppose not,' he sighed, 'but I don't seem to manage even that sort of outing these days.'

She placed a hand on his and smiled. 'The very next time I go to the village teashop, I shall call for you.'

He laughed, enjoying her touch. There was an agony of feelings going on inside him. Martin had fallen in love with Rebecca from almost the moment he met her, just as he had fallen for Fay before her. Fay was now completely unavailable, so Martin's fantasies were confined to Rebecca. It wasn't that he was fickle. It was just unfortunate for him that two such women should come into his life at more or less the same time. He could have loved either of them, for the whole of his life, and been happy with whichever one he married.

Unfortunately, he was a reticent suitor. He desperately wanted Rebecca to be his wife, but he found it impossible to do anything at all about it. He needed a woman to come up to him and say, 'Look, Martin, I know you're shy, but I'm head over heels in love with you and I think we should get married very soon.' Since it was highly unlikely, not to say impossible, that Rebecca would ever do such a thing, Martin was doomed to loneliness and frustration.

He said, 'I'm sorry. I'm just being pathetic. I'm always aware that when people look at me they see a vicar, rather than a . . . a person.' He had wanted to say 'a man' but decided at the last moment that it sounded too suggestive. He was terrified that Rebecca might think he was propositioning her.

'I see you as a person *and* a vicar,' replied Rebecca. 'Isn't that how it's supposed to be? Just as I see Chris as a man and a doctor.'

There, she had said it for him. She had called Chris 'a man' and himself 'a person'. It was his profession, no doubt about it, that formed a barrier between him and such women as this. Surely it was supposed to form a channel of easy communication? A parson was someone you should be able to talk to about anything, wasn't he?

Anything, Martin thought gloomily, but sex.

You talked to your vicar about matters of the spirit, even emotional problems, but you talked to your doctor about sex. Martin knew he didn't stand a chance while there were doctors – and men – like Christopher Bates around. Martin would only stand a chance if the whole of Britain's manhood was wiped out overnight, leaving him the only male around. Only then would the women turn and look at him and see the man behind the dog collar, and wonder about the manhood beneath the surplice and the cassock.

'Thank you, Rebecca,' Martin said. 'I'm glad I'm a person to you, too.'

'Of course you are, Martin – and a very nice one too.' Rebecca stretched forward and impulsively gave him a peck on the cheek. She then went off to see Kim, leaving Martin rubbing his cheek thoughtfully.

Two days later, at assembly, Amelia Sartour was present. She was wearing a puffed black silk dress which would have looked more in place during Queen Victoria's reign. On her head was a small black cap with a lace fringe.

To the staff she looked much frailer than at any time in the past. Her hair, swept back in a bun, was coarse and brittle. Her stick-thin arms poked from the sleeves of the grand dress, her wrinkled neck protruded from the collar like that of a turtle from its shell. Inside the dress her thin frame was a dry husk.

Her face showed that a spirit still burned within, though, and the eyes were still bright. But despite her animated features, to those who knew her well she seemed to be fading.

To the girls she appeared as she always had: an ancient crone with terrible piercing eyes that could stare into a young girl and see all the secrets of her soul.

Not that she was a tyrant, whose retribution and justice was meted out unfairly, but remote in her old age she was more myth than reality. She didn't know that she was held in quite such terrible awe and would have been upset had she realised.

Amelia didn't want to be feared in the least – respected, yes, but not considered a monster who preyed on the night terrors and ignorance of young girls.

The trouble was that the girls saw her so very seldom: mostly on open days and at important, away-game hockey matches. Home matches were watched, out of sight, from her study. The girls on the first team weren't aware of it, but Amelia Sartour knew all their names and faces, and all their strengths and foibles on the pitch. She knew everything about them which pertained to their skill at hockey. She studied them as closely as an entomologist might study individual ants in a nest.

So to see Amelia Sartour on the stage with the other teachers at assembly time, seemingly in a state of suspended decay, confirmed many of the girls' fears that she was a dreadful sorceress, a queen of night and magic, who would live for ever.

Amelia made the following announcement – an announcement which astounded most of the staff at the school.

'Girls, staff of Gradge Lodge School, I have something to say that may surprise you. It's been a long time coming, so I don't see why it should, but I have the feeling I'm considered part of the fixtures and fittings in the school. The fact is I feel ready to retire and wish to hand over the school to the person who I'm sure will deal with its management just as competently as I have myself – perhaps much better, since I don't consider myself to be a naturally efficient person. She's much, much younger too, which I'm sure can only be seen as an advantage from the point of view of you girls.

'You have no real interest in the retirement of an old lady –

someone who has already been here far too long and is getting a bit tired of shuffling bits of paper round a desk – but you will possibly have an interest in my successor.

'Well, I'm happy to tell you I've made provision for the school's future. I'm going to put the school, which means all of you too, not just the bricks and mortar, into the hands of the new owner as from today. As you know I gave up being headmistress some time ago and handed over the reins to Miss Knole, who has done an excellent job of turning raw young girls into ladies of knowledge. I like to think the girls of Gradge Lodge School present themselves to the world as ladies, except when they're on the hockey pitch, when they quite rightly revert to savages . . .'

Genuine laughter here, from both staff and girls.

'It is, however, not the headship of the school that comes into question on my death, but the *ownership*.'

Rebecca knew what was coming here and being on the back row of the two rows of teachers, she tried to shrink into her chair.

'Gradge Lodge is a private school, owned by me alone. Not unnaturally, I wish to keep the school in my own family, and I am fortunate to have a relation – a teacher – who will be ideally suited.'

Amelia cleared her throat. She was, like most schoolteachers and ex-schoolteachers, part actor. She enjoyed the attention, she knew how to keep an audience on the edge of their seats, and she played it for what it was worth.

'I hereby give notice,' she said, slipping into a formal address, 'that the new owner of Gradge Lodge School will be my great-niece, whom you already know, though I doubt anyone here knows of our family connection . . .'

Everyone leaned forward expectantly, from all sides.

'Mrs Rebecca Daniels!'

Though the rest of the school sat in stunned silence, apart from Helena Patten who looked serenely knowledgeable, and Amelia and Rebecca, there was one loud audible gasp from the games mistress, Priscilla Mohorty. For a few moments Amelia allowed the school to absorb what she had just told them, allowed them to stare at her embarrassed great-niece, then added a few words.

'Mrs Daniels was brought to the school for the express purpose of taking on the ownership. She will, however, so she tells me, continue to teach a little as well as managing the accounts and correspondence, and seeing to the general running of the establishment. Miss Knole will remain as headmistress. Miss Patten will continue to serve as secretary to the owner of the school, just as she has served me faithfully all these years. That is all I have to say. Now will Miss Dane please seat herself at the piano and strike up the first hymn?'

After assembly, Fay said to Rebecca, 'You sneaky old thing, you – why didn't you tell me you were going to be my boss?'

'I was asked not to. It won't make any difference to our friendship, Fay.'

'Of course it will – but not too much, I hope,' Fay laughed.

Martin said, 'Congratulations.'

'Thank you, Martin, I'm still in a state of shock – Amelia didn't tell me she was going to retire. I always expected it to be after her death, which I hoped would be a while in the future. She seems tired, doesn't she?'

Martin shook his head sagely. 'I don't think she wants to live much longer, Rebecca. She's old, in pain, and I think she's just about had enough of life. The hockey keeps her going a little, of course. But I've seen it in old people before. They start to say to themselves "Is life worth it?" and one day they answer "No" and just let go of it.'

'Well, now that I am about to take over from her, she can probably relax a little.'

Later, Rebecca went on request to Amelia's room and found Helena Patten there with her. Amelia was sitting in her chair by the fire in a dressing gown. Helena was tending to her hair and the nails of her left hand. There was a domestic glow to the atmosphere, which Rebecca might have found pleasing had it not been for Amelia's sour expression. In her right hand the present owner of the school held a letter. She was staring at it and was clearly distressed by the contents.

'What is it?' asked Rebecca, concerned.

'The damn parish council,' Amelia said. 'They want me to churn up my hockey pitches and grow carrots on them.'

Rebecca nodded.

Helena paused in her work and glanced across, saying tartly, 'You don't seem surprised, Mrs Daniels?'

'I'm not,' said Rebecca. 'I heard it in the teashop the other day – Mrs Floodgate told me. She's one of the prime movers.'

'They're jealous of me,' Amelia growled, 'because I'm an outsider in the village. You've got to have grandparents stretching back to Shakespeare, with all their descendants born in Hornchurch parish, before they'll accept you, this lot. Even the people in the next village are considered to be foreigners, let alone a dried-up old Aussie like me.

'They've always been against me. Well, they won't win. I'll fight them tooth and nail.' She stared moodily into the fire, which though it was still only autumn was banked high in the grate. Amelia felt the cold badly.

'How long will it take for this to come to a head?' asked Rebecca.

'A month or two,' replied Helena.

'Then, Amelia, you won't be here to fight them,' said Rebecca, 'not if you're handing over the school to me as from today. I shall be responsible for the playing fields.'

Both the older women looked up. There was a sharpness to Amelia's face not seen by Rebecca before now. The old woman stared at her great-niece, then asked, 'Will you fight them, Rebecca? I know you loathe hockey.'

'Whether or not I dislike hockey isn't the question,' replied Rebecca. 'I'm not fond of mathematics either, but it has to be taught in school, whether I like it or not. The question is, which is more important? The war effort, or hockey?'

'That's what I mean,' Amelia replied. 'Hockey is not important to you.'

'No, but it is to others in the school. I should have to weigh up whether that importance was justified. It would be up to me to make a decision on the hockey pitches.'

Amelia's thin features became distinctly hostile. 'But *I* want them to stay – I don't want there to be any question about it. I *need* them to stay.'

Rebecca said quietly, 'I don't want to upset you, Amelia. If you feel *you wish* to make the decision, then you must postpone the handing over of the school to me until after the question of the playing fields has been settled.'

'Or cancel the handing over altogether,' snapped Amelia. 'Perhaps I should have passed the school on to Helena after all, instead of placing so much emphasis on blood. Friendship is thicker than water too.'

'Perhaps you should have done,' said Rebecca. 'Perhaps you should still do that? I only know that if the school is in my charge, I have to be the one to make the decision. Of course I shall take your views into consideration, as well as those of others, but the decision must be mine. Otherwise I shall only be a token owner, with no responsibilities. I can't take on the responsibility without having the authority to back it up.'

Surprisingly, Helena came in here with a statement of her own. 'I don't want the damn school, Amelia. I don't mind doing the secretarial work, but essentially I want to look after you. What would I do with a school? I'm nearly as old as you are.'

Amelia threw her bony arms up into the air. 'Wonderful, rejected by my friend, scorned by my niece – what a marvellous time I'm having at the end of my life.'

Helena said, 'And you can stop that – you of all people – pretending self-pity. You couldn't give a damn about yourself really. You just want your own way as usual.'

Amelia scowled.

Rebecca smiled and said, 'It's difficult to stop being an autocrat, isn't it? King Lear had the same trouble.'

'Insults now, is it?' cried Amelia, failing to see the touch of humour in what Rebecca had said. 'I'm not an autocrat – I always ask the advice of my staff.'

'Then ignore it,' muttered Helena, combing through the old lady's long grey hair. 'Like all autocrats, you think you're being democratic simply because you tell other people what you're going to do before you actually do it. Nothing on earth would make you change your mind, though, once it's set.'

Amelia scowled again, glaring into the flames of the fire. Her ankles were blotched and ringed from the heat of the coals. She seemed about to go into a sulk and Rebecca wondered whether she should leave. She looked at Helena, trying to gauge something from the woman's expression. Helena continued to brush and comb the stiff, coarse hair.

Finally, Amelia growled, 'All right, I was just testing you, Rebecca – in a sense. I mean, I still want those pitches to stay where they are, but the decision must be yours. Let me ask you one thing at this stage. What is your inclination, right at this moment, to hand over the playing fields?'

Rebecca said, 'I've been thinking about it ever since I heard it in the teashop. I believe the girls should have somewhere to play their hockey. There are no parks around here, no other playing fields. Even the boys of the village sometimes have to sneak in over the school back fence to kick a ball around, when they want a game of some kind . . .'

'Football,' snorted Amelia.

'My sentiments exactly,' said Rebecca, 'but I still respect their need to play it. There are two hockey pitches and a running and jumping strip following the fence to the aerodrome. My inclinations at this stage would be to keep one hockey pitch, but to plough up the second pitch and start a gardening club amongst the girls. We don't have to hand over our land to the council – just use it to grow things. We would keep the strip by the fence too, for the athletics side of things. It would be a compromise.'

'A compromise?' grumbled Amelia. 'In my day we never even considered compromises. The word *compromise* was just an excuse for losing the battle.'

'This is not about a battle,' said Rebecca quietly, 'it's about a war.'

Amelia looked up and now her eyes showed some understanding of what Rebecca was trying to tell her. This was not just a personal fight between the school and the parish council. The general good had to be taken into consideration at the same time. Vegetable supplies to the school were limited. If they ploughed up one of the precious pitches, they would at least be able to reap their own harvest. It was not as if they had to hand over the vegetables to the detestable Mrs Floodgate: they could wave the turnips and swedes under the woman's nose and shout yah.

'The decision will be yours,' repeated Amelia. 'I hope you make the right one.'

'It'll be my decision, at any rate – not theirs,' Rebecca replied.

Amelia nodded and then said she would like to rest.

Rebecca left the room, but just as she was closing the door Amelia said, 'By the way, Rebecca, Miss Mohorty knows about this, but don't say anything to her about keeping the first pitch – not yet. Let her sweat for a while. It'll do her good.'

Rebecca closed the door quietly and thought about this remark on the way back to her own room. There was something hidden in there. Amelia would not be cruel to one of her staff without a reason, and Rebecca finally decided that Mohorty had been to see Amelia with a complaint about her, Rebecca, and this was her great-aunt's way of dealing with a staff member who tried to betray another behind backs.

'All right, Mohorty,' muttered Rebecca to herself as she passed the games mistress's room, 'this *is* a battle – and one I intend to win hands down, I'm afraid.'

Chapter Seventeen

Rebecca discovered that Mohorty had been trying to poison Amelia against her, without realising Rebecca was the owner's great-niece.

'She's a good games mistress,' Amelia said to Rebecca, as they were finalising the handover, 'but she has a horribly jealous streak running through her.'

Rebecca wondered whether Amelia knew of the affair between Mohorty and Dane and, if she did, why she chose to ignore it. Now it was her, Rebecca's, problem. The school was officially in her hands now. Her first act on taking up office was to send for Mohorty and Dane. It was early morning, before assembly.

Priscilla Mohorty entered Rebecca's new study while Julia Dane waited, sniffling, outside. Mohorty had a black look on her face. 'I resign,' were her first words.

'Now, why would you want to do that?' asked Rebecca. 'Simply because I'm sitting behind this desk? If you want to leave, I can't stop you, but I'd prefer you to stay.'

Mohorty looked at the new owner of the school with great suspicion in her expression. 'You'd prefer me to stay – so you can humiliate me on every opportunity.'

Rebecca sighed. This was going to be much more difficult than she had first envisaged. Mohorty was determined to fight every inch of the way, whether she was asked to stay or go, in order to give Rebecca as much trouble as possible. Rebecca believed there was never a more obstinate woman with such a blatantly obvious persecution complex.

Rebecca got up and went to the window. 'I don't want to humiliate you, Miss Mohorty. I understand from Miss Sartour that you are an excellent games mistress – she feels it would be a long time before the school got a better one . . .'

Mohorty's expression brightened at these remarks.

' . . . I know little about games, but I know my daughter thinks highly of you. The school can ill afford at this time to be trawling around for new teachers, when we've got perfectly good ones on the staff already. I would like you to reconsider leaving us, Miss Mohorty. I'm not going to beg you to stay – we both know what we think of each other, personally – but in my professional capacity I recognise your worth. I want to do my job as well as I can and I shall allow you to do yours. Now, what's it to be? Do you still insist on handing in your notice?'

Mohorty stood there with her bottom lip protruding, deep in thought, and then she said, 'I'll stay.'

Rebecca looked at her for a long time, until Mohorty realised that something more was required from her.

Mohorty said, 'You're waiting for me to say thank you. I'm not good at social graces, Mrs Daniels. I've had to battle for too much during my time as a teacher. As I said, I'll stay with the school – I appreciate your business sense – and I'll say thank you for this talk, that's all.'

Rebecca nodded, knowing that they were still enemies, but

since she was the school's owner she had the upper hand. She would not, as she had promised, try to get in Mohorty's way. They both had a role to play in the school and it would be better that their paths crossed as little as possible. There was, however, one more thing to settle. It was something that had been worrying Rebecca for some time and though her stomach churned with anxiety at having to raise the matter, it had to be settled, here and now, to establish her authority as the new owner.

'Would you mind asking Miss Dane to come in?' she said. 'And stay yourself for a few moments longer.'

Mohorty frowned, but went to the door and admitted a nervous and tearful Julia Dane. Dane clutched a little lace handkerchief which she kept twisting around her fingers. Her left shoelace was untied and she almost tripped on it.

'Miss Mohorty,' Rebecca said, 'close the door if you don't mind.'

'Are we being asked to leave?' cried the art mistress. 'Oh dear, I have nowhere to go – no relations – what shall I do with myself?'

'Try pulling yourself together,' muttered Mohorty.

Rebecca said, 'No, you're not being asked to leave, Miss Dane. As I've been saying to Miss Mohorty, your services are highly valued here at Gradge Lodge. Any unpleasantness between us in the past is forgotten. We must try to work together as best we can without too much abrasiveness.'

The art mistress glanced quickly at the confident Mohorty and unfortunately came to the wrong conclusion. Her air of pathos was replaced by a sly, knowing expression. She sneered at Rebecca. 'I see, Mrs Know-it-all – Miss Sartour has told you you can't sack us, is that it?'

Mohorty raised her eyes to the ceiling and walked away, saying, 'How someone so good at teaching art can be so bloody stupid is beyond me.'

Dane looked uncertainly at her friend and her eyelids twitched.

Rebecca snapped, 'Miss Dane, be under no false illusions – I'm in charge of this school now, not my great-aunt. Miss Sartour *advised* me to keep you, but there's nothing to stop me sending you packing right now, which I will do if you don't improve your manners in this office.'

Julia Dane went into the refuge she so often sought on such occasions: she burst into tears.

'Oh, shut up, Julia,' cried Mohorty. 'Now, you wanted to see the both of us together, Miss Daniels. Would that be in reference to our – relationship?'

'Yes it would,' replied Rebecca, relieved and grateful that Mohorty had been the one to open the subject. 'I don't want to labour this, but I want you to know that if you are not entirely discreet, if it becomes common knowledge amongst the girls themselves, then I really shall have to ask you both to leave the school.'

Mohorty nodded. 'Exactly what Miss Sartour told us.'

Rebecca was only mildly surprised to hear that.

'And of course,' she added, 'if there is one hint of actually involving the girls, I shall take the matter much, much further – I'll destroy you both, you understand. No compromises here, Miss Mohorty. No arguments either. I'm taking a huge risk with you both, because I don't know you – not that well.'

'No arguments,' replied Mohorty, stony-faced.

Dane said tearfully, wiping her nose, 'We respect what you

say, Mrs Daniels, but we're only interested in each other.'

'Good. Perhaps you'll go to your classrooms now? It's nearly time for assembly.'

Rebecca sang loudly and cheerfully at assembly that morning, before taking a class of her own. She told herself she was extremely fortunate. In less than six months she had come from the bottom of the heap to the top. She reminded herself that it was an inheritance, not sheer hard work, that had put her in such a position, but at the same time she was hard-working and any advancement in the world required a certain amount of luck.

Her class stared at her in awe as she came through the doorway into the room. Now *I'm* a goddess, she thought. The children will soon start to make up stories about my terrible rages.

'Class,' she said, 'take out your *Henry IV* Part Two and study Act Two Scene Three, where the Prince and Falstaff are together at the Boar's Head Inn.'

They did as they were asked without a murmur between them. The novelty of having the owner of the school teach the class English literature was not lost on them. Rebecca didn't usually give the class work and exempt herself, but today was special. It wasn't laziness on her part but she felt unable to cope with the concentration that teaching required. Instead, she sat at her desk and fell into a deep reverie.

Rebecca knew she should have felt completely fulfilled. She had a beautiful and healthy daughter, a wonderful position in life, her own health was good, and a handsome doctor seemed to be gradually falling in love with her . . . yet there was something missing. A source of joy had gone from her, which she had not recognised when it was there. In fact she had rejected it completely, though it had been offered to her.

In truth, Rebecca was missing Luke Adams. She had read all his poetry now and was ashamed of her erstwhile attitude towards him. From his poetry she could see that Luke had a deep and sensitive nature, was aware of the richness and sanctity of life, and though he hadn't the pieces of academic paper to prove it, his intellect was strong and keen. Rebecca had damned him as a simple farmer's boy. His poetry clearly showed he was more than this, and indeed, Bill had told her of his skills as a fighter pilot – a lecture she had chosen to ignore.

She stared at the sunlight streaming through the dusty windowpanes. Luke had gone now and she would never see him again.

'Please, miss? It's time for us to go to the next class.'

Rebecca jerked herself awake. Not that she'd been sleeping, but it was obvious to the class that she was not present in spirit. One of the braver girls had spoken and reminded her of the time.

'Thank you, Rosemary,' she said.

The rest of the class looked at Rosemary as if it were more than likely she would be struck by a bolt of lightning.

Rebecca said, 'What's the matter with you all? You know me – I've been your teacher for over a term now. I'm not going to turn into a dragon overnight, so you might as well start treating me as if I were just your class teacher again.'

The class stared at her silently.

'Well?'

'Yes, miss,' said one or two of them timidly, and looking

grateful when the bell sounded for change of lessons, they filed out as meekly as sheep.

Shortly after Rebecca had taken over as the school's new owner, Amelia became bedridden. Chris told Rebecca that Amelia knew her health was failing – her legs would hardly support her any longer – and that was probably why she had decided to retire. Rebecca went to visit her and noticed that the bed was close to the window, from which position Amelia could see the games of hockey and the practice sessions. Rebecca sat in the chair by the bed.

'What made you become so interested in hockey?' she asked. 'You surely didn't catch the craze in Australia?'

Amelia, looking like a pixie wasting away to nothing in her nightdress and bedjacket, creased into a smile.

'You make it sound like some terrible disease. No, I *caught* it when I first opened this school in 1901 – I was fifty-three at the time, so I wasn't much good at it myself, but I just loved watching the girls play. So much energy and vigour – look at your daughter Kim, out there now!'

'I'd rather not, if you don't mind,' said Rebecca primly. 'I had to watch a match the other day, you know, in my new capacity as owner of the school. When I was just the English teacher I could get away with not attending big matches, but now I suppose I'm expected to.'

'Naturally. That's how I caught it.'

'Well, I must be immune. I came away with the opinion that if we sent the girls' first team to France, we'd win the war in a week. I can only describe their behaviour as matching that of a clan of Scottish Jacobites charging down a mountain at an

English regiment – or perhaps a horde of Tartars? It was a frightening sight, whatever the comparison, and one I'll never forget.'

Amelia sighed. 'That's my girls,' she said proudly. 'Wonderful match, wasn't it? We slaughtered St Hilda's.'

Rebecca nodded sagely. 'Slaughtered is probably the word I would use myself, though not with the same relish.'

Amelia laughed. 'Anyway, child, how are you getting on with the running of the school?'

'There's a lot of administration,' admitted Rebecca, 'more than I imagined. Bills to pay, fees to collect, checks and maintenances, that sort of thing. There are endless letters and interviews with parents about this and that – I can't think how you managed to keep it up for so long, considering the state of your health.'

'But are you *enjoying* it?'

Rebecca mulled this over in her mind before replying. 'On the whole, yes. It's an unusual but nice feeling to be in charge – to be able to stamp one's own judgment on things.'

Amelia nodded. 'It is, isn't it? I liked the feeling of power too.'

Rebecca was a little shocked at this remark. She didn't like to think of herself as enjoying power. The image was not one which suited her view of herself. 'Oh, I don't know about liking *power*.'

'But that's what it is, isn't it? It's all right to enjoy a feeling of power, so long as you don't misuse it. If your judgments are fair and objective, if the power doesn't corrupt you as it has Adolf Hitler and his crew, then where's the problem? Don't let it go to your head, that's all.'

'I shan't,' smiled Rebecca.

She was silent for a minute, then raised something she had come across in the books: something Amelia hadn't mentioned.

'One thing surprises me – at least a quarter of our girls are non-paying students. Some of them not even scholarships. You seem to let in all sorts of girls, whether they're bright or not. Is that good business sense, Amelia? I mean, *I* certainly approve of it, but I wonder what makes a hardheaded businesswoman like yourself give away positions which families would cheerfully pay for?'

'My background,' sniffed Amelia. 'I've told you some of it – I'll finish the story some time. I like to give girls a chance – not just the brainy ones, the less capable too. I was like that myself once. Why shouldn't some of *them* have a good start in life? In a sense, I'm not paying for their education – the parents of the fee-paying girls are doing that. Are you considering a change in the policy?'

Rebecca shook her head. 'If we can afford it, then I'll keep to the same ratio. It helps me enormously to take on the grand position of school owner when I know there's some good being done without money going into my pocket. Money I don't deserve in the least.'

'Good. And what about Knole? Are you getting on all right with her?'

'We have our clearly defined territories – you saw to that – so there's been no clashes so far. I don't think she likes me very much, but I can see her point. A jumped-up young teacher from outside suddenly becoming the new boss. It's a bit hard to take, isn't it?'

Amelia wrinkled her nose. 'She's only been the headmistress herself a short time. She has a lot to be thankful for, so I don't think she should begrudge your good fortune.'

'Well, I hope she doesn't – perhaps I'm wronging her. Maybe she just doesn't like me as a person.'

'Perhaps. You're a bit too prissy-missy for a lot of the teachers here.'

This remark upset Rebecca. She had never had this image of herself. She knew she was cautious and slightly too moralistic for some people, but a prude? Was that really fair? She was actually quite broad-minded when it came to a lot of things. Look at the business over Mohorty and Dane. A lot of other women would have thrown them out of the school and not thought twice about it, while she had considered the matter carefully and decided to let them stay under certain understandings. Wasn't that broad-minded of her? And what about Fay and Bill? She didn't censure them, did she? Wasn't that very broad-minded of her?

'If they mean I disapprove of allowing morals to slip, then they're right,' she said to Amelia at last. 'I mean, I can *understand* some of the things that go on, but surely I don't have to approve of them?'

'My dear,' said Amelia, placing a scrawny hand over hers, 'the country is at war. Young men and young women are dying every day – old people too, but they're not so important and they tend to be more stoical. But the young people, well, they often don't expect to see the year out. New pilots of fighter aircraft have a life expectancy of a few weeks. Wouldn't you expect this to influence them? I would.

'Young men and women live for *now*, and their now, their

youth, is being taken away from them. Is it any wonder that they want to live riotously, without any thought for tomorrow?'

Rebecca said, 'I suppose not, but it wouldn't do for me.'

'No, it wouldn't, but I'm trying to explain to you why the others resent you. They see you as Miss Prim-and-Proper – and they're right, I'm afraid, you are. But it's nothing to be ashamed of. I think it's quite commendable.'

Miss Prim-and-Proper? Wonderful, thought Rebecca angrily. What was she supposed to do to prove she was as worldly as they were themselves? Jump into bed with Christopher Bates? Run naked through the streets? Get drunk and dance on the school dining-room tables? How did one prove to others that one wasn't locked tightly inside a cell of religious and moral principles? It just wasn't fair.

'I can't help being what I am,' Rebecca said.

'Of course you can't, my dear. There's nothing wrong with you, or the way you live, but I don't think others are ever going to see past what they feel is a disapproving mind. It's in the way you dress, the way you hold yourself, the way . . .'

'So I'm turning into an old maid, is that it?' cried Rebecca angrily.

'Just a little,' admonished Amelia gently.

Later, Rebecca spoke with Fay on the subject, as they sat drinking Camp coffee in Fay's room. Rebecca felt that the mere fact that she and Fay still sneaked into each other's room for a private chat, when really the owner of the school needed to remain aloof from the staff, was proof of her willingness to bend the rules. She waited her opportunity and then spoke to her friend in a frank manner.

'Do you think I'm missish, Fay?'

Fay stared at her friend and raised an eyebrow. 'Well – honest truth? – just a tiny bit. But we love you just the same, Rebecca – it's not one of those things that matter.'

So there it was, and though she was loved by some who knew her well, she would apparently always have this puritanical public image. It made her want to go out and do something really wicked, something that would make their hair stand on end, but she knew she couldn't. It wasn't in her nature. She couldn't change just to suit general opinion.

She would always be . . . Rebecca.

Chapter Eighteen

Rebecca's visits to Amelia's room became fairly regular. For one thing Rebecca felt a certain duty towards providing for her great-aunt's well-being and for another she often needed advice with regard to the running of the school. And she actually enjoyed her time with Amelia, who wanted to finish the story she had started about her life in Australia before the turn of the century. Rebecca was fascinated by this tale, which seemed to her to come out of some woman's novel. She listened spellbound, as Amelia provided her with the final episode to the saga.

Having reopened the Ragged School in Sydney, I felt fulfilled. However, running the school was a great drain on my resources, and if I wasn't careful I would end up being as broke as I was when I walked into the outback. I decided I would have to open a second school, a private one, the funds of which would provide for the education of poorer children.

In 1890 I opened a school called Gradge Lodge near Cairns. *Gradge* is of course an anagram of *Ragged*. Gradge sounds posh, even though it uses the same letters as Ragged, and I've stuck with the name ever since. It emphasises to me that there is really no difference between poor children and rich, except in the way they're organised. The parents of the children who came to Gradge Lodge School outside Cairns were wealthy farmers and businessmen who could afford a good education for their offspring. Most of the fees from Gradge Lodge pupils went towards paying to keep Sydney's Ragged School open. I spent six months of the year at each.

At Gradge we had our own particular problems. The climate was hot and sticky so we started school hours early – 6.30 a.m. and finished around noon. When the class went swimming we used to have to take some of the parents with us to watch for crocodiles. Once aircraft came along, they used our sports fields for landing strips, and it was the duty teacher's job to mow the grass short enough for the aircraft to be able to land.

I enjoyed those years, going back and forth from Sydney to Cairns, watching the children flourish. In those days I had a lot of energy – an enormous amount – and I thought nothing of travelling a thousand miles. It was exciting stuff and I had come a long way from the little ragged girl who ran the streets of Sydney in the middle of the 1800s. I was a well-off, respected person and, let me tell you, more than one man threw himself at my feet, though to be honest with you I was never a looker. It was more personality and money that pulled them in. I never took any of them – I wasn't interested.

I had no time for men after my old man had kicked the bucket in the outback. I certainly wasn't going to give up my work and independence to look after some bloke who thought it might be a good idea to take on a woman. It doesn't take long for a man to start putting his feet up, visiting the pub every night, and concentrating on increasing his beer gut. I'd seen women like me take on a man in middle·age and then rapidly become skivvies, fetching and carrying, scrubbing and cleaning. No, that wasn't for me, and no matter how hard they pleaded, how sorry I felt for them, I never gave in. They must have thought I was hard, but I wasn't, I was just very, very practical.

There's not much of the story left to tell, except that I came to England a while after the turn of the century, and founded this school, the namesake of the one in Cairns. I don't know why I came back. I loved Australia – it was my country – and I'm still an Australian citizen. I suppose it was something like the call of my ancestors, telling me to go back to Anglo-Saxon soil to die. When I first returned I thought I was already at death's door, but you see me now still sitting here, waiting for the final blow to arrive. It's disgusting how long I've lived until now. It shouldn't be allowed.

Now, my dear Rebecca, it's up to you to carry on here. You're just as I envisaged and perfect for the job. You're not frivolous in the least and you have a good sensible head on your shoulders. You don't like hockey, it's true, but then no one is *absolutely* perfect. I'm looking for a good manager for the school, not a sports fanatic. It would have been nice if you were both, but you're not. There's very few Amelia Sartours in the world, even if I say so myself.

So, there we are. I can die in peace.

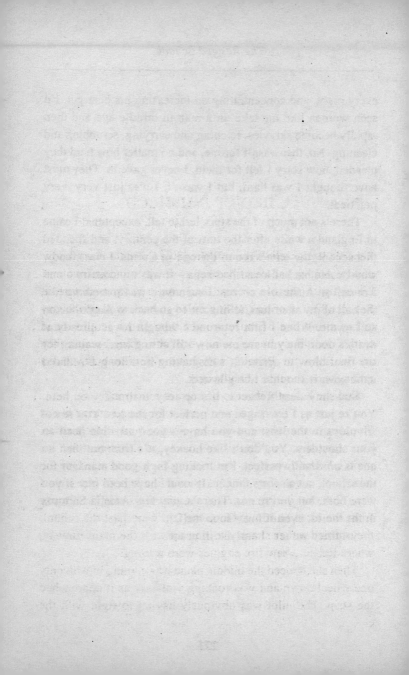

Chapter Nineteen

Rebecca left Amelia's room feeling like a middle-class fuddy-duddy. Amelia had described her as sensible and unfrivolous. Listening to the old woman had conjured up a picture in Rebecca's mind of herself. It seemed she was well on the way to becoming one of those women who show people round castles and stately homes, who work for nothing because they are working for Britain, who have shelflike busts and a grating, no-nonsense horsy accent.

Did she honestly want to be seen as a matron?

She went to the window on the landing and stared out at three Hurricanes which were coming in to land on the airstrip. Their formation was ragged, and it seemed to Rebecca that the middle aircraft was being escorted, or perhaps assisted, by the other two, since they didn't fly over the school but took a flight path on the periphery of the playing fields, well away from the main building. Once the trio were past the school, they turned rather sharply to line up with the main runway, where Rebecca saw fire engines were waiting.

Then she noticed the middle plane was coming in with only one wheel down and was rocking violently as it approached the strip. The pilot was obviously having to fight with the controls to keep the shattered aircraft from diving into the ground.

Rebecca's eyesight was good enough to see by its markings that the Hurricane in trouble was the one usually flown by Bill Ryker. Her heart was in her mouth as she clutched the edge of the window, watching as the plane seemed to float down like a misshapen seed in a high wind. She could now see the holes in the fuselage, presumably made by machine-gun bullets.

When it was almost on the ground the Hurricane veered sharply left, just missing a Nissen hut and a windsock. It soared over the roof of another hut, then disappeared from view. There was a *whumpf* sound, from the direction of the plane, then a column of black smoke curled from behind the huts. The noise of a fire engine's siren rent the air as it raced to the scene.

'Oh no!' cried Rebecca.

She stepped back from the window, the thought flashing through her mind that perhaps Bill wasn't the pilot of that aircraft today. Perhaps some other unfortunate airman had taken his place for some reason? Rebecca knew that this kind of thing happened, with the shortage of aircraft.

'Hello, Rebecca, what are you doing?'

Rebecca looked along the corridor to see Fay walking towards her. The sound of the fire engine was still faintly audible, but such emergencies were common at RAF Hornchurch. There was nothing unusual about a lot of activity and planes were coming and going virtually all the time.

Rebecca forced a smile on to her face. 'Er, hello, Fay – I've – I've just been having another chat with Amelia, about the school, you know.'

Fay laughed. 'Oh, I see – bosses' conference, eh?'

Fay suddenly noticed the noise from the airfield and a little frown appeared on her forehead. She drifted towards one of the landing windows. Rebecca called quickly, 'Fay? Would you like some tea? In my room?'

'What's going on over there?' asked Fay, staring out of the window. 'Is it a crash? My Bill's flying today.'

Rebecca shrugged. 'Oh, you know what they're like – probably some training exercise or something.'

Fay came away from the window. 'Maybe you're right – yes, let's go and have a nice little chinwag. I want to talk to you about the wedding. I wondered if you'd mind helping me sew my dress. I'm not much good at that sort of thing.'

Rebecca was not sure what she wanted to do with Fay, but it seemed a good idea to get her away from the window. If Bill had been in that crashed aircraft, they would hear soon enough. It was best not to anticipate any horrors. Better to let them arrive in their own time, if they were coming at all.

'Yes – yes of course,' she said, 'though I'm no great shakes with a needle myself.'

Rebecca managed to get Fay into her room, where the younger woman chattered about the arrangements for the wedding, which was to take place in two weeks' time. It had blossomed from the quiet affair that both Fay and Bill would have preferred to the full-blown knees-up Fay's parents wanted. They had persuaded Fay to have the wedding in the East End, so that all her relatives could be there. In the end, for the sake of peace and quiet, she had agreed. St Barnabas was the venue for the ceremony and the local Boy's Brigade

Hall was where the reception would be held, with Fay's female relatives doing the catering.

'It'll be stout and mild, lots of sandwiches and cakes, and a thoroughly vulgar day,' grimaced Fay.

The strain on Rebecca's nerves was enormous as she attempted to keep the light chatter going. 'Oh, you think I haven't been to some vulgar weddings?' she laughed, a little too shrilly. 'Why, there are coarse people in my family too, you know.'

'Coarse?' frowned Fay. 'Rebecca, are you all right? You look a bit tired.'

Rebecca wrung her hands in her lap. 'Little bit of a strain at the moment,' she confessed, 'what with taking over the school and all that.'

Fay smiled and nodded. 'Of course, I was forgetting. I suppose it must make you a bit anxious. Mind you, I wish it was me – I'd sack half the staff if I became owner. There's some real dead wood around here.'

'Now you know you don't mean that – at least you might do now, but if you actually did take over you'd probably change your mind. I'm almost sure you would . . .'

They were in the room three-quarters of an hour before there was a sharp rapping on Rebecca's door. She jumped up and opened it to find herself confronted by Helena Patten.

'Mrs Daniels,' she said. 'Is Miss Nelson with you? Only I can't find her anywhere and I know you two often take tea together . . .'

Rebecca's heart sank. 'Yes – she is.'

'I'm here,' cried Fay, coming to the door, realising something was wrong. 'What's the matter?'

Helena Patten remained calm. 'Flying Officer Ryker has had a crash in his aircraft . . .'

Fay half collapsed and Helena and Rebecca had to catch her.

'Before we have too many histrionics,' Helena Patten continued, 'it might be as well that you know he's not dead or critically injured.'

'Thank God,' murmured Rebecca.

Fay seemed to recover a little and asked, 'What – what's the matter with him?'

'I don't know,' Helena Patten said. 'He's asking for you, over at the temporary hospital just outside the airfield. I suggest you get over there.'

'Yes, yes, I shall,' said Fay frantically. 'Rebecca?'

'I'll come with you,' said Rebecca, grabbing their two coats from a hook behind the door. 'Here, put this on – it's chilly out there. Thank you, Miss Patten. I wonder if you would mind going to see my daughter. I was supposed to meet her in twenty minutes. Could you explain what's happened?'

'Of course, Mrs Daniels,' murmured the admirable Miss Patten, who drifted away into the heart of the school.

The two women took bicycles from the rack outside the schoolhouse and cycled round the perimeter of the airfield. On the far side, in a leafy avenue, was a large old house which had been employed as a hospital since the beginning of the war. It was close to the aerodrome, where most of the casualties occurred, yet not close enough to be seriously affected by any bombing raid that came from Germany for the express purpose of devastating RAF Hornchurch.

Once inside an anxious Fay asked a passing sister about Bill.

'Flying Officer Ryker? He's on the operating table at the moment. Are you a relative?'

'I'm his fiancée,' said Fay. 'How is he? Is he going to be all right?'

The sister put a hand on Fay's shoulder. 'I think you'd better talk to the doctor . . .'

'Is he going to be all right?' shrieked Fay, losing control.

Rebecca put an arm round Fay. 'Fay, Fay, he'll be fine. We have to wait until the surgeon's had a look at him before they know how serious the injury is. We'll wait here, Sister, if that's all right?'

The sister nodded. 'I'll send someone with cups of tea.'

Fay allowed herself to be sat down and quietly fussed over by Rebecca. A few minutes later a char lady came along with a cup of tea for each of them, and patted Fay's hand, saying, 'He'll be all right, love, you'll see.'

They waited there for two hours, during which time the population of the waiting room ebbed and flowed, as people came, waited and went. Eventually a weary-looking doctor came through the double doors and spoke to the nurse on duty at the desk. The nurse nodded towards Rebecca and Fay. He crossed the room and Fay got up to meet him.

'Miss Nelson?' he enquired.

'Yes – that's me.'

'I'm Colonel Radenski,' he explained. 'Please excuse this accent, I'm from Poland. I just finish operating on your boyfriend.'

'My fiancé,' corrected Fay. 'How – how is he?'

The surgeon smiled wanly. 'He is comfortable at the present, but it is his leg, you see. He has had bad accident with his leg. The right leg is broken in many, many places and there is a loss of the foot.'

Fay went pale and Rebecca supported her. Rebecca said, 'He's lost his right foot?'

'I'm afraid so,' said the doctor.

'Then why are you smiling?' cried Fay hysterically. 'What's the matter with you?'

'It is – unfortunate nervous complaint,' said the doctor. 'It has not anything to do with humour. I'm very, very sorry for what has happened to Flying Officer Ryker. I know him, you see. We are friends from the officers' mess. Only last night I was drinking with him in the canteen.'

Rebecca said, softly, 'We understand – Fay's just a bit distraught at the moment.'

'I'm sorry,' sobbed Fay, collapsing in Rebecca's arms. 'I just – I couldn't – he's going to be all right then? He's not going to die? Can I see him? Oh, he'll be so unhappy. He loves to fly. He won't be able to fly, will he? Not with only one foot? He won't be able to *walk* even, let alone fly . . .'

'We'll make sure he walks soon,' said the colonel. 'If you will excuse me now – I have another operation.'

'Certainly,' said Rebecca.

The colonel was starting to walk away when Fay called to him. 'Doctor – Colonel – thank you – thank you very much for what you've done for my Bill. I'm sorry for being silly.'

He shook his head slightly, his face still wearing that ghostly smile, then continued towards the doorway.

The two women waited at the hospital all night. Helena Patten came to see them and reported back to Amelia Sartour and Francine Knole. When morning came they were allowed in to see Bill, who was lying on a bed with a blanket-covered cage over his legs. He face looked strained, ashen, and there was a taughtness around the eyes, but he smiled at Fay.

'Kiss?' he said, offering his cheek.

She bent and kissed him. 'You bloody fool,' she snapped. 'What were you doing? Trying to be a hero?' Then she burst into tears and hugged his head for a moment against her breast. When she had sniffed back the tears, she sat down in a chair by the bed.

Rebecca sat on the other side of the room, feeling a bit superfluous to requirements. She promised herself she would get out of the room at the first excuse, in order to leave Bill and Fay to get over the initial stages of the trauma they were going through.

Bill said, 'I got shot up by a damned Junkers. Don't know what I was thinking of – momentary lapse in concentration, I guess. Lucky to get home.'

Fay said, 'You know – you know what's happened to you?'

'Yeah,' he said, looking over the top of the blankets to the cage that humped over his legs, 'my war's over.'

'I'm so sorry, darling,' said Fay.

'Just call me Long John Silver,' laughed Bill, but it came out too harsh to be natural.

'I'm just glad you're alive,' said Rebecca, 'I don't know what I would have done with her if you'd bought it, Bill. Will you go back to Canada now? When you're better, I mean?'

'Not if I have any say in it,' Bill muttered. 'I'll see the war out. That's what I came to do and I'll damn well do it, even if it's from behind a desk. We've got a wedding soon, too – unless Fay doesn't want a cripple for a husband?'

Fay jerked backwards as if she'd been struck. 'Don't – want—? Don't you *ever* say anything like that again, Bill Ryker,' she cried, genuinely angry. 'I'll slap you silly if you do.'

Rebecca said, 'I think I'd better leave you two to say goodbye. I'll wait outside, Fay. Don't forget the nurse said Bill's got to get some rest. He's just been through a big operation and he's probably in pain now.'

'I want to sit here, quietly, for a while,' said Fay stubbornly. 'Just for a while.'

'All right, I'll see you outside. Good luck, Bill.'

'Thanks, Rebecca.'

Rebecca stayed in the waiting room until Fay joined her again and then the pair of them cycled back to school. There was a message awaiting Fay: Amelia wanted to see her. Rebecca guessed that the old woman wanted to offer some words of comfort. She let Fay go to the meeting alone and went off to see Kim.

Kim's first words were, 'Has Mr Ryker been hurt?'

'Flying Officer Ryker is in hospital, dear, but the doctor has said he'll be fine. He – he might walk with a limp because he's hurt his leg very badly.'

'His foot's been cut off, hasn't it?' said Kim solemnly. 'Will he have a wooden leg?'

'They do some very good things with artificial limbs,' said Rebecca. 'Flying Officer Ryker will be fine.'

'I hope so,' said Kim. 'He promised to take me to the zoo one day.'

'Oh, he'll take you to the zoo, don't you worry,' sighed Rebecca. 'In the meantime we must be extra nice to Miss

Nelson, because she's very upset. Promise me you won't badger her with questions about Flying Officer Ryker.'

'Yes, Mum,' said Kim. 'I promise.'

Chapter Twenty

On 7 December 1941, it was broadcast on the wireless that the Japanese had carried out a sneak attack on Pearl Harbor in Hawaii, bombing ships and land bases of the American forces. The United States were retaliating and had thus entered the war. This momentous and historic event was completely overshadowed in Hornchurch by the debate over the Gradge School playing fields and whether they should be put to the plough in order to grow vegetables for Britain.

Rebecca received a note from a retired Major Crispin, inviting her to attend a meeting in the village hall on the evening of 9 December. Rebecca asked Martin if he would go with her for company and he agreed. Mohorty wanted to go too, since it was her department which would suffer if the outcome went against the school. Rebecca refused to take her.

'I need someone who won't get emotional over the words "hockey pitch" – Martin will do fine as a dispassionate adviser, thank you, Miss Mohorty.'

'I shan't lose my temper,' Mohorty said.

'Yes you will – you always do when you're arguing about anything to do with hockey. You're not coming, and that's final.'

Mohorty glowered. 'You're going to give in to them, aren't you? You're going to sell the school down the river.'

When Rebecca and Martin set out, at six o'clock in the evening, it was dark and cold. The trees in the street were bare and stark in the moonlight, covered in a sparse twinkling frost. A light ground mist wound its way along the lanes, around the trunks of the trees, and formed a shroud over the gardens as Martin and Rebecca made their way towards the hall, which stood near to the village green.

The hall, a prefabricated building with a corrugated-steel roof, was used for all types of meetings from Boy Scouts to the VPA to the Photography Club. The main room was heated by two small Primus stoves and was cold enough, but its toilets were equalled in temperature only by the Siberian plains. The men, of course, had to expose very little of their anatomy when taking a pee, but women were in serious danger of frostbite. Last year's winter had not yet found a way out of those frozen brick attachments to the prefab, let alone the current bitter weather. Rebecca had made sure she went to the loo before leaving the school, but she knew she would be offered tea which she would be unable to refuse and her kidneys always reacted to intense cold.

The hall windows and doors, like most village halls, were painted dark green. It was an offensive colour, but one that caused fewer arguments than blue, yellow or red. Rebecca went through the green doorway, with Martin close behind, to find the hall already occupied by a dozen people. They were sitting in folding wooden chairs around a rickety-looking table. The windows had already been blacked out and there was a hurricane lamp in readiness for an electricity failure.

Tea was in evidence on the table.

A brisk, dapper little man rose to greet them as they walked the short length of the hall to the table. He extended his hand and smiled, revealed two rows of obviously false teeth. Rebecca guessed he was in his seventies.

'Major Crispin,' he said, shaking Rebecca's hand. 'You must be Miss Daniels, the new owner of Gradge Lodge, and I know Martin here. Hello, Martin.'

'Actually, it's *Mrs* Daniels. I only correct you because I have a seven-year-old daughter, Major.'

The major's head went back slightly, as if he were surprised, and then he said, 'Oh, sorry.' He made a sweeping gesture with his hand at the group round the table. 'Mrs Floodgate, Mrs Dibbs and, er, well you'll get to know all the names I'm sure. I expect you've met some of them before. The vicar, Reverend Spinnaker . . . Martin knows the vicar quite well, don't you, Martin? Two Revs round one table tonight – we are blessed. Probably be a fight to see who says the grace, eh? Ha, ha. Except we're not eating anything but these stale cakes and biscuits Mrs Floodgate always brings – rejects from her tearooms, I shouldn't wonder . . .' The last sentence was delivered in a whisper.

Martin and Rebecca took the two free chairs that had been left for them and nodded to people around the table. It was obvious that the meeting had started some while before six and that strategies and tactics had already been discussed. Rebecca was outnumbered, outweaponed and had the added disadvantage of coming into the arena late. She placed her handbag by her elbow, undid her coat but, after one glance at the sputtering, ineffectual Primus stoves, kept it wrapped around her. A cup of tea was passed to her by a smiling little woman with a white bun and light blue eyes. This lady looked as fragile as porcelain, but Rebecca knew her to be as ruthless as a Cossack when it came to infighting over village matters. Both Rebecca and Martin ignored the plate of biscuits down their end of the table, taking the major at his word.

The major rapped on the table top with his knuckles. 'Ahem, meeting will come to order,' he said. 'If no one has any objection, I'll take the chair.'

No one had any objection, least of all Rebecca.

'Now, as you all know, this is an informal meeting of people from our village, though the parish council is represented by Mrs Floodgate and Miss Lovelace' (Miss Lovelace was the fragile-looking lady) 'and, of course, myself. We're here to discuss the possibility of persuading Gradge School to make a contribution to the "grow for Britain" programme. Mrs Floodgate?'

The major sat down. Mrs Floodgate did not get to her feet. Instead she looked around the table, at everyone except Martin and Rebecca, and made her little speech.

'I think it's a shame,' she said, 'that the householders in our pretty village have dug up their beautiful lawns and flowerbeds in order to plant vegetables – sorely needed by the war effort – when the school has acres of ground which is used only for young schoolgirls to go charging about after a ball. I think it's time a few sacrifices were made by outsiders to our village – people who've come here recently.'

Before Rebecca could say anything, Miss Lovelace said, 'I agree with Mrs Floodgate. The war effort should be taken seriously by all of us – not just those of us who have lived here all their lives, and their parents before them, but by everyone who comes to live in our village. I remember when Gradge Lodge was called Hallingham House, when it was owned by Mr and Mrs Davenport, who did a great deal for the village – if you remember they donated the bench by the church wall – and I never understood the need to change the name of their home. A school by the name of Hallingham House, which has been in our village for generations, would have been just as acceptable, I would have thought, and far more dignified.'

Rebecca thought it was time to speak.

'Mr Chairman,' she said, addressing the major who almost jumped out of his seat, clearly not expecting to be the medium between the warring factions around the table, 'people keep using the words "our village" as if the village belonged to them, as if they owned not just the houses in which they live, but the rest of the buildings too, including the school. Could you clear up a point please? Could you tell the meeting whether the rights of someone living here a hundred years are any different to the rights of someone who moved to Hornchurch yesterday?'

The major knitted the fingers of both hands together and cleared his throat. 'In law, I suppose, there's no difference whatsoever. However, the views of someone who has lived here all their life surely have a priority over someone who might come and go within a short passage of time? If a change is to occur it will affect those who remain within the environment.'

Rebecca said, 'Yes, but we're not talking about pulling down a church that has stood for a thousand years. My rights are the same as yours, whether I've lived here two days or two centuries. It is not *your* village, Mrs Floodgate, nor yours, Miss Lovelace. The village does not belong to individuals.'

'Yes, but surely . . .' began the vicar.

Martin interrupted with, 'I don't think there's any question about it. Can we get on with the main issue here, please? I understand there's a suggestion that the hockey pitches at the school should be put under the plough. That must be a decision for the owner of the school, Mrs Daniels here. She's willing to listen to anything this meeting has to say on the subject, but let me correct any earlier error by Mrs Floodgate – there are not "acres of ground" at the school. The hockey pitches consist of one point nine acres exactly. Now, has anyone else got anything to add to what's already been said?'

'I must say,' said Miss Lovelace, with tight lips, 'that some of the girls from the school have been most unruly outside the sweetshop recently.'

Rebecca turned to Major Crispin. 'Is this a forum for complaints about the school? If it is, I wish I had been warned, so that I could come forearmed.'

The major shook his head. 'No, no.' He turned in his chair a little. 'I'm afraid you might be out of order there, Miss Lovelace. We're really here to discuss the school playing fields.' Before he could be blasted by the very formidable guns of Miss Lovelace, he turned back quickly to Rebecca. 'Mrs Daniels, will you please tell us if you are prepared to dig up the school playing fields and plant vegetables for the war effort?' His face registered a plea.

Rebecca was beginning to want to go to the loo. The tea had done its work on her and the cold in the room was attacking her remorselessly. She wondered whether she could face the arctic regions of the toilets, or whether she could wait until she got back to the school. She decided on the latter, but things had to be concluded very quickly.

She said, 'What I'm prepared to do is this. I shall order one of the hockey pitches to be turned over to our newly formed Gardening Club, run by the girls themselves. The running strip alongside the aerodrome fence will also become a vegetable plot. However, the main hockey pitch will continue as a playing field. I hope this compromise satisfies everyone here?'

Mrs Floodgate drew herself up in her seat indignantly. 'It certainly doesn't satisfy me, Mrs Daniels.'

'Then I'm afraid I shall have to say hard luck, Mrs Floodgate, because I'm not going to deprive the school of all its games facilities for a few extra vegetables. The girls need to keep fit, they need the hockey pitch for morale purposes, and finally Miss Sartour is an elderly, ailing woman – hockey is her lifeblood, an interest I have to say I don't share in the least. If I were to take her hockey pitches away from her completely, I think it would damage her health. So I'm not going to do it, like it or lump it, Mrs Floodgate.'

'Well!' Mrs Floodgate stared around the table, gathering support for her indignation.

The major remarked, 'I have to say I consider Mrs Daniels to have been most fair.'

He received some daggers from the eyes of Miss Lovelace.

The vicar, clearly under the thumb of his female congregation, said, 'I, er, I'm not sure we've talked this through *thoroughly* enough . . .'

Rebecca stood up and buttoned her coat. She grasped her handbag and gas mask case. To the major she said, 'Thank you, Mr Chairman, but I have to get back to the school now. I hope at least some of you are satisfied by the outcome of this meeting? Good night.'

There was a stunned silence around the table as Rebecca pushed back her chair.

She walked quickly towards the door. Martin's chair scraped as he pushed it out. He hurried after her.

'You've made a few enemies there, Rebecca. I hope you realise that.'

'Let's face it, Martin, I wasn't going to do otherwise, was I? They were out for blood.'

'True, true. Still, you charmed the old major. I think he's in love with you. Expect a bunch of flowers within the next few days.'

'Turnips you mean,' said Rebecca. 'They don't grow flowers any more – remember?'

When they got back to the school, Mohorty was waiting for them, her arms crossed. 'I suppose you gave in to them?' she growled.

Rebecca pushed her aside. 'Out of my way, woman,' she cried, 'I have more urgent business than standing here satisfying your desire for self-mutilation of the spirit . . .'

Martin fell about laughing. Mohorty failed to see the joke and looked very put out. 'What did I say?' she asked Martin, almost plaintively.

'You didn't say anything,' Martin replied.

He then explained what had happened at the meeting.

Mohorty was both annoyed and relieved. She said it hurt her to lose one of her hockey pitches, and the running strip, but it wasn't as bad as she had feared. 'I thought she'd give them both away – she hates hockey, you know.'

'I'm sure you're right, but Rebecca isn't stupid, Priscilla – she knows the school needs to keep one pitch, whatever her feelings about the game. She's also a very fair woman. I don't know why you continue to treat her as an enemy.'

'You don't,' said Mohorty, 'but *she* does. We're just different types, that's all. We'll never like each other and there isn't a damn thing anyone can do about it, least of all the two of us.'

Martin shook his head in bewilderment and walked away, glad he was a mere male in this den of females.

Chapter Twenty-One

Rebecca, Kim and Martin were the only ones from the school who were going to attend Fay and Bill's wedding. Others had been invited, but with one thing and another couldn't go. Amelia was too frail to travel and Francine Knole saw her duties at the school as more important. Christopher Bates was also going: in fact he was driving the four of them to the church and reception.

Fay had wanted Martin to marry her and Bill, but Martin had gently refused. 'It wouldn't be right, Fay. Your own vicar should perform the ceremony – not just for you, but for the rest of your family.'

'The rest of my family haven't seen the inside of a church since the last time somebody died,' Fay had snorted. 'And they wouldn't know the vicar if he fell dead on their doorstep.'

But Martin had been firm. The truth was, he was still a little bit in love with Fay and it was bad enough going to the wedding without actually being the one who tied the knot for them. Martin was a good man but, like the God he served, he could be jealous. Although he did not advertise the fact, his family were landed gentry, and his pride was wounded too. A colonial had come over from Canada and snatched an admired woman from under the nose of a Berkshire Simkins. It was hurtful. Martin's family motto, carved above the fireplace in his father's house, was: *Love Well, Hate Well, Serve God, Fear No Man*.

The *Hate Well* was particularly apt for the Simkins family, who saw no reason to love their enemies.

Martin had successfully transferred most of his unspoken and unrequited love to Rebecca now and was going through the same sort of agonies over Christopher Bates as he had gone through with Bill Ryker.

He met Rebecca and Kim in the school hallway. They walked down the avenue to the gates to await Christopher and his car. They all had their gas masks with them, slung over their shoulders.

'Will I be allowed to wear a flower?' asked Kim of Martin.

'You mean a buttonhole? I should think so. We'll probably all get one.'

'Mum says the children probably won't,' remarked Kim.

Martin glanced at Rebecca and then said, 'Well, perhaps not. I don't really know.' Martin was not very good with the younger children: those under about twelve. They seemed to him to be more intelligent than he expected them to be. They were always one jump ahead of him.

'I could pick one, couldn't I?' said Kim brightly. 'From someone's garden.'

'Well,' began Martin, unsure of himself, 'it is winter, you know . . .'

'No you can't,' Rebecca said. 'If I see you picking any flowers, miss, you'll be in trouble.'

Kim pouted and Martin shifted his feet uncomfortably.

Shortly afterwards, Christopher Bates arrived with the car.

'OK, everybody?' said Christopher, leaning out of the window. 'Pile in then.'

Rebecca sat in the front, next to Christopher, while Martin shared the back seat with Kim.

'Let's play I-spy?' suggested Kim.

Rebecca said over her shoulder, 'Perhaps Martin doesn't want to play I-spy?'

'Oh, I don't mind,' lied Martin, who hated playing children's games.

The journey was torture for him. He really wanted to talk to Rebecca, who was deep in conversation with Christopher Bates, while Kim demanded his attention. If his mind wandered for just a few moments, Kim would snatch it back again very quickly with a precocious remark.

'Reverend *Simkins*,' she said, 'it's your turn and you haven't done very well so far, have you?'

Rebecca called, 'Don't talk to Martin like that, Kim – he's not one of your dorm pals.'

'That's all right,' said Martin desperately.

Eventually they reached their destination, a scruffy back street somewhere in the East End. They parked the car and walked to the church. This was red-leaded land, where the most important part of the house was the doorstep, on show to neighbours and strangers alike. All the back-to-backs had doorsteps which dipped gracefully in the middle, where they had been worn by the tread of a thousand feet. You could have the filthiest kitchen in the neighbourhood, in this district, but your front step had to be immaculate.

Glancing into one or two open doorways, Martin could see

bicycles in the hallways, washing hanging across landings, runny-nosed children staring belligerently out at passers-by, boots in lines, tools of trades, piles of old newspapers, a chamber pot waiting to go upstairs to bed, ceramic hot-water bottles like beer kegs, collars and braces hanging amongst the coats from hooks, shoe polish and brushes resting on a torn-out page of a magazine, children's toys dirtied with constant use.

Martin shuddered at the images. It was a world he had never known, the world of the terraced house, and he never wanted to come any closer to it than he was now. He caught a waft of the smell of boiled cabbage and potatoes from the hallways, and damp lino, and a multitude of other odours. In one house the back door as well as the front had been left open and he could see right through to the back yard, piled high with unimaginable junk from an old tin bath to a broken pram, and his mind reeled to think that someone had to look out of their kitchen window for hours on end at this sordid scene.

This was the world of boots and braces, of bottle-green jumpers, of shapeless jackets stinking of pipe tobacco, of monstrously pink women's bloomers which filled with wind on the washing lines to rival barrage balloons, of grey brassieres.

The church itself was an immense affair which had once been red brick, but the industrial revolution had marched all over its exterior and turned it almost black. The windows, made of clear but dirty glass, were high off the ground as if the church had been built for giants who wished to look out over the rooftops of London. There was a bell visible, hanging from an arch high up above the rear of the roof, and a wire cross eaten away by rust at the front. There was no churchyard that Martin could see, only buildings crowding in on the cramped alleys and a single scruffy tree in a circular plot on the pavement. Litter swirled in the breeze around the steps up to the double doors.

Martin hated churches like this. They depressed him. He was a country chapel man who liked the antique feel of pews rubbed smooth by the backs of rustics. City churches like this, a far cry from Westminster Abbey or York Minster, were his idea of purgatory. To have to serve as a minister in one filled him with absolute dread. He mentioned the austere aspect to Christopher Bates, who disagreed with him.

'Good, solid, working-class church,' said Christopher. 'Nothing wrong with that.'

'Craftsmen and farm labourers are working-class too, but they don't pray under such terrible conditions.'

He realised he was not going to get any agreement from Bates, so he turned his attention to the crowd outside the church. These were the neighbours who had not been invited to the service but who wanted to see something anyway. They milled around on the steps, hoping for a good look at the bride, in order to ascertain whether she was pregnant or not.

Martin, Rebecca, Kim and Christopher went into the church and were given buttonholes. There was one for Kim too, who looked up at her mother as if to say, *I told you so*. When asked whether bride or groom, Rebecca seemed to hesitate, so Martin said very firmly, 'Bride.'

Bill saw them. He was looking smart and well groomed in his uniform. His best man, who should have been Luke Adams, was a fellow pilot. Bill was sitting on the end of the first pew, a pair of crutches at his elbows. His face still bore the marks of post-operative strain. He waved to them.

'Hello, Bill!' called Kim.

Rebecca shushed her. 'Don't call out in church, Kim,' she said.

Martin said in her defence, quite loudly, 'I've always wondered why we have to whisper in church – I'm sure God doesn't mind us talking in normal voices.'

'God doesn't,' whispered Christopher Bates, 'but those old biddies over there do.'

Martin glanced a few rows down to see three formidable-looking East End ladies, in hatpinned felt bonnets that looked remarkably like German helmets, glaring back at him. They were solid women, with red, raw faces, who carried their gas masks as if they were looking for the opportunity to be provoked into using them like medieval mace-and-chain weapons. They were the sort of women that struck fear into the hearts of men like Martin and he fell silent immediately.

A little later, as the bridal march was struck on the organ, Martin prayed, *Please God, don't let there be a raid.* At present, Hitler was concentrating his bombing raids on 'Baedeker' cities – lightly defended English towns of historic interest that were featured in the *Baedeker Guidebook*. This was supposedly in retaliation for British raids on Rostock and Lübeck. However, Hitler was notorious for changing his strategy at a moment's notice and London was always a prime target.

Fay glanced towards Martin and smiled self-consciously as she came down the aisle on her father's arm. She looked radiantly beautiful and Martin groaned inwardly as his stomach melted. This woman might have been his to cherish, had he not been so tightly wrapped in his fussy little ways; had he been the slightest bit braver; had he made her aware of his love. Bill hadn't come along until Martin had known and loved Fay for at least a year. Now this dreamlike figure, this queen of the fairies, would be in another man's bed tonight.

The service went reasonably well, interrupted in the middle by the arrival of a bunch of airmen who had been unable to get off duty until the last minute. They winked and smiled at everyone as they tumbled quietly into the church and even the three old biddies didn't seem to disapprove. Martin realised that if you were young and cheeky enough you could get away with a lot more than someone as stiff and stuffy as he was himself. It was not a fair world, he told himself, not fair at all.

If the church had made Martin shudder, the venue for the reception precipitated convulsions. It was a dirty hut, near the arches of a railway viaduct. The smoke and grit from the steam trains had smeared the whole building with black soot. Fingers left marks on doorways and walls; dark flecks gathered on collars and dresses. Martin felt his scalp itching and knew he would have to wash his hair the moment he arrived back at the school.

'Well done,' he said, shaking Bill's hand. The former pilot was propped on his crutches, leaning on the doorpost as people went in. Martin tried, unsuccessfully, not to look down at Bill's feet. 'Congratulations, old man.' There was a pinned flap of trouser where a foot should have been.

'Thanks,' grinned Bill. 'Lose a foot, gain a wife.'

Martin thought this remark was especially tasteless, but Fay simply laughed. 'Oh, Martin,' she said, her eyes shining, 'how lovely to see you – thank you for coming, darlin'.' She kissed him lightly, full on the lips. His heart poured forth a mixture of sorrow and delight. He wanted to cry.

'Wrong man, Fay,' he said, smiling, his courage coming to the fore way too late to do him any good.

Fay shook her head, emphatically. '*Right* man, Martin – couldn't have been any other. Sorry.' Her eyes told him that she knew he wasn't joking.

So she had known how he felt, all along! Women were such secretive, devious creatures. How had she known when he hadn't given her any signs? At least he thought he hadn't given any signs. Was he so transparent to them, to women, that they knew his every thought? It felt like that sometimes, when they stared at him. He glanced at Rebecca's back as she moved before him into the grubby room. What if Rebecca knew how he felt about *her*? He might die of shame.

'All right, mate?' said a small, stocky man by his elbow. 'Get yerself a beer – plenty goin' over there. I'm one of the bride's bruvvers. Prefer brown ale meself, but there's all sorts over there. Get stuck in.'

Martin went to the pile of crates in the corner of the room and got stuck in. He selected a light ale and had the top removed for him by another smiling brother in braces, high-waisted trousers and big hobnail boots, his jacket already discarded.

Fay seemed to have brothers enough to form a horde of Visigoths. There were sisters too, it was pointed out to him by an unknown cockney gentleman, 'Smashers, all of 'em, just like Fay.'

Fay's brittle-thin mother was hidden under a welter of

make-up and frills and Martin did not feel he had seen her at all.

At the meal Martin found himself sitting next to a bridesmaid. She was seventeen in years and a hundred and ten in worldliness. Her name was Gloria and she had a face which looked as if it had been used to chop kindling. Under the table her hand brushed Martin's thigh, and she kept saying, 'Sorry – din't mean nothin' by it,' when she clearly did.

'I like older men,' she told him. 'They always know what they're doin', don't they?'

Martin could have argued all night with that statement, feeling as he did that he had never known what he was doing so far as women were concerned, and that he never would know.

'I'm a minister,' he told her, hoping to put her off. Then, seeing her puzzled expression, added, 'A clergyman – a *vicar*.'

'Oh, one o' them,' she laughed tinklingly, and he felt her hand slip on to his crotch and give him a squeeze. 'Nice.'

He almost choked on the sardine sandwich he was eating and excused himself, saying he had to go to the lavatory. He heard her laughter in his wake and died yet again.

As the afternoon wore on, there was drunkenness and revelry in some parts of the room, and cackling and backslapping in others. The mumbled, inadequate speeches were made, the best man's unrivalled for depth, the father of the bride's unequalled for smut. The cake was cut and eaten, the bride appeared in a cream suit, and then disappeared with her man. Someone drove the couple to a London hotel in a van normally used to deliver fish. The inevitable knees-up Mother

Brown was enacted. Fat women grasped Martin round the waist, urging him onto the floor; thin women clutched his arm, pulling him into conga lines. He drowned in blouses and flab, he was stabbed by sharp, pointed elbows.

Martin felt trapped by circumstances. He could not leave without Christopher Bates and Rebecca, and Bates was deep in conversation with some man who looked as if he delivered coal and never let his skin near water.

He finally found Rebecca, who was looking as lost as he felt himself. 'Time to go, do you think?' he asked her, hoping she might persuade Christopher Bates to leave.

'Oh, hello, Martin. Yes, I think I ought to be getting Kim back to school – it'll be past her bedtime.'

Bless you, Kim, thought Martin. 'Shall I go and rouse Bates, or will you?' he asked.

'I'll do it – Christopher's difficult after he's had a couple of drinks.'

Martin was alarmed by this. 'Do you think I had better drive then?'

'No, he won't be drunk, but he gets awkward. I'll go and see if I can drag him away from that discussion. He's probably talking politics or religion, judging by his face.'

You must know him very well, thought Martin jealously.

Bates was finally and reluctantly pulled away from his conversation. Martin found himself sitting next to the doctor on the way home and stared out of the window fixedly for the entire journey. Bates himself grumbled over his shoulder at Rebecca for the duration of the drive back to Hornchurch. Rebecca warded away the verbal blows easily and without rancour.

When they arrived back at the school, Martin thanked Bates for the lift, made his excuses to Rebecca, and went straight to his room to bed. He was exhausted, both mentally and physically, and vowed he never wanted to go to another wedding again.

Unless, of course, it was his own, to Rebecca.

Chapter Twenty-Two

February was a particularly cold month. The night raids frequently drove the occupants of Gradge Lodge School down into the shelters. Amelia was now so frail she refused to leave her bed and be carried out into the night. Rebecca realised this was the right thing to do: to remain in the warmer bedroom. Amelia was much less likely to die of a bomb blast than she was of hypothermia or pneumonia.

However, this gave Rebecca a personal problem. Someone had to stay with Amelia, to keep her company, even though the elderly woman insisted that no one should. Usually this person was Helena Patten, but there were times when Helena herself wasn't well enough to look after her employer. She too was getting on in years. Martin always offered to take Helena's place, but Rebecca said she couldn't allow him to do it every time, so she herself took a turn occasionally. She was, after all, the owner of the school, and the building and everyone in it was her ultimate responsibility.

Early one morning the air-raid warning siren wailed at two o'clock. The teachers gathered up their charges and herded them towards the shelters. A girl named Silvia McKinley, daughter of a local politician, was head girl at the time, and a particularly good one. Rebecca could rely on Silvia to take her place as head of her muster station, make sure all the girls were there and get them down to the shelters without any undue fuss. This night Rebecca decided it should be her who stayed with Amelia. Helena was in bed with a touch of flu and wanted to stay there. Rebecca informed Martin that she was remaining in the school, then went to the muster station where her group were gathered.

'Silvia, take over please, I'm staying with Miss Sartour and Miss Patten.'

'Yes, Mrs Daniels,' said Silvia, a tall girl with a commanding presence. She turned to the group of sleepy pupils huddled round the east exit. 'All right, I'm going to call the roster, then Daphne take the lead and I'll follow on at the back to make sure there's no stragglers . . .'

Rebecca waited with them while the roster was called. One girl failed to answer her name.

'Amanda? Amanda Swinburn?' called Silvia.

Still no answer, so another girl was despatched back to Amanda's dormitory. The rest of the roster was called and by the time it was complete the girl was back with a groggy Amanda Swinburn, who had failed to hear the call to the shelters and had remained asleep in her bed.

Once the girls were on their way along the narrow path that ran beside what used to be the second hockey pitch and was now a patch for winter cabbages, Rebecca made her way upstairs to Amelia's room. On the way she called in to see Helena Patten.

'Wouldn't you rather come in with us?' asked Rebecca of the hump in Helena's bed.

'No thank you,' came the muffled reply. 'I'm all right here.'

'As you wish. If you do feel the need . . .'

'Yes, yes,' snapped Helena irritably. 'Do go on.'

Rebecca shrugged and went to Amelia's room, where she told the old woman that Helena wasn't well and would be remaining in her bed. They had no light on in the room, but the fire was banked high and the flames lit the surroundings. The room was alive with shadows which danced around Amelia, making the old woman look gaunter than she was in truth.

'She should be in the shelters,' grumbled Amelia, speaking of Helena Patten. 'Since I refused to go down the shelters, everyone seems to be doing it.'

'Well, she does have flu. She would probably catch something much worse out there in the cold.'

'Can't you tell her to go under the stairs, or under the kitchen table at the very least?'

'I've tried telling Helena to do things before,' said Rebecca, 'it doesn't really work.'

Amelia sucked in her thin cheeks and stared at the ceiling in the firelight. There was a rumour that coal and gas were going to be rationed soon. The lean years were on their way and Amelia was making the best of the end of the fat ones.

Rebecca sat by the bed doing some sewing, squinting in the poor light. She had on occasion read to Amelia, but she didn't feel like reading by firelight tonight and since no request was forthcoming, she didn't offer.

The aircraft droned overhead, ground emplacements blattered away with anti-aircraft guns, and spasmodic machine-gun fire could be heard. It seemed the German Luftwaffe were going over them tonight, on to the heart of London, but that didn't mean they were home and free. The occasional bomber would often save one clutch of bombs to drop on his way back to the coast.

Even so, the ground shook as bombs began falling in central London. The ornaments rattled on the mantel and the windowpanes shook in their frames. Dust came from hidden crevices and shelves in the room to fill the air with a musty odour.

'What's happened with Christopher?' wheezed Amelia, during a lull. 'You still seeing him?'

Rebecca sighed. 'We still go out together occasionally.'

'Are you going to marry him?'

'That's a very personal question, Amelia. He hasn't asked me to.'

Amelia grunted, staring at the ceiling. 'Would you, if he did?'

Rebecca put her sewing down into her lap and looked into the flames of the fire. 'I'm not sure. I should like Kim to have a father, and he would make a good provider, being a doctor . . .'

Amelia cackled at this. 'You are so naive, young woman. What makes you think Christopher Bates would make a good father and provider? Has he ever given you the slightest cause to think that he likes children? Or dislikes spending money?'

Rebecca was a little put out by Amelia's manner. She shrugged her shoulders. 'It's not my business to enquire how he spends his money, but on the first count he's very good with the girls, when they're sick.'

'Well, that's in his professional mode. He's not so fond of kids *personally*. He's told me so. He's a good doctor, Christopher Bates, but he's no lover of children.'

'Men often don't like children in general, but dote on their own family.'

'That's true enough, but Kim isn't Christopher's child – she's yours. If you were to have a baby between you, maybe he would find it a fascinating creature, but I don't think so. I think he's much too selfish for that.'

A bomb fell about a mile away and shook the foundations of the house. Rebecca hoped it hadn't frightened the girls in the shelters too much. On the whole they were a pretty stoical lot. The older, braver girls laughed and joked through raids, keeping the nervous ones from going too much into themselves. Rebecca was not really concerned about Kim either, because her daughter had got used to bombing raids on Tilbury, which was attacked more frequently and more savagely than Hornchurch had ever been. In fact Kim couldn't remember a time when bombs were *not* raining from the skies, and like a lot of children tended to accept them as part of life.

When the house had settled, Amelia said, 'Have you been to bed with him yet?'

Rebecca plonked the sewing down in her lap. 'Now that *is* too personal, Amelia.'

'I told you about me and my man.'

'That doesn't mean I have to tell you about Christopher and me, now does it?'

'Well, have you?'

Rebecca sighed. 'No, not yet. I don't know what's holding

me back, because I'm very fond of him, despite . . .' She paused.

'Despite what?'

'Well, he tends to be a bit moody sometimes, especially over money. I think he's finding it hard to make ends meet during the war, but I keep telling him that once the war's over he'll have a fine and flourishing practice. I believe that.'

'Do you?' said Amelia, in a tone which implied that she did not.

'I don't see any reason why he shouldn't.'

Amelia simply grunted at this.

'You be careful of Christopher Bates,' she said, after a while. 'I don't usually warn women against him, because I like him – I like the fact that he's a raffish womaniser and a gambler – but you're my great-niece and you've got my school in your hands. Don't let him waste away what I've spent years building, now will you?'

'A womaniser and a gambler? I think that's stretching it a bit, Amelia. He's a single man, a bachelor, so of course he gets a lot of attention from young women. As to his gambling – he has a flutter now and then, that's all.'

'You're a bigger . . .' Amelia never finished her sentence. A whistling sound above the school interrupted her.

Rebecca dropped her sewing and threw herself over Amelia's body on the bed.

The next moment she was deafened by an explosion which seemed to take place somewhere in the room. The whole world rocked violently. Dust filled the air. Ceiling plaster came raining down all over the room. Chairs leapt and jigged and fell over. A vase toppled from a table and crashed to the floor. The wardrobe doors flew open and folded clothes spewed out on to the rug. Coats dropped from hooks like heavy ghosts. Books crashed in heaps from their shelves. Coals in the fireplace jumped and crackled.

When the room was still, Amelia cried, 'Have we been hit?'

But then she immediately went under her blankets again for protection against a fresh batch of ceiling plaster which fell like hail on her bed. Rebecca was covered in it, bits dropping from her shoulders and hair. Luckily the plaster came down in small pieces, rather than a big slab, or they might both have been hurt. As it was, Rebecca was merely shaken. Her pulse was racing, her ears were ringing, and she shivered with the shock of the experience, but she was not physically harmed.

She stood up.

It took her a few seconds to realise that they were actually all right and that the room was still intact. 'It might have missed us,' she said reassuringly. 'Perhaps it's hit the driveway or something.'

She first went to the window and peered under the curtain, her heart thumping, to make sure the shelters were all right.

To her relief the bomb hadn't damaged them in the least, though the occupants would have got just as much of a fright as had Amelia and Rebecca. Having reassured herself that Kim wasn't injured in any way, Rebecca went over to the door.

She found it stuck fast. The walls had warped, trapping the door against the jamb. Rebecca tugged the handle hard but couldn't shift the door, so she went to the fireplace and got the poker. Studying the door in the firelight she saw that the hinge side had a gap, while the lock side was part under pressure. She inserted the poker in the gap below the top hinge and, using the iron bar as a lever, she prised the door off its screws. There was a creaking and juddering, but the bomb itself had done most of the work and the door flew open, the wrong way.

Cold air struck her like a slap in the face.

The first thing she saw were pinpricks of light. They were way off, in the far distance, above dark waving objects. There was a puzzling vastness beyond the edge of the doorway.

It was a second or two before she realised that what she was looking at was the night sky.

She looked down and saw that there was nothing between the edge of the doorway and the ground. She teetered on the brink of the chasm, then managed to step back with her heart racing. Had she walked out into space she would have ended up down below on the broken timbers and rubble.

The bomb had destroyed a major part of the school.

'Is Helena all right?' wheezed Amelia from her bed. 'Go and see.'

With dismay Rebecca realised that Helena's room had been blasted to pieces. There was nothing left of it. She stood on the edge of the precipice and looked out into the night, with its faint glimmerings of stars, wondering what to tell Amelia. Overhead the German bombers were on a homeward track but still threatening. There would be those amongst them with bombs yet undropped. Freezing air from the raw night swirled round Rebecca. There was movement out on the roadway which ran past the school as people came to see where the bomb had landed.

'Watch that light!' yelled a warden.

Rebecca pushed the door, which was hanging from a single screw on the top hinge, back into the hole.

'What's he talking about?' grumbled Amelia from the depths of her blankets. 'We've got the blackout curtains closed, haven't we?'

'Yes we have,' replied Rebecca.

Amelia's face emerged. 'Damned cold in here,' she muttered. 'Well? What was the man on about? Has the school been hit?'

Rebecca dusted the plaster off the chair by the bed and sat down. She took Amelia's hand in her own.

'What? What is it?' cried the old lady.

'The school has been hit,' replied Rebecca, wondering if she could postpone telling Amelia about Helena.

'What about Helena's room?' asked Amelia, giving Rebecca no further choice in the matter.

Rebecca nodded grimly. 'It's gone.'

Amelia's face registered concern. 'Helena's hurt? You must try to find her.'

'I can't, Amelia – there's no stairs – there's no landing out there. There's nothing between the doorway and the ground. Some men are down there now. If Helena's there, she'll be found.'

The old woman stared hard at Rebecca. Incredibly, the fire was still burning and helped to light the room. Rebecca's eyes must have revealed her thoughts, because Amelia said, 'She's dead, isn't she?' The old woman fell back on the pillow and stared at the dark patches on the ceiling, where the plaster had fallen and the wooden batons were showing through. Her lean, yellow-brown face with its blue eyes set in a mass of wrinkles looked even more sunken than usual. The grey coarse hair stood out from her scalp in brittle clumps. Her head was like a husk.

After a while, she said, 'That bit looks like a map of Australia. Poor Helena. It should have been me. I'm ready to go – she wasn't. Why wasn't it me? Why didn't God take a useless, dried-up old biddy like me instead of someone with lots more life left in them?'

'It doesn't work like that, Amelia, you know that. The killing is indiscriminate. Helena was unlucky.'

'Poor Helena. She didn't feel anything, did she? Perhaps a few seconds of terror, but then you and I felt that too, and we're still alive. I hope I go as quickly as she did. If you have to go, it's best over in a few seconds, isn't it?'

Someone from outside yelled, 'Whoever's up there, put out any naked flames – there's gas.'

Rebecca got up and looked around. The jug of water had been knocked over in the blast and its contents spilt. She picked up a blanket, folded it until it was just a little larger than the fire, but with a thickness to it, and smothered the flames. The coals would be hot underneath, however, and she wondered how long it would be before the blanket burst into flames. Just then there was a rapping on the door.

'You'll have to knock it in,' called Rebecca. 'It's stuck.'

There was a crash and the door collapsed. A man in a helmet and carrying a fire axe was there – or, rather, half of him was – the other half was hidden below the doorway. He was obviously on a ladder.

'You two ladies all right?'

'Yes,' said Rebecca, 'but you'll need to extinguish this fire properly – I've smothered it with a blanket at the moment, but that might catch fire itself soon.'

The man disappeared down the ladder and then came back up with a fire extinguisher. He gave the fire a thorough going-over with the foam from the extinguisher, then turned his attention to the two women.

'Can you go down the ladder yourself?' he asked Rebecca.

'Yes, I think so.'

'What about you, Miss Sartour?' said the fireman, obviously familiar with Amelia. 'Shall I take you down?'

'I think you'll have to,' said Amelia faintly.

Once on the ladder, Rebecca's legs began to shake a little, but she made it to the ground. Christopher Bates was there. He took her in his arms, warming her. 'I'm sorry this had to happen,' he said.

Rebecca nodded, accepting a blanket from someone and wrapping it round herself. She looked back at the school. A quarter of the building had been destroyed – the whole of the south-west wing. It was possible that the school might have to be closed until repairs had been carried out.

When the other teachers and pupils came out of the shelters they still seemed stupefied by the blast, which had reverberated through the underground rooms and caused a minor panic amongst the girls. Rebecca found Kim and gave her a hug, telling her daughter everything was all right. Kim wanted to know if anyone had been hurt.

'Miss Patten,' said Rebecca. 'We think she's been – been badly hurt, Kim. But we don't know for sure.'

When the body was found a little later, under the rubble, and the bad news was broadcast to the rest of the school, Kim was dreadfully upset. 'Oh!' she cried, and the tears started to her eyes.

The reaction amongst the other girls was varied. Some of them wept, others took the news dry-eyed in silence. Miss Patten had not been a commanding presence around the school, but there were those girls to whom she had shown a particular preference. The pupils were either for her or indifferent to her. There was no one who actually disliked her. She had always told people that she was allowed to have favourites because she wasn't a teacher. Thus, some of them, like Kim, knew her extremely well, while others hardly knew her at all. Those who knew her would miss her.

Rebecca and Francine Knole, with the help of the other teachers, went about organising accommodation for those whose dormitories had been destroyed. Villagers offered to house girls who couldn't be squeezed into existing dormitories. Francine Knole insisted that Amelia took over her room, while she moved into Fay Ryker's smaller one.

Fay was away in Cornwall on honeymoon with Bill. She had announced her desire to move into rented accommodation with Bill when they returned, although Bill had to spend most of his nights on the RAF station. She had told Rebecca and Francine Knole that she wanted to set up home as best as she could, though it would be nothing like an ideal situation. Bill had been given a temporary desk job at Hornchurch, but there was the possibility that he would be posted elsewhere once his leg had completely healed. Since the wound was a particularly severe one, it was likely that he would be in transit for a long while to come yet.

The division of labour in the school still hadn't been sorted out to any definite degree between Francine Knole and Rebecca. Miss Knole as headmistress felt she should be in day-to-day charge of the staff, while Rebecca as the owner responsible for salaries felt that any changes in staffing levels, and any problems the teachers had, should be cleared through her. It was an unsatisfactory arrangement, which led to staff going to both of them whenever there was a problem, such as Fay asking permission to live outside the school.

Miss Knole was against Fay living outside the school, giving as her reasons the fact that teaching at a private school, during a war, was a twenty-four-hour commitment. There were after-lessons duties; there were air raids to consider: getting the girls down the shelters required all the staff to be present and ready to clear one section of the school. She still hadn't made up her mind definitely on the subject, but said to Rebecca, 'If all our teachers wanted to live outside the school, what would we do for evening supervision and air raids?'

'Fortunately they don't,' replied Rebecca. 'We must deal with probabilities rather than hypothetical uncertainties. The probability is that the rest of our staff won't request to live outside the school. However, I take your point.'

When morning came round the teachers, ragged with lack of sleep, reorganised their classrooms around the available space and decided to go ahead with the daily lessons. The alternative was to have a school full of restless girls idling away their time, which could result in more problems than actually setting to and teaching them.

Rebecca and Francine Knole met in the library to plan the future. 'My office is gone,' said Rebecca, 'so if you don't mind we'll have to share yours for the time being.'

'Of course,' said Miss Knole.

Francine Knole's physical appearance would not have excited a man, but women saw in her a very strong character combined with a compassionate nature. She made an ideal headmistress. She was firm but not overstrict with the girls and they respected and admired her, but had little affection for her. She was quite happy about this. She didn't feel comfortable with being liked, only with being looked up to and taken seriously.

Many of the girls had crushes on both Rebecca and Fay, and these two teachers dealt diplomatically with such situations, whereas Francine Knole would have been horrified to be the object of a young girl's immature infatuation, and would have considered it embarrassingly improper. Francine Knole felt that any excess girlish passion should be directed into French literature and Latin verbs, not at older women.

'Now, as you probably know,' said Rebecca now, 'we aren't insured against bomb damage. Any destruction which can be proved to be a direct result of the war doesn't fall within the terms of the insurance. However, we do have a reasonable amount of money in the bank – funds put away by Miss Sartour for just such an emergency – and we ought to set about rebuilding as soon as possible.'

'Are you sure we can afford it?' asked Francine Knole. 'You're not using anyone's savings, are you?'

'If I were, it would be Miss Sartour's and mine, which would amount to the same thing, since we're both determined that the school should continue to be successful,' said Rebecca firmly. 'But there is a special school fund, which was set up by Miss Sartour at the beginning of the war – it should cover us. What's not so certain is whether we'll be able to find any builders to come and do the work.'

Most young men were of course away somewhere, either in Britain or abroad. There were older men, builders, plumbers and electricians, who were available for rebuilding, but these were in high demand during such times. It was difficult to get anyone to agree to come and assess the damage, let alone put it to rights. There were also certain government restrictions on any rebuilding programme, though a school would be considered a fairly high priority after hospitals and military establishments. It was going to be a difficult time.

Francine Knole said, 'Well, I expect we'll get someone down soon to make safe the section that's been bombed.'

'Oh, we'll get that all right, but then we'll have to fight tooth and nail for a proper builder. I think we'd better roll up our sleeves and prepare for battle. Are you ready for it, Francine?'

The other woman smiled. In that moment the two were closer than they had ever been before and as close as they ever would be. In trying times, women reveal their flexibility.

'Ready and willing,' answered Francine Knole.

Chapter Twenty-Three

Arrangements for the funeral of Helena Patten were made very shortly afterwards. Amelia Sartour was taken to the church in a wheelchair, which she clearly hated. Martin conducted a moving memorial service, then Helena's body was to be sent to relatives in Cornwall where she had expressed a wish to be buried. This upset Amelia a little.

'I had hoped she could be buried in the local churchyard, so that I could visit the grave, but her will states she wants to be in Cornwall. I think that's a bit selfish of her.'

'You don't believe in respecting a person's last wishes?' said Rebecca, as she wheeled Amelia along the lane back to the school.

'Of course I do,' snapped Amelia. 'I shall honour the terms of the will – but what does she care really where her bones are going to be dumped? It's the living that count. We're the ones who suffer, not the dead. They're well out of it, thank you very much. Their final wishes should take *us* into consideration, not some silly romantic thought about one's corpse being on a windswept cliff overlooking a wild Atlantic Ocean one can't appreciate.'

Rebecca was torn. 'Oh, I don't know – isn't your place of

final rest important to you? It might seem silly to want a picturesque or nostalgic grave site, but it's a natural feeling to want to be in a place of your choice, isn't it? It might not be important to you *after* death, but it's important to you now, before death.'

'I suppose so,' grumbled Amelia, who actually wished she could be buried in the bright, wide-open Australian outback, somewhere near Ayer's Rock, rather than in a shady, gloomy churchyard full of dense yews and dark conifers somewhere in England. England was too cramped for her, too hemmed in by fussy copses, trees, brooks, hillocks and meadows. The Australian outback went as far as you could see, in every direction, and was so steeped in timeless mystery it filled you with a kind of fearful reverence for the unknown. 'But I still think she's selfish,' she grumbled.

'I think we all get a little selfish as we get older, don't we?' said Rebecca.

'Don't patronise me,' snapped Amelia.

At that point other people joined them, including some of the older girls, and they put the argument aside. Rebecca realised that Amelia was missing her friend very much and that she needed to talk about her, since she couldn't talk *to* her. There was anger at Helena, for going too soon, for going first instead of last. Helena was supposed to be the fit younger companion, who made Amelia's passage into death a little easier to handle. Amelia needed to argue with her old friend about this and she could only do so through someone like Rebecca. It was possible that if Amelia didn't give vent to her grief, even if it took the form of anger, she might just fade away before everyone's eyes. It was Amelia's style to rant at something she feared, like death.

Once they heard about the bomb, half a dozen parents decided to remove their daughters from the school. Those who lived in the countryside, away from any target for German bombers, were horrified that their children had been so close to death.

Rebecca was upset by the loss of the pupils, but Francine Knole told her not to worry too much.

'I guarantee most of them will be sent back within a few months. Once they find out what fees others schools charge, and what they're getting for their money, they'll be asking you to take back their precious daughters. Most of the parents are mothers on their own and unless they want to send their offspring to a state school – a prospect that horrifies them even more than a stray bomb – they won't have much choice.'

So Rebecca put the matter out of her mind and concentrated on getting the school rebuilt.

The standing brickwork and timbers of the ruin were quickly made safe. The rubble was sorted into heaps and any valuables recovered. A huge tarpaulin was then draped over the bombed section of the school, but this would not withstand a high wind. Birds like magpies, pigeons and seagulls were making a mess of the covering. For some reason it seemed to attract them, as a roost, and they were covering it in splashes of lime.

After a lot of telephone calls and badgering, asking around the village and sending letters, Rebecca managed to secure the services of a local builder who said he had his two robust daughters to assist him. One of the daughters was a carpenter, the other an electrician. Steven Jarvis lived on the far side of the village in a shiplap shack which was no advertisement for his skills as a bricklayer. He still used a horse and cart for carrying his materials, so Rebecca knew it was going to be a slow job, but Mr Jarvis charged reasonable prices and she was reliably assured that he would do the job just as well and probably better than anyone else.

Amelia was impressed by the words on the side of Mr Jarvis's cart: S. JARVIS AND DAUGHTERS – BUILDERS.

'I don't have to prove my worth,' he told people. 'I know what I can do and I get on and do it.'

Rebecca visited Mr Jarvis at his cottage, to discuss the terms. When she met the daughters, who were surprisingly slight and pretty, she began to feel doubts. It was not that she considered her own sex to be short on skill, but building surely required a modicum of physical strength. The two sisters looked as if they could just about lift a lipstick to their lips. True, they weren't the giggly sort, and seemed serious enough, but their muscles looked as undeveloped as Kim's.

Mr Jarvis caught Rebecca staring at the girls and knew instantly what she was thinking. He took his pipe out of his mouth and said, 'It's not the strength, it's the knack. Them girls have got the knack.'

'But I can't begin to imagine either of them carrying a hod full of bricks,' said Rebecca truthfully.

'Hod don't have to be *full* for a starter,' explained Mr Jarvis after another puff on some foul-smelling concoction. 'An' it's the way you lifts it up on to your shoulder that matters. There's a knack to it, see, and them girls have got it. Have you ever seed a woman playing golf?'

'No, I haven't,' confessed Rebecca.

'Well a little-bitty girl can knock a ball just as far as a six-foot man, if she's got the knack, see. 'Course, some of them champion golfers is different, but you take one of my daughters, put a golf club in her hand and she'll knock spots offen some man who uses his brute strength to whack the ball. You mark my words, them girls have helped me often enough afore. They'll do fine, Mrs Daniels, you'll see.'

But Rebecca was not going to be allowed to see how expert the two sisters were when it came to building. She received a badly typed letter, with several of the letters chopped in half where the carriage on the typewriter had slipped, telling her that Mr S. Jarvis and Daughters could not do the job after all, since the parish council had intervened.

'Look at this,' she stormed, showing Francine Knole the letter. 'What do you make of it?'

'I'd say Mrs Floodgate and her crew have stepped in,' muttered Francine Knole. 'You made some enemies over the hockey pitch.'

'I compromised, didn't I?' cried the aggrieved Rebecca.

'You compromised, but what they wanted was outright victory. Mrs Floodgate and Miss Lovelace want to see you crawl, Rebecca – and they probably have some hold over Mr Jarvis.'

Rebecca put on her coat and went to see Mr Jarvis.

'Can't help it,' he said, waving his smoking pipe in the air. 'Sorry and all that, but the council's got me over a barrel, Mrs Daniels. If I goes against 'em, they'll do all sorts of things to me, like withholding planning permission for houses I want to build, and not giving me the jobs they normally puts my way

– public buildings and such. There's the local infants' school comin' up for an extension. I need contracts like that to keep me head above water.'

'But this is monstrous,' said Rebecca. 'They can't *order* you not to assist me in rebuilding the school. There must be laws against that sort of coercion.'

'Probably is, but what you got to do is write to your MP or summat, to get some action. That's all going to take time. When you gets the law on your side and I'm seen to be doing it all against my will, why then o' course I'll do it.'

'And that's your last word on it?'

'Can't do nothin' else about it, or I would. I told you, they got us over a barrel. Be like cutting me own throat.'

Once more the world seemed to be heaping injustices on the head of Rebecca Daniels, but by now she was used to the world being a harridan and she simply gathered herself together and went out to do battle.

She found Mrs Floodgate behind steamy windows in her café. Mrs Floodgate didn't close for the winter, unlike Devon or Cornwall teashops, since her clientele were not tourists but farming people and villagers. She remained open all year and was proud of it.

'Mrs Floodgate,' Rebecca said, after marching in, catching her enemy coming through the doorway to the kitchen with two cups of tea in her hand and confronting her, 'I wish to know why you have ordered Mr Jarvis not to carry out rebuilding work on my school.'

Mrs Floodgate was clearly at a disadvantage, having to hold the two teas without spilling them, and do battle. She tried to pass Rebecca, who stood steadfastly in her way, knowing the woman would try to retreat to the kitchen with only a Parthian shot over her shoulder. The kitchen was Mrs Floodgate's sanctuary and no one from the café side dared follow her there.

'I don't know what you mean,' she cried, drawing herself up and slopping tea into the saucers despite her efforts to retain her balance.

Rebecca kept her ground. 'You know very well what I mean – Mr Jarvis had agreed to rebuild the school. Now he tells me the parish council has warned him off.'

Mrs Floodgate smirked. 'There's more than me on the council, you know.'

'Of course – perhaps I should consult some of the others then?'

Mrs Floodgate had laid herself open to that one and she went pale. Rebecca knew then that the teashop owner had taken it on her own shoulders to speak to Mr Jarvis. It had probably been more of a hint than an outright order, that should Mr Jarvis go ahead with the repairs to Gradge Lodge School he might find himself coming second when presenting tenders for work with the council. Mrs Floodgate was quite capable of underhand behaviour and of usurping more authority than she could officially muster.

'You can speak to who you like,' she replied to Rebecca. 'I merely suggested to Mr Jarvis that another, more lucrative building programme was coming up, and that he shouldn't tie himself down too much with fiddly bits of work.'

The customers, two local women, were still waiting for the tea which had been arrested in its progress by the human barrier between them and their succour, but at the same time they were clearly fascinated by the fight that was going on in front of their eyes. A choice had to be made between refreshment and curiosity. Curiosity eventually won. They would rather thirst and see the spectacle of two female gladiators hacking away at each other with blunt words. They did nothing to assist Mrs Floodgate in the way of relieving her of the teas. Were they to do so, that particular combatant would slip away to safety behind her castle walls and they might not witness the final outcome.

Rebecca said, 'Mr Jarvis gave me the distinct impression that the *whole* council was against this project . . .'

Mrs Floodgate's eyes narrowed. Her arms were becoming tired. She was getting very frustrated. If she didn't do something soon she was going to drop one, or both, of the teas. It was intolerable to her that this woman could come barging into her shop – *her* shop – and start throwing her weight around.

'I don't give a damn about the rest of the council,' Mrs Floodgate cried. '*I* don't want you to get Mr Jarvis. There, are you satisfied? You made me look a fool over that other affair – and you two can stop gawking,' she screeched. 'Take these rotten teas out of my hands, for God's sakes, or I'm going to drop them all over the floor.'

One of the customers stood up and reached around Rebecca for the teas, but she looked Mrs Floodgate straight in the eye as if to say, 'This is the last time we'll come in here, thank you very much – we don't pay for insults, we pay for tea.'

Once the teas were out of her hands the formidable Mrs Floodgate wiped her fingers on her pinny and glared at Rebecca. 'You can damn well do what you damn well like about it, Miss Fancy Knickers. I don't care what the rest of them think, Celia Lovelace and myself will block you every inch of the way. You won't get away with what you did last time. I'm going to grind your nose in the dirt and believe me I'll enjoy it.'

'This tea's cold!' called one of the customers.

'I'm not bloody surprised,' shouted Mrs Floodgate, throwing all caution to the winds in her fury. 'If you'd have wound your necks in and took them off me, they wouldn't be cold, would they?'

The customers rose majestically and, with handbags held before them like wardens holding collecting pouches in a church service, they went to the door of the shop and stood outside.

Mrs Floodgate glared at them. 'Still rubbernecking. Can't bear to leave in case they miss something.' She turned back to Rebecca. 'As for you, don't you ever dare set foot in my shop again, or I'll throw you out myself.'

With that she flounced back into her kitchen and crashed a few pots and pans around to let people know she meant business. Rebecca, feeling she had been defeated this time, went out of the shop and past the staring ex-customers. She was not through with Mrs Floodgate, though. Not by a long chalk.

Chapter Twenty-Four

By the time Fay and Bill returned from their honeymoon Francine Knole had accepted Rebecca's argument that the other teachers in the school would have no reason to live outside the premises and agreed that Fay should be allowed to do so.

'But, Mrs Ryker,' she told Fay, 'you must fulfil your extra duties in after-lessons hours.'

'Of course,' replied Fay. 'After all, Bill . . .'

'Your husband?'

'Bill, my husband, will be working quite long hours at the RAF station.'

'That's no concern of mine,' said Francine Knole primly, clasping her hands in front of her. 'What your husband does is of no consequence. It is your duties I am concerned with.'

'Yes, Miss Knole.'

Fay came out of the interview with the headmistress and, seeing Martin in the corridor, blew a curl away from her forehead to indicate that it was a relief to have the meeting over with.

'Tough, eh?' said Martin.

'Well, *firm* anyway.'

'How's Bill?'

Fay frowned. 'He's fine – well, his leg's not so good. He's got to go back into the hospital for physiotherapy for a while. In the meantime I shall look for some accommodation for us. You don't have any ideas, do you?'

Martin had no desire to help choose a love nest for the woman who wanted – who *had* – another man. But he was the eternal friend. He knew that most of the teachers regarded him as asexual, even those who were desperately shy about their own sexuality. *Good old Martin*, was the common cry. Fay had guessed of his passion for her, so she was still special to him. He reluctantly agreed to help her search for some rooms.

'Just two would do,' said Fay. 'A small kitchen and a bed-sitting room.'

'I'll ask around,' said Martin. 'The local vicar might know something. I preach for him occasionally, so he owes me one or two favours. Let me ask him.'

'Thank you, Martin, you're a dear.'

'Of course I am.'

Fay had been shocked when she saw what had happened to the school in her absence. She was even more shocked when Rebecca told her of her encounter with Mrs Floodgate.

'You mean the old witch is determined to stop us rebuilding the school?'

'She hates me,' confirmed Rebecca. 'The business over the hockey pitch has done it. I think she would side with the Germans if she thought it would cause my downfall.'

'She can't be that bad, surely?'

'Worse,' said Rebecca gloomily. Then she changed her

tone and expression. 'Anyway, how was your honeymoon? Did you have a wonderful time?'

'Bude is such a nice little seaside town,' sighed Fay. 'Quiet and peaceful – the loudest noise is the fishermen unloading their catch in the morning. The mist comes up from the shore . . . You know we stayed at a lovely little inn . . . could have stayed there for ever.'

'Of course you could,' smiled Rebecca. 'And you didn't argue at all, you two?'

Fay's dreamy, sunny expression clouded a little. 'You bet we did – he can be the most insufferable person at times. I never realised Bill had such an ego . . .'

Rebecca laughed. 'I'm sure he's thinking the same thing about you, Fay. It's just a man and a woman – two different individuals – trying to live together, that's all. It's not easy, is it? Sorting out the boundaries, giving up most of your privacy, having to compromise on almost everything.'

'Was it like that for you?'

'I thought it was going to be heaven with Alan,' said Rebecca. 'Then I realised it was *my* heaven I was expecting, not understanding that he had an idea of heaven too, which didn't exactly dovetail with mine. So these two people who had certain expectations of marriage had to give ground, retreat in certain areas, and they didn't want to retreat, either of them, not an inch. We had some unholy rows at first, but gradually we sorted it all out, arriving at some sort of middle ground in the end. I expect it's much the same with everyone.'

'I thought we had so much in common before we married,' grumbled Fay. 'There must be *some* perfect people around, surely?'

'I doubt it. You hear these couples say, "We've never had a cross word in fifty years." Actually it's usually only one of them that says it, while the other sits and nods. I suspect both of them are as empty-headed as dolls and wouldn't know how to disagree if you gave them lessons in it.'

Fay sighed. 'Well, there was lots that was nice about Cornwall, and some things that weren't.'

'A bit like ordinary life?'

'I suppose so. Anyway, I'm looking forward to setting up home now,' said Fay brightly. 'Knole has given me the go-ahead to live outside and Martin has promised to ask around about some rooms.' She sighed. 'It'll be heaven.'

'Yours or Bill's?' smiled Rebecca.

'Now don't spoil my pictures,' laughed Fay.

Later, Fay visited Bill at the hospital to find out how he was getting on with the physiotherapist. The physio turned out to be a young woman of twenty-seven with a pretty face and a nice figure. Fay said to her grinning Canadian husband, 'We're getting you out of here as soon as possible – I don't like the look of the staff. They seem the sort of people who provide too much care for their patients and create dependency.'

'Yeah?' laughed Bill. 'Oh, they're OK.'

'I'm sure they are,' Fay said primly, 'especially your physiotherapist.'

At that moment Fay's mum and dad walked into the ward and shouted greetings to Fay and Bill. Fay's mum wanted to know all about the honeymoon. Fay's dad chatted to Bill about men's subjects like soccer and cars. They had just come for a quick visit, at the insistence of Fay's mum, and were taking the bus straight back to the East End afterwards.

At one point, Fay overheard her dad say to Bill, 'It was you, wasn't it?'

'Was me what?' asked Bill.

'You sent the note yerself, didn't you – saying you was shackin' up with my Fay at the pub?'

'No, Joe – it must have been someone I knew.'

'Garn – it was you, I know it was. You *wanted* me an' Fay's brothers to come after you, so's she'd 'ave to marry you.'

Fay, who had been halfway through a sentence to her mother, stopped and stared at Bill. It was obvious to all three visitors at this point that Joe had blundered into the truth. Anger flooded into Fay's heart.

'It *is* true, isn't it?' she said to Bill.

Bill gave her a wry smile. 'Best of intentions, darling – you know how I felt about you? I hated all that sneaking around corners. I wanted it to be all above-board.'

'Joe, see what you've done now,' whispered Fay's mum.

'What did I do?' said Joe, shrugging.

Fay was still glaring at Bill. 'You bastard!' she finally said.

Joe cried, 'Hey, hey, that's no way for a daughter of mine to speak. An' that's yer husband you're yellin' at, hussy. Bill, give 'er a clout around the 'ead for that one, or you'll never keep her down. She's a wild one, she is.'

'I did it with the best of intentions,' Bill insisted.

'You tricked me,' said Fay, infuriated. 'You blatantly lied to me.'

'But you promised to marry me once I stopped flying – well, the foot did that.'

'You had your crash after the wedding was arranged.'

'True, but – does it really matter, Fay? I mean, we're married now. All right, I tricked you into marrying me. I love you, girl. I had to do something. I was going crazy. Jesus. What was I supposed to do, lie down and take it? I fought. It was the only way. The only way.'

His eyes pleaded with her to forgive him, but she was just too angry to do that. She felt humiliated. He had made her his wife, but she was a fool of a wife. Her feelings and wishes had not been taken into consideration. The men had got together and tricked the woman. It was a big joke. Her father would go home laughing his head off at how stupid his daughter had been to be taken in by such a scheme. He would tell his mates at the pub and they would all have a good laugh about silly women, about how you could pull one over them at any time.

Fay's mum said quietly to Joe, 'We'd better leave.' She stood up and tugged his arm, leading him towards the door.

'Wait a minute – it's *her* what wants to get her ideas straight. You *wasn't* married, you know,' he shouted at his daughter as he went out of the door. 'You was no better than a hoor. If somebody's got to trick you out of that, well it's a blessing, not a sin. You was the one who was at fault, girl . . .' Fay didn't hear the end of it, but she knew her father would still be ranting and raving at her all the way to the bus stop.

She turned again on Bill and this time there were tears in her eyes. She hadn't wanted to cry, but she couldn't help herself. 'You're despicable,' she said.

Bill tried to take her into his arms, but when she struggled to get out of his reach he let her go. He stared at her miserably. 'I'm sorry,' he said, 'it was the wrong thing to do. It's ironic that if I'd have waited a couple of weeks, you would have married me without all that. I don't know what to do now, honey, to make it better. I want to make it better.'

She dried her eyes on a handkerchief and stared at the floor. 'I – I can't forgive you just yet. You don't know what you've done, Bill. You were someone *honest* to me, and now you're not. I'm wondering what other lies, what other tricks you've fooled me with.'

'None,' he said emphatically.

'Well' – she dried her eyes and looked at him frankly – 'we'll see, shall we? I'd better be getting back to the school now . . .'

'Aw, hell,' cried Bill, losing his temper for once, 'stay for a while longer, damn it!'

'No, I really do have to be getting back. Rebecca's in trouble and I want to help out. You know the school was bombed while we were away? Rebecca had a builder who was prepared to do the rebuilding, but Mrs Floodgate stepped in and ordered him not to do it.'

'Mrs Floodgate? What, that sweet little old lady at the ye olde teashop?'

'You know so little about women, Bill.'

'Hey, let's not be so free with the insults, eh? I know I've been a bad boy, but I'll make it up to you.'

Fay shook her head. 'I'm not being insulting – you really don't know how powerful or how ruthless some women can be in certain situations. Mrs Floodgate holds a lot of sway here in Hornchurch, believe me. If she doesn't want a local builder to do a job, then it won't get done. There's so much work around for builders at the moment that she can keep placing priority demands on his time.'

'What's Rebecca going to do about it?'

'She can't do anything,' said Fay. 'Not directly. We've got to find some way round Mrs Floodgate.'

Bill stared at his wife, desperate to get back into her good books once again. 'Or meet her head on,' he murmured.

'How do you mean?'

Bill paused for a while in thought, then said, 'Leave it to me, Fay. Rebecca will get her builder.'

Chapter Twenty-Five

Rebecca planted a greengage tree in the grounds of the school and had a little plaque made to go in front of it. When it was in place, Rebecca went and fetched Amelia from the house and took her to see the tree. It was a misty March morning with a weak pale sun struggling to penetrate the veils drifting over the Essex fields.

Amelia grumbled the whole while as she was being wheeled over the grassy area to where the greengage sapling stood. Fine spray from the dew-covered grass dampened her ankles below the tartan blanket. Kim came with them and chattered.

'It's a *lovely* tree, Auntie – you'll be ever so pleased with it.'

'Will I?' growled Amelia.

'Yes, and if there's blossom on it this year, we'll get some fruit, won't we?'

By this time the tree was in view and Amelia, on noticing how small the sapling was, said, 'Any fruit on that poor object will break its back.'

However, by this time they were close enough to read the plaque, which read: *In memory of Helena Patten.*

Amelia's face softened immediately and her eyes glistened with tears in the grey light of the early day. 'A memorial tree,' she said. 'How thoughtful of you, Rebecca. It's because we couldn't have a grave, isn't it? But why a greengage?'

'Oh, two or three reasons really. I once heard Helena talking about her childhood – how her grandparents had an orchard full of greengage trees, and how these days you see so few of them. I thought it would be appropriate.'

'Quite right – and the other reasons?'

'Practical,' replied Rebecca grimly. 'After the business over the hockey pitch and growing for Britain we ought to be seen to be *producing*. This is a fruit tree, not an ornamental one like our cherries. Helena is growing for Britain.'

'Bravo!' said Amelia huskily. 'Any more?'

'Yes, most fruit trees need their blossoms to be pollinated. Albert Thackery's allotment just over that hedge has two greengage trees at the bottom. I think the bees will be able to find their way over here, don't you? It's only a couple of hundred yards or so.'

'Excellent,' murmured Amelia. 'What a clever woman you are, Rebecca. I'm glad you're looking after my school for me – I really am.'

Rebecca was touched by the compliment. 'Thank you, Amelia, but I seem to be making a bit of a mess over the rebuilding at the moment.'

Amelia waved a gloved hand. 'Oh, don't you worry about that – it'll all come out right in the wash. I've been having battles with the council for years. Officials! You can spit 'em and roast 'em for all I care. Everywhere you go you get bureaucrats sticking their noses into people's business. You'll get round Mrs Floodgate somehow, you see.'

'Officials,' repeated Kim, disdainfully, and spat on the ground.

'Kim!' cried Rebecca, horrified by her daughter's display of bad manners. 'What do you think you're doing, young lady? Is that any way to behave?'

'Aunt Amelia said we could spit 'em,' answered Kim, with some justification. 'So I spat 'em.'

'She didn't mean that,' Rebecca said, as Amelia broke out into a husky laugh. 'That's a dirty habit. Don't let me see you doing it again.'

She went on to explain to her daughter exactly what Amelia meant by spitting and roasting the councillors and found herself grimacing at the images she was putting in her daughter's head. Halfway through her explanation Kim was distracted by a flight of aircraft coming back to base. Rebecca was thankful that she didn't have to finish her description of Mrs Floodgate being skewered on an iron spike and turned over an open fire.

'At least now I'll be able to come out here and think of Helena sometimes,' said Amelia, staring at the tree. 'That's nice. Who needs a grave? This is much better.'

Rebecca was only half listening to Amelia. She was watching the Spitfires coming in low over the village. It puzzled her.

'What are those pilots doing, Amelia? They usually approach high over the school when the wind's in this direction – now they seem to be hedge-hopping houses in the village.'

Amelia strained her poor eyes and nodded. 'You're right –

they're coming in low over the teashop, one after the other. That'll upset our Mrs Floodgate. Don't understand why they've changed the pattern, but they must know what they're doing, I suppose. You get these sudden alterations in policy. I suppose we should be pleased – we won't get so much noise now.'

However, Rebecca doubted it was a change in policy that was responsible for the new flight path. Such things as aircraft runway approaches were decided on scientific and technical data, not on policy. There was something very peculiar going on, which would probably only reveal itself after a passage of time.

After school was over for the day, Rebecca went to meet Christopher Bates. She had at last decided to go to bed with him. It was a cold decision she had made, in the early hours of the morning, and it seemed to be the right one. Christopher had avoided any talk of marriage, though he had expressed a desire to make love to Rebecca properly. She had resisted until now for reasons she actually didn't understand herself, but had now decided she was being stupidly prim.

I do find his body exciting, she thought to herself, as she walked down the avenue of trees. He's a very exciting man altogether. What am I holding back for? Certainly not my virginity. Because people might talk? Well, do I really care about *that* when the war rages around us and any one of us might be killed at any time? No, I don't.

I think I'm entitled to a bit of life too. I don't think I'm a bad mother to Kim – she's not going to suffer because her mother goes to bed with a man out of wedlock. Certainly Amelia doesn't approve of Chris, but she wouldn't care about us not being married. She'd be a bit hypocritical if she did, after telling me *her* life story. She doesn't approve of Chris because she believes he wastes his money. Well, that's his to waste if he wishes, isn't it? We're all too eager to judge one another, find fault, tell people how they should live.

No, I really think it's time I loosened up a little and let myself enjoy life, instead of mooning around grieving over Alan for the rest of my days.

Nevertheless, by the time she reached Christopher Bates's house she was experiencing a mild anxiety. Her stomach was in a tight knot. *Was* she doing the right thing? She stared up and down the empty street, gathered herself together, and then slipped down a path still covered with last autumn's dead leaves, to knock on the door.

There were footsteps in the hall behind the door's coloured-glass panel that showed a boat and a plough interlocked, then the door opened. Chris stood there, dressed in a casual jacket and tieless shirt, with grey slacks and claret carpet slippers. He motioned for her to enter, smiling broadly. Then he glanced out of the door before shutting it firmly behind her.

She undid the belt of her coat. 'You're worried someone will see us?'

'Only for your sake,' he murmured, smiling, reaching for her coat. 'You have a reputation to consider – the owner of Gradge Lodge School. Parents wouldn't like it.'

'Yes, well, they're not starved of a physical relationship like I am, are they?' she said.

'Like *we* are,' he murmured. 'Anyway, there's *my* reputation to consider too. I'm the local doctor. Sick people like to think their doctor is considering their condition twenty-four hours a day, with no distractions.'

He hung her coat on the knob at the bottom of the stair rail. 'Hooks pull coats out of shape,' he said, 'and we'll be using the bed, won't we?'

He placed a warm hand on her bare shoulder as she entered the living room. She trembled involuntarily, surprising herself by feeling a shiver of lust go through her body. In a large mirror above the fireplace she saw that Chris was regarding her greedily. She was wearing a low-cut black dress, with a black slip beneath. Rebecca knew that black suited her and made her look desirable – Alan had often told her so – and she had decided that if they were going to do it, then she was going all out for it, with all the trimmings, including lace-topped stockings.

'Are – are we eating first?' she asked.

Chris seemed to tear his eyes away from her. 'What? Oh, oh yes.' He busied himself then, fetching her a drink. 'It's old cask sherry,' he explained. 'My father bought several crates of the stuff and never drank it himself. It's rather dry but I like it.'

She took a sip and found she liked it too.

In the dining room, Chris drew back a chair from the table, which had been laid with a white cloth, candlesticks and two intimate place settings. There was more wine on the table. Was this more secret contraband from his father's cellar? She hoped it wasn't illicit fare, purchased by Chris on the black market. Rebecca detested the black market.

She took her seat at the table and waited with growing anxiety while Chris went out to fetch the chicken he had roasted. When he returned with the dish, the smell of which made Rebecca's stomach churn with apprehension rather than appetite, he lit the candles and turned out the main light. Steaming potatoes and cabbage were brought from the depths of his unseen kitchen. He fussed around with the table, then with her chair, making sure she was completely comfortable. One or two things about the state of the room seemed to bother him and he had to put them right before returning to his main task of serving the meal.

A second glass of sherry made Rebecca feel a little light-headed. The atmosphere between her and Chris had altered subtly. There was little talk between them now and the atmosphere was strained. He broke off conversation awkwardly to sharpen a knife in such a thorough and considered manner it nearly drove her crazy. Then he proceeded to carve the chicken. His actions were very slow and deliberate.

Finally Rebecca cried, 'I can't stand it – let's go to bed now – please, Christopher. I want to get it over with.'

He looked up in surprise. 'Get it . . . What do you think's going to happen? It's not surgery, you know.'

Mortified by her own outburst, Rebecca lowered her head. 'I'm sorry. I'm just wound up, that's all. I want you. I can't wait until we've eaten. I'm sorry if the meal will be spoiled, but I can't sit here making polite chitchat for another hour. I want to go to bed *now*.'

'Fair enough,' he said quietly, putting the carving knife and fork carefully on the edge of the serving dish. 'Would you like to follow me?' He took her hand.

When they were in the bedroom, where a faint light came from the landing through the open doorway, he took her in his arms and kissed her. She responded passionately, covering his mouth with her own, her breath hot and musty in her nostrils.

'Hey,' he said, gently, 'is that the sherry talking?'

'A little bit,' she said. 'Do you mind?'

'If you need Dutch courage, who am I to say nay?' he said. Then he let her go and began to take off his clothes without looking at her.

Rebecca watched him for a second, then moved awkwardly away, turning her back to him, and unbuttoned the black dress. She let it drop in a heap around her ankles and found she couldn't go any further. She could see herself in the dressing-table mirror, the light from the hallway outside shimmering on her black silk slip, and she was horrified to realise she had put it on inside out. She could see the ridge of the seam running down one side.

She turned, stepped past Chris, and shut the door with a bang.

'Hey?' said Chris from out of the darkness. 'I wanted to see you . . .'

'Next time,' she said quickly. 'I'm – I'm a little shy in front of you at the moment.'

Why had it upset her so much, that her slip had been the wrong way round? It really didn't matter and in the circumstances, in his state, Chris probably wouldn't have noticed. And what if he had? It wouldn't have bothered him, she was sure. Yet it bothered *her*. Rebecca was a careful dresser and it was indicative of the state of mind she had been in when preparing for the evening. There was something not quite right about what she was doing with this man.

Still, she told herself wryly, it was too late now. She might as well enjoy all the physical contact she could get out of it tonight and worry about her doubts in the morning. She removed the rest of her clothes and almost launched herself at him across the room. He fell on the bed with her, laughing, still wearing his socks and vest, and she climbed on top of him in her eagerness to have him inside her.

Once there, she lost all her inhibitions and her anxious drive. They made love slowly and gently at first, gradually building up an explosion of passion between them, until they were rocking violently, using each other's bodies as anchor points. Rebecca reached her climax twice before Chris groaned and went limp in her arms. They lay on the top of the bedcovers, the perspiration growing cold on their bodies, for some time afterwards. Then Chris got up and dressed.

'Can I use your bathroom?' she asked him in the darkness.

'Of course,' came the answer.

She grabbed her clothes in a bundle, opened the door and found her way to the bathroom. Once there, she washed under the basin taps. There was no hot water but she managed. Then she dressed as smartly as she could in the cold air of the bathroom before going down to help Christopher warm up their interrupted meal.

'Well, that wasn't too bad, was it?' he asked an hour later, putting his knife and fork down on his empty plate.

'It was fine,' smiled Rebecca.

'And we're both fulfilled, in more ways than one?' he questioned.

'Let's say I feel a lot better,' she said. 'I hope you enjoyed it too.'

'Wonderful,' he confirmed, leaning back in his chair. 'Now

tell me, how are you managing with the school? What about this damage? Is Jarvis going to rebuild for you?'

'He *was* – until Ma Floodgate put her oar in the water.'

'Hmmm,' Chris looked thoughtful. 'Well, I'll have a word with her, but you know what she's like when she gets a bee in her bonnet. I can't put any pressure on her – the damn woman's never sick. I mean if she had TB or something I could refuse to treat her until she changed her attitude towards you . . .'

'Christopher, that's not funny.'

'Oh, it works, I can assure you. Anyway' – he leant forward in his chair – 'if you like, I can manage Jarvis for you, once the thing is allowed to go ahead. I mean, I can probably get a cheaper price out of him. If you let me have the money, I'll see what I can do to reduce the costs.'

Rebecca shook her head. 'That won't be necessary, thanks – I can manage it. I'm capable.'

'I'm sure you are, but being an old resident of the village, I could do better. If it embarrasses you that I'm willing to do it as a friend, we could agree on some sort of commission – say, ten per cent, for me to act as your go-between. I think that's the usual fee for a consultant in the building trade.'

Chris was leaning forward now, staring at her intently.

'Chris, I've just told you, we don't need any help.'

He looked irritated. 'Of course you need help – you're a woman trying to handle men's affairs. If you'd just let me give you some assistance . . .'

'No, thank you,' she replied emphatically. 'Why do you have to spoil a perfectly delightful evening with this silly talk about women needing help? I'm fine, I tell you.'

A sour expression crossed his handsome features. 'Fine – sure you are. You're so fine Jarvis is going to start work tomorrow, isn't he? That's how fine you are. If you'd just let me handle it, it *would* be fine. You really don't know how to deal with these people. I do. I could have the man there before noon tomorrow morning.'

'Not because you've just made love to me and feel tender towards me, but because you need a ten per cent commission?'

He slammed the flats of his palms down hard on the table, making the cutlery and plates clatter.

'That's not fair. Of course I want to do it for you because I'm fond of you. But look – I'll be frank with you, Rebecca, because I know you'll understand. I have certain financial commitments – difficulties – that have to be overcome. Once they're out of the way, I'll be all right. You could help me with this, as a friend . . .'

'As a lover,' she corrected.

'All right, yes – as a lover. You could help your lover out of a hole. After all, it isn't as if it was your money, is it? I mean, it's the school's. I'm not suggesting you give it to me, or even lend it – you could employ me. It would all be perfectly legitimate and above-board. It's something you could do for me, Rebecca.'

Chris had never been this forthright over money before and Rebecca wondered whether he had brought the subject up now because he felt he had a hold over her. They had made love just an hour earlier, and she had enjoyed it. It had wiped from her mind for a short time all her worries and concerns. She felt physically relaxed for the first time in many months. She hadn't even thought of Alan while they were thrashing around on the bedcovers. At the time the absolute ecstasy, the beautiful thrills that ran through her, were all she had cared about. Now they were over and she was being manipulated by the man who had produced them.

'Christopher,' she said evenly. 'I don't owe you anything, do I?'

'Owe me anything?' he repeated in a high voice. 'Of course you don't *owe* me anything. I just thought . . .'

'I do not want a go-between,' she said emphatically. 'If you want to borrow money from me, then I'll be quite happy to lend you some.'

'Then I'll just owe *you*, instead of the bloody bookie,' he grumbled. 'No change in the status quo.'

'I can't *give* it to you – not if it's as large an amount as it seems to be. I don't have that much and I have a daughter to think about. How much is it?'

He mentioned a sum and she winced. 'I can lend you half that much, take it or leave it, but you are not managing my affairs for me.'

He sighed in a bitter fashion, as if it were her fault that he was in debt in the first place. 'Oh, I'll take it, thank you very much. When can I have it? Tomorrow?'

'I'll draw it out in the morning.'

'Thank you.' The sullen expression vanished as he suddenly grinned.

He lifted a half-empty wine glass. 'Hey, here's to us. Look, I may be a bad lad where finances are concerned, but heck, I'm nice to beautiful women, aren't I? Did I ever tell you you're the most beautiful woman this side of the Thames? It's been a great evening, hasn't it? Have some more wine.'

'No, I'd better be going,' she replied, getting up.

'It's not because . . .'

'No, no, I really do have to be getting back. Where's my coat? Oh, on the banisters. Thank you for a lovely meal, Chris – you're a good cook, aren't you?'

'Not bad. I do my own housework too. I'm not afraid of women's work.'

She forced a smile. 'Actually, it's just *work*,' she said.

Walking along the avenue in the darkness, back to the school, with the March wind soughing through the trees around her, Rebecca was terribly disappointed and very unhappy. She knew she couldn't see Chris again, not in a romantic way. He wasn't the man she had thought him to be. She knew she was a harsh judge, but it mattered to her that a man was open and honest from the start, and didn't try to use her to get what he wanted before throwing himself on her mercy. If he had come to her in a dignified fashion and asked her to lend him money, she would have had more respect for him. Or would she? No, she had to be honest with *herself*: she would have been disappointed in him however he had handled it – because the truth was, she didn't really love him. If you love someone, she told herself, *nothing* matters. But if you don't love them, *everything* matters. There was the truth of it. She had thought she was growing to love someone, but she was wrong.

But the future was going to be bleak. If there was no Chris, then there was no love to look forward to. She knew Martin was interested in her, but she could not respond to him. Martin was the universal friend, but not to be contemplated in the role of lover. He was too – well, he was dear old Martin.

When she got back to her room she took down a copy of Luke's poems from the shelf and, after reading one or two of her favourites, she cried herself to sleep.

Chapter Twenty-Six

Janet King, one of the teachers, was retiring from the school and Francine Knole had put an advertisement in the newspapers for a replacement. She had asked Rebecca if, as owner of the school, she wished to assist in the selection of a replacement teacher. Rebecca, conscious of Francine Knole's feelings about a head teacher needing to manage without interference from others, decided to let Francine handle it on her own.

'No, the staff are your responsibility, Francine. I'll accept whoever you choose.'

Amelia Sartour shook her head when she heard the decision. 'You'll regret it, Rebecca. It's always wise to see who the head teacher's bringing into the school. You should leave the actual selection up to her, but you should be present to prevent any catastrophes occurring.'

'Well, I've given her a free hand now,' said Rebecca. 'I can hardly go back on it.'

The truth was that Rebecca was far too busy trying to sort out the rebuilding of the school. She was surprised one morning when Mr Jarvis and his two daughters turned up saying they were ready to start work.

'What about Mrs Floodgate?' asked Rebecca.

'Ah, well, you see,' rumbled Mr Jarvis in his deep Essex accent, 'that's all been sorted out. Seems the planes can't fly over the school till the repairs 'ave been done, on account of the structure of the walls being weak. So they 'ave to fly over the teashop, causin' all sorts of havoc. Mrs Floodgate's losing her custom over the noise, she is. It were all explained to her by one of the pilots from the camp.'

'What was explained to her?' asked Rebecca, feeling a little out of her depth.

'That the school had to be repaired afore the planes stopped flying over the teashop,' said Mr Jarvis patiently.

'Plates was fallin' off the Welsh dresser,' chipped in one of the daughters.

'Trays of teacups was spillin',' said the other.

Rebecca shrugged. 'Well, I don't really understand why the aircraft had to go that way round, or why they believed the school wasn't structurally sound, but I'm very happy you've come to work on our repairs. I'll make sure you're supplied with tea throughout the day, then you won't need to go dashing off to Mrs Floodgate's and suffer all that noise.'

Mr Jarvis smiled. 'Ar, very important that,' he said.

Rebecca went away from the meeting feeling in a very positive mood. She saw Fay talking to Christopher Bates in the corridor and managed to duck into a doorway until he had gone. Fay came by her and Rebecca stepped out.

Fay jumped and put her hand on her heart. 'Gosh, you startled me.'

'Sorry,' said Rebecca. 'I – er – I noticed you talking to Dr Bates.'

Fay wrinkled her nose. 'Yes, he was coming on a bit strong, as usual. He doesn't seem to realise I'm a happily married lady these days.'

Despite her new feelings about Chris, Rebecca was a little shocked. 'What do you mean?' she asked. Fay was unaware of how deeply Rebecca had become entangled with Chris, since she was so engrossed in her new married life.

'Well, you know how he is, always trying it on. I never took him up on his offers *before* I got married, so I don't know why he should think I would now. Unless he thinks I'm not happy with Bill. Well, I soon put him straight.'

'Offers?' repeated Rebecca faintly.

Fay said, 'Rebecca, you are dense sometimes. You must have had a sheltered upbringing. Christopher Bates has been trying to get me into his bed ever since I arrived here. That or borrowing money from me. He's incorrigible. Surely you've been told all this before, if not by me, by someone else.'

Rebecca was stunned, but there was a growing fury in her, directed towards herself and her own stupidity. This was mingled with a sense of relief, that she had got out of a situation before she was too enmeshed. Only just in time though, she thought. Yes, I *am* dense.

'Well, I suppose Amelia did try to warn me against him.'

'Anyway, I sent him away with a flea in his ear – you haven't been lending him money, have you?' asked Fay, with sudden realisation.

'Well, yes I have,' admitted Rebecca. 'I lent him some the other day.'

'You'll be lucky to see that back.'

'I'd better. It was rather a lot,' said Rebecca. 'I can't afford to let him walk away with it.'

Fay shook her head. 'You'll have to fight tooth and nail for it, ducks.' The blonde-headed teacher then stared out of the window, down into the courtyard. 'Oh, good – Jarvis has started at last, has he? Bill's plan worked then?'

'Bill's plan?' repeated Rebecca stupidly, feeling she was being bombarded with revelations concerning her own ignorance.

Fay laughed. 'Yes, he told all his pilot pals to fly low over the teashop, instead of high over the school. It was a bit dangerous and the CO got shirty about it, because they were coming in on a slight crosswind. Ma Floodgate's convinced they had to do it, though. She thinks the school's in such a fragile state it might fall over with the slightest gust of wind or loud noise. Wonderful, my Bill, isn't he?'

'The best,' nodded Rebecca. 'Now, have you any more bombshells for me this morning, or can I safely go on my way and know that I'm up to date on all the schemes and plans for the welfare of the school and my private life.'

'You are in a funny mood,' laughed Fay. 'Yes, there is something else. Actually, I've been looking for you all morning. Do you believe in miracles, Rebecca?'

Fay was obviously brimming with some kind of news. There was a smile hovering around the corners of her mouth and a sense that she was anticipating a strong reaction from Rebecca. Rebecca hated this kind of tantalising, which she knew some people thrived on, the *guess what*? game, which was supposed to make the listener eager and excited. It simply made Rebecca frustrated and she let Fay know it.

'Don't toy with me, Fay. What is it?'

'*Don't toy with me, Fay,*' growled Fay in mock echo, refusing to allow her humour to be dampened by Rebecca's brisk manner. 'Why shouldn't I *toy* with you – you pompous old thing? I've got good news – *very* good news – and I'm going to tell it to you in my own way, so you can jolly well relax a little, Mrs Daniels.'

Rebecca sighed. 'Oh, all right – but I've got a lot of work to do, Fay – honestly.'

'It'll wait for this, I can assure you.'

'For goodness sakes, what *is* it?' cried Rebecca.

Fay's eyes were shining. 'It's *Luke* – he's alive and well – relatively well. He's in a POW camp. Bill heard through the Red Cross. Seems he was picked up by a ship on its way to Singapore. He was ill in hospital for a long time, from head injuries in the crash . . .'

Rebecca was stunned for the second time that morning.

'That's – that's wonderful news,' she said at last, the joy flooding through her with the realisation of what Fay was saying to her. 'Luke, still alive. I can hardly believe it – it is a miracle.' After a few moments, however, the irony of Luke's situation hit her. 'But the Japanese overran Singapore – oh, that's what you meant by being in a POW camp? Luke's a prisoner of the Japanese.'

Fay's expression changed to a serious one 'Yes, I'm sorry, Rebecca. But he's *still alive*, when we thought he was dead. God must be looking after him, mustn't he?'

'Oh, Fay, I hope so.'

Having waited agonising hours and days for news of Alan from the beaches at Dunkirk, only to be told in the end that he was amongst the dead, then for information on her father and uncle, subsequently to learn they had been killed in the Channel, Rebecca was tuned to expecting only bad news from the war.

'Luke – still alive,' she whispered, half to herself, though Fay obviously heard her.

'You're very happy, aren't you?' said Fay. 'I mean, more than you would be just for a friend of mine.'

'Any human life . . .' began Rebecca quietly.

'Yes, yes, I know *that*,' laughed Fay impatiently, 'but Luke means more than just any human life, doesn't he?'

Rebecca's voice dropped even further, so that Fay could hardly hear what she said.

'I think I'm in love with him, Fay.'

'Think?'

'Well, I fought against it for a long time, wouldn't let myself be . . . in love with Luke. I don't know why.'

'I do,' Fay said, gently. 'It's because you're a rotten snob, Mrs Daniels. Just like Martin. It's a pity you couldn't have fallen in love with Martin – you're so much alike . . . no, on reflection I don't think that's really fair. Martin gets infatuated easily, while you fall in love with enormous difficulty. You fight against it for some reason. I think, deep down, you're a very passionate person, Rebecca, only you let shallow things get in the way of that passion. I think you're frightened of the primal woman inside you.'

Rebecca smiled. 'You know me so well, Mrs Ryker. Yes, I suppose I am – or was – a snob. But just before Luke went on that last fateful flight, something happened, inside me. We were standing – here – almost on this very spot – talking. I felt

– oh Fay, I *wanted* him, you know? It frightened me. I'd never allowed myself to have those sort of feelings, physical feelings, in a public place – but I couldn't help myself. I wanted Luke, and I knew then that it was more than physical.'

'Metaphysical, you mean?' joked Fay, still teasing her. 'Oh, I'm sorry, Rebecca – you are funny. Why shouldn't you get those feelings? You're not a nun. I should think even nuns get them, anyway. But I'm so glad – of course I'm glad about you and Luke. My two best friends, in love with one another. You knew he loved you, didn't you?'

'Did he?' asked Rebecca eagerly. 'You're sure? I sort of felt, well – he seemed to chase me quite a bit.'

'And you ran away quite a bit. Of course he was in love with you – desperately in love. Did you get to tell him about how you felt – before he . . .'

Rebecca went red with shame. 'No, no – I – no. But I must write to him now. I shan't tell him yet, of course – just establish contact again.'

'Just establish contact again,' repeated Fay, shaking her head sadly. 'Oh, Rebecca. Well, if you want to do it that way, face to face, then it's your choice. Personally I'd send him a letter that would burn down the post office, but still, that's me, not you. You must do it in your own way. Good luck, lovey. I think it's wonderful, that Luke's alive and that you love each other – even if you're the only one that knows it. I'm sure it'll all work out in the end.'

'I hope so, Fay – I just hope he survives that POW camp. I just hope . . .'

'Luke?' snorted Fay. 'It'll take more than a prison camp to finish him off. You wait and see. Got to go now. I'll see you later and we can talk some more. All right?'

'All right,' smiled Rebecca. 'And thanks – thanks for the best news I've ever had.'

'Yes, it is, isn't it?'

Rebecca stood in the same spot for at least ten minutes, staring out through the window at the beautiful Essex countryside that was emerging from the mist. The sun had some strength in it now and was driving away the morning haze with some determination. Trees were unclothed, hedgerows appeared, and houses materialised slowly and shyly from their secret hideouts. In the distance a brook glinted like a silver snake.

Luke was alive. It was wonderful news. After reading through his volumes of poetry Rebecca felt she knew Luke almost as well as she knew herself now. Underneath the casual, cheerful exterior Luke was a sensitive and intuitive observer of the natural world and its human inhabitants. His insight sometimes startled her with its incisiveness. Luke could look at a scene and find the beginnings or the end of an empire, such as in his poem 'Last Hours'.

Having got to know the real man, Rebecca was deeply in love with him. Yet she realised she had blotted her copybook for ever. He had offered friendship and she had rejected it, for the worst of reasons – because she was a bigot.

It's true, she told herself, I didn't want anything to do with him because I believed he came from a lower class. I felt myself to be his superior, intellectually and in station. Well, it was possible that both were true – he was not an *intellectual* poet, more of an instinctive one – but his enormous talent was evident in his work.

And what if it weren't? Would she still be entitled to look down on him because of what she had seen as his failings? Of course not. She had acted in a crass and despicable fashion and she was thoroughly ashamed of herself. It had made her miserable and she knew she deserved to be so. It made her realisation of love that much harder for her.

Suffer, you worthless woman, she told herself. *But try not to enjoy that suffering too much.*

She would write to Luke. It was possible she might be able to salvage some sort of contact with him. He might not write back, but he was a forgiving soul and there was just a chance he would.

With this hopeful prospect in mind Rebecca at last unfroze herself from the spot and walked the length of the corridor, pausing to glance into the classrooms at the teachers and their pupils, enjoying the peacefulness of the morning after a night when the Germans had overflown the village in their droves.

She turned the corner of the corridor to come face to face with Francine Knole accompanied by a man. She recognised the man immediately – she could never forget that nose – and she felt the blood rush to her face. It took him a few seconds longer, but then he too showed by his expression that he remembered who she was. He smirked: a particular habit of his which had always infuriated her. His face told her a great deal at that moment. He believed he was encountering one of the more junior teachers in the school he was visiting and he had no need for deference.

'Ah, Rebecca,' smiled Francine Knole, 'I'm glad I've run into you. We would have been coming to see you later, once I'd shown Mr Sinclair round the school. This is Mr Sinclair.

313

He applied for the vacant post and amongst the candidates, most of whom were unqualified I have to add' – Francine gave a little shudder indicating how she felt about people who tried to enter her profession without the relevant training – 'Mr Sinclair seems the most suitable. He has been the headmaster of a state-run Tilbury school and I think we'll be lucky to get him.'

'Mr Sinclair and I already know each other,' said Rebecca, savouring the moment. 'We taught at the same school.'

'Indeed we did.' Sinclair smiled greasily. 'I was the headmaster as I recall, and you taught one of my classes.'

'What an extraordinary coincidence,' said Francine Knole. 'You were previously both at the same school?'

'Mr Sinclair was my superior,' admitted Rebecca. She was ashamed to feel relish as, after a short pause for effect, she said deliberately, 'How strange that our roles should now be reversed.'

The condescending smile left Sinclair's face immediately, to be replaced by a puzzled expression.

Francine Knole enlightened Sinclair with, 'Mrs Daniels is the owner of Gradge Lodge School.'

Sinclair stared blankly for a few moments, then said, 'But – but the notepaper heading?'

'Oh yes, my letter,' laughed Francine Knole. 'Well, this is wartime you know, we have to conserve our paper supplies. That was the old headed notepaper, from when Miss Sartour was the owner of the school. Mrs Daniels is Miss Sartour's great-niece and though Miss Sartour is still alive Mrs Daniels has inherited the school. Miss Sartour is quite elderly now and was pleased to hand over the responsibility. Now, if you'll

314

follow me, Mr Sinclair, I'll show you the rest of the school . . .'

It was an unhappy, shambling Mr Sinclair who followed the headmistress along the corridor. He glanced back once at the triumphant Rebecca and then walked on looking as if someone had just removed a few of his internal organs and tossed them on the rubbish heap. He sagged, he dragged his feet, his large head had sunk low on his shoulders. He seemed hardly to be paying attention to Francine Knole's lecturing voice, but appeared more interested in his own distant feet and the path they trod.

Later, Francine Knole came to the office she and Rebecca shared. 'Well, what do you think?' she asked Rebecca. 'I mean of Mr Sinclair?'

'Is he really the best qualified of the applicants?' asked Rebecca.

'By far. We've had one ex-postmistress, two elderly teachers who were almost falling over their feet – Amelia could have beaten them in a race up the school drive – and a seventeen-year-old girl who was fit and healthy, but again, no qualifications. This is wartime, Rebecca.'

Rebecca sighed. 'I know, I know. I have to tell you, Francine, that man was responsible for me leaving my last school. He's a predator, he's vindictive – he's a multitude of things that I despise in a man. We must protect our girls.'

Francine's face fell. 'Oh, I didn't realise.'

'Is he still here?'

'Yes.'

'Let me have a word with him on my own please, Francine. I know I said I would leave the recruitment to you, but I think under the circumstances I need to speak to this particular applicant alone. Would that upset you?'

Francine shook her head. 'No, of course not. We must be sure we're getting the best of what's available for the school, but we can't employ people who might be more trouble than they're worth. I'll send him in.'

Francine went out and a few moments later Sinclair came through the doorway. He closed the door quietly behind him. Rebecca thought he looked a beaten man. His face was grey and the muscles flaccid, causing his jowls to droop. His shoulders slumped. He moved his tall, heavy frame as if it were a difficult task to get it to do as he wished.

Sitting down, he said, 'I'm a good teacher.'

'Your teaching qualifications aren't in question. It's your character. You know what I think of you, and I feel I'm quite justified in those thoughts.'

He looked away from her and she saw that he had tears in his eyes. 'I'm a damn good teacher,' he said again. 'No one can take that away from me.'

'Why are you leaving Tilbury?' asked Rebecca.

He drew himself up and stared at her haughtily. 'I felt it was time to gain more experience in the private sector. I'm getting older and I would like to teach as long as I can. It would be pleasant to end my days at a sedate private school.'

Rebecca stared at him and repeated her question. 'Why are you leaving Tilbury, Mr Sinclair?'

His face collapsed again. 'They're showing me the door – pushing me out.' Stephen Sinclair started to sound angry, like the Sinclair of old. 'After all these years,' he growled bitterly. 'They're forcing me to leave.'

'Why? And no fabrications this time, because I'll certainly make enquiries. Why are they sacking you?'

'They're not *sacking* me,' he growled. 'I'm leaving because they're making it intolerable to work there. They're appointing teachers without consulting me, they're reorganising my curriculum for me, they're telling me how many children the school can cope with in terms of numbers in the classroom. All my responsibilities are being eroded. I won't stand it. If you don't give me a job here, I'll find somewhere else.'

'It'll be difficult for you.'

'I don't care. I won't be dictated to by a bunch of shopkeepers.'

She knew he meant the school governors.

'You'll be dictated to here.'

He looked up, his expression frank. 'That's different – here I *choose* to be one of the staff. If I'm to go back to teaching classes again, then I'll do it, to the best of my ability. That's quite a different position. I'd take a job as a park keeper rather than be bullied.'

Now you know what it feels like, thought Rebecca.

'Are you sure you're not being dismissed for some other reason? You know what I mean. You gave me a hard time when I was at that school, with your unwanted attentions and *your* bullying. I don't want to recommend your appointment to Miss Knole then hear that some young teacher has been molested.'

He looked at her sharply. 'There's nothing like that – you can check if you like. Look, I've nowhere else to go. I've tried other schools. They're all suspicious of a headmaster taking a step down to teaching again. I haven't bothered anyone – not since you. You – *excited* me. I'm sorry, I know it wasn't your fault, but I would have done anything to get you – even ruined my own life. Silly, but there it is.'

'And what about now?' she said, feeling slightly flattered by what he had told her, and hating herself for it. 'We'll still be in the same school.'

'I think I've learned my lesson,' he said grimly. Then more truthfully: 'I don't like you much now anyway, Mrs Daniels. You're too – too ready to be *right*.'

Rebecca accepted this without a blink. 'This is a *girls'* school, Mr Sinclair. How can we be sure we can trust you?'

He looked disgusted. 'I'm not a damned paedophile, Mrs Daniels. I don't chase after little girls.'

'Mature women only?'

Sinclair sighed. 'Even mature women don't interest me much these days, Mrs Daniels. I need a job, not complications.'

When she was satisfied she had got every ounce of truth out of him, Rebecca told him she was going to recommend his appointment. 'We need a good teacher. You'll be on probation for a year . . .'

'A whole *year*?'

'Yes, a whole year. Then if you've proved yourself to be suitable we'll retain your services. The least hint of any unsavoury behaviour on your part and you're out. I hope you understand that? There won't be any inquest. I'll just tell you to leave. If you feel you can come to us under such an arrangement, then I'll speak to Miss Knole.'

His pallor and demeanour improved after these words. 'I'll

do my very best, I can assure you. I understand you have another male teacher at the school?'

'The Reverend Martin Simkins.'

'I shall look forward to meeting him. Presumably our rooms will be close to each other, in the same wing?'

'You'll probably have to bunk with him for a while, until the repairs to the school are completed. Will that give you a problem?'

Sinclair raised his eyebrows. 'No, no,' he said after a while, 'this is wartime after all. I saw the damage as I came up the driveway. A stray bomb, I understand. Awful thing to happen. The Germans are making it hell for some of us.'

'Certain locals are slightly worse than the Germans at making it hell for us, Mr Sinclair, as you'll probably find out.'

With that enigmatic remark in his ears, Stephen Sinclair left the office in search of Francine Knole.

Chapter Twenty-Seven

Skirts were getting shorter due to the scarcity of material, much to Francine Knole's disapproval. She disliked her staff virtually showing their knees. Legs were not conducive to the dignified image of the school. She said she would be glad to contribute some of her own clothes if it meant that her staff went about properly and appropriately attired. Francine Knole was a fussy dresser nearly a century behind in her ideas of fashion. It was not surprising that no one took her up on her generous offer. Fay almost died with embarrassment at having to refuse a frock offered her by Francine which she later remarked would have drowned her in frills and lace.

Another shortage had the pupils of Gradge Lodge School reeling in horror. There was to be sweet rationing. Those girls whose rich parents provided them with unlimited pocket money paled at the prospect. The playing fields were being levelled: princesses were forced into equal shares with peasant maids. The less well off decided eventually that it was a good thing.

Annette Bailey, a third-year girl, said it was the start of Communism in Britain and that Karl Marx would soon be as revered as Shakespeare.

Sarah Biggs, a second-year hoarder and one of the school's best hockey players, began a reign as queen of a flourishing black market in sweets.

Fay and Bill were found a little cottage by Martin. It had been empty for some time and needed work on it to drive out the cold and damp, but the pair were delighted with it. There was a prospect of Bill being posted away from RAF Hornchurch now that he could no longer fly, and they wanted to make the most of their time together. Fay had announced her intention of following Bill wherever he went, but though this romantic ideal was laudable, it was impracticable. It was more than likely that Bill would be sent somewhere Fay could not go: perhaps the Middle East or Burma. The couple busied themselves decorating, cleaning, repairing someone else's property with the enthusiasm that only newlyweds can produce.

Stephen Sinclair seemed to settle at the school without any problems. Amelia, the only person who knew the full story apart from the two involved parties, had been shocked at Rebecca's decision to allow him on the staff.

'What if he attacks one of the teachers? Or worse still, one of the girls?'

Rebecca was spoon-feeding Amelia the medicine she disliked taking and avoided when she could. 'Open wide, Amelia!'

'I'm not a child.'

'Then stop acting like one. Oh, Sinclair isn't a sex maniac – he just forced his attentions on *me*. I don't think he's going to jump on one of the staff and rape them. If he tries anything – anything at all – he's out. He knows that. I've told him there

322

won't be any inquest to establish innocence or guilt – I'll take the word of others against him.'

Amelia swallowed the medicine with a look of disgust on her features. 'Well, I hope you know what you're doing.'

Rebecca shook her head. 'Of course I don't know what I'm doing. I'm brand new to the job of managing a school. But I have to make decisions, one way or the other. I hope Sinclair behaves himself, but I'm certain he's not going to go around squeezing breasts or anything as crass as that. He's a good teacher too, believe it or not. The girls don't seem to find him as sleazy as women like you and me.'

'I've never met the man,' protested Amelia, 'and I'm sure I don't want to. He sounds a boor. I don't have to either, these days – that's your job. How are the school repairs coming along?'

'Wonderfully,' smiled Rebecca, putting down the sticky spoon and medicine bottle. 'Jarvis and his daughters are working away like mad. He's quite fit for such an old pers . . .' She stopped her sentence halfway through.

Amelia said, 'You may well pause in your words, miss. Jarvis is twenty years younger than me.'

Rebecca laughed. 'Yes, of course. But the women are magnificent too. They work like Trojans. You should see them carrying hods of bricks up and down the ladders. It makes me wince just to watch them.'

'No thank you. You forget, I was once good at masculine pursuits. I was the best shot in the outback. That's how I got my first man.'

'*First* man?'

'There's still time for another one,' snapped Amelia. 'Now,

323

this fellow Sinclair, you say he's quite good-looking for his age and he's not fussy about his women?'

Rebecca laughed. 'Amelia, you are a terrible lady. Anyway, what do you mean, not fussy about his women? It was me he set his sights on.'

'That's what I mean,' joked the old woman, clearly enjoying herself. 'Not fussy at all.'

Rebecca reached for the medicine bottle and Amelia growled, 'Pax!'

The talk then went on to the discovery that Luke Adams was still alive, though a prisoner of war.

Singapore, a terrible defeat for the British, had fallen under the swift onslaught of poorly equipped but resourceful Japanese soldiers on bicycles. It was an ignominious reverse for a nation with a fading empire: one they would never fully live down. Singapore's big guns had been facing out to sea and the enemy had come down the Malay peninsula through dense jungle at breakneck speed. A hundred and thirty thousand British troops were now prisoners of the Imperial Japanese Army on a small island in the Far East.

'They'll treat him well, won't they?' asked Rebecca anxiously.

'It's difficult to know,' said Amelia. 'You have to understand the Japanese mentality. They are taught, like the Spartans, to die rather than surrender. When a man is taken prisoner he loses all honour, becomes less than human, becomes a low kind of animal which can be treated with contempt. I'm afraid they might be brutal.'

'How do you know this?'

'There were Japanese immigrants in Australia. I got to

know some of them very well. Deep down, people are basically the same – some decent, some not so decent – but during times of war it's the surface customs that prevail. Soldiers are always under observation and the guards on the camps will do what they believe is expected of them publicly, even if they abhor their own behaviour privately. Luke's in for a bad time, my dear, and we must pray that he'll be strong enough to come through it all.'

That evening Rebecca took Amelia's advice literally. She went to the little room that had been turned into a chapel under Martin's guidance and prayed to God that Luke would survive his trials. She had heard it said that the Japanese were forever short on supplies and the prisoners starved, thus exposing them to disease.

'Please God,' she whispered, 'don't let him die.'

'Rebecca? Oh, I'm dreadfully sorry – I wasn't sure what was happening, the light in here is poor . . .'

Martin had entered the chapel and now turned to leave.

'Don't go, Martin,' she said, not getting off her knees. 'Just come and kneel by me for a few moments, would you?'

Martin returned quietly and, rather self-consciously for a priest, knelt down beside Rebecca. He put his hand upon her head, gently.

He asked quietly, 'What are we praying for?'

'For Luke Adams, in a Japanese POW camp,' said Rebecca.

'Dear Lord,' intoned Martin, still in the same soft voice, 'we ask for the safe keeping of our brother, Luke Adams, now in the hands of our enemies. Keep him from the evil that men do unto their fellow men. Keep him from the ravages of disease and hunger. Bring him safely back to these shores again, that we might rejoice in his homecoming. We ask it in the name of the Father, the Son and the Holy Spirit, Amen.'

'Amen,' whispered Rebecca.

She stood up and walked to the entrance to the chapel and Martin followed her.

'Thank you.' She smiled at Martin. 'I feel much better now. We can't do very much, can we? It just seems to be a matter of hoping and praying.'

'I'm afraid so,' Martin replied, his eyes on hers. 'But praying is quite a lot.'

'Yes, I know.'

She went back to her room and began a letter to Luke which she hoped would reach him through the Red Cross. In it she made no mention of her newly discovered feelings for him, but told him about the trials and tribulations of village life, described to him the seasons they had seen since he went missing, and talked about people with whom they were both familiar. It might have been a letter from a friend or a relation, but it was not a love letter. She guessed from her treatment of him in the past that Luke would know she was feeling much more tender towards him, whatever she wrote, simply because she had bothered to send a letter at all. He would know how she felt, she was sure.

The following day, after classes were over, Rebecca took Kim to see Bill and Fay's new home. The cottage was at the eastern end of the village and backed on to a copse. The exterior cladding was of shiplap boards painted white, with crooked windows set in the planks as if they had been added as an afterthought. The front doorway was so low that Rebecca had to duck on entering, before finding herself in a tiny living room. The kitchen-scullery was attached at the back of the house, there were two bedrooms up the twisting wooden staircase, and the toilet was a privy out in the yard. It could have been the castle of a fairy princess so far as Fay was concerned.

'Don't you think it's absolutely gorgeous?' she breathed, her hair tied up with a scarf like a factory girl's and a smudge of whitewash on one cheek. 'Don't you think it's the nicest little place you've ever seen?'

Kim said with great childish enthusiasm, 'I think it's really super, Mrs Ryker. I think I would like to live here.'

'Thank you, Kim.'

Rebecca looked around her. 'Well, you've certainly done wonders with it, Fay. What are those bricks for in the corner of the room?'

'Oh, those. Bill's going to do some makeshift bookshelves with them – and a couple of planks.'

'And where is the hero of our story?'

Fay laughed. 'Up on the roof fixing some slates that have slipped. I worry about him doing things like that with his leg, but he still insists. I can't get him to come down even for a bite of lunch.'

'Shall I call him?' asked Kim.

'Yes, he might come down for you,' said Fay.

Kim went to the door and called, 'Mr Ryker?'

Bill's voice came back from somewhere above, 'Speak O angel of the Lord, thy servant heareth.'

Kim giggled. 'Don't be silly. Mrs Ryker says you're to come down for lunch. We're here to visit you.'

Bill came down a ladder outside the back window a few

moments later, moving awkwardly. He was carrying a hammer and box of nails. Greeting Kim with a smile, he said, 'Good heavens, I thought it was a cherub calling me.'

'Cherubs are baby boys,' admonished Kim. 'I'm not a little boy – I'm a girl.'

Bill looked genuinely surprised. 'Are they boys?'

'Yes they are,' said Fay. 'You don't know your theology very well, do you, Mr Ryker?'

'I guess not,' he said. 'Gee, so that's right, eh? Boys. I'd never have guessed it. Little boys with wings.'

'Just like you pilots . . .' began Rebecca, then she visibly bit her lip and looked down at his leg. 'I'm sorry, Bill.'

'Heck,' he laughed, 'I'm not worried. I'm not one of those guys who can't bear to do an ordinary job. When I had all my bits, I was prepared to fly for King and Country, but I ain't pining over the fact that I can't go up into the clouds any more. Guys are getting shot down from up there. Why should I want to be where guys are being killed? I got a good excuse.' He tapped his new metal appendage.

'We're going to have cheese and pickle, would you like some? And some tea?' asked Fay.

'Heck no – no tea. Have we got any coffee?'

'No, I'm sorry, darling.'

'Well, I'll have milk then – and cheese and pickle. Bread? Good. How about you, angel face,' he asked Kim, 'you want some milk too?'

'Yes please, Mr Ryker.'

'That's Bill to you – Uncle Bill if you like. Auntie Fay's the one over there with the apron on. Let's not have any more of this Mr Ryker stuff.'

'Well, are we going to eat, or starve?' Rebecca asked.

'Eat,' said Fay. 'Come to the dining table, it's all laid out for a banquet.'

The cheese and pickle, with some wrinkled apples, were spread on a cloth covering a couple of orange boxes. They sat on the floor, cross-legged, to eat and drink. Kim chattered happily to Bill, who was clearly her favourite for the moment. Fay and Rebecca talked about matters more serious, and eventually touched on Luke's misfortune. It was a pleasant little meal marked by a sudden thought which came to Rebecca as she looked around at her daughter and friends.

It occurred to her that they were eating in much the same way as a Japanese family might eat in their own home.

Chapter Twenty-Eight

In October that year El Alamein turned the tide for the Allies. General Montgomery had beaten Rommel in a head-to-head tank battle for the African north. There followed a period of both triumphs and defeats, but the list of the former was growing and the latter diminishing.

Rebecca and her school struggled through the next year, which was a wearing time for the whole population of Britain. The repairs were completed and the school was back to normal – as normal as it could be in wartime – but those parents who had removed their girls because of the bombing of the school never sent them back again. The war seemed to drag on and on and it was a testing time for those trying to keep the home fires burning. In September 1943, Italy surrendered unconditionally. This was cause for celebration and the school had a party.

'If the weather's good on Saturday,' said Francine Knole, 'we'll set up tables on the driveway. What do you think about that, Rebecca?'

They were having an evening staff meeting, with all the teachers present except Fay Ryker, who had gone with her husband Bill to the railway station to see him off on his journey north. He had been posted to somewhere in Scotland. Fay had said bitterly that they couldn't have posted him further away if they'd tried. It was pointed out to her that Burma was quite a lot further away than Scotland. So was North Africa. She began to realise that at least he had been posted to a relatively safe region and was somewhat cheered.

Rebecca replied, 'I think that sounds good. Some of those dining-room tables are very heavy though. Miss Sartour bought them as a job lot in Buckinghamshire. They're made of solid oak.'

Stephen Sinclair said, 'Don't worry about that – Martin and I will be able to lift them, won't we, Martin?'

Martin nodded and sighed. 'I hope so – otherwise the male of the species will suffer a deadly blow in the war of the sexes.'

'Women don't judge you by your strength, man,' growled Priscilla Mohorty. 'They judge men by their . . .'

'Sensitivity?' suggested another female teacher.

'No,' said Mohorty, 'by the shape of their bottoms.'

'Shouldn't have thought it would make any difference to *you* what shape my bottom was,' said Sinclair.

'I meant women as a whole,' snarled Mohorty. 'You're right – I'm personally not interested in men at all. They're a bunch of no-hopers. They bore the pants off me.'

'I can assure you if your pants had been bored off you by *me* you would certainly be interested,' countered Sinclair.

'Absolutely not. Wrong plumbing altogether,' crowed Mohorty.

Francine Knole was horrified by this exchange of sexual innuendo before the whole staff, some of which she only partly understood. She had thought Mr Sinclair quite a gentleman until now and she was upset and shocked to find him engaged in such a conversation. Although she was aware of Priscilla's preferences too, she didn't like this sort of thing advertised and brought out into the open.

'Please,' she said with a pained expression.

'Sorry,' said Mohorty briskly.

'Yes, my apologies too,' murmured Sinclair silkily. 'No offence intended.'

Rebecca watched all this with some amusement. She was about to make further suggestions regarding the party when the head girl burst into the common room. 'Miss Knole,' the child gasped. 'One of the girls is missing.'

'What do you mean?' asked Francine Knole.

'She's not in her bed, Miss Knole. I think she's run away from school. We can't find her anywhere.'

It was not the first time a girl had run away from the school, but it was a rare occurrence. Usually it was trouble at home and the child was trying to get back to her parents. Or it was due to bullying, which was stamped out as soon as it was discovered by the staff. One fifth-year girl had fallen in love with a circus hand and disappeared the night the circus closed. When they found her she was sent home to her parents but subsequently discovered to be pregnant. The school had taken a long time to recover from the row which ensued after that one.

Francine Knole was on her feet in an instant. 'What is the name of the girl?' she demanded.

'Its Pietra.'

'Pietra Magdalini?'

'Yes, miss.'

Rebecca groaned. 'Of course – we should have thought. This Italian business. Pietra has Italian origins.'

The head girl looked nervously surprised. 'Oh, of course, ma'am. I hadn't thought. She's – she's just Pietra to us.'

Francine Knole said sternly, 'You're not aware of any bullying or teasing in respect of Pietra, are you? Because of her Italian background?'

'No, miss,' said the sensible head girl.

Pietra Magdalini's parents lived in London. They had arrived in England before the war and ran a successful furrier's shop in the West End. The parents took out British citizenship just as the war broke out and, though taken in for questioning several times, had not been interned. They protested their loyalty towards the Allies, saying that many of their relations were American immigrants fighting against the Italians and Germans.

Francine Knole said, 'If she hasn't been bullied, why has she run away?'

'I think it's the whole business,' replied Rebecca. 'Pietra knows she's of Italian blood and here we are having a party to celebrate the downfall of her old country. Just think how you would feel if you had married an Italian and taken out citizenship there – would you enjoy a party celebrating the downfall of England?'

'No, of course not,' Martin said. 'Let's not stand around here talking – let's get out there and look for her. When did she go missing? Do you know that?' he asked the head girl.

'After lights-out, I think. I took one last walk through the dorms, to see that they were all quiet, and saw that her bed was empty. We checked the washrooms and lavatories.'

'Right,' said Francine. 'Let's search the school first. Rouse the girls. I want to speak to her dormitory. Perhaps someone knows something.'

The teachers all went their separate ways. It helped on these occasions that they had muster posts for German raids and that each teacher was in charge of a certain number of pupils and covered a particular area of the school. A search for Pietra began immediately and even Amelia's room was examined, in case the girl had sneaked in there while Amelia was asleep. A thorough examination of the school revealed nothing. Friends of the missing girl revealed that Pietra had been unusually quiet the last few days, but hadn't told anyone of her intention to run away. The teachers met again in the staff room.

'I'll alert the police, the Home Guard and the ARP,' said Martin. 'I suggest the rest of you form small parties and search the immediate district – she won't have got far if she's run off over the fields. If she's managed to catch a bus or train, then we'll leave it to the police to ask questions of the bus driver, whatever.'

Rebecca wondered why Martin seemed to be taking command of the situation when she felt it should be herself or Francine Knole, but since he acted with confidence and authority she allowed him to continue. It was possible he had some experience of this sort of thing, and in any case he didn't seem to realise that he was usurping her position, so she assumed it was some sort of natural reaction.

Rebecca teamed up with Fay who had returned. Mohorty and Julia Dane said they would check the houses and gardens in the village, along with two other teachers. Rebecca and Fay were to concentrate on the farmland to the north-east.

The pair fetched some torches from a storecupboard and set out into the darkness of the September evening. There was a strong smell of bonfire in the air, sharpened by the odour of fermenting apples. The two women clambered over the fence at the back of the school, Fay catching her precious stockings on a nail and tearing them. 'I'm glad the girls can't see us now,' she said. 'I think we'd lose a few dignity points.'

Fortunately both women had changed into sensible shoes, but nevertheless they found themselves in a cornfield where the stubble had not long been ploughed back into the ground. There had been a lot of rain over the last few days: the clods of soil were slick and slippery. It was hard going over the uneven ground and Rebecca slipped over twice, getting herself covered in mud.

'We'll be lucky to get out of this without breaking an ankle,' she said. 'I suppose we should have planned it a bit better. Why don't we make for the edge of the field and walk round the ditch?'

With the aid of their torches they found the foot-wide grassy patch between the edge of the field and the ditch and kept to this path. It was pitch black around them. They called Pietra's name as they went along, feeling that if she *were* out in darkness somewhere she would probably be glad to be found.

Trees loomed out of the darkness, tendrils of bramble bushes seemed to jump into their way and raked their legs as they passed. Rebecca was grateful that it wasn't raining, though there was a warm dampness to the air which suggested that rain might not be far away.

'If we're not careful,' muttered Fay, 'we're going to get lost ourselves.'

Rebecca realised this was a very real possibility. The torches only allowed them to see the immediate path ahead. Since the blackout was operating, there were no lights in the surrounding countryside to guide them to habitations.

'This was a bit silly in the first place, coming out here,' Rebecca admitted. 'I don't know what we expected to find. I mean, if poor Pietra is out here somewhere, we could miss her very easily in the darkness. If she's hurt herself and can't hear us for some reason . . .'

'Don't think about it,' said Fay, shuddering. 'Let's just get around this field and then make our way back to the road – I'm sure it's that way.' She pointed.

Just then they heard the distant wail of a siren going off in the opposite direction to where Fay was pointing. A few moments after the sound had died away there was the drone of aircraft overhead. Then a light suddenly sprang out of the ground a few yards ahead of Rebecca, dazzling in its brilliance. It cut through the darkness like a white knife, illuminating the packed skies above. To Rebecca's terror an earsplitting pounding began close by, explosions punching holes in the night with rapid regularity.

'What's happening?' cried Rebecca, wondering whether to stand still or run. 'What is it?'

'Searchlight. Anti-aircraft battery,' yelled Fay. 'It's over there, behind those bushes.'

Rebecca realised how stupid she was being. 'Oh, of course,' she said.

The two women made their way to the anti-aircraft gun,

which was manned by four soldiers. When they stepped into the enclosure of sandbags, a corporal saw them. His eyes widened and he almost dropped the ammunition box he was carrying.

'What are you two doing here?' he yelled.

The pounding of the gun filled Rebecca's head and she could hardly bear to think, let alone talk. She shook her head and pointed to the gun. The corporal shrugged and motioned for the two women to sit on a rough seat which had been installed in the enclosure. They did as they were told and the corporal yelled something incomprehensible to the other three soldiers. They turned to glance at the women, then went back to the business of trying to shoot down German bombers.

A few moments later the bombs began screaming down and exploding on and around Hornchurch airfield. Rebecca was aghast at the sound of the explosions, which rocked the ground beneath them. She prayed none of the bombs would hit the school, or indeed go anywhere near it. She wondered if there had been enough teachers in the school to get the girls into the shelters in time, since many were out searching for Pietra. She was especially concerned for her daughter.

Staring into the darkness at the airfield, about half a mile away, she could see two red flares burning on the ground. She wondered if they were incendiary bombs, dropped by the Germans, or something to do with the RAF station itself. Maybe the fighter pilots needed some sort of guidance when they went up? It was a puzzling aspect of the whole scene, but one which would have to wait for explanations.

At the present time all she could do was press her hands to her ears to avoid being deafened. What with the big gun just a few feet away and the bombs raining down on the airfield, it was like being imprisoned in a large empty oil drum and having someone drop fireworks through the hole at the top. Each bomb explosion made her head feel as if it were going to burst. And the gun still kept blasting away, its empty brass shell cases clanging on to the ground, their smoking tubes letting out an acrid stink. Rebecca's eyes watered and her nostrils stung with the gases from the shells. It was hell.

In spite of her own discomfort, Rebecca was more worried about Kim; Rebecca could only hope that no harm was coming to her. This was the most savage raid any of them had ever experienced. She knew she should be back at the school, reassuring Kim.

After a time the bombers had all passed over and the gun stopped thumping out its rounds. Rebecca cautiously took her hands away from her ears. Her head was ringing. She looked at Fay who seemed to be in just as bad a state.

The corporal came over to them. 'What the 'ell do you think you two are playin' at?' he grumbled. 'Come on, let's see your ID.'

Luckily both women had their identity cards on them.

'This place is out of bounds to civvies. You should know that,' he said, inspecting their cards by the light of a torch. 'What're you doin' out here anyway? On a bleedin' hike? Why aren't you carrying your gas masks? You know you're s'posed to carry 'em at all times.'

'We're teachers at the private school – one of our girls has gone missing,' explained Rebecca. 'We're out looking for her.'

'In the pitch black?' cried the corporal. 'You must be bonkers.'

'You haven't seen a schoolgirl, I suppose?' asked Fay. 'She looks . . . Italian.'

A strange look came over the corporal's face and he glanced over his shoulder, out into the fields. 'Funny you should say that. Jack did see somethin' when we was stood down. Italian, is she? We're at war with them bleeders, ain't we?'

'Not any more,' snapped Fay, 'and certainly not with a twelve-year-old child.'

The corporal pursed his lips. 'Jack, tell the lady what you saw.'

'Saw something moving out there,' replied one of the soldiers, who seemed to be more articulate than the corporal. 'There was some movement by the oak tree. It was too big for an animal – say a fox or a badger. I caught sight of it at the beginning of the raid, in the momentary light of the explosions – I just caught a glimpse of something crawling out of the ditch.'

'Which way is the oak tree?' asked Rebecca.

'You can't go out there now,' the corporal said sternly. 'You got to stay here until an officer comes.'

Fay said haughtily, 'Who do think you are, Corporal? My husband was one of the pilots at Hornchurch – I know the CO there and . . .'

'Don't care about that,' interrupted the corporal. 'My orders is to detain anyone out here tonight. Somebody let them flares off at the ends of the airfield so's Jerry knew where to drop his bombs. Could've been a woman just as easy as a man. Or a child. Maybe it was you, or even this Italian girl you keep talkin' about? Sounds likely, dunnit, Jack?'

'You mean,' Rebecca gasped, 'the target was marked for the Germans?'

'S'about it,' said the corporal. 'Jack,' he called over his shoulder. 'Keep your eyes on these two, while I call the sergeant.'

Jack, the well-spoken soldier, came and sat in front of the two women. He had his rifle at the ready. 'Don't do anything silly, ladies,' he said.

Fay protested, 'You can't honestly believe we had anything to do with laying flares to guide the enemy to the target,' she cried. 'Look, there's a girl out there somewhere.'

'Perhaps there is,' acknowledged the soldier as the corporal spoke into his field telephone, 'but I think it's a very foolhardy thing to go out looking for her during a blackout with just a couple of battery torches. There'll be an officer here before too long. You can explain it to him.'

Rebecca got to her feet. 'I'm not waiting here while one of my girls might be lying in a ditch, cold and perhaps hurt, terrified out of her life. I've got a daughter back at that school and I need to get back to find out if she's all right too. You can shoot me if you wish to – I'm going out to that oak to see if Pietra's still there. Fay, you stay here and talk to their officer . . .'

Rebecca switched on her torch. She jumped the gun emplacement sandbag wall, the hem of her frock catching the soldier's face. Then she began running along the edge of the ditch.

'Hey!' he yelled at her. 'Come back.'

But no shot came out of the darkness. Her heart was beating wildly and she realised that if she didn't slow down she would soon be out of breath. The fear and excitement of breaking away from the soldiers had pumped adrenalin into her veins and her tiredness was swept away. Keeping strictly to the grassy verge of the ditch, she walked quickly and surely until the beam of her torch struck the trunk of a large tree.

'Pietra,' she called. 'Are you there? It's Mrs Daniels. Answer me if you can hear. I've come to take you back to the school. Everything's all right. You won't be in any trouble, I can assure you of that . . .'

There was no answer. Rebecca stopped a few yards from the tree. Her legs were caked with mud up to the knees and she kicked one heel of her shoe against the other to dislodge some of the clay. The beam from her torch swept round the base of the oak, where there was some blackthorn undergrowth. Shadows chased each other in and out of the tangle of thornwood. At the point where the oak stood, the ditch had been filled in. It was probably a crossing place for the farmer. No doubt a pipe ran under the roots of the oak, carrying the water from one ditch to the next. Rebecca made her way to this earthen bridge.

Fallen twigs cracked under the soles of her shoes. There was a rustling in the grasses, beneath the blackthorn. Rebecca's torch beam searched this spot, but the bushes were so thick here they were impenetrable by anything larger than a rabbit or one of its predators.

'Pietra!' she called again. 'Where are you?'

Still no answer. In the distance came the sound of a motor vehicle. The officer had probably arrived at the ack-ack emplacement. To the south-west the sky was lit with the fires caused by the German bombs. Fire engines were busy at work, the noise of their activities floating to Rebecca on the wind.

Around her, though, out here in the fields, was a cone of near silence. Nothing else moved after the rustling in the bush. The only movement was a slow trickle of water in the ditch. Then a small warm breeze swept through, possibly caused by the backdraught from the airfield fires, and fluttered the leaves overhead. The wind soughed through the branches of the oak.

Rebecca swept the beam upwards, like a searchlight, almost accidentally. The thick boughs of the oak reached majestically out over the edges of the fields. Her torch caught something in the crutch of one of these giant boughs: a figure crouched there in a hunched position. It startled her and she gasped, recalling childhood stories of trolls and goblins. It did indeed look like some gruesome creature from the pages of the Brothers Grimm.

'Pietra?' Rebecca cried.

'Don't move – don't make another sound,' said a voice in very precise English. 'If you do either I shall be forced to shoot you.'

Her torchlight glinted on something in the hand of the speaker. It was a pistol. She could now make out the pale features of a man wearing a raincoat. He stared down at her, his eyes glinting in the beam from the torch. A shiver of fear went through Rebecca and she almost turned to race away into the darkness. She would have done, had the man not spoken again.

'Get that light out of my face. Listen, I can kill you like a rabbit on the run. I'm very good with weapons. Just stand where you are.'

A realisation came to her as she lowered the torch. 'You're

the one who put down the flares. They're out looking for you, you know. You can't get away.'

'You could be right,' said the man, dropping heavily to the ground, yet still keeping his gun pointed at Rebecca. 'I made a stupid mistake in the darkness, otherwise I would be on the main road now and fairly safe . . .'

'You sound English – why are you doing this?'

He laughed grimly, without humour. 'I'm not English. Come on, quickly – lead me back to the road, away from that damned gun emplacement over there. Quickly now.'

'I don't know the way to the road – I came out here looking for a lost schoolgirl. You heard me calling for her.'

He stared at her for a moment, as if he were making up his mind about something. In those few seconds Rebecca knew he was going to kill her. She saw now that there was a knife in his left hand, as well as the gun in his right. He was going to murder her quietly, so that the soldiers a few hundred yards away wouldn't hear it. She gasped and backed away from him.

'I'll scream,' she cried. 'I'll bring them here.'

'Shut up,' he hissed. He stared at her again, then folded the clasp knife with one hand and put it in his raincoat pocket. 'All right, walk ahead – go on, I'm not going to hurt you.'

'Yet,' she said.

'That's right – not yet. Now walk. I can assure you that if you do scream, I'll shoot you. I'll have nothing to lose. Do you understand me?'

'Yes,' she replied.

He forced her to scramble ahead of him. They struggled back over the ploughed field, the way now dimly lit by the fires on the airfield. Rebecca realised the man was retracing his former route in order to pick up the fork where he had gone wrong. She also realised that the army would not expect him to be near the aerodrome, not so long after the raid had finished. They would believe him to be on a train or in a car, getting as far away from the camp as possible.

Rebecca thought about making a run for it, out into the blackness of the night. She knew he would get at least one shot at her and she weighed the risk of being hit by that shot against the possibility of escape. He was probably very accurate with his pistol; Germany didn't send untrained agents into Britain. And while the rough ground might hold him up, the slippery furrows would also slow Rebecca down. In the end she decided it wasn't worth it. She would have to wait until a better opportunity presented itself.

Finally, a grunt of satisfaction told her that the man had found where he had gone wrong earlier.

They were very close to the perimeter of the airfield at this point, where men were clearing up the debris after the raid. Again Rebecca wondered whether to risk breaking away, or shouting, but she knew the man was doubly alert now that they were within calling distance of British servicemen.

'Over here,' he hissed, motioning her to come closer to him and pointing the gun at her.

They walked in this way, Rebecca never allowed out of range of the pistol, until they reached a hedge. Rebecca knew that this was the hedgerow which followed the road. Just as they came to it, a car swept round the bend, its headlights sweeping through the night. The man ducked, waving his gun at her. Astonishingly, the car stopped its engine, by a five-barred gate, and Rebecca could hear voices.

'What do you think, Martin? Would she have found her way back here?' Rebecca recognised the voice as that of Christopher Bates.

Someone opened a car door and got out. They went to the gate and stood on the bottom bar, looking out over the fields. Rebecca couldn't tell if it was Martin or Chris. She kept her eyes firmly on the man who had her captive. He in turn had the gun pointing at her face, ready to pull the trigger if she so much as breathed a word.

They stayed this way for what seemed an age, Rebecca and the agent crouched down beside the hedge on one side, and the two Englishmen on the other. Then she heard Martin's voice call out, 'Can't see anything. Maybe she walked north . . . ?'

The door slammed again and the car moved off along the lane. Rebecca felt immensely disappointed. Surprisingly, the fear had left her now, even though she knew she was probably going to die. Now there was no one around to hear her screams. She had no threat with which to keep the man at bay.

'I suppose you're going to kill me now?' she said dully.

There was no answer from the man. He simply reached inside his coat for his knife. Once it was in his hand he advanced towards her. Rebecca shouted, 'Help! Help! Over here!' But help was too far away. In a few moments it would all be over. She should have screamed earlier. At least he would have been caught. Now she was going to die and the agent was going to get clean away.

Suddenly, out of the night, a flying shape hit the man around the waist.

The agent spun sideways and dropped to his knees with a yell of pain. There was a struggle. The two figures grappled in the mud, one trying to force his gun into the face of the other. Rebecca kicked out hard at the agent's hand and he gave a yell of pain as the pistol flew away into the field.

From down the lane the lights of the car returned.

The agent suddenly flung his assailant aside and looked towards the car that had drawn up again by the gate. Then he staggered off, out into the field. Neither Rebecca nor her helper attempted to follow him. In the lane the car horn was sounding now, blaring out their position. Searchlights mounted on vehicles out near the airfield sprang to life. They remorselessly illuminated the darkness and the agent was caught in their glare, a stark figure in the middle of the ploughed field. Rebecca could see the man was not going to escape.

She watched him try to run away, with mixed feelings. Perhaps he was not as afraid of death as she had been, but he looked like a retreating hare, desperate to outrun the guns. She empathised with the feelings of a creature at bay. It was only a few moments since the agent had been the hunter and now he was the prey. She wondered what he was feeling and thinking.

Perhaps his heart was racing ahead of him in his fear? Perhaps his legs were moving of their own accord, acting simply out of terror? Perhaps he was thinking of his loved ones, back in his own country?

Or maybe he was just a cold, hard creature who was not afraid to die?

When he reached the end of the field she could see him clearly transfixed in the lights of the advancing army vehicles, churning their way over the furrows, determined not to let their quarry get away. There was a shout from one of the trucks.

The man turned and fired his pistol, three sharp cracks, into the glaring brightness of the searchlights. Glass shattered. There was more shouting.

Rebecca saw a soldier take deliberate aim with his rifle, a single shot followed, this time louder than the three previous reports. The agent fell backwards in the mud.

He lay there, very still, twisted at a peculiar angle. Rebecca somehow knew from his position that he was dead, that he would never move again. His dark raincoat was now a shroud. In just a few moments he had gone from slaughterer to slaughtered. Despite the fact that he had been her enemy, prepared to take her life, Rebecca felt a pang of sorrow for the dead man out in the field.

She felt tired and drained and leaned against her rescuer, who she now saw was Martin.

The first question she asked was, 'Is Kim all right?'

Martin reassured her on this point, and she felt a surge of relief. There were other questions to ask, about the raid, but they could be answered later. Martin was very patient with her, considering her agitation.

'Why did you stop?' she asked wearily. 'Whatever made you stop?'

'There was a car parked up against the hedge – who would park a car in a dark lane in the middle of nowhere? There isn't a house for half a mile. It looked strange enough to stop and investigate.'

'Oh, I didn't realise he was trying to get back to his car. But – but how did you know I was here?'

Martin smiled and said, 'I could smell your perfume – I'd know that fragrance anywhere. I knew you were there, and either too injured to call out, or you were being held captive – the army told us there was an agent on the loose – so I decided to send Dr Bates away and just wait for a while.'

She rested her head on his shoulder. 'Bless you, Martin – you're – you're a saviour.'

'Yes,' he said solemnly. 'I am, aren't I?'

He walked her back to the car where Christopher Bates was waiting to take her home.

Chapter Twenty-Nine

In the car on the way back to the school Rebecca felt too numbed by her experience to talk. On their return she immediately went and found Kim, and hugged her. Kim seemed a little embarrassed by this demonstrative behaviour, as she always did, but was happy to put up with it for her mother's sake. Rebecca reflected afterwards that her young daughter appeared to be nerveless during bombing raids. She put this down to the fact that Kim could recall no other life. The world had been at war for as long as the child could remember. Rebecca, on the other hand, was becoming increasingly unnerved by the attacks.

Once in her room, with Fay and Martin sitting with her, she thawed a little from her numbness.

'Pietra?' she asked.

Fay said soothingly, 'She's fine. Mohorty found her curled up in a barn – safe, warm and dry. Some of the girls *had* been teasing her and Francine Knole is sorting that out at the moment. I think it's best left to her.'

Rebecca nodded. 'I want us to cancel this victory party. Of course we're all pleased now that Italy is out of the war, but it's not worth the pain it's going to cause Pietra, and possibly

351

her family, when they learn what's happened.'

'I think we all agree on that,' Martin said.

Rebecca turned to him. 'Thank you, Martin, for saving my life,' she said. 'That was an act of pure courage.'

Martin grinned and shrugged. 'Oh, not really. Instinct more than anything else. I saw what he was going to do and just reacted. My rugby days certainly came in handy – that tackle was one of the best I've ever done.'

'Well, I don't know how to thank you.'

'My pleasure,' he replied.

It was an awkward moment for her. Rebecca knew that the clergyman was more than fond of her, but he was a man who fell in love easily. She had no romantic feelings for him, but she liked him immensely and valued him as a friend. Hopefully, she told herself, he could fall *out* of love just as easily. She knew he had been in love with Fay, before she was married, and had since switched his affection to her now that Fay was unavailable. He was such a nice man that Rebecca wanted him to have all he craved for himself: a wife, a family, a good home life. It was just that *she* couldn't be that wife.

She knew she mustn't dwell too much on her gratitude or Martin would take it for something it was not. So she switched her attention to more general matters.

'No bombs hit the school then?'

'We lost the damn vegetable patch,' growled Fay. 'Direct hit on Mrs Floodgate's victory project.'

'Really?' said Rebecca. 'I bet Mohorty is pleased.'

'Ecstatic. Ten feet to the right and she would have lost her number one hockey pitch. As it is, the pitch just got showered with stones and earth – won't take much to put it to rights.'

'What about Amelia? Did she get frightened.'

Martin laughed. 'Oh come on, Rebecca – you know Amelia doesn't scare that easily. The girls were frightened but Amelia was fine. Francine Knole sat with her all through the raid.'

'All's well that ends well, then?' Rebecca said. 'But still, I can't help thinking about that poor man.'

'Poor man?' snorted Fay. 'He would have killed you without any compunction whatsoever.'

'I don't think so,' said Rebecca. 'I mean, I know he would have killed me, but not without feeling. Somehow he seemed to me to be like a trapped animal, doing what was expected of him in order to get away. I don't know. Maybe I'm wrong, but I just got the impression he wasn't a man who could kill without remorse – not in cold blood.'

Martin said, 'I agree with Fay. He set those flares at the airfield.'

'But that's a legitimate military target – it's not like murdering a civilian out in the middle of a dark field. Anyway,' Rebecca sighed, 'it's all over bar the nightmares. I expect I'll get a couple of those in the future. Do we know who he was – where he came from? He spoke like an Oxford don.'

'Bulgarian, according to the army,' said Martin. 'Who knows what his reasons were for working for the Germans? Money probably. Or some misguided idealism. He was raised here, in London, by an aunt. Educated at Cambridge.'

Both Rebecca and Fay blinked. 'How do you know that?' asked Rebecca.

Martin said, 'The army found a letter in his pocket – a very old one. It was from his aunt, congratulating him on getting a Cambridge blue, for athletics – the hurdles. Strange thing war, isn't it? The fact that he bothered to carry that letter meant he must have been proud of the fact that he got his blue. Yet he was trying to destroy the people who gave it to him. I don't really understand it. Not at all.'

'Well, his loyalties must have lain elsewhere,' said Rebecca.

Fay said, 'In his wallet perhaps.'

The earlier bombing of the school and now the attack on the aerodrome, from which the school escaped only with luck, frightened many more parents. The sad consequence of these near misses meant that they began to take the children away. By March 1944, just as the 'forgotten army' was striking back at the Japanese in Burma, most of the girls had left and Rebecca was forced, temporarily, to close the school down.

She called a meeting of the teachers and explained to them that they could remain in residence, ready for the time when the school would reopen.

'What will we live on?' complained Stephen Sinclair.

'Well,' said Rebecca, 'I admit that's going to be a difficulty. I obviously can't pay your salaries while there are no fees coming in. I'm simply telling you that you can remain here because I wouldn't like to think of anyone not having a roof over their heads. However, if you can obtain a post elsewhere, and you wish to leave, then of course you must. If you choose to stay, your rooms will be rent-free, but you will have to provide money for your food.'

'I think we should be entitled to a bit more than that,' Sinclair grumbled, 'severance pay or something.'

Martin said angrily, 'You've only been here five minutes.

Some of us have taught here for years. Mrs Daniels owes you nothing. She gave you a job when you were desperate. What more do you want from her?'

This attack seemed to shock Sinclair into silence. No one had ever seen Martin so angry before and Sinclair knew that he had overstepped the mark, simply from Martin Simkins's reaction.

The other teachers had mixed feelings about remaining at the school. Mohorty and Dane were going to stay. Fay said she wanted to be nearer to Bill and so started putting out feelers for jobs in Scotland, though their quite separate education system meant she was considered underqualified for positions north of the border. Martin was staying. And it was in Francine Knole's interest to remain until the school reopened: she was not likely to get a headship anywhere else at a moment's notice. She told Rebecca she was just beginning to enjoy the benefits and privileges of a head, as well as the responsibility, and didn't want to relinquish any of these. The rest of the teachers either left for other parts of Britain, or answered advertisements for posts in and around London.

The school settled into dormancy while it awaited the end of the war. Amelia Sartour was very upset by this but did not blame Rebecca for the situation. Though bedridden now, she had still enjoyed the noise, the yells, the shouts of laughter from the girls walking past her door. Her bed was near the window, but there was no hockey to watch.

Only a ghost pitch remained on the playing fields, occasionally used by Mohorty and Kim for a knock-about. This latter activity was essential anyway, to keep Mrs Floodgate from swooping down and demanding a further vegetable garden. Mohorty still liked to keep her hand in and she was certain Kim would make the Essex team one day, if not play for England, and in that respect Mohorty saw herself as the girl's manager and coach.

Kim herself attended the local state school.

In Burma the Allied force known as the Chindits, or 'mighty lions', were driving deep into the Japanese lines. British soldiers and Gurkhas were inflicting heavy casualties on the enemy, as were the new forces of Chinese and American soldiers. Rebecca was especially interested in this area of the war, because of Luke Adams. He had never replied to any of her letters, but she guessed he was still being held in Singapore's Changi jail, if he was alive at all. General MacArthur was returning, as promised, to the Philippines to smash the Japanese who had driven him out in 1942. It seemed as if the Far East was opening up a little and that the prisoners in Singapore might be freed before too long.

Martin came into the staff room one morning, his face shining with excitement. 'It's begun!' he said dramatically.

'What's that?' sniffed Mohorty. 'They started shooting the miners at last?'

The miners had been on strike, on and off, since early March. At one time there had been as many as 156 out of 200 pits closed down. Mohorty was in favour of lining the strikers up against the wall and shooting them. She made no pretence of being anything but two steps behind Hitler in her views on the workforce and its place in society.

'No, you dope – the invasion! It's started.'

Mohorty dropped her book and stared at Martin. Rebecca paused in the act of taking a sip of tea. Julia Dane simply gawped into his animated features. They had all been expecting this – the invasion of Europe – but it had been so long in coming it seemed almost like a miracle now it was here.

'It's the biggest seaborne invasion force the world has ever known,' continued Martin in awed tones. 'I mean, I'm a man of peace of course, but I can't help being caught up in the excitement of it all.'

'Contain yourself, man,' said Mohorty authoritatively. 'Xerxes attacked Marathon Bay in 490 BC with almost eight hundred thousand troops. I don't think we've put that many men ashore.'

'A hundred and fifty-five thousand,' replied Martin, sounding a little disappointed. 'But they said it was the biggest ever seaborne invasion.'

'The newspapers? The BBC? They're as thick as a navvy's ears that lot,' snorted Mohorty. 'They make things up for effect. I can assure you there have been far greater invasion forces throughout history than the one led by Eisenhower. Monty should have been in charge anyway – we all know that. Monty could have done the job with half the men.'

Rebecca said, 'Montgomery is certainly a good commander.'

'The best,' snapped Mohorty. 'Nobody to touch him. How's the invasion going, Martin?'

'It said on the news that the British and Canadians are pushing forward, but the Yanks are stuck on Omaha Beach.'

'Omaha? That's in America, isn't it?' said Julia, looking up from her knitting. 'What are they still doing in America?'

'No,' Martin explained patiently. 'Operation Overlord,

that's the name of the invasion. They gave the landing points code names. Sword, Juno, Gold, Utah and Omaha. The American forces are bogged down on the beach called Omaha.'

'Told you so,' snapped Mohorty. 'Monty would never have allowed that. He'd have planned it better.'

'Well, some of the Yanks are doing all right,' replied Martin in defence of the Americans. 'Apparently on Utah Beach they only lost six men. Then the Germans ran away.'

'Probably Polish and Czech slave troops,' snorted the games mistress. 'Germans don't run away from Americans.'

Mohorty wouldn't give any foreigners credit for the repulsion of the German army. If Brits hadn't done the work, they'd been behind those who had, the Canadians (who were almost British anyway). Several days later Mohorty was still arguing with Martin over the French and Polish contribution to the invasion when a strange droning sound was heard in the skies outside the school. It sounded as if it might be an aircraft, yet it was a noise completely new to them. Mohorty, Francine Knole, Julia Dane, Martin and Rebecca went outside to see what it was.

The day was overcast and very dull. Black clouds hung rolled like tanks over the heavens above them. A storm was threatening to break. Birds were retreating to nests and perches out of reach of wind and rain.

Rebecca strained her eyes, seeing a kind of flare travelling across the sky. 'What is it?' she asked the others.

'Looks like some kind of aircraft,' said Martin, straining his eyes against the poor light. 'It's heading towards central London.

He had barely finished speaking when the flare spluttered and went out. There was a moment of eerie silence, then the strange aircraft dropped out of the clouds and hurtled towards the earth. The five teachers watched the descent in horror.

'Good God!' cried Mohorty. 'I hope whoever's inside can get out.'

But no parachute blossomed like a white flower in the air above Hornchurch.

The winged object continued its descent and landed about a mile away in the fields. A tremendous explosion occurred on impact. A whole oak tree was flung like a toy high in the air. Earth and flints showered the countryside. A thin column of smoke crept upwards like a long-imprisoned genie escaping from a bottle.

Martin was white-faced. 'A bomb,' he said.

Rebecca said, 'It couldn't have been a bomb. I mean it was flying. There must have been a bomb on board. Perhaps it's a new German weapon – a fast aircraft that delivers a single bomb – it *was* travelling very fast.'

'Maybe you're right,' Martin replied. 'That sounds more logical.'

But he should have stuck to his first impression. It *was* a bomb. A pilotless flying bomb, which would come to be known as the 'doodlebug'. What they had witnessed was one of the first Vl rockets to be sent to bomb London. Later, pilots from Hornchurch would be sent out to turn the doodlebugs round, so that they crashed at sea, or shoot them out of the air.

RAF Hornchurch was flourishing; more equipment and new aircraft were arriving at the station daily. At first Rebecca was pleased to see this happening. It meant that things were improving at last: that Britain was winning the war at home as well as abroad. Then one day in December, just as a series of ring roads and green belts were proposed by the government, she received a compulsory purchase order issued on the school.

'Oh no,' she groaned. 'Not this.'

It appeared that the authorities needed the land on which the school stood for expansion of the airfield. A new runway was to be added and the school stood in the path of the proposed development. Since there were no pupils in the school the local council saw no reason to oppose the purchase.

'Mrs Bloody Floodgate,' growled Rebecca. She took the letter to show Martin, who whistled softly under his breath.

'The buggers,' he said. 'We'll have to fight it of course. But this isn't just the local council – this is central government.'

'Yes, but the council didn't help, did they? Why didn't one of them come to me and give me some warning of this? Mrs Floodgate must be crowing right now.'

'I think you're probably right,' said Martin sagely.

'We have to keep this from Amelia, until we can't hide it any longer,' said Rebecca. 'The news would kill her.'

Martin agreed, though he felt they ought to tell Mohorty and Julia Dane, who might want to look elsewhere for work now that the school was under threat.

They didn't. Mohorty was her usual intractable self, prepared to be unyielding and uncompromising in her defence of the school. 'We'll fight them,' she thundered. 'We'll fight them on the lawns, we'll fight them on the driveway . . .' She parodied Churchill's famous speech for them, over dinner, until even Rebecca felt a little more hopeful. Mohorty was a pain in the neck when she was against you, but she was very good for morale when she was *with* you. Rebecca began writing letters of protest to the government straight away, saying her school was just about to reopen and that pupils would have nowhere else to go. She was stretching the truth several different ways, but this was war and all was fair in that.

The occupants of Gradge Lodge School managed to keep the news from Amelia, despite the fact that though the old lady was bedridden she had a way of ferreting out information without having to leave her room. It seemed to come to her in the air, and she sifted and evaluated such information far more thoroughly than anyone else, possibly because she had more time to ponder, more time to analyse.

Rebecca was determined, however, that this was one piece of information that would be withheld from her patron. The staff were sworn to secrecy on the matter. Amelia mustn't know about the proposed fate of the school under any circumstances.

It was at times like these, when all seemed against her, that Rebecca fell back on Luke's poetry. His volumes of verse were like touchstones to her. They were the one sane set of values in a world of madness. His poems spoke tomes of truth to her, from depths of hope. She sat up into the late hours with them, poring over their short, brilliant lines, wondering if Luke himself was being sustained by his own internal strength at a time when the world had gone *beyond* madness for him.

She prayed for his safety and well-being.

Chapter Thirty

Rebecca went to see Mrs Floodgate in the vain hope that she might have put her grievances behind her, but Mrs Floodgate was a woman who swelled with revenge. She stuck out her chest like the sail of a man-of-war and with her cannon mouth boomed out a reply. Rebecca took the attack broadside.

'You made your bed – now you can lie in it,' thundered Mrs Floodgate.

Her voice was full of righteous satisfaction. She blossomed with smugness. Rebecca could have cheerfully cut her throat with one of her own butter knives.

'Made my bed?' repeated Rebecca. 'What on earth are you talking about? The government are taking away my school. I have nothing to do with it. What if they were to tell you they were taking your teashop? Would you call that justice?'

But the government *weren't* taking Mrs Floodgate's teashop, so she could afford to thunder. Rebecca went away feeling it had been a dreadful mistake to believe that Mrs Floodgate had anything approaching a heart. Mrs Floodgate's circulatory system worked with a stainless-steel pump.

Now the doodlebugs were coming over in droves, but at least you could hear them and take cover. You could listen to their jet engines as they cruised overhead and when the sound stopped you ran for the nearest shelter. But there was a newer, more silent threat. Its explosion was more powerful too. This monster was the V2: the *Vergeltungswaffe Zwei*. It travelled at nearly four thousand miles an hour and carried a one-tonne bomb in its nose. Instead of flying horizontally across the channel, it went up in an arc, high into the outer atmosphere, then plunged to earth.

In November, Churchill admitted that more than a hundred V2s had landed on London. The V1s had already killed 6,000 people and destroyed 25,000 houses. Until the Allies overran Holland, the rocket bombs could not be stopped.

There was a terrible tragedy in Deptford–New Cross when a V2 landed on Woolworths on a sale day. The place was packed with customers: men, women and children. Some were blasted into smithereens, nothing left of them but a single item of clothing, like an odd shoe. Bodies of others lay around the devastated store like pale angels, completely whole and seemingly unmarked, the breath simply sucked from their lungs by the vacuum caused by the explosion. This attack, even at the end of a bloody war, shocked the British people.

Rebecca spent her time going to London, seeing MPs, trying to gain support for herself and her school. No one was interested. She was told that the fate of one building in a land where buildings were being destroyed every day was not a national crisis.

'You're being financially compensated,' she was told by her own MP at his monthly surgery. 'Find another schoolhouse.'

'But there are no suitable buildings in the area. I want the school to stay in Essex, yet close to London. It's important that if we have to relocate it's local to where we are now . . .'

'Well, if you're determined to be fussy,' she was told, 'we can't help you. Next!'

Rebecca wearily trudged back to the school again. The date for the bulldozers was set for a month hence. If there was really no possibility of stopping them, then Rebecca knew she ought to find another house, wherever it was, and get Amelia settled into it. That meant telling Amelia what was happening and Rebecca was not looking forward to doing that.

'Better start taking down the curtains,' she told Martin when she got back. 'The politician supposed to be concerned with our interests was about as helpful as Mrs Floodgate.'

The doughty Mohorty was still not willing to give up the fight, even at this late hour. 'There's still one or two people who owe me favours,' she snapped. 'They're not terribly influential, I have to admit, but they might be able to help. There's a cousin of mine who works in the Ag and Fish. I'll go and see him tomorrow. He's a bit of a drip, but he's scared of me.'

'Any cousin would be bound to be a bit of a drip next to you,' Martin said, 'and they're probably *all* afraid of you.'

Mohorty grinned, taking this in good part. 'I can be a bit formidable,' she agreed.

Julia Dane said in her breathless way, 'I'll come with you, Priscilla, dear. My brother is a bank manager in Tottenham. We can see him too.'

'You expect him to give you a wad of money, do you?' retorted Mohorty.

'No, of course not, Priscilla,' replied Julia Dane nervously.

'But as a bank manager he's quite an important person.'

'Well, I'm sure he thinks so,' sighed Mohorty. 'Personally I wouldn't give you tuppence for a whole basketful of 'em.'

Francine Knole, surprisingly, stuck up for the financial profession. 'It's one of the oldest in the world,' she said. 'And one of the most respectable.'

Mohorty snorted. 'There's an older one and it's probably on a par with bankers for respectability. And if we don't find a way out of this hole, we may all find ourselves following that profession – except Martin of course. He hasn't got the right plumbing for it.'

Martin went bright red and stared out of the window.

It took a while for the intelligence of this remark to sink into Francine's naive brain, but when it did, she gasped. 'Priscilla Mohorty, you are not a very nice woman. I'm glad the girls weren't here to listen to that remark.'

Mohorty grinned again, enjoying herself. 'No, I'm not, am I? Well, it takes all sorts, doesn't it? Anyway, if the girls were here, we wouldn't be in this fix, so I wouldn't have said it in the first place. Come on, off your backside, Dane, let's get into the Big Smoke and see what we can do about this business.'

When she had gone, Francine said to Martin, 'I really don't think Priscilla Mohorty had a very genteel upbringing.'

'Actually,' Martin replied, 'her parents were *very* genteel. Her father was a bishop and her mother came from an Oxfordshire peerage. Surprising, isn't it?'

'I would never have believed it.'

'It's true. I found out quite a while ago, when her father was alive and still the Bishop of Bradwell. Mohorty asked me if I wanted her father to give me a leg-up, as she put it, in the profession. I'm not sure if he would have done it – obtained me a higher post, mean – but Mohorty was willing to badger him on my behalf. She's a formidable woman, as she admits.'

'Good Lord – there's not corruption in the Church too, is there?' said Francine faintly.

'There would be if Mohorty had her way. She sees that sort of thing as quite legitimate. If you're in a position of power and can help a friend, well, you do it. It means stretching the rules of privilege, but that's all in the game to her. Her heart's in the right place – I'm just not sure about her soul.'

'Amen to that,' breathed Francine Knole.

Christmas was both a happy and a sad time for the occupants of Gradge Lodge School. It seemed as if the Allies were winning the war at last, but on a personal note the school was condemned. All efforts, including those of Mohorty, had ended in failure. The most Mohorty had managed was a stay of execution. The demolition of the building had been put back to February 1945 and they had to be out of the house by then.

'I don't understand what they want to extend the runways for if the war's nearly over,' grumbled Mohorty at a meeting on the subject. 'I mean, if Hitler's going to be defeated soon, why do we need bigger airfields?'

Martin said, 'I suppose they don't want the same thing to happen again. I mean, we were caught with our pants down in 1939. I expect they want to ensure we have enough aircraft and airfields to protect Britain in the future.'

Rebecca nodded. 'I think Martin's right. The military is feeling very powerful at the moment, basking in favouritism.

They've won a war and the government is bending over backwards to show them it's appreciated. They're going to grab all the land they can get while they're on top. Let's face it, we've lost the fight. We'll have to tell Amelia.'

The date set for informing Amelia of the disaster was Boxing Day. Rebecca wanted to get Christmas dinner behind them first, otherwise it might be a miserable affair. All the current occupants of the schoolhouse were there, including Kim. Sinclair had returned, with holes in the bottoms of his shoes, having beaten the pavements of London in an effort to find a post – and failed. Christopher Bates had been invited. Francine Knole and Rebecca had managed to get two chickens which had been stuffed with chestnuts. It was to be a magnificent feast – the Last Supper, Mohorty said – with no expense spared. Kim, Rebecca and Julia Dane had made paper chains with torn strips of coloured newspaper and flour paste, and Mohorty had found some tinsel.

A Victorian crib was brought by Christopher Bates, who set it up on the sideboard of the staff room, where they were having their feast. It featured the usual shepherds, sheep, three kings, Joseph and Mary, and of course the infant, but all the figures were made out of cast iron. Christopher told them the set had been a present to his great-grandmother from none other than Isambard Kingdom Brunel and was fashioned from the same batch of iron that had been smelted for the building of the *Great Eastern* steamship. The set was extremely heavy, since the figures were six inches high, and the sideboard creaked under the weight.

Holly was fetched from a local spinney by Francine Knole, who liked 'natural things' around her. Sinclair had added some mistletoe, purchased in London of all places, in the vague hope that he might be asked to kiss someone pretty. Rebecca, in a moment of cruel revenge for past deeds, said her stomach churned at the thought, but Francine Knole simply hmmm'd and stared out of the window, giving Rebecca cause for thought.

At the appointed hour Amelia was carried down by Martin and Christopher and placed on a sofa.

'Lot of fuss,' said the old woman, 'I like it.'

Before dinner Rebecca read out some general mail from former teachers at the school, including a letter to her from Fay. Fay was having a grand time in the Scottish highlands, which had captured her heart. She said she was preparing to be snowed in for the winter with Bill and was looking forward to it immensely. Kim took the Christmas cards once their contents had been read and placed them round the crib on the sideboard.

'One more card,' said Martin, as the sideboard groaned ominously, 'might be the straw that breaks the sideboard's back.'

The Christmas dinner went well. They even had some crackers which had been made by Francine Knole. When it was all over and they were sitting in armchairs, smoking cigarettes and drinking sherry, Amelia suddenly spoke.

'All right,' she said, 'will someone tell me what's the matter?'

'Matter?' asked Rebecca, taken aback.

'Yes,' replied Amelia, adjusting the blanket over her legs. 'You've been hiding something from me. All that whispering in corridors. You think I'm daft or deaf?'

'Neither,' muttered Martin.

'Well then, let's hear it.'

No one said anything. They simply stared at the old woman, who stared back with a look of annoyance on her wrinkled features.

Finally, Kim said, 'They're going to take our school away, Auntie.'

The silence continued; Amelia stared at the faces in front of her, knowing she was hearing the truth.

'Who's going to take the school?' she asked at last.

'The government.' This time it was Rebecca who answered the question. 'They want to build a new runway for the aerodrome and we're in the way. There's a compulsory purchase order out on the school. We've already been given an extension. We have to be out in two months.'

'Is that a fact?' grated Amelia, more to herself than anyone else in the room. 'Well, we'll see about that.'

'You can't do anything – we've tried all the avenues,' said Martin. 'The whole thing's wrapped up and on its way through the post. There's nothing more we can do.'

'We'll see about that,' repeated the flinty woman, her mouth a tight line, her eyes glinting. 'We'll bloody well see about that.'

'Auntie!' gasped Kim. 'You swore.'

'Sorry, child,' said Amelia, reaching out and stroking Kim's hair. 'Strong measures call for strong words. Martin, Christopher, get me to the phone.'

'It's Christmas Day,' said Rebecca, thinking that Amelia must be turning a little senile. 'There's no one in the offices at the . . .'

'I'm not going to phone their damn offices,' snapped Amelia. 'Just do as I say.'

Martin shrugged and nodded to Christopher, and together they chair-lifted Amelia to the telephone. Actually, one of them could have carried her on their own, since she was as light as a husk. They put her in a chair next to the instrument and waited while she dialled a number. When the phone was picked up at the other end, Amelia gave the name of a high-ranking member of the government. A few moments later, she was clearly speaking to the person she had requested.

' . . . they're trying to take away my school,' she told the Cabinet minister. 'You know what my school means to me. I want you to stop them.'

There was a long pause, then Amelia said, 'Bless you. I knew I could count on you. What? Oh, yes, yes, I'm quite well. How's the family? Lovely. Well, have a good Christmas – remember me to the children. 'Bye.'

She turned triumphantly to the rest of the room. 'That's that – no more talk about my school being taken away.'

Rebecca was astounded, as were all the others. That is, everyone except Kim, who thought her auntie was a goddess, immortal and omnipotent. All that work they had put in, trying to stop the order being carried out! And Amelia had put paid to the mighty forces of the public planning and building departments with one single short telephone call. It was wonderful, but it was also galling.

'I can't believe it,' said Rebecca. 'We spent weeks – all of us – running ourselves ragged over this.'

'Should have come to me in the first place,' snapped Amelia. 'Didn't trust the poor old woman, eh?'

'We didn't want to upset you,' said Martin.

'Upset me? Pah. You think things like this *upset* me? It's crises like this that keep me alive. I'm only sorry it was an easy battle. Too easy really. I like something I can get my teeth into. Good feeling of satisfaction when you come out winning from something difficult. Still, I'm glad we're back on course again. War should be over soon. Then we can open the school again. I want to see it full of pupils once more before I die. Then I'll go. In the meantime, if you get any more crises, you let me in on it from the start. It'll save you a lot of heartache and it'll give me something to do.'

Later, Christopher Bates murmured into the old woman's ear, 'Amelia, did you have an affair with that Cabinet minister?'

'Mind your own business,' she snapped.

He laughed out loud, causing the others to stare in their direction. Amelia giggled. She was enjoying herself.

When the party was over, and Amelia was back in her room, Christopher managed to get Rebecca on her own for a few minutes, as they cleared the dining-room table. 'How are you getting along?' he asked.

'Oh, I'm fine. Kim's doing very well at school at the moment. I'm keeping myself busy with various things.'

'That's good,' Christopher said, nodding hard. 'I – I just wondered if you were missing me at all.'

Once Rebecca saw where the conversation was going she tried to stop it. 'I don't think we'd better discuss this – it's over between us, isn't it? What's the point?'

'The point is, *I've* never considered it over, even though you may have. I've been thinking lately that we might get back together again. Give it another shot. What do you say? I mean, whatever it was you disliked about me might have changed for good.'

Rebecca sighed. She didn't want to tell Christopher that it was his character which put her off. She believed the problem was inherent to Christopher and was not likely to have 'changed'.

'Look, Chris, I'd much rather we didn't talk about this. It was just as much my fault as yours. It's not just a matter of me accepting you. I've got faults, too, that you wouldn't be able to live with . . .'

'Let me be the judge of that.'

'Chris, you don't love me,' she pleaded. 'You only think you do.'

His face went scarlet and his eyes turned opaque. He clenched his fingers into fists. His breath sounded harsh. In a choked voice he said, 'Don't *ever* assume you know my feelings better than I do myself.'

'I'm – I'm sorry. You're right. It was very arrogant of me. Look, Chris, I've had a nice time today and I hope you have. We can be friends in each other's company . . .'

His face looked brittle. 'I don't want to be friends. I want us to be – to be together, for always. I want you to be my wife, dammit. I can't be friends with you.'

'In that case I have nothing more to say to you.'

He gripped her arm and stared into her eyes. There was such pain in them she almost melted. She didn't doubt at that moment that he was in love with her, or had been, and that he was suffering for it. She knew what it felt like: it was hell. She hated the thought that someone was going through torture because of her. Fortunately, before she could say anything, Martin came into the room and prevented her from doing something she would definitely have regretted in the long run.

'Chris, I am so very sorry,' she said softly. Then she pulled away from him and began clearing the dishes from the table. Christopher stood for a moment, then left the room without a word. Martin took his place at her elbow.

'What was all that about?' Martin asked.

'Something that happened a while ago.'

'It looked pretty nowish to me.'

'Well, it was, but it's settled, so don't worry about it – I don't want you to get involved.'

Martin, the protector, grunted. 'He looked as if he was hurting you.'

She touched her arm where Christopher had gripped it. There would be a bruise later. She had not realised at the time how hard he had been squeezing her.

'No, I rather think it was the other way round, Martin. Anyway, let it alone. It's over.'

Martin shrugged and helped her gather up the dishes. 'Sometimes,' he said, as they left the room together with their hands full of plates, 'when I see something like that, I'm glad I'm destined to be a bachelor.'

'That won't stop you from getting hurt, Martin.'

He sighed, staring at the floor. 'I suppose you're right.'

When they got to the kitchen there was a bun fight going on, started by Mohorty, and the floor was covered with bits of soggy bread and cake. Rebecca looked around her in amazement. The air was still full of missiles. Mohorty was shrieking with laughter. Kim was hiding behind the cooker, then rushed out to spray Stephen Sinclair with lemonade. Julia Dane was wiping jelly from her hair and flicking it at Mohorty. Only Francine Knole stood aloof from the fray, her hands behind her back.

'Oh, honestly,' cried Rebecca, 'I'm beginning to think Kim's not the only child around here . . . Francine, couldn't you have stopped them? Look at the floor – and the walls – honestly . . .'

She got no further. Francine Knole brought a hand from behind her back. It contained a wodge of blancmange. This was flung in a very determined manner and hit Rebecca squarely between the eyes, followed by a handful of raspberry jelly. The jelly went down the front of Rebecca's dress, slid down between her breasts, and rested there, unpleasantly cold.

'Oh God!' she cried. 'Francine!'

'Yes?' smiled Francine Knole. 'Is it a surrender I'm about to hear?'

'Not on your life,' yelled Rebecca. She scooped some cold mashed potato from a dish and let fly.

It was a wonderful end to Christmas Day 1944.

Chapter Thirty-One

The victory celebrations at Gradge Lodge School on VE Day were marred by the fact that Amelia was desperately ill. Kim attended a street party in the village, but Rebecca remained at Amelia's bedside. It was during this bout of illness that Amelia procured a promise from Rebecca.

'I want to be taken to Australia,' said Amelia. 'I would like my ashes to be scattered in the outback. I'd like to think of my dust mingling with the dust of the oldest race on earth, in the most mysterious place on earth. Can you do that for me, Rebecca? Will you send my ashes to Australia?'

Rebecca fought back the tears. 'I'll take you there myself,' she said. 'We'll go together.'

'You don't need to do that.'

'I want to do it. I want to see what kind of land produced a warrior like you. It must be a magnificent country.'

'It's a continent, girl – a magnificent continent – and you'll love it.'

Amelia recovered a little from this particular illness, but sank again three months later. She died on 6 August 1945. She had many souls for company on her way to the afterlife: it was also the day on which the atomic bomb was dropped on Hiroshima.

It was a day for counting the war dead. The USA had lost a quarter of a million servicemen. Britain had lost five hundred thousand; Germany, three and a half million; Japan, two and a half million; and the USSR a staggering thirteen million. Millions of Jewish and non-Jewish people had been murdered in concentration camps, and thousands of civilians killed in air raids on both sides of the English Channel.

Rebecca was in the room at the time of Amelia's death, but she couldn't say for certain when Amelia breathed her last, for she went without a sound. Rebecca had been reading a newspaper report about Clement Attlee's new Labour government. The country was in economic ruins and Harry S. Truman was warning Britain that the US Lend-Lease agreement was at an end. It seemed that shortages of food and clothing were going to be worse in peace time than they had been during the war.

'Amelia,' Rebecca said, 'have you read this?'

There was no answer from the bed. Rebecca looked up, sharply. Amelia's face was drawn, her jaws wide open, her eyes staring. Rebecca knew immediately that the old woman had at last given up her grip on life. She closed her eyes and mouth and went to call Christopher Bates.

The funeral was three days later. Amelia's body was cremated and her ashes put in a jar which Rebecca took back to the school. She was sorely tempted to scatter the ashes on the first hockey pitch, feeling that this was just as suitable a place as Australia for Amelia to rest in. Her conscience, however, wouldn't allow her seriously to consider this option and she booked a berth on a ship sailing in the late autumn, bound for South Australia.

* * *

Once the war was over Rebecca and Francine Knole set about advertising the reopening of the school. There was a good response. Many daughters and younger sisters of former pupils applied and were accepted. Rebecca refused no one at that initial stage. Soon the school was up and running again. Mohorty got her second hockey pitch back, despite the fact that food was just as short as it had been during the war. The phrase 'the war effort' no longer applied and people were fed up with being told what to do with their land.

'Martin, keep an eye on Kim for me while I'm in Australia, will you?' asked Rebecca one day, when he was in her office.

'You've decided not to take her with you then?'

'I've spent hours agonising over this but I've finally decided I don't want to interrupt her education again. These children have had such a rough time over the last few years, in and out of school. I think it's best she stays.'

Martin shrugged. 'Of course, but I think you'll miss her – you know she might gain a lot from the trip. It's a geography lesson in itself.'

'Yes, I know all those arguments, and I agree with some of them. If Kim had had an unbroken education so far I wouldn't have hesitated, but I really think she needs some consistent learning now. No, I'll go alone.'

'All right. When will you be back?'

'I'm thinking of coming home next spring, just as the Australian winter is starting.'

Martin chuckled. 'Good thinking – get the best of both summers, eh? Well, I'll look forward to your return. Francine will make sure the school is running well for you while you're away, and the rest of us are mostly old hands, you know. You need have no worries about your business.'

She smiled at him and touched his cheek. 'You're such a nice man, Martin. I wish – I wish . . .'

'Don't say it,' he sighed. 'We both know it won't do any good. By the way, you know Sinclair and Francine are – well, they're probably going to tie the knot.'

Rebecca's eyes opened wide. 'No! I sort of guessed she liked him, but it's gone this far, has it? She's a braver man than I am, Gunga Din.'

'Rose-tinted glasses, I suspect. I hope she doesn't regret it.'

Rebecca nodded. 'I know what you mean. Still, you never know, she may even make a decent human being out of him – she's not a weak woman, by any stroke of the imagination.'

'Let's hope so. Have you heard from Fay?'

Rebecca nodded again, warmly this time. 'Yes, she's coming to see us before she goes to Canada with Bill. It's funny she's heading off west and I'm going east – it's an exciting world now the war's ended, isn't it?'

'Well, it is for *some* people,' Martin said, wryly. 'For others it's the same old Hornchurch.'

Rebecca laughed. 'Oh, you love the old village really, don't you? And the villagers – even Mrs Floodgate.'

Martin said, 'What would we do without our Mrs Floodgates? Now *there's* a person who makes life exciting in dull old Hornchurch, Essex. Without Mrs Floodgate the place would sink into the depths of boredom, wouldn't it?'

The next Saturday afternoon, Fay and Bill arrived unexpectedly, the date for their sailing having been brought forward. 'Well, how was Scotland?' asked Rebecca.

Bill, Martin and Fay were in Rebecca's room. Bill was in an animated conversation with Martin: they were talking fishing. Rebecca was perched on the arm of Fay's chair. All of them were drinking home-made beer, which Mohorty had recently taken to making and distributing amongst the staff, much to the horror of Francine Knole, who had a holy fear of rumours reaching parents about drinking orgies on school premises.

Fay replied, 'Scotland is a wonderful country.'

Fay was blooming. Her eyes shone with well-being and her complexion was remarkable. It seemed that life north of the border agreed with the London-born woman. More importantly, she looked happy. Rebecca was glad of that, for many wartime marriages had soured. Rebecca had noticed that there was a kind of manic euphoria during the war, induced by a sense of unreality. Each day was a gamble, a kind of Russian roulette, no one knowing whether they would survive the next twenty-four hours. A cocktail of boredom and high excitement was swallowed time after time, and men and women married on a whim, only to regret it bitterly later.

'Must be something in the air up there,' Rebecca said to her friend. 'The heather must be good for you.'

Fay laughed and patted her abdomen. 'Well, it might have *happened* in the heather.'

Rebecca stood up, took a step back and stared at Fay's shape. 'You're having a baby?' she cried.

'Hmmm,' smiled Fay, clearly delighted with her condition.

'How wonderful!' Rebecca kissed and hugged her. 'When's it due? You don't look very far gone.'

'Two months – two months gone that is.'

'Congratulations, both of you.' Martin shook Bill's hand stiffly, then pecked Fay on the cheek. 'If you need someone to be shipped over to do the baptism . . . ?'

Bill put his arm round Martin. 'If there's any chance we can get you there, we will.'

'Hey, I was only kidding,' protested Martin. 'None of us is that rich.'

'Well, I plan to be one day,' Bill said. 'We're going to have a big house in Vancouver and we want all our friends to come and stay with us for as long as they can stand it.'

'Canadian hospitality,' said Fay, wrinkling her nose. 'Actually, he also wants a house in Quebec, Saskatchewan, and various other places in Canada. We'll have to be millionaires to fill the list.'

'We shall be,' promised Bill. 'You wait.'

'I don't want us to be millionaires,' said Fay seriously. 'I think it would spoil what we have.'

'What do we have, honey?'

'You have a beautiful, untarnished love,' said Martin, surprising them with some gentle poetry of his own, 'the kind that no amount of money on earth can buy.'

'Exactly,' said Fay. 'That's what we have – so what do we need money for?'

'To live?' suggested Bill.

'Oh, anyone can get enough money to live on – that's all right. I don't mind that much.'

Rebecca had noticed that Bill still walked with a heavy limp and would probably do so for the rest of his life. No doubt there would be a small disability pension to compensate him a little for losing his foot, but she felt the missing limb had been replaced by something else: a sort of iron determination not to be held back in life by an injury. She knew that Bill's talk about becoming a millionaire was real to him. He meant it. Rebecca hoped this ambition would not cloud the relationship of her two friends in the future. It was all very well to work hard, to strive for something better, but there was no point in sacrificing love and marriage to it.

Later she said to Fay, 'I – I hope Bill doesn't become disappointed. He seems a little . . .'

'Unfulfilled?' finished Fay. She sighed. 'I know that's right. I don't want a bitter man for a husband, so I'm going to have to handle things very carefully. I'll give him lots of slack and let him run with his dreams. But if they start to turn sour on him, or he's working too hard to see his wife and children, I'll reel him in. He's a big, tough man outside, but inside he's a softy, you know. If he thought I was angry with him, or hurt by what he was doing, he'd come to me.'

'Are you sure about that?' asked Rebecca anxiously.

'I know it.'

Fay's conviction that she could control her marriage was as strong as her husband's certainty that he was going to become a rich man. Rebecca feared for them, but at the same time she knew they were devoted to each other. There would be storms, she could envisage that, but they would weather them, though they came through at the other end with tattered sails. Fay, coming from the East End, was used to battling with tough, violent males. If she could handle the entrenched hard cases, she could surely deal with any workaholism or obsessive ambition the more sensitive Bill might bring home with him.

The four friends spent a happy evening together. Rebecca asked tentatively if Bill had heard from Luke at all; he said he hadn't but that didn't mean that Luke hadn't written. Mail was still slow and unreliable.

'The Japanese have handed Singapore over to the British again, so Luke must have been released from Changi jail – if he's still alive.'

'Why shouldn't he be?' asked Rebecca quickly.

Bill replied that they had to be realistic. Life inside a Japanese prisoner-of-war camp must have been hell. Dysentery, malaria, other tropical diseases were rife. Malnutrition was the least of the prisoners' problems. They had to accept that Luke might not have survived the war in jail.

'I suppose we should be positive,' Bill finished, 'but I don't want any false hopes. I'm prepared for the worst.'

Rebecca nodded. 'The ship calls at Singapore on its way to Australia. I intend to ask questions there. It may be that Luke stayed on for a while when he was released, otherwise I'm sure we would have heard from him.'

'I think you're right,' Bill said. 'Good luck. I hope you find him. But if you do . . . what then? I mean, what's your personal stake in his future?'

Rebecca stared at Bill, then at Fay. 'I know what you're all thinking – I did my best to put him off when he was here. That's true. I had some strong ideas of what I wanted for Kim in those days. Those ideas seem strange to me now and not at all important. Perhaps – I mean – maybe if Luke still feels he would like to know me better? Well, we'll see.'

Fay said, 'Be careful, Rebecca – you don't know what

POW camps have done to him. Luke might not be the same man he was when you saw him last. He's probably changed a great deal, possibly for the worse. I don't mean just physically, but mentally and without a doubt spiritually too. He might be impossible to live with, you know. No one would blame you if you walked away from a man who wasn't right in himself. Don't go and do something for Luke because you pity him.'

Bill and Fay left the following morning. Rebecca mulled over Fay's words, knowing her friend was right: Luke would most certainly be altered in many ways. A man could not return from hell unscathed. There would be scars, perhaps even raw wounds, inside as well as out. It was as well to prepare herself for somebody who might be a stranger to her.

Oh I hope he hasn't lost his poetry, though, she prayed silently that night. I hope he still has his poetry.

Chapter Thirty-Two

The SS *Devonshire* left Southampton on 6 November with Rebecca on board. The hugs and kisses with Kim, and her feelings of guilt and regret, were still with her. Perhaps she should have taken Kim with her after all, she thought miserably, knowing she would miss her daughter. Or perhaps the trip ought to have been postponed until the child was older? But Amelia's ashes ought to be scattered as soon as possible. Kim hadn't seemed *too* concerned at the break. She was remaining in the same environment and had dozens of people to watch over her.

Alan's parents had been another thing altogether. When Rebecca telephoned them and told them about the trip, they had accused her of abandoning their granddaughter, threatened to come and take her away from the school, and were generally abusive. Rebecca told them that any attempt on their part to abduct her daughter would ensure her immediate return to England and a court action.

'You wouldn't do that?' hissed her mother-in-law.

'Watch me,' snapped Rebecca.

By the time the telephone conversation was over, her mother-in-law was in tears and Rebecca was consoling her.

She knew the two of them would never actually carry out their threat to abduct Kim: they were too ensconced in their comfortable rural way of life to attempt anything so energetic and illegal.

Rebecca had a small cabin down in the bowels of the ship, below the waterline, but that suited her fine. She couldn't open the porthole, but the ship didn't rock quite as much down there as it did on the higher decks.

The Bay of Biscay was stormy when the *Devonshire* ploughed through it, and many of the passengers were seasick. Rebecca was among them. She kept to her bed, eating only dry toast, wondering why she had paid for expensive meals when she was clearly not going to eat a thing on the whole voyage. After the second day, she decided that she would probably perish within the first week if the ship continued to be tossed and dropped into the hollows of waves.

Once, she struggled up the gangways to the top deck, to get some fresh air. There she witnessed the dark, monstrous waves for herself: the mountainous peaks and deep troughs. The sea foamed and raged around the small P&O liner, as it was lifted up high, then plunged down in watery chasms. Sea birds abandoned its rigging as if they expected the worst. She went below again, convinced that no one would survive the trip. The ship was doomed to end its days rusting on the bottom of the Atlantic Ocean somewhere between England and southern Portugal.

Yet, by the time they approached Gibraltar, the *Devonshire* was still forging its way through a sea now as calm as an Essex canal. Rebecca decided the smell of the cabin was revolting. She had lain there for several days and the air was stale and nasty. Once more she staggered up the gangways to the upper deck and leant on the rail, letting the fresh sea air blow away the last of the sickness. She still disliked the throbbing engines, which reverberated throughout the vessel night and day, but now she actually wanted to live a little longer.

A steward appeared at her elbow, saying, 'Would you like a drink, madam?'

'Yes please – an orange juice or something.'

'Might I suggest a game of deck quoits? Or perhaps some canasta in the lounge?'

Rebecca placed a hand on his starched white sleeve and said, 'A drink of orange juice is a major step at the moment – games may come later after convalescence.'

He looked at her oddly and then went off to fetch her drink.

They hove into Gibraltar on a bright cool day. Rebecca stayed on the ship. She felt that having just gained her sea legs she might risk losing them again. When they reached Malta, however, she did go ashore, and strolled through the narrow limestone streets of Valletta, absorbing its long and troubled history. The gates to the walled city proclaimed that no Turk had ever passed through its portals, a message that dated from the time of the Turkish Empire. The words might well have mentioned Germans in the same breath, for the George Cross island had withstood a terrible bombardment from the German bombers and submarines without surrendering an inch of its sparse soil.

The ship then slipped past Cyprus and eventually entered Port Said, bustling with feluccas and bum boats. Arab traders swarmed around, sometimes managing to get aboard, selling everything from bullwhips to pencil boxes. There was a magician too, called the Gulli-Gulli man, who entertained them on the deck of the ship with his tricks. Then they entered the quiet waters of the canal, gliding down its narrow channel to Port Suez and the entrance to the Red Sea.

Rebecca made a few undemanding friendships on board. She played cards, and eventually deck games, and read a lot. At Aden, at the other end of the Red Sea, many of the passengers disembarked. The barren rocks of the colony, with its stark volcano cone rising out of the dust, looked uninviting to Rebecca. She thought of Amelia, a six-year-old Amelia, whose parents had caught a deadly fever in this land, which had carried them away and left her great-aunt an orphan. The dry, rocky landscape did not look particularly deadly now, but Rebecca felt no desire to test its atmosphere.

Finally, after six weeks, the *Devonshire* reached Hong Kong, another bustling harbour, this time crowded with sampans and lighters, junks and kaidos.

She left the ship at Hong Kong to spend two nights in Kowloon's Peninsula Hotel: a breath of luxury. Nathan Road, which ran past one side of the hotel, was the main shopping street and it was thick with people. Rebecca felt a little claustrophobic in the small colony, damp and cold at that time of year, and she was glad to be on her way south again when the ship departed after a three-day stopover. She was becoming impatient to reach Singapore now and she asked the purser how long they would stop there.

'About four days, madam,' said the purser. 'Do you have friends to visit?'

'I'm not sure. He was a prisoner of war – in Changi jail. He may still be on the island.'

The purser was a tall, elderly Scot with a kindly disposition and he favoured single women travelling alone, for their company and soft manners.

'Perhaps I could make enquiries for you, by radio, before we reach the island? What's his name?'

'Luke Adams – he was a sergeant. I'm not sure if he's been discharged yet.'

'Demobbed. Well, we'll give it a go. If he stayed on as a civilian, what might he be doing?'

Rebecca said, 'Well, he's a poet actually.'

The purser raised his eyebrows. 'A poet? Can't think why a poet should want to stay in Singapore, unless it's to recuperate after his ordeal. They had it pretty rough, you know, the POWs there. The Japs weren't particularly good to them, so I understand. I'll do my best.'

'Thank you.'

When they docked at the lion city, the purser came to Rebecca's cabin and said, 'There's a man by the name of Luke Adams who's been staying at the Toc H – that's a cheap hostel run by a religious organisation. You'll find it at this number off Orchard Road – just give it to a rickshaw boy and he'll take you there.'

'Oh, well done,' said Rebecca. 'I really am grateful.'

'Glad to be of service,' smiled the purser. 'Perhaps we could have a drink together later?'

'You can count on it,' replied Rebecca.

Once again, she decided to taste of the best the colony could offer, and booked into Raffles Hotel. Then she took one of the new trishaws – three-wheeler bikes which carried passengers – to the Toc H. It was a small, rather pretty building in a garden of its own, surrounded by palms and frangipani trees which had scattered their white blossoms all over the lawn. She saw exotic birds in the bushes as she passed, dipping their beaks into the bright red trumpets of blooms. The whole place had an air of peace.

A small Chinese lady wearing a cheongsam met her on the steps up to the double doors. 'Can I help you, missy?' she asked.

'Do you work here? I'm looking for a man – a Sergeant Luke Adams. Have you heard that name?'

The Chinese woman frowned. 'Mr Adams? He lef' three days gone, missy.'

Rebecca was intensely disappointed. 'Oh, really? Oh heck – I'm just that little bit too late. Do you know where he went? Did he leave a forwarding address?'

'No address.' The woman shook her head sadly. 'He go back England, I think. No sure. Mr Adams still little bit sick from Changi jail. I watch him, each day. He eat one orange, slowly, piecie-by-piecie. He eat all. Last bit . . .' She made a gesture with her hands like a ball.

'Rind?' suggested Rebecca.

'Yes, the rind he eat too – all very slowly. Hands, shaky-shaky. No much food in jail, missy. He very sick man one time.'

'I understand,' said Rebecca. 'What's your name? Did you know him well?'

The lady stood aside as if inviting Rebecca up the steps and smiled at the Englishwoman. 'You take jasmine tea with me?'

'Yes – yes, I'd like that.'

'My name Ah-li – you call me Ah-li. I manager this place.'

'Call me Becky,' said Rebecca, knowing her full name would be difficult for someone who spoke Hokkien Chinese.

'Bei-ki,' smiled Ah-li. 'Nice name.'

Ah-li ordered a servant to bring them the tea then settled down to answer any questions Rebecca might have – and to ask a few of her own.

'Mr Adams you boyfren'?' asked Ah-li.

'Not really. That is, we're very good friends. I admire Mr Adams's poetry very much. Did you know he wrote poetry?'

'Oh yes,' laughed Ah-li, with the scent of jasmine on her breath, 'he all time scrib-scrib in notebook.'

Rebecca smiled. 'I'm glad about that. I was afraid he might have somehow lost the motivation to write. I'm glad he's still writing his poetry. How did he look? Was he very thin?'

'Like stick-man,' said Ah-li, shaking her head sadly.

Rebecca spent a pleasant hour with Ah-li before she realised she was probably keeping her from her duties. She stood up and said her goodbyes, saying how nice it was to have met her and that she hoped they would meet again. It struck her then that Ah-li was an extremely pretty woman and she wondered if there had been anything between her and Luke. Her eyes must have given her away, because Ah-li smiled.

'You in love with Mr Adams, yes?'

Rebecca decided on the truth. 'I – I think so.'

Ah-li snorted delicately. 'You no think so – you in love with Mr Adams *definitely*.'

'Perhaps. I'm not so sure about him being in love with me, though.'

'He in love with *one* woman – Ah-li know that much.'

Rebecca asked, 'How do you know?'

Ah-li nodded knowingly. 'He no look at other girl. All men go down Bugis Street. Mr Adams no go down Bugis Street.'

Rebecca stored this piece of incomprehensible information in the back of her mind and made her way back to Raffles Hotel. Once there she had lunch out on the balcony from where she could see a game of cricket in progress at the cricket club. There were beautiful shrubs below the balcony: rich red and purple blooms hanging like blown lanterns in the sultry noon. Birds flew from tree to tree and called in musical tones to each other. The sea sparkled out on the harbour. On the way back to the hotel Rebecca had passed peaceful jungle kampongs – villages on stilts – where Malays and Chinese lived their daily lives.

It was very difficult to imagine that a whole hell of pain had occurred on this beautiful island in the recent past.

That afternoon she took a flying taxi – a taxi that stopped for passengers like a bus – from Singapore city to Changi. There was a village at Changi and an RAF station. There was also the infamous Changi jail, with its high walls and watchtowers. She was allowed to visit this site of so much human despair. She sat in the small prisoners' chapel and prayed for the souls of those who had ended their lives within the prison's walls. She prayed for the guards, too, and for the Japanese dead at Hiroshima and Nagasaki. The simple chapel, made of aged softwood, bamboo and palm leaves, seemed to have a power of its own that was as potent as that of any soaring European cathedral, as if its walls had witnessed and absorbed the years of human suffering.

There were notes and names left around the altar of the chapel and Rebecca sought for signs that Luke had left his mark there. Indeed, she found it, a short poem carved into one of the roughly hewn pews.

> Whenever I see
> raindrops
> on a high chain-
> link fence,
> glistening like
> force-farmed tears
> hung up in hundreds
> to dry,
> I can't free
> my mind
> from the fact
> of the fence.

The poem was signed with the initials L.A.

She left the chapel and the jail with a profound sense of how terrible life must have been behind those walls over the last few years – indeed over the whole history of the stockade, which she was now distressed to note was a civil prison once again, for criminals. It hadn't been granted even a brief respite, but seemed an eternal monument to the incarceration of men. High, dark walls with round watchtowers, a massive gate higher than the walls themselves, and an internal piece of ground visible only to captors and captives. The whole experience had shaken her considerably.

Back at Raffles she regained her composure enough to go down to dinner and there she met the purser from the ship. He was delighted to see her and suggested they have a drink in the famous long bar after the meal. Rebecca accepted.

With their Singapore slings in their hands, Rebecca recounted her afternoon at the prison, and remarked how much the atmosphere of the place had affected her.

'I know,' said the purser, 'I've been too. My brother was in there. He never came out.'

'I'm sorry,' said Rebecca, then in an attempt to lighten things a bit said, 'I think I'd like to see Bugis Street.'

The purser almost choked on his drink, went bright red, and then seemed to collect himself. 'The – er – the *Jungle* Club is in Bugis Street. It's an infamous watering hole for wild seamen – and others.'

'Just that? A drinking den?'

'Well,' said the purser, coming clean, 'you can get a woman there too. Down Bugis Street.'

'You mean prostitutes? How sad for them. I suppose there's a lot of poverty around?'

'Indeed there is,' said the purser. 'Not only women – there's the *kai-tai* too.' Now that he had started he seemed to want to reveal every sordid aspect of the notorious street. 'That's men who dress up as women and sell their bodies to other men. It's not a place for a lady like you. Mind you, there's some good restaurants down there, but you wouldn't want to mix with the clientele.'

'Why not?' asked Rebecca. 'They're just people, aren't they?'

'There's people and people.'

In the end the starchy purser refused outright to take her to a restaurant in Bugis Street, but they took a trishaw and went along it. The dirt road was full of colourful Chinese women and European sailors, all arm in arm, drinking, eating out on the open-air verandas of ramshackle restaurants. Strings of lighted paper lanterns ran from one end of the street to the other, via telegraph poles and palm trees. There was gaiety and laughter, not all of it false, and drunken yells. A British soldier ran the full length of the street chased by a Chinese cook wielding a chopper. The soldier paused only to vomit briefly in the gutter before outrunning his pursuer.

'Didn't pay his bill,' remarked the purser, with some authority, and Rebecca guessed that he was no stranger to the street himself.

She went back to the hotel with mixed feelings about the island. In the morning she would be back on board ship, headed for Sydney, and she wished she had longer to explore Singapore. She had seen three of its faces, Ah-li's Toc H, the jail and Bugis Street; four, if she counted the expat community which used Raffles Hotel as their meeting place, and she wanted to see more. She had the idea that she was probably missing the best part of the island: that it had many, many faces, some of them good – like Ah-li's Toc H – and some of them not so good – like the jail. She was not prepared to judge places like Bugis Street, but accepted them for what they were.

She fell asleep, her thoughts jumbled.

Chapter Thirty-Three

By the time the SS *Devonshire* steamed into Sydney harbour, Rebecca was a complete sailor. It had taken her the whole trip to become used to the sea, and now that the journey was over she felt she had been born with a deck rolling beneath her feet.

Sydney looked a beautiful city, enhanced by a harbour with hundreds of pretty coves.

Rebecca said goodbye to the purser, who shook her hand and said that he hoped when she returned to England she would do so on the *Devonshire*, so that they might renew their acquaintance. Then she left the ship to be met by two customs officials who began to go through the contents of her suitcase, spilling her underwear all over their trellis table without the least regard for her modesty. Eventually one of them pulled out the jar that contained Amelia's remains.

'What's this?' he asked, holding the ceramic container up and looking suspiciously at the wired stopper.

'My aunt's ashes,' Rebecca replied.

'The ashes?' cried the other official, deliberately misunderstanding her. 'They're already here, ain't they, Jim? Australia won the last Test if I'm not mistaken . . .'

Rebecca rolled her eyes. 'Not the Test cricket ashes – the ashes of my aunt's body.'

The official who was holding the jar almost dropped it with a look of disgust on his face. He placed it carefully down beside Rebecca's suitcase and looked at his partner, Jim.

'I dunno if this is allowed, do you, Jim? Bringing the burnt remains of corpses into Australia? Sounds a bit macabre to me.'

'What do you expect me to do with it, now that I'm here?' asked Rebecca. 'Throw it in the harbour? I can hardly take it back to England again, can I?'

'Well,' said Jim ponderously, 'yeah, you can. You can leave it here and pick it up on your way out.'

'But I have to scatter the ashes in the outback.'

'What?' cried the other official. 'You're bringing dead people from Europe to mingle with our exotic outback? Not on your life, lady. You take it back where it comes from.'

Rebecca said, 'The lady in this jar is an *Australian*.'

Both men blinked and looked at each other, then Jim said, 'Why didn't you say so before? An Australian, eh?'

'Yes, it was her last wish to be brought back here to her homeland, which I've done at considerable expense. Circumstances took her to England, but her heart was always here in the old country – sorry, the *new* country. She never liked England very much. Too – too jolly-hockeysticks for Amelia. She was an outback person – rough and ready manners – not one of your china-teacup brigade.'

Rebecca knew she was laying it on thick, but they seemed to be enjoying it.

'Didn't like living amongst you poms, eh?' grinned Jim. 'Can't say's I blame her.'

Rebecca could have hit him, but she smiled and nodded instead. 'Amelia's father was at Gallipoli in the Great War – an Anzac,' she lied. 'He was killed going over the top – leaving his wife pregnant with Amelia.'

'Oh God, she died pretty young then, this Amelia. That's a crying shame,' said the other man.

Rebecca did some quick mental arithmetic and realised that that would indeed make Amelia about thirty years old now. 'Yes,' she said, picking up the jar of ashes and keeping the date of birth and date of death covered with her hands, 'and she was engaged to an Australian airman too.'

'Aw, Christ,' said the second official. 'How did she die?'

'A – a German bomb – on VE Day, would you believe?'

Jim said incredulously, 'The Germans flew a bombing raid on VE Day?'

'No, no,' said Rebecca hastily, realising she had gone much too far, 'an unexploded bomb from a previous raid. It was under her garden shed. She – she was potting some chrysanthemums and suddenly . . .'

The two officials exchanged another of their secret looks, then Jim immediately put a chalk cross on the side of her suitcase, winked at her and said, 'G'day, lady.'

She pushed her underwear back into the case, closed the lid and walked through the customs hall, her heart pounding.

Why did I do that? she asked herself. Why was I playing silly games? They might have refused to let me in. I must be going potty or something.

She found a free taxi which took her to a mid-range hotel near the Catholic cathedral. There she unpacked and had a shower before putting on some light clothes. It was very h in Sydney and there were none of the sea breezes she was used to on board the *Devonshire*.

After a short nap she went out into the city and strolled through the shopping area, replenishing her depleted cosmetics and buying some clothes. There was not a great deal in the stores, but then England was suffering terrible shortages too, probably more than during the war itself. The world had spent vast sums on killing several million people – mass death was an expensive business – and it would take some time to get back up to strength again. Factories had to be turned around once again, from producing guns and shells to making everyday items.

That evening Rebecca went to a church service and then retired early to bed.

The following day she did the sights, ending up at noon at the harbour again, in an area known as The Rocks. There she discovered, as expected, on a stone lintel over a doorway, the words *The Ragged School*.

Well, here I am, she said to herself. Is this where Amelia went to school in the middle of the nineteenth century?

She went inside the cool building and found herself in a cramped classroom. The tiny wooden benches, rickety and carved with hundreds of initials and symbols, were still there. The Ragged School was now a little museum of sorts, with all kinds of small antiques and artefacts on display, not all to do with the school itself. There was a curator there, a woman in her late fifties, who sold her a ticket.

'My great-aunt was a teacher here,' said Rebecca. 'In fact she was a pupil too – in the middle of the last century.'

'Really?' said the curator. 'What was her name?'

'Amelia Sartour.'

'Oh, yes – I've seen that name in the school records – Sartour. Have a look around. You might find something interesting . . .'

Rebecca spent some time there, but it was mostly in absorbing the atmosphere, trying to sense old ghosts. She tried to imagine what it would be like as a six-year-old in the 1800s, coming fresh from a middle-class background in England and landing up in this small classroom. She couldn't. It was impossible. It was beyond her grasp.

As she left she was invited to sign the visitors' book and did so with only half her attention. Suddenly she gasped and must have changed colour, because the curator said, 'What's the matter – are you feeling ill?'

'No – this signature – it was signed today?'

The curator stared at the book and then replied, 'It's today's date – must have been. Do you know him?'

Rebecca did indeed know him: it was Luke Adams.

'I think so – unless there's two people with the same name – no, I'm sure it's him. The address is the Blue Mountains Hotel. Do you know where that is?'

'One of these back-street places, I imagine, going by the fancy name. Ask a taxi driver. They'll know.'

Rebecca almost ran out into the street and hailed the first taxi she came across. 'Blue Mountains Hotel?' she asked.

'Where?'

She repeated the name but the driver had to stop at a news stall and ask the paper-seller for directions. Eventually the taxi drew up in a narrow street, outside a building not much bigger than a large house. She paid the driver and went into the hotel.

It had a little hallway with a stairway off the side and a counter at the end. She rang the bell on the top of the counter. A little old lady came out of the back of the house.

'Full,' she said shortly. 'No more rooms.'

'I'm looking for someone,' said Rebecca. 'A Mr Luke Adams. He should be staying here. Do you have a guest of that name?'

The little old lady looked Rebecca up and down. 'Does Mr Adams know you're coming? I mean, you might want to see *him*, but does he want to see *you*?'

'Then he *is* here,' breathed Rebecca, the joy welling up inside her.

At that moment a voice behind her said, 'Rebecca? Is that you? Good God – Rebecca?'

She turned. Luke had come silently down the stairs and was standing before her. He looked painfully thin in his khaki shirt and slacks, almost emaciated, but his eyes were bright. They stared at one another for a moment while the old woman fidgeted with something at the counter. Then Rebecca walked towards him.

'Luke,' she whispered. 'Oh Luke, it's so lovely to see you again.'

'Is it?' he asked, his eyes serious.

'Yes it is – it's wonderful. I never thought we would see each other again. I called into Singapore to try to find you – I found Ah-li . . .'

He grinned. 'Ah-li – she was a brick. Did she tell you she smuggled food into Changi for us prisoners? Risked her life to give us a few scraps every day. She was a washerwoman then – now – well, you know, don't you? – she's in charge of the Toc H.'

'Luke, can we go somewhere to talk?'

He shrugged. 'Sure – how about the park?'

She went ahead of him through the narrow doorway and out into the street. He followed her. Outside, he asked to take her arm, clearly still a little frail. Her heart melted. The robust, cheeky country boy she had known was now a thousand years old. It was in his face, in his mood. He had seen the other side of hell, daily had watched men die, had wasted away in body and spirit himself.

'You look – wiser,' she said, as they walked slowly along the sunlit street.

'The kind of experience I've been through doesn't give you wisdom, unfortunately,' said Luke. 'I may look like a sage, but actually I think I've *lost* a bit of mental power, not gained it. Starvation doesn't do anything for you except make you think about food all the time. Constant diarrhoea does even less for one's mental agility.' He looked at her. 'I'm afraid it's all rather sordid. I would like to tell you that my powers of meditation and knowledge have increased and that I'm now a great philosopher with wonderful insight into the human condition. I can't do that – it was enough to stay alive, never mind gain anything on the way to where I am now.'

'I understand,' she said.

'No you don't, but it doesn't matter. I did write some poetry though – and I shall write again when I'm fully recovered.'

'I wrote letters to you,' she told him, 'many times.'

'I never got them,' he replied.

'Oh, I thought you didn't reply because you hated me.'

Luke said, 'I did – but that wasn't the reason for my silence. I didn't get word, so I thought you were indifferent to me, an my fate. You always gave that impression.'

'I know – I'm sorry.'

'Don't be. It's human nature.'

When they reached the park he sat on a seat in the shade and she slipped down beside him. Luke asked her what she was doing in Australia and she told him. He then asked how she had found him and she told him about his name in the visitors' book at the Ragged School. He nodded, as if to say that it was all quite logical. Then he asked her about Christopher Bates.

'We didn't hit it off,' admitted Rebecca. 'He – he wasn't the man I thought he was.'

'Perhaps none of us ever are,' said Luke. 'Maybe you women are looking for something that doesn't exist?'

'I'm not looking for perfection,' she replied, 'but I need a man to have certain values – integrity.'

'And Christopher failed you there?'

'I'd rather not talk about him, if you don't mind. It didn't come to anything and I'm glad. It's something that's well behind me now. Lots of things have happened since.'

'You've had new beaux?'

She laughed. 'Not at all – the only man who's paid any attention to me since you left was an elderly Scottish purser on the ship. He was friendly to me. Apart from him, no one has turned a head in the street.'

'I can't believe that,' snorted Luke, almost his old self again. 'Looking like that? I could eat you, m'darlin'.'

Rebecca glanced down at herself. She was wearing a white frock, because of the heat, and she knew it made her look irginal. She supposed she did look quite cool and attractive, especially to a man who had been incarcerated for years.

'Well, one or two wolf whistles from building labourers, perhaps,' she smiled. 'Now what about you, Luke? How do you feel – about me, I mean? Do you still love me? You said once that you did. It's been a long time, I know. You've been through so much since then.'

He straightened at her directness and stared into her eyes.

'Love you? Love *you*? I've loved and hated you in turns. You've made me utterly miserable at times.'

'That wasn't all my fault – I didn't set out to do it on purpose. I was following something I thought was right, for Kim – and, I suppose, for me. But I didn't *make* you miserable. You did that with your own feelings.'

He grunted and looked away, towards a group of palms.

'Of course I still damn well love you,' he said at last. 'How fickle do you think I am? I thought of nothing else while I was in that bloody jail. Just you, in your damned white dresses, looking like ice cream. I thought about you *too* much, sometimes, if you know what I mean – *without* the bloody dresses on – does that disgust you?'

'Not at all,' she said quietly. 'I came to love you too, Luke, through your poetry. Perhaps I loved you all the time, but wouldn't listen to myself? I don't know. What I do know is that I don't want to let you go again. If we walk away from each other once more, we might both end up alone, regretting. I don't want my autumn years to be soiled by regret, do you? Luke, will you marry me?'

He stared hard at her. 'You're not doing this just because you feel sorry for me? Because I'm – like this?'

'Luke, men are not the only ones who lie in the dark

thinking about making love to someone who's absent. I *want* you – badly. And I want you, for ever.'

Tears came to his eyes. 'It's happened,' he said. 'I dreamed of this moment – ten thousand times. Sometimes I told you to go to hell and walked away feeling bitterly proud. Sometimes I just grabbed you and made love to you. Now – now I just want to hold you for a few moments – hold me, will you?'

They went into each other's arms and Rebecca felt like crying herself. She was sure her heart was going to burst. His arms were stronger than she'd expected they would be and she realised how much strength a man like him must have to survive such a terrible ordeal. She was going to help him build on that strength, put the war behind him, become whole again.

'Yes,' he whispered in her ear.

'Yes what?'

'Ah, you've forgotten already? You just proposed to me.'
She laughed. 'So I did.'

They remained on the park bench for several hours, talking, discovering, planning. When they stood up again it was evening, and they walked slowly back to Rebecca's hotel. There they remained for two whole days. They talked about Amelia's death and the reason why Rebecca had come to Australia in the first place, to scatter her great-aunt's ashes in the outback.

'She was a marvellous woman,' said Luke. 'I admired her grit immensely. While I was in Changi I thought of her – told myself how she would cope with life in a POW camp. I mean, Amelia went through hell as a *six-year-old* – starved, stole scraps from waste bins, was beaten and abused, and still came out with a spirit the size of Ayer's Rock. I was a grown man.

Surely I could survive an experience, not the same, but certainly no worse than Amelia's? It helped me.'

'Yes, she was a warrior.'

On the third day they hired a car and drove into the outback. They scattered the ashes near a group of gum trees, out in the wilderness, under the throbbing sun.

The silent, ancient landscape, covered with malformed rocks and broken, white-trunked eucalypti sloughing their bark, made a strange grave for the remains of Amelia Sartour. It was where she wanted to be, though, part of that antique land, and Rebecca was happy to grant her last wish.

Luke and Rebecca spent three months touring Australia, touching the land that had touched Amelia, and then booked a passage home to Essex. One harrowing adventure – the Second World War – was over for them.

Another great adventure had begun.

Rebecca could have hit him, but she smiled and nodded instead. 'Amelia's father was at Gallipoli in the Great War – an Anzac,' she lied. 'He was killed going over the top – leaving his wife pregnant with Amelia.'

'Oh God, she died pretty young then, this Amelia. That's a crying shame,' said the other man.

Rebecca did some quick mental arithmetic and realised that that would indeed make Amelia about thirty years old now. 'Yes,' she said, picking up the jar of ashes and keeping the date of birth and date of death covered with her hands, 'and she was engaged to an Australian airman too.'

'Aw, Christ,' said the second official. 'How did she die?'

'A – a German bomb – on VE Day, would you believe?'

Jim said incredulously, 'The Germans flew a bombing raid on VE Day?'

'No, no,' said Rebecca hastily, realising she had gone much too far, 'an unexploded bomb from a previous raid. It was under her garden shed. She – she was potting some chrysanthemums and suddenly . . .'

The two officials exchanged another of their secret looks, then Jim immediately put a chalk cross on the side of her suitcase, winked at her and said, 'G'day, lady.'

She pushed her underwear back into the case, closed the lid and walked through the customs hall, her heart pounding.

Why did I do that? she asked herself. Why was I playing silly games? They might have refused to let me in. I must be going potty or something.

She found a free taxi which took her to a mid-range hotel near the Catholic cathedral. There she unpacked and had a shower before putting on some light clothes. It was very hot in Sydney and there were none of the sea breezes she was used to on board the *Devonshire*.

After a short nap she went out into the city and strolled through the shopping area, replenishing her depleted cosmetics and buying some clothes. There was not a great deal in the stores, but then England was suffering terrible shortages too, probably more than during the war itself. The world had spent vast sums on killing several million people – mass death was an expensive business – and it would take some time to get back up to strength again. Factories had to be turned around once again, from producing guns and shells to making everyday items.

That evening Rebecca went to a church service and then retired early to bed.

The following day she did the sights, ending up at noon at the harbour again, in an area known as The Rocks. There she discovered, as expected, on a stone lintel over a doorway, the words *The Ragged School*.

Well, here I am, she said to herself. Is this where Amelia went to school in the middle of the nineteenth century?

She went inside the cool building and found herself in a cramped classroom. The tiny wooden benches, rickety and carved with hundreds of initials and symbols, were still there. The Ragged School was now a little museum of sorts, with all kinds of small antiques and artefacts on display, not all to do with the school itself. There was a curator there, a woman in her late fifties, who sold her a ticket.

'My great-aunt was a teacher here,' said Rebecca. 'In fact she was a pupil too – in the middle of the last century.'

'Really?' said the curator. 'What was her name?'